I0747647

Lifting the Veil is a work of fiction. Names, characters, places, and incidents either are the product of the author's imagination or are used factiously. Any resemblance to actual persons, living or dead, events or locales is entirely coincidental.

2023 Paperback Edition

Copyright © 2023 by Kate Church

All Rights Reserved

First Edition 2023

ISBN PAPERBACK: 978-1-7358183-4-4
ISBN EBOOK: 978-1-7358183-5-1

Printed in the United States of America

Illustrations by Kate Church

Cover Design by Getcovers

No part of this publication may be reproduced, stored in, or introduced into a retrieval system, or transmitted, in any form, or by any means (electrical, mechanical, photocopying, recording or otherwise) without the prior written permission of the author.

the

Kate Church

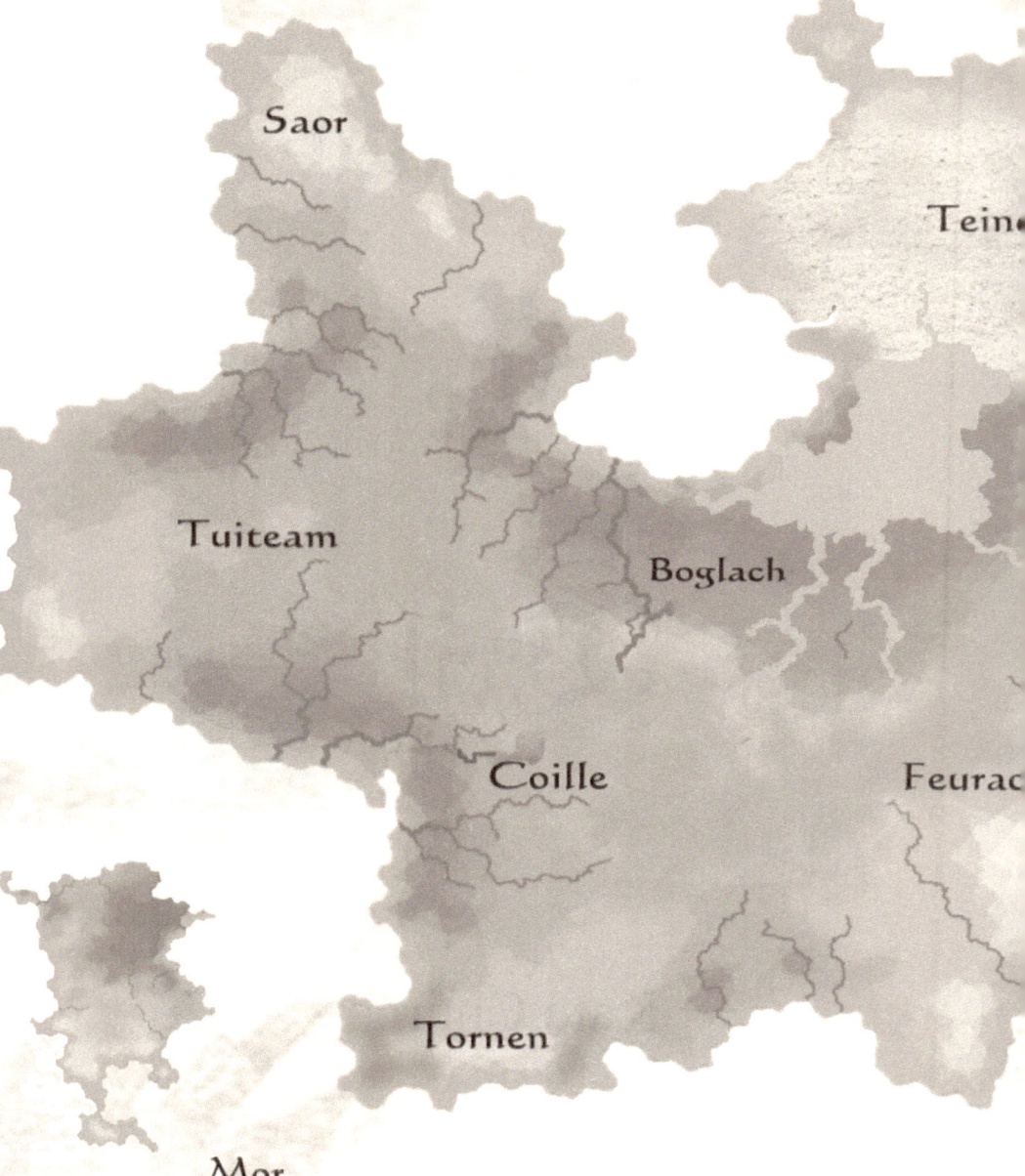

Caladh

Saor

Teine

Tuiteam

Boglach

Coille

Feurac

Tornen

Mor
Tawel

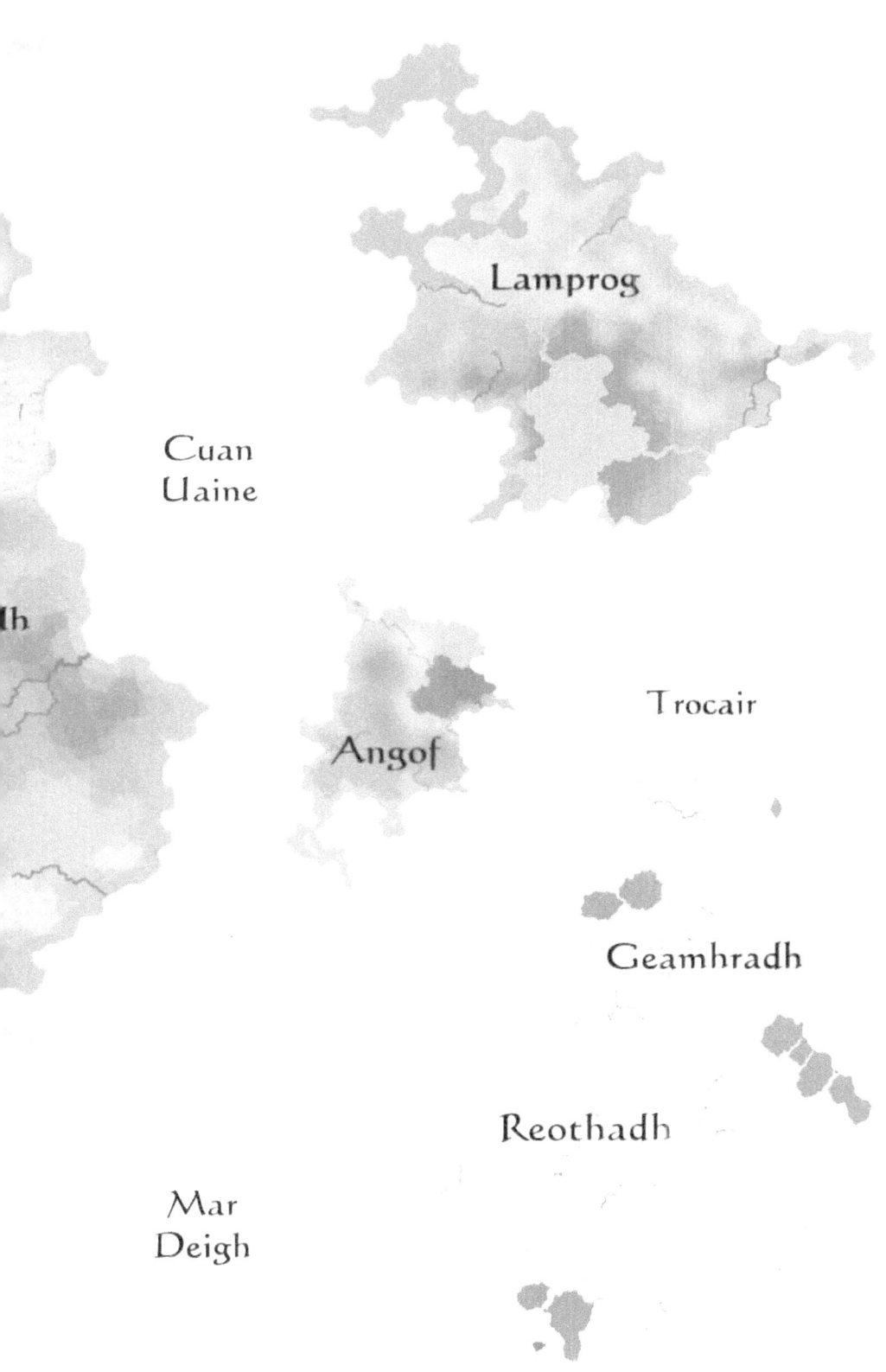

Lamprog

Cuan
Uaine

Ih

Angof

Trocair

Geamhradh

Reothadh

Mar
Deigh

Drayk

    While I removed myself from their presence, my thoughts never left her. With each blink, all I could see was her face and I found myself struggling to keep them open, not wishing to see her eyes or the tears that were found streaming nearby. From the warm embrace I received to the look of betrayal that became written upon her face, I was finding it all more difficult to shake than I had anticipated. Refusing to let myself become consumed over the pawn I was tasked to retrieve, I diverted my attention elsewhere for the squabbles of man held little fascination for me, only coin. Although, Haxa and I vacated the room, we were never out of range from the turmoil and strife that now flooded within.

    You did well, Drayk. King Ferand is quite pleased.
    As are you I sense.
    You have yet to disappoint me, but I must admit, even I thought this task would have presented a challenge, even for you. However, it appears I was mistaken.

It was not without difficulty, as you must know.

Oh, of that I am certain. Your concern for her is almost as remarkable as their desire for one another.

I glanced towards her with a look of disapproval before returning my attention towards the chamber.

Perhaps given more time and you could have claimed the King's jewel for yourself.

And how do you know I did not?

For you smell of frustration and soot, not of her.

I glanced towards her briefly to find her grinning forcing my attention to be drawn back to the chamber.

Besides had you claimed her, I believe even you would be tempted to save her from King Ferand's licentious intentions.

Even though we could not see her, we could hear her weeping and it tore at my heart, if but briefly.

You feel something for her when you should not.

What I feel is her soul crying out, not my heart or my loins aching for her. Do not let your own twisted version of the truth dilute what is truly there. Affection should never be used as a weapon nor should there ever be a need for it to be taken from another. If it cannot be freely given or accepted, then one does not deserve it. I know it is not my place to save her, though I feel compelled to for this reason alone. I feel what King Ferand desires, whether her body or Conall's pride, taking her affection in this way will hurt his cause.

My thought was broken when we heard shouting echoing throughout the chamber forcing our discussion to be tabled for another time. Upon re-entering the chamber, we found Conall now covering Eira with his body and a sandy King Ferand hovering next to them with his sword drawn, shouting obscenities and hollow threats. The situation took both Haxa and I by surprise as neither of us would have anticipated the strength and agility Conall would have needed to accomplish such a task in the few moments they had alone together. They were stronger together and with that, I now understood the late King Baylon's desire to seek out others of their kind. Had they both been healthy, King Ferand would have already met his demise and the powers of myself and Haxa alone would not be sufficient to contain them.

"Call my guards and restrain him!" King Ferand shouted through panted breaths, "For his insolence, I will make him watch as I ravage his beloved."

His beloved? Could it have been that King Ferand noticed something I did not or was he merely hopeful that Conall's posturing was that of a lover?

"Beshrew thee Ferand!" Conall spat, "I would sacrifice my beating heart before I will permit you to bed her."

I turned towards Haxa who was clearly focused upon Conall, dialing up her energy until Conall's mind was nearly at the breaking point. Her debilitating mind blare was as if tapping one's fingers upon a tabletop and each tap was a little stronger than the last. At first, he would still be able to speak but there would be a humming noise filling his ears. Within moments, that humming would increase to the shrieking cry of a siren, taking away his voice and the breath he held. Just before the end, Conall would hear a sound so forceful and penetrating that his minor blood vessels and eardrums would rupture, forcing him to submit to the pressure or be consumed by it. He barely finished his sentence before Haxa went to work on him and from what I could see he was beginning to redden from the pressure. Although, he appeared determined to shield her from King Ferand, his body and mind would not hold out much longer.

"You say this as if you have a choice in the matter," King Ferand uttered sounding rather pleased with himself.

King Ferand grinned as he pulled Eira into his arms just before Conall collapsed on the floor before him. Though he reached for her, he could not maintain his grasp. He was soon found cowering before us all while clutching his throbbing mind and crying out for it to stop. Haxa, unwavering in her assault, did not falter at the sound of his blood-curdling cries. I watched as the crimson from within Eira trickled down and onto the cavern floor into a pool that would soon be all that was left of her should King Ferand have his way. While I care not for the vile and depraved desires of man, unless forced, I refuse to bear witness to these acts. Seeing King Ferand's desires now unfolding before me caused something from within me to stir once more, pulling at my throat, insisting this must be stopped when my gaze found hers. Just above tear-stained cheeks, but beneath the embers I had grown to seek in the dark were her bright honeycomb eyes. They were pleading with her *beloved,* as King Ferand so eloquently put it, to save her. Conall could do nothing to stop the madness. Their pain, even though part of it was my own doing, still tore at what was left of my cold heart.

"Have her if you will, King Ferand," I shouted, "but not

like this!"

In my sudden outburst, all eyes were now upon me. I focused my energy on King Ferand as I knew I would have little effect on the minds of the others. I needed him to relent, even if it was just for today.

"I am certain Your Majesty would rather this maiden be a willing participant than the fearful and battered one that presently is before you."

His eyes narrowed slightly at my suggestion, but in the mere moments following, Haxa's voice broke through the silence.

"Drayk is right, Your Majesty," she grinned. "Let us mend her if but temporarily and explain the situation. Perhaps she does not yet understand what it means to be in the presence of a king such as yourself."

I felt the tension in the room lessen significantly at this notion and while I knew Haxa spoke falsely, I was unsure as to her purpose for agreeing with me. Having been in her presence many times over the years, I knew her to be merciless in a way that was unlike my own. I would kill any target without so much as a second glance, but she relishes in destroying those from the inside out by breaking their spirits and bending them to her will. She would have loved nothing more than to bear witness to King Ferand defiling Eira all the while knowing that it would be Conall's spirit that was truly being the one tested and broken. I may have been an assassin, but she is the one we should all fear. Her hatred and malice know no bounds.

"Have her mended and cleansed to my liking before bringing her to my bedchamber," King Ferand ordered. "And

Haxa, your presence will be required in the event she has a change of heart."

King Ferand pulled her in tightly against himself before placing his lips upon hers, ever watchful of Conall in the distance, who was now rising to his feet, breathing heavily.

"Relax Conall," King Ferand grinned once more, "I will return her to you."

Lowering one of his hands on her hip, he began tugging at the leathers that barely covered her body. With each tug, I could see Conall's jaw clench ever so slightly, and it was then that we all found his weakness. It was her. With each caress of King Ferand's fingers upon her flesh and each time his lips touched hers, Conall's demeanor changed. The connection between them was remarkable to say the least and had I not known better, I would have assumed they were long lost lovers with the way they were willing to leap into great peril for one another. However, that would not explain the innocence she exuded during our time together. Everything about her behavior suggested that she had been untouched by man, yet she was willing to risk her life for this one and he was willing to do the same for her. A revelation that was not only apparent to myself, but to Haxa as well for she grinned with delight as she watched the scene unfolding before us.

"If you claim her on this day or any other you will condemn our kind to death!" Conall shouted clearly fed up with King Ferand's antics.

King Ferand tore his lips from hers before casting her aside as if she were a ragdoll, where she once again was greeted by my arms before collapsing within them. I looked upon her now in the same manner that I had when she collapsed before me just beyond the Ice Tower, complete wonder. I was completely taken with her, but as a pain began to consume my chest my thoughts returned to the ones waging war over her virtue. Out of my peripheral vision I watched as King Ferand rushed towards Conall stopping only inches from him.

"What is this madness that you speak of?" King Ferand spat, clearly flustered.

Conall closed his eyes and inhaled deeply before opening them again.

"You know naught of what you have sought, and you reek of that ignorance," he insisted, voice stern and breathing steady.

King Ferand placed a hand upon the hilt of his sword with clear intention to draw it but did not. They stood there as two statues waiting for either fear or fury to break their stance, but it did not. I pulled my focus back to Eira whose once bright eyes were growing terribly dark. Placing one arm under her legs and another behind her back, I lifted her into my arms. Her body melted against mine and the memory of her in my arms within the nook of the cog flashed before me. The pain in my chest grew stronger, more demanding if you will and I was forced to look away from her. I stepped towards them, nearly upon them before their concentration broke forcing them to turn towards me in near perfect unison.

"Conall speaks the truth," I added.

"How do you know it as such?" King Ferand leaned in towards me clearly astonished at my sudden support of

Conall's claim.

"For deception is the way of man, not beast," I sneered.

"Then take her to the rack," he snarled. "We know his weakness, now let us see what we can learn of hers."

I nodded just before throwing Eira up and onto my shoulder, where she would remain unless there was a need to subdue her further. However, with the amount of crimson that had pooled onto the chamber floor and the amount that had run down upon me, there would not be a need. Just as I vacated the room, Haxa stepped forward to inflict her wrath upon Conall until he no longer protested or until King Ferand was satisfied, but all I heard was his silence. His willpower was as I anticipated, or he would not have survived as long as he had without one as such. Yet, it was his connection to Eira that was stronger than anything I had seen before. Despite only one encounter, she risked her life on the dismal possibility she could save his and now he would endure a warlock's version of vengeance just to keep her from being bedded by King Ferand. Unfortunately, his efforts may be in vain for the desires of King Ferand are rarely forgotten, merely postponed. With his feelings as they were on the subject, it might have been kinder just to kill her swiftly rather than witness what may be returned to him.

As I began carrying her up the long spiral stairwell, I pondered the conundrum that was their connection further. Was it possible for them to have bonded in what little time they were given or was this a connection that they all feel for one another? I thought over this carefully as truly understanding it could provide valuable insight to how they interact with our world or those that are familial to them. My mind then thought of unconventional thoughts. Perhaps, they knew each other, and it all was a ruse. While they were defensive of one another, they did not appear or speak from knowledge. Had it been a ruse and in her flustered state she would have undoubtably slipped up by speaking his name or by using the past tense. Then I thought of that morning by the stream, she was seeking someone other than Conall, but took to him without a second thought. It confirmed my suspicions that the males I had once encountered may still be amongst the living. King Ferand would pay considerably for this knowledge.

Just before reaching the mouth of the stairwell, I turned sharply to push through the hidden opening where I was greeted by a couple of sewer rats that King Ferand refers to as members of the royal guard. Both donning full armor, according to King Ferand's demands, but not appearing quite battle ready should there have been an immediate need. After the recent attack upon the city and the missing prince, they were looking considerably unwell. For being as young as they would have been, their eyes were sunken within two very deep and large black grooves accompanied by something clearly cultivating its way across the lower portion of their faces. Being elven there has never been a need for shaving of facial hair or rest, but man requires both and frequently or they start to appear as the two of these men do. It took them a moment to stand at the ready when I entered the room, but just as they were about to react to utter what would certainly be nonsense, their attention was pulled elsewhere. Seeing the long soft legs that have set up camp upon my shoulder brought some life back to them and upon their faces grew grins from nearly ear to ear.

"Would you look at that?" one of them muttered.

"I see King Ferand has sent us a gift," the second one sneered with delight, "I will make sure to thank him personally."

I quickly extended one of my arms in their direction, releasing a dagger from beneath my gauntlet and into the air. To my amusement, they leapt away from the blade and could now be found hunkered down towards the floor with their hands covering their eyes. As if that would have served any purpose against a blade. Some royal guard King Ferand has.

"Begone with you heathens," I bellowed, "or by my troth, the next one will not be a warning."

They scurried about like goblins and fled the chamber, leaving the two of us alone once more. Pulling her down from my shoulder I laid her upon what the late King Baylon dubbed the rack before tilting her up towards me. It was a large wooden plank surrounded by several restraints, pulley systems and plates. It was designed to break the body from the inside out and though I witnessed only brief moments of Conall's time on the rack, I felt confident she would not hold out as long. I watched her once more as I did many times before, searching for the answers her body and mind were unwilling to give. Her eyes opened to me once more, still quite dim, but very aware of whom she was looking upon. With each restraint I cinched down, her eyes began to glow brighter than the moment before and her flesh, though ghoulish from the poison now waging within, was beginning to boil.

Our eyes now watching each other incessantly were speaking volumes to one another. Without it even being asked of me, I brought my body back towards hers once more as I had in the passageway and watched as her breathing became erratic. Her eyes widened greatly, but I kept mine as they were hoping hers would soon follow suit as I meant her harm. With each breath, I drew closer to her and though she felt the sting of betrayal, I felt her body relax ever so slightly with my body next to hers. I brought my lips in towards hers and witnessed a subtle flutter of her eyelashes. In her anticipation she was distracted. I thrust a handful of luaithre against the opening I created from the nathair's fang. Luaithre is an ash like substance known to singe broken flesh and prevent healing. In the case of shapeshifters, it is invaluable against preventing unwelcomed transformations. It is what King Ferand would have used on Conall the night we found him on the chamber floor. Had he been able to transform during the torture and he would have been able to endure so much more, as would she. I wished to save her from that if I could. As her body lay tightening from the sting of the burn, the blood from the wound slowed. If she had not already, she will soon understand the gift that I have given her, though she may not see it as such.

I returned to my work when I felt the air in the chamber change. Haxa had finished with Conall and had come to check on the King's jewel.

She is not as strong as her male counterpart nor as old, pity really. Still, she will prove useful provided she can be persuaded to lay with Conall.

King Ferand's intention is to breed them?

Aye, well of course. King Baylon originally caged Conall as a novelty since he could never hope to control him, but with the female held tightly within our grasp any bairns he is able to sire will become ours for the taking. Surely you must have known.

I know naught of what you speak.

Come now Drayk, no need to be deliberately obtuse.

I looked upon her now with disdain as I was growing tired of her trickery despite its usefulness. It was then that I gazed into Eira's eyes once more. Filled with so much emotion they now glowed brighter than a hunter's moon found in the night's sky. If my cold heart had the ability to love another, it would have been her, but alas I am not capable of such. I turned to step towards the far wall just as King Ferand entered the chamber.

"Let us begin."

Conall

It was the sound of the cavern door swinging ajar that woke me many hours later. As I rose to my feet, the memory of it all came rushing back to me in a wave that made my chest grow tight and my heart ache. In my distress, I quickly scanned the room for any sign of her, but there was nothing. Eira has been lost to me once more. Fearful of what may have become of her and what was to become of me, I stood at the ready and waited to meet my foe. To my astonishment, it was Drayk that entered while carrying a very pale Eira over his one shoulder as if she were a sack of grain to be milled. She was lifeless and the ache I previously felt when I awoke turned to a pain that was beginning to devour my chest and my mind. I wished he never found her as a death in the tower would have been more merciful.

I threw my hand out before me, "Come no further for you are not welcome here."

He scoffed, "My choice of profession leaves me

unwelcome nearly everywhere." He paused just before pulling Eira from his shoulder, "So, never presume your preference affects me in the least. Besides, I thought you would appreciate having her returned to you."

"How thoughtful of you to return the corpse of my kin," I uttered with spite and a fair amount of sarcasm.

I tried desperately to look away, but the pain in my chest was growing. I wanted to hold her once more and bear the pain of her loss for as long as my body could withstand it. It was then when I heard it. A low, faint thud followed by another and then another. She was alive. My attention was pulled back towards his face. I scanned it for any sign of emotion or remorse for his part in all of this, but there was nothing. Just the same stern expression that he greeted me with the day we met. Perhaps she was just a pawn to him as he wished for me to believe or maybe he was immune to her charms, but it mattered little now. What was done could not be undone.

"Was she…" I began to utter, but my voice trailed off, unwilling to finish the question knowing how much the answer may pain me.

"No," he said frankly, "I made sure she was not."

I felt my lungs give way with the breath I had been holding, clearly relieved that this part of her had remained unscathed. I thought surely Ferand would have renounced my claim and taken her to his bed moments after leaving the cavern. He does not appear to be the type that could have his wicked intentions reasoned with, but if I have my say there will not be a next time. I reached for her, pulling her from his arms and into mine. She felt terribly cold, and I grew fearful she would not survive. Drawing her near, I could feel her exhale ever so slightly, but I could no longer hear her in my mind which troubled me greatly.

"If vengeance, as you claim, is what you seek…why return her to me?"

"Come now Conall," he cocked his head to one side, "do you truly believe that Tuiteam would go through such trouble just to slay her in the night? Or you for that matter?"

There were pieces on the board, but some of them still remained amongst the shadows, leaving holes in the game we had found ourselves within. Had we known the rules or the key players and Ferand would not have the means to succeed. He needed to keep the remaining pieces hidden until the board was fixed in his favor. We were the pawns he focused the remaining pieces around. King Baylon kept me here to strengthen his army, not to protect his house from invading ones. I felt sure of that, but I was unsure how if kept hidden like a dirty secret that would be accomplished. Drayk, unlike Ferand, was no fool. He could not be easily swayed to reveal coveted information should I press him, and I was unsure of how much he could have even been privy to. He was a lorvisad assassin slinking about in the shadows of Tuiteam after all.

"No, I do not," I uttered, "for we are the pawns the game is built around."

"Then you understand," he said firmly, gaze fixed upon mine.

"If we are just pawns to you—"

"She was a mark to me, a target, NOT a pawn," his tone

sharp and defensive.

Though his expression had not changed, the tone of his voice echoed loudly with emotion. He felt something for her and this time I was sure of it.

"You," he growled, "mean NOTHING to me. You were never my target and I have little use for pawns. So, do not presume to think that I care in the least for Tuiteam's intentions or blanket me as one of them based only upon the understanding that I accept their coin."

I had struck a nerve, however unintentional.

"Why did you stop him?" I insisted, my gaze intensifying.

"The answer you seek will not comfort you," he insisted before dropping his gaze upon her face, "nor will it save either of you from your fate."

"I care not if it comforts me!" I shouted feeling my flesh ignite.

"Then perhaps you should get used to disappointment," he said sharply.

"Leave us," I demanded. "We are done here."

"I decide when we are done, not you!" his voice demanding and insistent.

I rushed towards him with Eira in tow, burning from the fire that was now raging from within.

"If you so dare, cast your vengeance upon me here and now," I growled. "Or leave us of your own accord for you know naught of who you challenge."

Clearly not accustomed to being challenged, he glared at me for several moments with a gaze that never faltered.

There was something he came for, but it had yet to be revealed. Perhaps, he was hoping to see something he had not before. Frankly as the moments wore on, I grew tired of the chase and turned away from him. I ventured towards the far side of the cavern where it was the darkest, but the water trickled in clear. It would be there that I would wait for her to return to me if it be her will. While I had walked away, he did not falter in the slightest. It was then that I realized I no longer cared whether he remained as it would change little for me. I knelt near the back wall and laid her on her side, before brushing her long locks back from her face. Each strand felt softer than I remembered and though her flesh had felt colder than the rock that now surrounds us, I never felt more hopeful. From the moment I heard Tuiteam was seeking her until now, my heart never stopped calling out to her. I was confident it would do so until I could see her eyes open again.

I did not hear Drayk leave his position, but as the door to the cavern began to close, he spoke once more.

"Though her will may not be as strong as yours, she held out longer than even I anticipated." I listened intently unsure of what his parting words would be when he continued. "Please thank her for me," he paused, "as we may have never known or found Bryn without her."

I felt my breath catch as the door closed behind him just before the locks returned to their rightful place. Though her virtue may have remained intact, her pride certainly will not and the fate of her kin, well our kin, now hangs in the balance. Not willing to linger in the troublesome thought of yet another one of us trapped within these walls, I returned to where I had awoken the day before. It was there that I picked up the cloak we laid upon before, dusting it off and turning back towards her. As I turned, I noted something that had been lain within the angel's grasp. Reluctant to accept anything from Drayk, I was hesitant at first, but I soon opted to take it within my grasp. It was heavier than expected and warm to the touch. Unwrapping it slowly I found it to be a bread of sorts accompanied by a large chunk of pork if my senses were still working correctly. The sweet scent of it filled my nasal cavity and made my belly ache for it. Although I was tempted to devour it, I decided to save it for when she wakes once more. She will need it more than I.

Upon returning to her, I dropped down against a nearby wall before pulling her up through my legs and onto my chest. She did not utter a sound. I wrapped the cloak around us and my arms around her feeling the sting of her chilled flesh against the heat of my very own. The sensation caused my heart to race, but I soon realized that it was her fingers that had begun to tighten against my chest that made my heart race, not the temperature difference. As I lay there with her, I felt my heart calling out to her once more. It was willing her eyes to open to me and provide me with a reason to be hopeful once more. Though they did not, it did not discourage me. I found comfort in the beat of her heart and her breath as it danced across my chest in slow, brief twists and turns. With each beat, it was becoming harder to remember life before her. I felt myself growing concerned over what would become of the heart she had mended should I be forced to venture on without her. Isolation is a fickle mistress after all. When you seek solitude, you do not feel alone or yearn for the companionship of others, but once you have been given a taste, you cannot bear to part with it. It was in those thoughts and concerns that I found myself drifting off to sleep.

Through broken dreams and the sounds of her weeping in night, we struggled onward, never waiting to hold onto what once was or what may never be again. Despite my attempts to shift about, she clung to me like a wee bairn to their mother in a desperate attempt to banish the fear from her mind. I did not refuse her for I knew all too soon she may leave my side. Laying there in silence, only counting the beats of the other one's heart, we weathered the storm. Though she had been maimed by others during her time, whether man or beast, what she experienced here was something quite different. It may take time for her to come to grips with it all. The world of man was undoubtably crueler than she could have imagined, I would be interested to know what it was that broke her. Although, I would never have the heart to ask her.

My eyes re-opened for what felt like the first time in days to witness Eira still delicately wrapped within my arms. Her breathing was returning to a normal rhythm and the effects from her torment were subsiding. While her recovery was far from over, I felt she was on the mend, and I could rest easier now. Looking down upon her, I noticed she had turned in towards my chest forcing her long locks to fall forward, covering her breathtakingly beautiful face. I reached for them and drew them back before running my fingers alongside her cheek and down onto her neck. She felt softer than I remembered. With each touch I felt something deep inside me stirring, forcing my breathing to change and my heart to race. The sensation was of fear and desire that quickly spread throughout causing a shiver to follow shortly thereafter. There was no denying I greatly desired her, as any man would, but she would be safer away from me. It was the strength we had together that Ferand desires of that I am now certain. Though I am not certain how he would have known that would have been the outcome of our union.

As I lay there attempting to calm those feelings, I felt her fingers gently begin twirling their way through my long locks. The gesture drew my attention back towards them and to her where I felt a smile attempting to appear upon my face. Her fingers, small and thin, where curling my hair between them as a bairn would during their younger years before they had learnt to curb that anxious behavior. I was tempted to break the silence when I heard her thoughts once more.

For years I have lived in relative isolation never thinking of another, but now nearly my every thought is consumed by thoughts of him. With each touch he makes my heart flutter, pleading for more. Just as his touch excites me, I can hear his heart racing each time we are near.

I tried not to utter or think anything direct as I did not want to complicate her already anxious mind, but my thoughts were overflowing with emotion. Her fingers stopped twirling my locks between them when she felt my gaze upon her. She turned her head slightly, bringing my gaze into view and while my gaze may have been on hers, her focus had fallen towards my lips. The simple shift of her gaze drew my attention downward as well. As I watched her teeth slide forward slightly before biting her lower lip. The sensation I had felt previously was growing and I became slightly aroused with anticipation. Even while attempting to control my thoughts, I knew my enthusiasm would soon become very difficult to conceal as her body was still very near to mine. I wanted to say something to diffuse the tension. However, as I thought over our time together, it had been there from the moment we met, relentless and irrefutable.

What I would give to bring back that moment when his lips touched mine that morning in Coille. Though I had not wished it, I would not change it and my mind will not let me forget it.

I dare not wait another moment for I felt as she. Placing one of my hands just behind her neck and the other behind her back, I drew her closer to me. I held her there just to feel the rise and fall of her chest, as her breathing and the beat of her heart increased as the moments drew on. I leaned in and placed my lips upon hers once more. While our bodies are already alarmingly warm, compared to man, they now felt ablaze. The sensation forced a surge of energy to rip through my veins that I had not felt in weeks. Her thoughts were running away with her, struggling between the pain she felt and her own desires, but she made no attempt to stop. Her mouth opened to me and in a clash of tongues and teeth the desire only deepened. Her hands pulled at my flesh, urging me to bring myself closer to her though I was not sure how. Thoughts of fear had found her, and she was reliving me being taken once more. Shouting at someone unseen, but I was here with her now. Her breathing had become labored, and she was struggling to maintain control over her body and emotions.

Rolling her over onto her back I climbed on top of her, bringing myself dangerously close to her. The gesture, though bold, calmed some of those emotions and her fearful thoughts soon subsided. Her eyes smiled at me briefly, and I found myself lost within them. My lips found hers once more, but they did not remain there. I soon found myself wandering onto her cheek and down onto her neck. She twisted her fingers into my locks and pulled at them gently, insistent I continue. Now, it was my own desire that concerned me. Through persistent kisses became an unyielding hunger and I felt myself beginning to pant between each one that was lain upon her flesh. The urge and desire that started out faint was turning primal. Soon we would become slaves to our animal instincts.

"We must stop," I uttered through panted breaths.

Though in truth I did not wish to stop, but something inside me pulled at me, telling me this was not the way. I wanted to deny that feeling, cast it aside and take what it was we both desired.

"Conall," she uttered breathlessly.

I pulled away from her slightly and watched her eyes widen with surprise.

"Eira," I leaned in and kissed her lips gently, "you cannot bond with me this way," I muttered through panted breaths. "Our bodies are misleading us, and you deserve to bond with someone of *your* choosing."

"I know what it is my body wants and I am in control of it," she whispered softly. "You need not worry," she added.

Though I was not entirely convinced, I did not wish to

part from her so suddenly nor did I wish to hinder what one day might be. I wrapped my arms around her tightly drawing her towards me just before rolling onto my back. It was with delight that I watched her fiery locks drop onto my chest just as a faint giggle escaped her. A sound few focus upon or perhaps even remember until it is heard no more, but we all are capable of such. It was that giggle I found myself concentrating on. Though faint, it echoed throughout the cavern and in my mind, making me long to return to the outside world. It was not until I heard it that I realized I could not remember the last time someone giggled in my presence. I found myself distracted trying to think of it and I soon realized it did not matter. Regardless of when or whom it may have been from, the only voice I wished to hear now, was hers.

Pulling away from her as I did moments ago appeared to calm the primal urges we were feeling, but in drawing her back towards me, I felt those embers ignite once more. I found her gaze once more unwavering from mine and I could not remember why I wanted to pull away from her. In a blink, we were drawn back into a sea of passionate, deep kisses that felt never-ending. It was then when I felt fear pulling me back from her. Not because I was afraid, but because I was not unafraid. I tore myself from her and turned away where she could not see my face. I did not wish for her to see me in such a light. I was conflicted and my emotions were running recklessly away with me, a feeling I was not accustomed to in the slightest. I felt her pulling herself towards me, clinging to my back the way she did when we first met. I wanted to turn to hold her once more, but I could not bring myself to turn back towards her.

"What are you afraid of?" she uttered sounding concerned.

I sat there, arms wrapped around my legs with my face buried within them, trying to think of what it was that made me turn away from her. I wanted her to want me, almost desperately, to which she did, but that was not enough. I felt every fiber of my being pulling me towards her, but upon the brink of ecstasy my body was screaming for me to wait. Why? Then I thought of everything again. We are immortal spirits. We have been known to spend centuries searching for one to bond with. Once bonded, I knew naught if we were able to bond with another. We are not impulsive in our choice. Our actions just now screamed impulsive, but having already felt the bond with another, I knew naught why my call to her was so strong. It was then that I knew what was truly bothering me.

"That nothing is what it seems and what we feel for one another is merely an illusion created from the beast blood that surges within us."

I felt her arms wrap around me just before she placed her cheek against my back as she had done that morning in the stream. Her thoughts were wandering, toiling over if it was something she did or if her mind and body could have been mistaken in their choice. I decided to ease her burden.

"Eira, I am a broken man, heavily battered and worn by centuries of loss. Though we can let desire consume us and greet tomorrow with whatever may come. My past and my heart insist I not be so hasty with such a matter."

I reached for her hand and stroked my fingers across the smooth flesh that lay upon them. It was the sound of her breathing, steady and effortless, that relaxed my troubled heart. I closed my eyes to focus upon the sound, when the beat of her heart joined into play an unsung melody that was beginning to be all that I needed.

"There is a war now waging within us," I continued. "Do you believe you can separate what Caladh demands of us versus what you know in your heart to be the path of your choosing?"

"Aye, for the demands of Caladh mirror what my heart already desires," she uttered softly.

I felt her hand slide my long locks aside gently before placing her lips upon the back of my neck, kissing it softly. I felt my thoughts vanish and the words I intended to utter lost within my throat. The force I felt previously pulling me towards her was resurfacing once more. It was commanding in its presence, demanding I heed to its call by remaining with her and protecting her. It forced me to feel desperate at the thought of losing her, a feeling that made me weak. However, the strength I found by just being near her was remarkable. My conflicting thoughts and desires refused to be deciphered so easily. Whether this feeling was my traumatic past misleading me or it was leading me towards the one person I was destined to embrace, the line dividing them was marginal.

"I do not wish to take you as a beast in the night," I uttered more forcefully than I intended, "as it feels presently. For though we can become beasts of our choosing, it is your flesh upon mine that I wish to savor should that be to your liking. For centuries I have felt my heart calling out, searching for what will make it whole again then I found you. There is no world of which I would choose to live that you do not exist and should we long to bond for eternity, it can wait one more day."

She kissed my shoulder ever so softly before whispering, "I wish I could have been birthed sooner, so that your heart might not have ever been broken."

I turned back towards her to take her in my arms once more, kissing her softly. Though she was not the one who broke my heart, she was the one willing to love it as it were with no thought or agenda for a different tomorrow.

After the events of the last few days, I longed to remain within his arms. It was there that I found the comfort I desperately needed. It was there I felt safe and the torment that ailed me melted away. I found myself lingering upon his every breath, fearful that one day he, too, would be taken from me again. Each time I thought of it I felt ill. Though it would appear we had just met, nothing about him felt foreign to me. It was as if I was connected to him in a way I did not yet understand or maybe was not ready to understand. Bryn, a man I considered my companion for many years would not hold a candle to the internal flame that burns for this man. In a moment of fury, he offered his beating heart to King Ferand to protect me. One does not make such an offer for mere kin, but somehow, I knew if it had come to that, he would do just that and I the same for him. A thought both endearing and frightening.

Retracing that moment in my mind, I lay there in

anguish of Drayk's betrayal as the nathair's poison began to surge throughout my body. With each beat of my heart, it clawed its way through me forcing the pain to grow stronger. As if the poison was an extension of the beast itself, motivated and continually seeking to kill. The tear of my flesh from the nathair's fang felt mild compared to the fire that was now racing through my veins, burning all within its reach. The pain demanded my focus, and I could think of little else. Through strength I could not comprehend, Conall pushed through the warlock's debilitating mind blare and charged towards King Ferand. His body struck into King Ferand's torso with enough speed and force that he was launched across the sandy floor before crashing into the stone wall that lay beyond. I knew not of what he had hoped the action would accomplish, but in doing so it bought us time. Time we may not have had should he not have persisted. As I lay there, grimacing from the pain, Conall placed his body upon mine, shielding me from the wrath King Ferand would unleash provided he was able to return to us. The moment was grim, but with his arms at my sides and his eyes staring into mine, I felt the world around us temporarily grow silent. His eyes were beautiful and unwilling to turn away from mine, like the sun breaking through the clouds on a summer's eve. Persistent and pleading. I willed the moment to linger, but I knew it would not. Feeling the tears welling up in my eyes, my heart began to race knowing I would soon be taken from his arms. It was then when I felt myself flinch, breaking the memory.

Eira, are you unwell?

I had not realized my eyes had been closed until I heard

his voice, drawing them open once more to be met with his. With no other thought, just the feeling that arose within me from finding his eyes as I opened mine, I already felt the tension of the nightmare dissipating. I turned slightly to lay my head upon his shoulder and exhaled slowly trying to slow my frantic heart that once more was racing. I felt him wrap his arms around me before drawing my long locks back from the nape of my neck, where his fingers returned to caress my flesh. Though rough around the edges, his touch was like no other and it soothed me greatly.

What troubles you?

I felt compelled to answer but decided to remain as I was. Continually toiling over what we could not change seemed futile and it was only a memory now after all. Yearning to distract myself with the thoughts of a euphoric induced haze or anything that would make the dismal chamber we now found ourselves in disappear, I thought of Bryn. I had not realized how little I had thought of him until this moment. It made me wonder if he, too, had someone caring for him and comforting him as I did. It was in thoughts of him when I felt Conall's breathing change. I could not tell what it was that disturbed him or if hearing my thoughts of Bryn that worried him, but I did not wish to toil over anything more than was necessary.

Tell me of the world you remember. I long to hear of a time when our people were many and there were no cages to hold us.

The land was lush and plentiful with life not so long ago. While there was some darkness, as is always required for the light to prevail, it was rarely seen, and we did not fear it. The world belonged to the fae, and they took pride in their creation. Vast mountains covered in never-ending greenery and a sky that never seemed to grow dark. Even when the weather would turn cold or cast a storm upon us, all of Caladh remained at peace. It was there we could flourish and roam about in the light versus disappearing in the shadows as we do now. Other than fearing the mischievous actions of a nearby lurking brownie clan, there was little to cause a fuss over.

I was born in the fields of Feurach just as the morning sun broke through the horizon on a midsummer's eve. I remember little of the one's who greeted me, but it was the hum of my mother's lullaby that I can still remember. It was there I made my home and there I intended for my bairns to be birthed. The fields were bountiful with wildflowers of nearly every variety, and one could lose their self within the flower's fragrant embrace. They blanketed the peaks and valleys with an array of colors, that changed frequently throughout the year, but they were nearly always there. One could find themselves lost in a sea of them for days without being disturbed by others. It was in those fields that I took my first steps and, in those fields, where I would later come into my own. I remember laying in those fields, a soft breeze shifting overhead carrying seedlings off to make anew nearby accompanied with the scent of the sea just to the east of me. Had I but known the comfort of my homeland would not last and I would have lingered in those fields longer.

The fields were no longer as he described, not even remotely. Although, I can remember seeing tiny white flowers billowing in the breeze as the tall grass in Feurach would sway in unison, I remember naught of the fields of color he spoke of. My time spent in Feurach was lengthy, for it was the safest of regions outside of Lamprog for us, but I frequently found myself saddened just by being there. I knew naught the cause. I wish I could have seen it as it was, unspoiled by man. It sounded lovely.

What of your family? Surely a few must have remained after the great divide.

Aye, that they did. Most of my family were taken during the torrent of fire and brimstone that erupted into our world, fracturing it at its core. The ones that did not perish then would soon thereafter. Within the next century, man had been birthed from within Boglach and were thriving. They took advantage of Caladh's kindness and soon began devouring anything that the torrent of fire did not. My sister was the last to be taken from me. We had returned to the fields I loved so much only to be greeted by a pack of Jagare lying in wait for our return. Though I do not believe they understood what we truly were, they only saw us as elves that had strayed or were abandoned by our kin. Both young and naïve in a world that very rarely gave second chances. They saw my sister as an object of their desire, ripe and ready for the picking. It was there they took her from me. One by one they had her just before and leaving her body for the darkness to feed upon. It was in the night she had passed on and her spirit vanished before me. I never saw her or felt her presence again.

I felt his body shudder, no doubt reliving the memory in his mind. Despite the memory being from so long ago, he

31

would never fully be rid of the torment. He carried it close to his heart, as a badge of honor and as a warning to be mindful of the choices he makes. If I did not fully understand his actions before, I could see the purpose behind them more clearly now.

Before her death, I took no pleasure in taking the lives of men. I believed they were defending and feeding their own as we were, but after that I would leave none alive if given the chance. Perhaps that makes me cruel, but upon their arrival they have sentenced all unlike themselves to death or worse, imprisonment as we are now.

As I looked upon him, eyes pressed tightly together, I could sense he was in pain. A pain that could not be silenced or healed by any magic elves could possess. I placed one of my hands upon his cheek where I felt him lean in to kiss it softly as I nuzzled his other cheek with my own.

"You must miss them all terribly," I spoke softly breaking the silence.

He nodded.

"When the world erupted in fire and brimstone, was it ever known what truly happened to cause such?" I asked trying to distract him.

His body relaxed somewhat when I heard him speak for what felt like the first time in ages.

"Dark magic," he said frankly, "what it did not destroy, it poisoned."

"Boglach," I muttered.

He nodded once more.

"But by whom? No one has that kind of power."

"It was believed to be the elves of Tiene, though I am

not convinced."

"It could not be," I felt my voice upturn with surprise just before I pulled away from him as I rose to my feet. "They raised me from my birth until I fled in search of another like myself. They could never have done this."

"That was just what was believed and over the years the tale continually changes." He stood quickly just as I began pacing. "No one knows of their true power, not even King Aldon as they remain isolated in a world of intense fire."

"Even if they could, I do not believe they would," I insisted. "There is no purpose behind breaking open the world. Nothing good would come of it." He stepped before me, stopping me where I stood. "I have pledged my undying loyalty to the elves as I believe only they can protect us from man."

I felt myself spiraling and suddenly quite ill over the matter. After all, it was King Aldon who had kept me safe until now and the elves of Tiene who raised me. Neither of them had given me a reason not to trust them. It was in thinking of the possibility that I had been misguided or even betrayed once more when I thought of Drayk. Just thinking his name pained me and brought memories of his bright eyes forward in my mind. I found myself once more drawn to him, curious to see behind the mask he clung to so desperately. I wished to know what he was hiding from the world. The pain intensified. I placed a hand upon my brow trying to stop the pain when I felt his hands grasp my arms, pulling my attention back towards him.

"Only we can protect ourselves from man," he sounded

confident.

"I do not believe we have been doing such a good job of it up until now," I mumbled.

"Together," he clasped my hands within his, "we can and regardless of who released the dark magic into our world, we were not the only ones who have suffered."

I wanted to exude his confidence, but looking upon his face now, I could not.

"We must get out of here," I whispered, "or they will surely torture us until our bodies are abandoned by our spirits."

"That may not be possible, for the way out is sealed by magic, not just iron as I would have hoped. Of course, now that you are here, they will never open the door without Haxa for it would be too risky for them."

"Then we must think of something else," I mumbled.

I ran my fingertips across the scar on his lip before looking into his eyes. They were once more heavily focused upon mine and glowing brightly.

"It pains me to think of them hurting you. Had I arrived sooner, and you might have been spared."

He sighed, "Had you arrived any sooner and you would have either bore witness to the act or placed at my side to endure it with me." He frowned, "Ferand is a varlet masquerading as a king. He knows little of its demands or how to manage those demands properly. There would have been no stopping him."

I felt my heart sink and with that my expression. With a gaze that rarely falters, he watched me carefully as I felt his hand running just underneath the leathers that barely covered my belly. It was there he glided his fingertips back and forth across the puncture wounds. It both tickled and pained me to feel his touch as it were. The poison from the nathair could easily have remained there and even as he touched me now, I still felt it ache more than I believed it should.

"Their poison is powerful I have been told," he uttered.

I nodded, "The pain from it was like nothing I had ever felt, and I was certain it was going to claim me within the Ice Tower. I never imagined I would have been strong enough to withstand its power twice."

"The will to live is a powerful one," he uttered, barely above a whisper, "but you are wrong about one thing."

My focus was broken, "I am not sure what you mean."

"Although King Ferand will without a doubt attempt to break us, he will not kill us. He needs us in order to stack the game in his favor," he said frankly. "However, the purpose I was once led to believe, is no longer founded and Ferand's true purpose alludes me. Man has never wasted time on compassion, so protecting us will never be out of the goodness in their hearts."

"What is it you believe they want?" I felt my words catch in my throat, fearful of the answer, but once again my curiosity would not cease.

His arms wrapped around my lower back pulling my body against his. I could once again feel his every movement, from the tightening of his muscles to the blood surging through his veins. The heat that he exudes forced my flesh to flush from the sudden surge. It was then I could see him and understand him in a way I could not before. Everything we do and everything we feel, the other one experiences. There is no denying it or escaping it. It was clear his strength was returning to him, but with that his apprehension was growing.

"I do not understand," I mumbled feeling my gaze tighten slightly in confusion.

"I know naught of their true purpose for us, but I know they want us together. We are stronger that way. Surely you must feel it," he spoke confidently once more.

I nodded briefly, "Aye, that I do," I paused, trying to place my thoughts and feelings for him together within my mind before uttering them aloud. I could utter nothing more than the simplest of responses was all I could muster at the moment. "What I feel with you…and for you is like nothing I have felt before."

There was so much more I wanted to say. I wanted to tell him that I knew him, without knowing him. That up until now, I felt my spirit had been sleeping and when I heard his voice that day it had awakened. That every time he gazed upon me with those bright golden eyes, I felt my heart was going to break through my chest just to be closer to his. Of course, none of those words had escaped me when I needed them to, and I felt cowardly for not being bolder in my manner. I wrapped my arms around his neck before nuzzling him with my nose and cheek. It felt instinctual and one of the few animalistic traits that seemed to carry over into my elven form. The simple act, while soothing, once more stirred something within me. It felt primal and possibly familial. Once again, the questions began nagging at my mind. How did he come to be in this place? If what we were feeling was primal or possibly familial, then why did I not feel this with Bryn? Are there others out there like us? The questions felt endless and just as more were starting to break through, I heard him speak.

"I was taken in Boglach by the Warrior Prince and his men. After a heated and prolonged battle, I sought refuge in the brush, where I collapsed and changed back to my elven form. Since they did not witness the change, they believed me to be a lorvisad and sought the opportunity to extract secrets of the elven kingdoms. There is only one other to my knowledge, and I believe that person to be Bryn that you spoke of." He paused for several moments, "And this feeling, the rush between us, I cannot fully explain it. I believe it is amplified, nonetheless, by nature's continual desire for us to exist despite the challenges that persist."

I felt my thoughts stop in utter disbelief and my body stiffen. His response surprised me to say the least, forgetting all too soon that he can hear me without even a word being uttered. Yet as I listen for his thoughts, there is often nothing. How can that be?

"Over time you will learn to control it," he paused, "and even though I do not long to hear your every thought, they are quite thunderous at times."

I withdrew my cheek from his just before pulling back enough to where my gaze could meet his without discomfort.

"Pardon?"

He smiled briefly before responding, "Highly passionate people tend to think and live boldly." He raised himself slightly before leaning forward to kiss my forehead. "Besides, I enjoy them greatly."

I felt slightly uncomfortable at knowing my thoughts were no longer my own, but relief soon followed. In knowing those thoughts, it would be easier for us to understand one another. In thinking of that, I felt like slightly less of a coward for not speaking my thoughts earlier. It did not take long for my thoughts to return to his words when I recalled him mentioning Bryn by name.

"You know of Bryn?" I blurted out suddenly.

"Aye, perhaps not initially, but he is the only other one I have seen in quite some time."

"You have seen him?" I uttered with a desperation in my voice that I had not intended.

"Aye, I must admit that I was surprised to see one of our own in such a position of power. I had wondered if he was there against his will, but after watching him for some time, he did not appear ill at ease."

"Do you recall where you saw him? Was he in the Kingdom of Light?" I pressed him.

"Aye, it was," he responded sounding very hesitant. "Nearly a year ago now, he held a position in King Itheal's high court. From what I was able to infer, he was masquerading as an ambassador of sorts for King Aldon. He did not appear distressed in the least."

I felt my head spinning at the suggestion he was living out in the open as it were, yet I was unable to find him in all my time searching. It was there that he was taken from me and there he requested I find him. What was going on in Losgadh that kept him there? Could it have been a situation like what we had found ourselves in? What if it was all a trap?

"When we met in Coille that morning, that is who you were seeking?" He spoke softly and though his words may have come out questioning he by no means was searching for me to answer. "If you knew where he was, why were you in Coille?"

I shook my head briefly, "I only know that is where he wished for me to find him, not that he was already there. Had I known he was in plain sight all along and we would have been reunited ages ago."

"Then why venture towards Tuiteam at all?" he sounded genuinely curious now.

"I was misled by my own foolishness. Had I but lingered just a little while longer as Yew encouraged and both of us might have remained free."

Intrigued by my response, he prodded me to tell him more. We sat down upon the chamber's floor, where I told him the dreaded tale of how I came to find myself locked within this chamber with him. As I retold it all from the beginning, it felt as if a lifetime had passed, but in truth it had only been days. Thinking over it all now, I should have probably given us both a bit more credit for what we withstood. The turmoil and torture that found us would have surely killed nearly anyone else, but we were still here. Badly beaten and soon to be heavily scarred, but we were alive. It was not long before he encouraged me to stop and rest with him. As he tucked me into the nook of his arm and against his chest, I barely blinked before all went dark. It was there that I awoke a short time later, still carefully tucked within his tender embrace. With his breathing steady and mind at ease, I looked upon his face and once again felt an all too familiar feeling overwhelming me. It was then when an unfamiliar memory came forward in my mind.

      Late one eve, as we were lying in the fields of Feurach, I gazed upon him resting peacefully under the moonlight. His flesh glistening from small droplets of water that clung to him. His breathing was deep, as if he had just returned from a hunt, yet he appeared content. There was a faint smell of salt floating within the breeze and with each gust, hundreds of white petals went dancing through the air, like snowflakes in winter. As I glanced around us, it was clear we were surrounded by hundreds of the flowers those petals were taken from. Clasping a few of the petals within my grasp, I indulged in their velvety softness and long to fall into a deep sleep in a bed of their creation. It was in that thought that my gaze returned to him.

      I did not hear anything spoken, but as I watched him, his bright eyes opened just before shifting to meet my gaze. Through half-lidded eyes he watched me, and I watched him. He began to utter something, but it was not the words that caught my attention or what kept it. It was the sound of the soft laughter that followed. He was happy. As he turned towards me, I noticed there were no scars upon his face and the mind that has been so terribly troubled by loss, was in a state of bliss. The scarred face I had come to know, and was beginning to love, was not the face I was seeing now. It was different. He was different. He appeared euphoric, untouched by the darkened world we now found ourselves in. I felt my breathing quicken, my flesh tighten, and my heart race just looking upon him as he were. I wanted to lean towards him, so that he could take me in his arms. Unfortunately, as I reached for him, he vanished from my sight.

My eyes opened, surprised to realize that it was all just a dream. I did not have a moment to think as his gaze was once again seeking mine. When our eyes met, I felt the same flood of emotion that I had felt hours before. As if there was nothing to extinguish the embers inside me that burned passionately and only for him.

"Conall," I spoke softly as I gently began tracing an unseen shape upon his chest as a means of distracting myself. "I...I..." my voice trailed off and I felt the courage that was once so strong, fade away out of fear.

"Eira," he spoke softly with a gaze to match, "what is it?"

"I just saw something...or dreamt it really," I buried my face within his chest. "I am no longer certain, but it was so real. I could feel the breeze upon my flesh and smell the white flowers that grow in the fields of Feurach as they fluttered upon the twists and turns of the breeze. I wanted it to be real."

I heard my voice turn airy and I closed my eyes willing my mind to take me back to that place. I wanted to see his face as it were, untouched by trauma and exhilarated at the sight of me.

"What was it you saw?" he uttered barely audible and sounding quite unsure of what my response may be.

"We were together in the fields of Feurach, resting beneath a starlit sky, your body glistening in the moonlight. You spoke little, but I will never forget your face. Untouched by the burdens you now carry, yet, I have never seen you happier."

"You saw that just now?" he spoke with angst in his voice.

"Aye, that I did," I uttered breathlessly, feeling a wave of emotions wash over me.

"Are you certain that moment was what you saw?" the concern in his voice was rising along with his heartbeat. He sounded desperate.

Opening my eyes quickly, I forced myself to pull away from his chest where I looked up in search of his gaze. When I found it, I could see tears welling up in his eyes. Something about this dream bothered him greatly and I longed to know the reason behind those tears.

"Conall," I reached up to wipe them away, "are you alright?" I paused slightly before continuing as I was unsure if it were my dream that upset him or something else. It was then that I believed dropping the matter would have been for the best as we have not the strength to toil over such trivial things. "Forgive me," I added, "we need not dwell on it as it was just a dream."

He swallowed hard several times before speaking.

"That is not a dream you had," he uttered sounding surprisingly out of breath, "but a memory."

I felt his gaze resting heavily upon me, almost in disbelief.

"Is it even possible to recall someone else's memory?" I uttered feeling lost.

Without uttering another word and before I felt I could blink; I felt his lips upon mine. They were deep, passionate kisses that were filled with such emotion that I felt physical pain within me when his lips would part from mine. Yet, I did not wish for them to stop. Our bodies melted together in a blaze of heat and with each scrape of my flesh upon his, I felt his heartbeat race even more than before. Each touch of his hands pulling my body towards his and each kiss that I placed upon him felt even more powerful than the last. I often felt distracted in his presence, lost in the thought of him or the feelings that were washing over me. In being with him as we were now, consumed my very existence. Neither my body nor my spirit felt like its own, only as if it were part of his. With his aid, we removed the leathers that once covered my body, and I watched as his eyes gazed upon my flesh with wonder. His eyes hungry. Had that look been given by anyone other than him, I would have been frightened, but I trusted him in a way I trusted no other.

I sat up, pulling myself closer to him. It was there where I began to tear at the breeches that no longer could conceal his desire. I willed them to no longer be between us. Of course, the one moment we needed to be rid of them quickly and they just would not give. When they failed to yield to my demands, he pulled at them, tearing them, and casting the remains aside just before lowering ourselves onto the chamber's floor. He hovered over me, clearly savoring the moment and feeling the warmth of my body beneath his. He was the most relaxed I had ever seen him even though I could feel my belly begin to tremble with anticipation, his thoughts were only of my comfort. He ran his fingers down my side and onto my belly making it tremble even more, causing me to let out a soft giggle in surprise. This made him smile greatly. As he glided his fingers back and forth across my flesh, I felt more at ease. It was then my body shuddered one final time, presumably sloughing off the last of my apprehension. It was there when I saw the face that I had in my dream, looking back at me filled with euphoria as I ran my fingers through his long wind-braided locks. With each kiss, he was asking for my permission and each time I answered by only pleading with him for more.

Our bodies now panting with anticipation and with each pant our lungs exhaled, the air danced upon our flesh in a failed attempt to cool our overheated bodies. Our mouths opened to one another through deepened kisses and dancing tongues, furthering the desire for one another. It was then I recognized that it was not just our bodies clinging to one another, but our spirits. They were willing us to make the bond and be one with each other. As the moment drew closer, I felt myself waiting for a sign of his apprehension or a thought of hesitation as there was before, but there was nothing. His thoughts were only of me. While they were once just verbalizing what he was feeling, they were now pleading with me, worshiping me in a language that had never been known to me, all the while calling me his *ionuin*. In hearing his lips utter that I was his beloved, I could wait no longer. I prayed to him and pleaded with him to solidify the bond I so desperately desired. Wrapping an arm around me, cradling my head in his hand, while kissing me softly. It was then I knew he could wait no longer, and I felt the world around me begin to change. It was in his embrace I abandoned all that I had and all that I was to become one with him in a sea of fire.

It had been days since Prince Berenger was pulled from the depths of the marsh and brought to the Kingdom of Losgadh. Had it not been for the courage and might of one man, he surely would have perished that day. Though the tale of their misadventure was told through the scattered sputters of a frightened man, it was still unclear to us as to what or who had sent the vessel away that would have carried them safely to us. We attempted to gather more information from the young man, but our attempts were futile. The only detail that we were confident on was that the man's name was Kenric, as he would not stop repeating it upon their arrival. They were both badly shaken and neither has said little since their arrival. Prince Berenger was a deeply broken man in the throes of a battle between life and the other side. We were unsure which side would emerge victorious. Frequently Prince Berenger would cry out in agony or be seen pleading with the hallucinations of his weakened mind. It was in the deepest trenches of his anguish that my darling Rose flocked to his side to tend to his every need despite her father's growing disapproval over the matter. She claimed it was her duty and for the love of her betrothed, Ferand, that she cares for him. In truth, I believe this was just a means to distract her already troubled mind.

While we had lost none of our desire for one another, it was proving to be quite difficult keeping each other at arm's length when in the presence of others. Through stolen kisses and trysts in the moonlight, I no longer doubted her love for me, but it was her duty that still troubled her with each passing day. With the arrival of Prince Berenger, I could not bear to press her over the matter, nor could I bring myself to tell her of the lies and secrecy that surrounded her conception and birth. However, the time would soon come when I could wait no longer as there was once more stirrings of the betrothal growing cold. King Itheal would never have it be as such and was beginning to toil over the matter at all hours of the day and night. Should it be his intention for the betrothal to move forward as planned and we would soon be expected to depart for Tuiteam along with Prince Berenger. Forcing Prince Berenger to depart before he has mended was just the means to ensure that King Ferand's heart had not swayed in our absence or the hand of my darling, Rose, may be promised to another. King Itheal would never tolerate such a violation of their agreement, but of what I know of King Ferand, I would put little past him.

With thoughts swirling of the impending voyage looming in my mind, my thoughts once again turned towards Eira. I had not been able to locate her since she stumbled upon the enchanted grove. Attempting to extend my reach towards her only brought me more pain and with each failed attempt King Itheal became further irritated with the delay. Each time yielded an additional piece, but nothing that appeared to be of any use: a sandy floor, an angelic statue, a man with locks of caramel heavily scarred and bloody. Had I not witnessed the angelic statue, I would have assumed she was in a prison of sorts. Of course, had it been a prison she was in and there are only a few located on the mainland. None of which I can recall that appear as this one. If there was even a remote chance I could find her again, I would need to keep struggling regardless of the dangers the task posed to me.

I waited for the moon to begin its ascent into the night sky before laying down to try once more. Closing my eyes, I thought of her yet again: her honeycomb eyes, the twists and turns of her locks as they billowed in the breeze, and the way her skin appeared to glow brightest in the presence of a sunset. I drifted to her quicker this time than in times past which caused a great feeling of concern within me. Whoever had been watching over her previously has either since moved on or they wanted me to see what I was about to see. Her face came into view, and she was once again not alone. I found her wrapped within a man's arms, but this time it was clear this man was not man, rather elven for his ears were unmistakable. To my disliking, they both appeared distraught and quite unwell. There was a greyish tone to her skin and the way he clung to her frightened me in a way I had not felt for some time. I longed to reach for her to comfort her. Unfortunately, as the thought entered my mind, she faded from my sight once more.

I sat up sharply feeling a surge of thunder strike in my mind forcing me to return to my previous position. Seeing her as she was changed something within me, although, I am unsure why it would have.

Just as I was drifting off into a sea of mystery, my attention was snapped back to the present when there was a knock at the door.

"Lord Bryn," the voice called out, "King Itheal has requested your presence."

I groaned slightly as I sat back up, willing the page to be silent. When I did not respond right away, he knocked again, only more insistent this time.

"Lord Bryn!" he shouted.

"Aye, aye, I heard you!" I shouted back almost immediately wishing I had not.

I brought my feet to the floor and struggled to gain a footing as I stood, weary legged and unsteady. Despite the dizziness I was experiencing, King Itheal could not be kept waiting. I needed to tell him that the key he had been seeking and waiting for may not be coming. I could not say that for sure, but something about the way I found the two of them made me question if they were in a place that they could flee or if they were choosing not to. Making my way towards the door, holding my head in my hands, I used the wall and door for support before opening it and stepping out into the long, dim hall. The page looked upon me with concern and in my frustrated state I snapped at him.

"Wipe that look off your face before I do it for you," I paused, "this does not concern you."

He nodded vigorously but did not utter a sound just pointed in the direction he wished me to go. I heeded his instruction without barely more than a second glance. As I stumbled my way through the halls following the page's guidance, he scurried behind me as if there was a remote chance he could have carried me should there be a need. Upon reaching King Itheal's study, I swiftly composed myself before opening the door and stepping inside, making sure to leave the page behind to nearly be struck in the nose with the door.

King Itheal smiled, "Lord Bryn," his smile was slowly fading, "you look unwell. It appears this situation we have found ourselves in is taxing you as well."

"It is not without difficulty, Your Majesty," I responded pleasantly.

"Indeed," he gestured for me to come closer. "However, it is not without reason that I summoned you here this eve."

I stepped forward just before nodding my understanding, eager to know where his attention had been drawn.

"While it may be against the advice of my counsel, I have decided it is time for the Lady Rosalyn to move forward with her betrothal. Along with returning Prince Berenger to his homeland for further aid and recovery."

Although, I knew this moment had been coming since Prince Berenger had arrived, I had been hoping it was further off and a look of surprise found its way upon my face.

"Ah," he paused, "I see you are not pleased with my course of action either."

I attempted to recover from my momentary lapse. "Not in the least, Your Majesty. I am here to assist you in any way you see fit."

He did not appear convinced.

"You depart just after sunrise and unless doldrums set in, you should reach Tuiteam's port by first morning's light on the morrow. To which they will be expecting you."

I nodded pretending to understand. Though, I was unaware as to how they would be expecting us with no word sent when another thought entered my mind, Rose. If she had intentions of backing out of the betrothal, it must be now. Should we arrive in Tuiteam, and they will never permit her to leave. I was about to turn and exit the chamber when Eira crossed my mind as well. Against my better judgement and without it being asked of me, I decided to probe King Itheal about the place I now found Eira to be.

"If it not be a burden, might I ask Your Majesty a question?"

"Proceed," he said sternly.

"The key you seek has been taken," I paused, "to a place unknown to me as I am not as knowledgeable of the mainland as you are."

"This key," he paused, "how do you know it has been taken?" he responded.

I glanced around the room briefly, deciding to tread carefully with the information that followed considering those present.

"For it no longer heeds to its master's call."

"Are you certain of this?" he probed.

"Aye, I make attempts daily and have been met with resistance. Perhaps I might share some of what I saw?"

He gestured for me to continue.

"Angelic statues found above a dimly lit sandy floor with stone walls of nearly an identical shade. Does that mean anything to Your Majesty?"

I watched him carefully for any sign of acknowledgement but only confusion graced his face. A sign that did not bode hope within me. Dropping my head slightly in disappointment, I was about to vacate the study when I heard one of the guards pipe up.

"It is the Hall of Everfall to which you speak," his voice echoed across the study, drawing the attention of all present.

He promptly knelt before King Itheal, "Forgive me, Your Majesty, for it was not my place to speak without your permission."

He remained as he was, waiting patiently for King Itheal to grant him amnesty for his contribution.

"Rise now, for all is forgiven," King Itheal asserted. "Where is the location of the hall you speak of?"

"While I cannot say for certain, it is believed to be beneath Tuiteam's castle."

"Tell me of this place, how do you know of it?" I insisted, forgetting my place as well.

King Itheal glanced at me briefly in surprise but uttered nothing. Regardless of the information I sought or may have been presently, I was rarely, if ever, this bold in my manner. It was not wise.

"Even soldiers speak to one another from time to time.

Had you not mentioned the sandy floor I would have been as lost as the others."

"I do not understand," I added.

"Tuiteam's castle rests largely on a bed of old caverns formed in the sandstone," he paused searching our faces for understanding when he continued. "Over time, the stone has shifted and broken, creating the caverns we know to be there and leaving sandy beds around and even under the castle's walls."

"Why proclaim it as the Hall of Everfall?" King Itheal interjected.

"For it is there that they lay their dead," he added solemnly.

"Then it is a tomb?" I questioned.

"Only for those of their choosing," he added. "It is said that anyone not of their bloodline is turned to ash and given back to Caladh. That is why no graves are to be found there."

I felt my face tighten in confusion as I have never known another city of man to treat their dead in such a way. It was then King Itheal turned his attention back towards me despite my concentration still upon this.

"Lord Bryn," he snapped his fingers, pulling my attention back towards him. "At the conclusion of the coronation, I suggest you fetch this key and return it to me with all haste."

"Aye, it is understood," I responded promptly.

I bowed before him and promptly exited the study before beginning a brief descent into madness as the questions flooded my already strained mind. As I brought my pace to a stroll, I felt each one of those questions pulling at me with an insistence I was not prepared for. What brought her to Tuiteam? Who was the elven man that now clings to her so desperately and who was he to her? What of Rose…should I tell her of her lineage or permit her to travel to Tuiteam even though I was advised against it? If so, how would I be able to endure watching her wed another when I feel as I do for her? The questions seemed never-ending. As I grasped my head in my hands once more, I pleaded with them to stop. Though they did not.

It was not without difficulty, I reached my bedchamber and slammed the door behind me, just before lowering myself to the floor in anguish. Unsure of how I was to make decisions such as these, I sat there for what felt like a lifetime in contemplation over them. When no logical or rational course of action presented itself, my mind wandered to irrational ones and then back again. The only choice that I could focus upon would be to tell Rose the truth and hope that her love for me was enough for her to flee from her homeland with me. However, in doing so, I could potentially become a lorvisad and she would undoubtably be executed as a traitor to the crown along with abandoning Eira to her fate. I do not believe this is a battle I could win. No matter the choice, someone would be lost to me or worse, I could lose them both.

I turned to note the moon was now nearly at its peak in the night sky and the candles in my bedchamber had since burnt out. If I was waiting for a more opportune time to be alone with Rose, there would not be one. Soon she would be endlessly surrounded by guards until she was presented to King

Ferand and lost to me forever. I must go to her while there was still time. Standing swiftly, I cast the door aside and rushed towards her bedchamber nearly colliding with her lady's maid moments after rounding the last corner. Unsure as to her purpose there at that hour, I tried to brush off the encounter with a brief bow. Unfortunately, her hand landed firmly on my forearm forcing my gaze to meet hers.

"Lord Bryn," she gave a brief smile, "having trouble sleeping?"

"Aye, madam," I nodded, "thought a late-night stroll might cease a weary mind."

"Walk with me, would you?" she uttered softly before turning to walk down the hall of which I just came.

I exhaled heavier than I anticipated but turned to follow her out of respect.

"It appears you have not informed the Lady Rosalyn," she glanced at me briefly, "for had you and surely, she would have fled the castle with you by now. She is quite taken with you."

"Madam, I assure you, I know naught of what you speak."

"Come now, Lord Bryn," she glanced at me once more, "I have watched you work tirelessly to follow the breadcrumbs that were lain before you."

I felt my eyes widen in surprise. "It was you," I whispered feeling a sense of confusion and irritation over the matter. "How do you know of such matters?"

She stopped just before turning towards me, "For I have lived many years within these walls, leaving little that occurs within them unseen by me."

I grabbed the back of her arm and pulled her towards the nearest chamber, closing the door behind us gently.

"Unhand me Lord Bryn," she insisted.

I released my grasp and watched as she rubbed her arm where I grabbed her. While it was my intention to be forceful, I had not intended to cause her discomfort. I was attempting to apologize for my actions, but my thoughts were already being pulled elsewhere.

"Why divulge this information to me?" I whispered, "What purpose would it serve?"

"Lord Bryn," she sighed, "I greatly care for the Lady Rosalyn. In doing so, it would pain me to watch her beheaded or worse, tortured for her deception."

"But it was not of her choosing that everyone was deceived," I insisted.

"A moot point, as I am certain that detail will not matter in the least to King Ferand."

"Does anyone else know that she is elven, at least in part?"

"Of that I cannot say but should someone know or her betrothed discover this for himself upon looking at his bride's bright blue eyes and there will be no mercy for her." She touched my forearm once more, "I have watched this tale unfold for many years and there shall be no happy ending."

"As there was not one for her mother..." I felt my voice trail off, saddened by the thought.

"I knew Queen Drusilla quite well, almost as well as the elven noble who came to covet her in the moonlight. Both of which I would expect to be appalled at all that has happened since that fateful night."

"What night are you referring to?"

"The night they were discovered of course." She sounded surprised at my inquiry but leaned in closer to me clearly willing to tell me the tale. "They were found caressing one another down by the waterfront early one morning when an onlooker recognized her and summoned the royal guard. While she was taken and imprisoned for her indiscretion, her lover suffered a fate far worse than death. He was tortured relentlessly for months, first by King Itheal and then undoubtably by King Aldon. I knew not of what became of him until I saw him many months later. Unbeknownst to me, he managed to arrive on the day of Queen Drusilla's execution. I caught a glimpse of him perched on a building nearby, just out of sight for any potential onlooker. It was there where he watched his bairn be cut from the womb of his lover moments before her own life was taken from her. Somehow, he had found his way back to her, but while his eyes still shone brightly in the light, his heart had grown cold."

I felt my heart sink within me and while previously I believed I understood the danger loving Rose posed, hearing this tale tells me I truly did not.

"And what of the Lady Rosalyn?" I uttered.

"She was stripped of her elven ears and cast aside for some time as King Itheal could not bring himself to look upon her face."

"Striped of her ears, I do not understand," I spoke softly.

"They were cut," she paused, "to make her appear more as one of us," she said frankly. "Aside from Queen Drusilla's execution, it was the vilest act I have ever known to be committed in the Kingdom of Losgadh." She paused for several moments, clearly reliving the memory in her mind. "King Itheal was not himself nor has he been the one I once knew since that day. Her betrayal changed him in a way no one could have predicted."

"And you are certain she knows naught of this?"

"Aye," she paused, "few were permitted to witness that act for fear of the populace turning against him."

"Then she is not truly safe anywhere," I frowned.

"Perhaps not, but I fear for you both should she side with duty over her heart's desire and consummate her marriage with King Ferand."

"I dare not think of such things," I closed my eyes tightly willing that thought to be banished from my mind when I heard her speak again.

"Then take her from this place with all haste. For though he would not admit it, King Itheal only wishes to be rid of her and rid of the pain he feels when he looks upon her face." She paused with an unsettling look now upon her face, "And to King Ferand, she is just a vessel, nothing more."

I stepped away from her and began pacing in the enclosed space, concerned over all that I had heard.

"What if she will not leave with me?"

"Find a way to make it in her best interest," she added with a nod, hinting at something that was to be understood, "without disclosing the truth to her."

"That may not be possible, for one's duty is not so easily evaded."

"Find a way or abscond now, thereby leaving her to her fate or releasing her from it," her voice insistent.

I placed my hand upon her shoulder and lightly touched my cheek to hers as a means of thanking her for the tale she had risked so much to tell me. As I turned to leave the chamber, my hand found the latch, but I felt paralyzed by the weight of it. Standing there as a statue, I pondered the options that lay before me, understanding more clearly than before the cost of one's duty. In that moment, I released the latch from its resting place and took my first steps towards my darling Rose. While the path I was choosing was not without risk, it was the only one that may permit both Rose and Eira to live while fulfilling my duties to all those involved. We would set out for Tuiteam at first light.

Prince Berenger

It was in the moment their screams for mercy ceased to be heard when I found myself amongst the living once more. The last moment I remembered I was being pulled into a darkened pool found within the marsh. The cries of my men had been burnt into my memory and I longed to be released from their painful screams. Unfortunately, it was a burden I must bear for leading them to their death. Although, my memory of the events of that day were quite vivid, as I attempted to open my eyes, the light would not find them. Why was I still surrounded by darkness? I could not presume to understand where I had found myself or why I would have been kept in such darkness. All the unknowns were causing me to grow frantic, a feeling I was not acquainted with nor welcoming to.

In an effort to distract myself, I leaned upon my other senses for guidance, hoping they might reveal something that my eyes could not. The room felt surprisingly warm, similar to that of a greenhouse, but while the space was warm, it was not from rays of light directly upon myself. I carefully extended my fingers before permitting them to creep across the surface I found myself laying upon. It was soft and felt of silk rather than the cloth or the furs that were to be found upon the beds in Tuiteam. Once beyond my fingers reach, I began to stretch my arms, extending them over the soft surface only to be met with the sharp pains of a heavily battered body. The sudden rush forced me to recoil and halt my pursuit. The pain may have begun in my shoulder, but it was the pain I felt deep within my chest that nearly took my breath away. It was in my struggle when I heard it. Just when I thought that I was alone, the silence was broken by a woman's gasp.

"Who are you?" I paused unsure of to whom I might be addressing when I heard the strain in my voice. I quickly tried to clear it before continuing, "Where am I?"

"Shhh, try not to speak," the woman's voice spoke softly, "you are safe here."

"But where is—" I began to prod when I felt the tips of her fingers lightly touch my lips.

"Calm yourself Prince Berenger," she spoke once more, "the Kingdom of Losgadh welcomes you."

She removed her fingers from my lips, but I had yet to understand all that happened or how much time had come to pass.

"Where are my men? How did you find me? What day is it?" A rush of concern washed over me. I sat up quickly not fully understanding the limitations I would be met with forcing me to return onto my back.

"Prince Berenger!" her voice heightened clearly concerned, "Please rest for you have only just awoken and I fear for your life should you persist."

I had intended to rebuttal. However, when I felt her hands upon my chest that lay bare, insisting I remain as I am, I did not wish to persist in my intended course.

"Forgive me, milady," I paused clearing my throat once more, "I know naught of where my manners have gone."

She remained silent, but I felt the surface next to me shift slightly. I reached for the cause of the change when my hand found her. Unsure of who she might have been or where my hand just touched, I recoiled it swiftly out of sheer embarrassment.

"Forgive me once more," I paused, "I wish to know what became of me and my men." I uttered softly unsure of what she may have been privy to.

"Of course…" her voice trailed off.

She shifted from the place she had been, and I soon heard light taps across a stone surface. By the time I noticed she was moving I was only able to count ten, maybe twelve, steps before I heard a metal latch turn or possibly lift from its resting place. It was then I heard her speak once more. Her tone quite different than that of which she spoke to me, but she was not addressing me. Unaccustomed to being without my sight, my hearing was not as in tune as I would have hoped causing me to only catch a handful of the words that were spoken. Someone was to fetch someone or something of that I was certain. It only took a moment to utter before I heard the latch shift once more and the tapping began again. She reached the bedside and sat down upon the edge, very near where my hand now lay. Her manner was a bit more unconventional than I was accustomed to. More than likely, this was a cleric and not someone of nobility, so I did not protest.

"I hope my somewhat complicated and dramatic arrival did not trouble King Itheal."

"Fear not, for there is little that troubles him," her voice slightly higher this time, she must have been smiling if but a little. "However, your recovery did prevent me from sleeping as sound as I am accustomed to," she paused, "but I did not mind."

"Regardless, it was not my intention."

"Please do not stress yourself over the matter. It was my pleasure really," I felt her hand upon mine but for a moment before it was recoiled. "We do not often have guests here in the castle, so although I did not wish you ill will during your journey, I welcomed the chance to care for you."

I felt her lean in towards me, placing her fingers upon my brow just before stroking my curly locks away. I was confident the gesture served no purpose other than for her sheer pleasure as the state of locks held little concern for me.

"Then I am indebted to you milady," I spoke firmly just before reaching to place my hand upon hers.

The gesture surprised her, and I felt her fingers trembling slightly under my touch. Although I was unsure as to the reason, I quickly withdrew my hand as to not further her discomfort.

"Forgive me once more," I uttered feeling slightly uncomfortable now as well.

"No, please do not apologize…it was entirely my fault." She began stumbling over her words and it amused me more than I would have anticipated, "I, I…"

I felt myself smile slightly for the first time in ages and just as I did, a faint giggle escaped her. Though, I could not see her face, I had hoped she was smiling at the folly that had occurred between us. Being a prince of Tuiteam, we are granted the privilege to touch whoever we wish but not to be touched without prior consent being issued. This understanding was set forth long before my birth but maintained as a means of keeping us above the populace. It was a custom I longed to be rid of amongst many others. I was about to speak once more when I felt her hand sliding alongside the back of my neck just before pulling me towards her when I felt the chill of stone against my lower lip.

"Please drink something," her voice soft, but encouraging.

I did not feel parched, but I found myself wanting to please her for reasons unbeknownst to me. I attempted to nod just before I felt the liquid dripping slowly into my mouth. It was crisp and light with a hint of honey that lingered upon my tongue. I had not tasted anything quite like it, but through her patience and my tolerance, I received several more tastes of it over the next few minutes just before the door to the chamber opened once more.

"Prince Berenger," a deep, mighty voice bellowed, "I am pleased to see you have awakened."

"Aye, that I have," I responded unsure once more of to whom I may be speaking with. "I greatly desire to know what became of me and my men."

"Hmm…" the man uttered louder than I am sure he intended, "I should have expected nothing less of Tuiteam's Warrior Prince."

"I am complimented that my reputation precedes me, but what of my men?" I insisted.

"There was only one survivor other than yourself that came to us. Though badly shaken, he is relatively unharmed."

The woman lowered my head back down and removed her hand from my neck just before I nodded with understanding.

"And what of my sight?" I added.

The room fell silent.

"Prince Berenger," he paused, "of that I do not know."

"Kenric," the woman spoke once more, "the man who we found in your company insisted the waters of Boglach had taken it as a means of preventing your escape."

"The perils of Boglach appear never-ending," I muttered.

"Perhaps your mind and body just need more time," the woman interjected. "What you endured cannot be undone in only a matter of days."

"Trust in her, Prince Berenger, for my daughter, though youthful, is wise beyond her years," the man spoke once more.

"Losgadh truly is blessed to have such a wonderful cleric amongst its people." I spoke softly wanting to appear appreciative even though the message she had delivered comforted me little.

"Prince Berenger, I will forgive the misunderstanding

for you are without sight presently, but it is no healer you are in the presence of," the man's voice said sternly.

"I do not understand," I responded.

"You are in the company of the Princess Rosalyn and have been since your arrival," the man added.

I attempted to bow my head slightly, but the gesture shot pain down my back forcing me to stop as I were. I felt humiliated at my ignorance and then again for my behavior. My cheeks were undoubtably burning brightly from it all and I had begun to perspire as if I had just been placed in front of the hearth.

"Forgive me Princess Rosalyn for I did not see."

"Prince Berenger, there is nothing to forgive," she responded.

"My daughter has tended to your every need since your arrival—"

"King Itheal, please forgive my ignorance and inappropriate behavior—" I blurted out in surprise as I now understood the man in my presence to be his majesty.

I felt the Princess Rosalyn's hand upon my shoulder now rubbing it ever so gently.

"Calm yourself Prince Berenger, for my father was aware that it was I who requested to tend your every need and that your lack of sight would have prohibited you from understanding the company you presently keep."

"You are too kind, Princess Rosalyn," I added feeling the slight sense of relief that I desperately needed to counter the overwhelming humiliation I had just endured.

"You are an honored guest amongst my people and

being as such, she took it upon herself to tend to you. She has not left your bedside for more than a few moments since your arrival," he paused. "If you have not expressed your gratitude towards her as of yet, it would be customary for you to do so now."

"There is no need father, he has already done so, and I have accepted it."

"Very well, I will leave you to your rest," he pivoted and stepped back towards the door. "Should you desire anything to make your stay more comfortable, you have only but to ask."

"King Itheal?" I strained to call his attention back towards me. "Even though I am grateful for your aid and the present company I keep. There is a matter in Tuiteam that demands my attention, and I would like to get back to it if I am able."

"Very well, Prince Berenger," he said sternly before the latch on the door was lifted once more and he vacated the chamber.

"Prince Berenger," the Princess Rosalyn spoke once more. "I know it is not my place, but do you believe leaving in your current state is wise?"

"King Ferand has tasked me with escorting you back to Tuiteam," I uttered. "We should not keep him waiting."

"Is this the matter that concerns you? Certainly, King Ferand would care more for your recovery than our betrothal. Would he not?"

I thought over her questions carefully for having my requests questioned or critiqued by others was, also, something

I was not accustomed to. Could this have been their way or was she audacious due to her nobility? Though Ferand will not be fond of her bravado, that may be all that will protect her from his pretentious nature.

"No, it is not," I insisted.

I decided it would be kinder not to tell her that my brother cares little for my wellbeing as this would only hurt her, I sensed. In addition, I refrained from saying anything further regarding the state of unrest that I left Tuiteam in. I believed this would not bode confidence in the woman that is presently residing at my side. It is best that she not be made aware unless it becomes necessary as a means of protecting a betrothal that was long overdue.

"Milady, to what is the hour?"

"Oh," she sounded taken aback, "it is late, and the moon is still high in the night's sky." I felt her shift along the bedside. "Though you may not be able to see it, it is lovely on this night. Perhaps a parting gift sent to me by the Gods."

"Then might you describe it to me," I said hopeful. "If it would not burden you."

"Not in the slightest," she responded. "Tonight, we have been blessed with a sky of deep blue with ribbons of plum and midnight painted throughout. These ribbons adding to the contrast of the golden stars that find themselves scattered about and shining brighter than usual. Despite their love of the spotlight, the moon will always outshine them for its light is a mere reflection of all of theirs in its glasslike appearance." She stopped briefly before continuing this time with a sadness in her voice that I had not heard previously. "Even though I have never left the confines of these walls, I know there is no where I shall venture to that will provide the light that is found here."

I reached for her more out of instinct than desire when my hand grazed a portion of her dress just as she rose from the bed. There was something about the way she spoke of the moonlight that struck me as it had not before. I had never heard someone describe it as such or with the passion for it as she had. She spoke as if she were one with the sky and not of our world. Something that made me hopeful yet trembling with fear for her. Tuiteam's populace is not fond of those that do not behave as we and basking in the moonlight would not go unnoticed. However, the part of me that was hopeful longed to see Caladh as she does. Through her gaze, the world was beautiful and caring. It was nothing of the world I had come to know. It touched me greatly that she had remained unaffected by the cruelty Caladh has bestowed upon so many.

"That sounds breathtaking," I uttered, unsure of what else to say.

"It is," she paused, "I will miss it greatly."

"The moon is never far even in Tuiteam, but I cannot recall it ever appearing as you just described. Perhaps, I do not see the world as you do, or the moon reveals itself to you in a way that it does not share with others."

I heard her sit down in what I presumed was a chair very near my bedside.

"Well, should you ever wish to see the world as I, you have only but to ask. I will be your eyes, until your sight returns to you."

"Princess Rosalyn," I uttered more as a question than I

intended, "do you believe my sight will ever return to me?"

"I am hopeful that it will, but not knowing of how they once appeared limits my understanding."

"My eyes have always been quite dark in color. Bordering on molasses as I have been told."

She stood from the chair and returned to the bedside.

"May I take another look?" she asked.

"Of course."

She leaned in towards me once more, hovering a portion of her body very near to my face. With each breath I could feel the warm air exiting her body as she unwound a ribbon from just below my brow that I had not even realized was there. When she finished the ribbon fell upon my chest and once again her fingertips found their way onto my face. Resting them carefully near my eyes, I felt her pulling lightly at the surrounding tissue.

"Of what do you see?" I asked growing impatient.

"They are no longer as you described nor has their appearance changed since your arrival."

"Of what do you see?" I insisted, hopeful that she was mistaken, but fearful she may not be.

"Your eyes are no longer your eyes Prince Berenger," she spoke sharply. "The darkness has been consumed and they are now filled with light." She paused, "I am sorry to say that I do not believe your sight will be returned to you," her tone softened significantly.

I felt the air catch within my chest and though I wanted to cry out in anger, I could not. I reached up and clasped her wrists within my grasp to which a gasp escaped her. I did not wish to harm her in any way, but I needed a moment to collect and control my thoughts. I released her wrists from my grasp a moment later and returned my now trembling hands towards my sides.

"Is there nothing this land does not wish to take from me?" I did not intend to pose this as a question to her directly, but more to myself as I felt plagued by misfortune.

"I do not believe Caladh only seeks to take things from you, but all who reside here. For this is what it requires to maintain balance."

"Forgive me Princess Rosalyn, but you understand little of the misfortune that has fallen upon me," I uttered sharper than intended.

I felt her lower herself next to me once more, taking one of my hands in hers, squeezing it gently.

"Then permit yourself to unburden that pain upon me now."

"It is not my wish to burden you, milady," I muttered just before feeling tears begin streaming down my face. "Please turn away from me now," I insisted. "I wish to be alone with my thoughts."

"And what if I refuse?" she said sounding determined.

I raised a hand to wipe the tears that were now streaming down my cheeks. I had not realized my eyes would have still been capable of such. It was then when our hands met, drawing my attention towards her once more. Though I could not bear to utter a rebuttal, I somehow knew it would not have been accepted even if I had.

"I feel Caladh resents my birth for reasons

unbeknownst to me and will stop at nothing to rid me of what little joys that have been found during my time here."

I felt her place her an arm around my neck, pulling me towards her just before placing her lips upon each of my eyelids, kissing them softly. She smelt sweet like honey with skin the texture of flower petals. Though I longed for her to remain as she were, I feared what that longing might represent. Taking a moment to remind myself that she was promised to another, I willed myself to pull away from her of which I was met with resistance as she clung to me in a way that felt both desperate and comforting. It was then that I realized perhaps I was not the only one who needed comforting. I reached for her, pulling her towards me as she wrapped her arms further around me, permitting my tears to fall freely as they would not have otherwise. Though the touch and care she provided for me on that night and the days before I awoke was permissible, the simple act of drawing her near to me as I did was unforgivable. No one in Tuiteam would see the gesture as anything but disloyalty towards their King. However, in this moment, I cared not for the perceptions of others.

Kraciun

After spending days in the mountains of Geamhradh followed by a brief stent in the frozen tundra just beyond them to the south, we were finally venturing home. The mystery of the wolf's escape had continued to bewilder me, along with her ever eluding presence. Without any trace evidence to support her survival, my mind remained convinced that she had passed on shortly after her escape or was taken by a greater beast during her trek through Glacial Pass. Commander Elgar was not so easily convinced of course, but had it been my neck on the chopping block and I might have insisted otherwise as well. Before this incident, never had it been known that a prisoner could escape the tower, let alone disappear from the land entirely. It was as if she never truly existed. I toggled the pieces of the unforeseen puzzle about in my mind daily to no avail, but I never gave up on the task. While it may not have been my duty in doing so, I felt a sense of urgency pulling at me whenever I thought of it.

Commander Elgar strolled just ahead of me in relative silence, undoubtably pondering the explanation that King Edric would require for our failed excursion. Though the journey was not without merit, neither would see it as anything other than a failure since the task was not completed. As we walked in silence I looked down upon my hands, tattered and torn from the ceaseless climbs and frigid temperatures. The men around us looked equally as battered by this excursion. Too long have the people of Reothadh lain dormant on an island of ice and snow, waiting for our Queen to return or our King to bring us peace. The wilds here were growing and no amount of training could prepare us for the claims we were attempting to hold over this land. Should I be given the choice and I would flee to a new world. With that thought in mind, I reached for Commander Elgar.

"Commander," he turned towards me, "forgive me, but I can go no further. I must return to the Ice Tower."

"Kraciun," his brow tightened, "you shall accompany me to Castle Trocair as I am certain King Edric will wish to speak to you."

"I cannot I am afraid," I released his arm from my grasp, "for it is there that something beckons me."

Just as I turned to flee, I felt his hand grasping my upper arm firmly, locking me in place, forcing me to glance back at him. His eyes were narrow. He had not taken kindly to my sudden defiance. It was not my intention to defy him directly nor so openly, but the thought of my own wish to flee made me think that the wolf or its elven companion may have had a similar idea. Returning to the Ice Tower's port may provide us with the answers we seek and though it is unwise to deny my duty, denying my gut instinct has proven far more perilous. Jerking my arm from his grasp abruptly, I began rushing in the direction of the Ice Tower when I heard him shout threw the trees that surrounded us.

"Kraciun! You will stop," he paused, "or suffer my wrath you shall!"

My gait slowed to a snail's pace. Though he may seem like a lion in winter, I do not believe he would follow through on his threat. Of course, had I not stopped, and he would have been forced to make an example out of me to protect his authority amongst the men. I heard his footsteps rushing towards me.

"You will turn and face me this instant!" he bellowed.

I turned quickly towards him and noticed his expression had not changed in the slightest.

"You will accompany me to Castle Trocair as this is not a request. Is that understood?" his voice echoed loudly through the air as all others had already fallen silent at my defiance.

"Commander Elgar, the vessel is the key," I paused, "for that is why we have found naught of them."

To my surprise, his expression changed from hardened and agitated to oddly optimistic and curious.

"Explain," he insisted.

I leaned in towards him and whispered, "We have been deceived for the wolf and the elf never left the south on foot."

"But you informed me the guards and serfs had been questioned," his voice angered once more.

"Aye, that we did," I paused, "but never was it known

to us where the vessel came from or where it was going. Perhaps, their escape was planned, and the men aboard that vessel had vested interest in keeping their presence aboard a secret. I must attempt to barter passage on the next vessel for where it lay berth may hold the answers we seek."

"Aye, I see…off with you now," he commanded casting a hand into the air, signaling his permission for me to part from his company.

I nodded in return and quickly returned to my hastened step with a few foot soldiers now in tow. While I did not believe we could maintain this speed for an extended period, the idea of a warm bed and seat by the fire surely helped us along. The mountains may have been brisk, but they greatly shielded us from the elements during our time there. Something I would have given about anything for as we continued our trek south. Though I was unsure whether this gamble was worth the risk, in this moment, I needed to believe it would be. After all hope was all we had left. Holding on to that thought and the possibility of a brave new world before me held me over until the Ice Tower was in sight. Just shy of dusk, we staggered our way up towards the land that we had recently become our home to be greeted by laughter and chatter radiating from within. Either the tides had shifted in our favor, or the mice were enjoying their time while the cat was away.

Upon entering the foyer just shy of the main chamber, the noise that had previously been diminished, now echoed uncontrollably throughout the chamber, and made my ears ring from the sudden change. We stowed away what gear we could spare and trotted in to join the others. They were drinking ale while ribbing one another and it brightened my spirits to see them not wallowing in our recent defeat. Of course, it was understood by all that the merriment would not last, but I refused to walk away from it. We sat near the fire to rest our weary legs and fill our bellies for they were quite empty from the day's journey. Had I arrived here on nearly any other day and this chamber may have been vacant for the duties of the men at the tower never cease. I opted to remain there as long as my body would permit me, and it was into the wee hours of the morning before I found myself willing to part with the joy the evening had brought me.

It was in the barracks I found myself when I was able to pry my eyes open later that morning. Glancing around the chamber slowly as my eyes adjusted, I found no others in my presence. Could the hour have been that late? I turned and brought myself into an upright position when I finally felt my body rebelling against the search for the wolf. With each twitch and turn, not just my muscles cried out in pain, but my very bones felt as if they wanted to shatter. I had not felt a pain such as this in quite possibly years. Sitting there, now slumped over with my head in my hands as I could not bring myself to stand. Not just yet anyway. I concentrated on my breathing, trying to pull my focus back to the task at hand, knowing all too well that my window for execution of this was limited. Casting doubt aside, I rose to my feet, steadier than expected. With the feeling of being hit with a hammer heavily weighing me down, I took each step a little slower than usual as I forced my way back to the main chamber.

Much to my disappointment it was not nearly as cheery

as the night before, but there were several men taking a momentary pause there. I fetched some stew from the main pot and sat near them to be brought up to speed with anything that may have happened in my absence. The report was brief, so brief in fact, that I barely finished my meal before they had concluded with the matter. I struggled to stand once more. This time was easier than the last and returned my dishes to the kitchen for the squire to tend to. We rarely kept them on hand, but in recent months they have been found to be quite useful with remedial tasks that would have otherwise been ignored. One of the boys took them from me without question and rushed away. I returned to the main chamber where I began plotting the best course for my *escape* when I was greeted by a familiar face.

"Kray! What brings you back home to roost?!" the voice chuckled.

"Bart!" I exclaimed. "You know Commander Elgar prefers the spotlight to only be on him." I grinned before wrapping an arm around him and giving him a gentle squeeze.

"Aye, that he does," he grinned. "So...what brings you back so soon? I was under the impression that you were not to return for weeks or possibly months."

I leaned in towards him and whispered, "Can you keep a secret?"

He nodded.

"Then follow me," I added.

I turned and fled the room to a dark chamber just off the main chamber. Unsure of its intended purpose, we mainly use it to lock away deserters while King Edric ponders their fate, but it will suit us for the moment of privacy we need. We slipped inside before quietly closing the door behind us. Bart looked more interested than concerned, but then again, he always has been one for a bit of cloak and dagger.

"I need your help to get me aboard the next vessel that docks here."

"Why not just request permission to board?"

"For we do not know of whom pays the piper and I am certain that is how the wolf and elf evaded us."

"Then you do not believe it was one of us?"

I shook my head, "It could not have been for the weapon used to slay all those men does not appear to be manmade. I believe the answer lies where the vessel lays berth."

"But that could be anywhere," his voice rose slightly. "What if the thing you seek is not found at the end of this journey and you have no means to return?" he sounded concerned, if but briefly.

"Then we shall part as friends and perhaps, the land I find myself in will bring me a happiness I have not found here."

He stared at me for a moment before turning to pace about the room, pondering all that was just laid before him. There was something further he was mulling over in his mind, but he did not utter a sound for several moments.

"We may barter passage off this island as mercenaries or pose as serfs. Either would save us from being viewed as deserters which they would most likely not permit aboard."

I nodded.

"Fair point." I cocked my head slightly thinking over what he had just said when I uttered, "What do you mean *we*?"

He raised an eyebrow at the ridiculous notion that I ever thought he would not be joining me.

"Like it or not, you cannot handle this task alone and better to have aid then find yourself alone on the mainland."

I rolled my eyes and exhaled louder than expected forcing his gaze to greet mine with a significant amount of disapproval.

"This coming from the man that pulled me into a secret plot of subterfuge and potential treason should King Edric be informed."

I rolled my eyes again knowing all too well that he was right, as he so often is.

"Very well," I extended my hand for him to take to seal the deal. He took it without any further questions or concerns noted. "We tell no one of this and we depart on the first vessel that will accept our offer."

"Take only what we can carry," he then tugged at his tunic, "and lose these."

"Aye," I nodded once more, "for we will not find pleasant greetings as long as we wear them."

As luck would have it, another vessel arrived there just upon the morrow. Bart and I fled the tower as the men were chiseling away at a daunting list of tasks. Undoubtably, the easiest distraction that one of authority could create. No one would miss us for hours, giving us the time we need to board the vessel. Once free of the tower, we strolled towards the cliffs that surrounded us and searched for the rope that once clung so desperately to its edge. While it would be no better than scaling the frozen edge by hand, it would mask our escape more than just walking out the front door and leaving a trail of breadcrumbs for all to follow. I opted to dropdown first as we both knew I was lighter and the better climber of the two of us. Additionally, should the rope snap, I am more capable of recovering from the impact than he.

Lowering myself over the edge, I did my best to limit the commotion my ascent would cause as the sounds of ice fracturing may have been normal to our ears, but voices echoing against the ice and across the Mar Deigh would not be. A sliver of a pathway was noted hugging the base of the cliff and that would be where we would need to change our garb before venturing closer to the vessel. It would not provide much cover, but it was all we had. I began my descent down the rope while listening to the ice upon it crack and creak with each bend and twist it made. It was my hope that the sheathe of ice that encased it would have fallen mere moments after I wrapped my body around it, but alas, it did not. Clinging to it like I did only further strained and irritated my already battered and callused hands.

Several feet from reaching the rope's tattered end, I scanned our surroundings once more to find everything just as it was, but I felt a chill dancing upon the back of my neck. As I hang there, positioning myself for the drop, a large wave threw itself against the rock and ice tossing my body about as if I were a ragdoll being fought over by two bairns. For fear of being pulled into the sea, I clung desperately to the rope ever hopeful the wrath of the Mar Deigh would revoke its oath for vengeance and just leave me bitter from its warning. However, just as the water of the first wave had finished raking its icy claws across my flesh another followed in its wake. I glanced above to see a concerned Bart watching from on high, when a second wave overthrew me. Again, my body was thrown, and I felt my fingers giving way. I would not be able to withstand another jolt from the waves without falling uncontrollably towards an uncertain end. As the wave recoiled into itself in preparation for another assault, I reached for my axe and released the rope from my grasp.

While I feared being taken by the sea, I refused to resign from life so easily. I felt myself begin to freefall, permitting the gap between the rope and the path to close in a mere blink and just as my feet grazed the surface, a third wave came thrashing in. With no time to catch my breath, I cast my arm backwards, lodging my axe into the ice just as the wave dropped in overhead. The Mar Deigh's might tore once more at my flesh, drawing me towards the icy rock my world clung to and then back towards its core in a violent display of its unyielding power. Holding my position, I signaled for Bart to follow my lead and make his descent. There was not time to decipher all the muttering his mouth appeared to be making before the next wave came in, but it would not be long before he found himself either thrown into the sea or smothering me from his sudden descent.

With the tide turned suddenly violent, we would have to act quickly to flee from the waves and compose ourselves before attempting to blend in with the nearby serfs. A feat that would not be without its challenges, but the least difficult of the two options we plotted for. As Bart slowly made his way towards the path below, I used my axe as an anchor to pull my way across the icy surface. Each time I repositioned it and slid towards it, I felt weaker as my muscles were beginning to seize from the bone-chilling waves that continued to thrash and claw their way onto me. I had hoped this path would be the lesser of two evils, but I suppose we all are permitted one oversight now and again. In what felt like hours, I had crept my way free of the spiteful waves and was now guiding Bart towards me. In this case, his larger frame worked to his advantage as even the Mar Deigh has been known to have difficulty shifting boulders when a limited amount of time is offered.

Upon reaching my side, Bart collapsed from exhaustion if only for a few moments before we heard shouting rebounding off the ice towards us. The men from the vessel appeared to be venturing towards us, probably following the sound of my axe splitting the ice beneath me, but that may be giving their ears more credit than they deserve. Unable to wait for a better moment to find us, I began to strip off the armor I once felt so honored to don in light of a new identity and cast all but my bracers into the sea. Hiding them along with my daggers and axe carefully under a worn tunic and equally worn doublet. We were ready to venture towards the vessel to join the others. Bart trailed just slightly behind me but finished donning his new garb just in time for us to be spotted by a few of the men just off the forecastle of the vessel. They did not appear alarmed nor interested in our sudden appearance, merely just aware of us.

In order to divert attention away from us, we fell in line

like so many before us to begin picking up and loading the cog that had clearly been here longer than I was aware. While there was an obscene number of crates scattered along the water's edge, I was bewildered by their sheer mass. Even being a trained soldier in King Edric's army, they posed challenges for both myself and Bart as evident by the strain that soon washed over our faces. Being close to Commander Elgar granted me certain privileges but even I did not know the contents of these crates. Over the last several months our shipments had increased, but while my focus remained on the goods these vessels brought, rarely was I aware of how many left Reothadh as chock-full as these were. Something else I would need to ponder should I get the chance, but for now, we would need to keep our heads down and whisper a silent prayer for our presence to go unnoticed. I had intended to barter passage, but as things are now, that may no longer be required.

We worked in silence with barely more than a few upward glances as the day drug on and just as the sun had nearly fallen completely out of the sky, the crates had vanished, leaving only large grooves in the ice as the memory of what was once there. To our surprise the officers paid us no never mind as they appeared to only see the men below their status as bodies rather than men of their equal. It was the first time I could feel someone watching me, but when I turned towards them, their eyes did not appear to see me, only through me. These men were different from those found in Reothadh, their hearts were colder than the rock and ice we now stood upon. If given the chance they would sacrifice anyone available to save themselves. While I still intended to board the cog to see this through, I already knew the land of which these men haled from…Tuiteam.

 Commander Elgar

My men and I had returned to Castle Trocair late in the day to find a very ill-tempered King Edric waiting for us there.

"Commander Elgar" he bellowed across the land that lay before the main doors to his castle. "What news do you bring me of my wolf?"

I raised my hand into the air as a request for cease fire as I was not prepared for the barrage of questions that would soon be cast upon me. As I ventured closer, he took that as his sign I was ready to discuss the matter, but in truth, no one is ever prepared to deliver unfavorable news. I felt his hand land heavily upon my shoulder before we turned towards the main doors. Gesturing for the remaining men and guards not to follow, we stepped inside.

"So, tell me Commander Elgar," he uttered in a gruff voice, "why have you returned to me without the beast I tasked you to fetch?"

"King Edric, you know I would not have had I been

given a choice in the matter," I said boldly.

"You disappoint me Elgar," he uttered just before making a clicking sound behind his teeth. "I suppose there is a first time for everything."

"King Edric, the men were given an insurmountable task to say the least. Given more time, perhaps we would have found her, but there was no sign of her anywhere on the island."

"Do you expect me to believe that she just vanished without a trace?!" his voice agitated.

He stepped in front of me, forcing our eyes to meet and stopping me within my tracks. His brow furled and eyes now narrow.

"The task given to us was a fool's errand, King Edric," I argued.

"You dare challenge me Elgar," he growled, "for if you do, it is you who will lose."

My gaze narrowed to match his own. It was then and there I felt that a line was being drawn. Should I choose to step across it and there would be no turning back. I weighed my options carefully and though I knew I was not a man who should be king, I needed to make room for one that could be. King Edric's days were now numbered, but it would not be wise of me to make that known just yet.

I softened my gaze before speaking once more, "Let us discuss the matter in your war room."

I held out a hand in the direction of the chamber and waited patiently for him to accept. He scoffed just before turning and stepping towards the war room where at least we would be behind closed doors before discussing what really happened during my time away. Reluctant to disclose more knowledge than was necessary, but during these fickle times there was no room to be coy with the King of Trocair. As we approached the war room, the doors opened to us before closing swiftly behind us, leaving us alone in a guarded chamber. I watched as he paced his way across the chamber repeatedly without uttering a word. Though Trocair is not much for customs, I waited patiently for him to speak first in order to keep his temper appeased. It was sometime later when he opted to break the silence.

"A fool's errand...is that what you think of me after all this time? That I am a fool?" His voice still gruff but softened in a way that I had not heard in some time.

"King Edric," I sighed heavily, "we were all deceived while seeking the wolf." He stopped pacing but did not turn towards me. "It was not a wolf we were seeking and that is why we found nothing of her."

"Are you suggesting that we captured a member of the fae?"

I shook my head trying to give him a moment to see what I had only come to terms with just after Kraciun's departure.

When he did not produce a reply for several moments I added, "I believe our thoughts were misplaced before in thinking the elf and the wolf were two separate beings, but what if they were one in the same?"

"A shapeshifter," he turned sharply with eyes now wide, "but that is impossible."

"More like improbable," I muttered openly.

"If this were true, then explain the pile of men that were slaughtered by an elvish blade," he challenged.

"Perhaps, an elf from Lamprog was tasked to retrieve what they believed was their kin, but more than likely they knew the beast to be a shapeshifter."

"That would explain how they were able to infiltrate the tower and flee without others taking notice," he said quite frankly. Foregoing that twinge of surprise in his voice that once was.

I rushed towards him just before pointing to several locations on his war table.

"Regardless, I do not believe we are the first to know of their return and if one could remain hidden all this time, odds are there will be others."

My gaze, direct and unwavering, rose to meet his. This thought had clearly occurred to him before as he did not appear taken back in the least at the mention of it. I could not tell if he was hiding something or if he just happened to recover from the news quicker than I expected.

"The men stationed in the tower offered no other pearls from the search? Perhaps an insider knew of what she truly was?"

His gaze began to wander around the room and his voice significantly softer than before. He appeared to be diverting attention away from the idea that there could be others, but I know naught why.

"The men of the tower were questioned. If there is a subversive, then they are still eluding us. No other pearls were uncovered during our search."

"But you believe the shapeshifter broke free of the tower alone?"

"I did at first, but without aid, she would not have been able to defeat those men with a blade. There are none of that quality within our possession." I pointed towards Lamprog, "Only the elves of Lamprog wield blades capable of such finesse and violence."

He began pacing once more.

"King Aldon's men have not breached our borders in many years," he insisted.

"That may have been true at one time. However, the wounds on the men that have now passed on were clearly not those of a beast. Only one of King Aldon's men could have done this."

"Are you certain?"

"Yes," I spoke frankly before pointing towards Tiene. "No one of this region could have survived the tundra."

"King Aldon knows of the shapeshifter we are seeking. I am sure of it."

King Edric strolled towards a large chair nestled in one of the corners of the room where he sat, mulling over all that had been said. I watched as his battered fingers stroked what was left of his tattered grey beard clearly deep in thought. Although, he did not utter a sound, I could hear the questions swirling about in his mind, further clouding his already weary mind. Watching him as he was now, brought memories of what once was back to me. We met as young men, training for what would unquestionably be the war to end all wars, but the war we continually trained for never came. For years we were promised an invasion of the mainland, but the promises soon fell short forcing the soldiers that remained to become restless. Edric and I were amongst those men. I knew then that there would be no stopping his lust for the mainland and even now, he is consumed by it.

It was not long thereafter when he spoke of overthrowing our King. I had hoped the hollow promises of the man before him would melt away in his reign, but they never did. From the moment he made his intent to usurp the throne until now, I never left his side, nor did I doubt his intentions. We fought side by side for many years and we won many battles. I can still recall the day that we laid claim to the isle of Angof, to which now lies in ruins under his leadership. He was supposed to unite us and bring us a chance at new life. Yet, we remain in this frozen wasteland ever hopeful he will fulfill the promises that were made by him as a young man. It was then I acknowledged the doubt that begun several days before had taken root and my allegiance was shifting to the hope of someone new.

"We cannot attack the elves of Lamprog," his voice echoing towards me from across the chamber, "nor can we inquire about such a matter with King Aldon. There must be another way to find out if there are others like her and who else knows of them."

"I do not believe this would be information others would speak freely of, but there could be stirring in amongst the whispers."

He nodded.

"If the beast is under King Aldon's protection, there will be no chance of her being returned to us. Lamprog's borders are well guarded as you know." His eyes now fixed upon me. "Where is Kraciun?"

I met his gaze and kept mine unwavering to prevent any potential stirrings of disloyalty within him.

"He returned to the Ice Tower," I spoke firmly.

"Despite my orders to have him return with you?" he growled.

"Forgive me, King Edric, but he was needed on a more pressing matter there."

He rose from where he sat quickly and stormed his way towards me.

"Commander Elgar, you have disappointed me once more. What could possibly be more pressing than following the orders of his King?"

"Of that I cannot say," I uttered quickly, knowing all too well that I knew exactly what drew him back towards the Ice Tower.

"Commander Elgar, you will release the answer from your throat or find yourself in irons!"

It was a poor choice on my part to attempt to withhold vital information from him. King Edric knew me quite well and could always sense when I was being dishonest.

"He believes the vessel is the key!" I shouted just as his large hands met my armor, shoveling me backwards violently.

My body crashed against the war table with such force that I felt the table itself shift. The war table, large and carved from solid stone, took six men to bring into the room. So, shifting it was a monumental feat. As my body connected with the edge, I felt something within me split forcing me to wince. Upon adjusting myself upright once more, the pain only increased, but now was not the time to appear weak.

"Though I do not believe the elves would have been able to barter passage aboard the vessel, he believes there is something to be found there." I added while trying to push through my discomfort.

King Edric stood there huffing, clearly frustrated by the situation.

"He is mistaken," he spat.

His response shocked me.

"King Edric," I paused still trying to understand why investigating the vessel would irritate him so before I continued. "Kraciun is one of our best. If there is an answer to be found, he will find it."

"No, you must call him back!" he spat again, clearly more irritated this time.

"I cannot!" I spat in return, unsure what he could possibly be afraid of.

"I order you to call him back," he growled just before leaning in towards me.

"King Edric," I paused, "even if I should depart this instance and ride on the back of Lavin, I would not reach the Ice Tower in time to order his return."

I placed a hand on one of his shoulders, attempting to soothe the angered beast within him. It was then that I started to pull together more of the jagged pieces of this ragged puzzle.

"Kraciun was ordered to investigate the wolf's

disappearance, as was I, and that is precisely the matter he is tending to."

I removed my hand from his shoulder and turned to walk around the war table. Once along the opposite side, it would be difficult for him to express his disgust by such physical means.

"You will seek him out and tell him to call off the hunt. I wish to let the matter rest."

"No," I growled. "It was you who sent me and my men out to scour the frozen tundra and climb the mountains of Geamhradh in search of the wolf. Now you want to let the matter rest." I felt my voice turn dark and drop into a lower register, "As Knight Commander, I demand an explanation!"

I watched his breathing deepen and his nostrils flare with each angered breath that exited his body. His gaze fixed on mine once more. Just when I thought he intended to utter a response, I felt the table before shift once more as his fists came down upon its surface, fracturing the stone beneath them. Upon the stone, grew streams of crimson, but his fists did not falter from the point of impact.

"You have no authority to demand anything as such of me," he spat. "You have forgotten your place. Perhaps a night in irons will remind you. For it is I who was willing to slay my King and take his throne, not you and it is I who wears the crown, not you."

Never would I have believed he would be willing to take the matter that far. Standing there in shock, I soon felt the blood draining from my face. I dare not plead for forgiveness for he would know the words I spoke were false.

Unfortunately, there was little time to react before the doors to the war room were opened and several soldiers marched inward.

"Take him to the vault," he ordered.

Their faces soon became painted with the same look of shock I had upon my own, but soon we nearly all had recovered. The guards attempted to pull me within their grasp, but I pulled away from their touch. While I understood they were just doing their duty, I needed not an escort.

"Touch me again and I will break those hands," I spat. "I know of where I am headed."

They withdrew their hands, pulling them upward slightly in defense. As I stepped beyond them and through the doors to the war room, they followed in closely behind me. With each step that was taken towards the throne room, I could feel all eyes upon me, watching me, fearful of what I had done to anger their King. Not being entirely sure why mentioning the vessel would have changed his mind so suddenly but my confidence was growing. There is something about all this that never settled well with me, and the reason was starting to unfold before me. Was this all a test? Resembling some elaborate game to prepare the men for something greater or had King Edric been fraternizing with the enemy all along in our wake? Either suggestion turned my stomach sour and forced my tired mind to grow achy toiling over the all the unknowns that were now in play.

Upon entering the throne room, all points of entry were soon shut, further ensuring the vault's entrance remained hidden. Once sealed within the room, I was permitted to step towards the vault's entrance that was carefully concealed just behind King Edric's throne. There was no particular mechanism used to open it and it was not magical. One simply needed to apply the correct amount of pressure on two trigger points before the latch would lift. Once lifted, the plate can be slid back beneath the throne to reveal the stairwell beneath. The vault was not a place one would choose to go willingly as the perpetual darkness has been known to drive some mad with delirium. I, too, would not choose to venture here had it not been King Edric's wish. There was little I could do to change the matter now. As we stepped downward into the ever-growing darkness, there was no more than the sound of our own footsteps to greet us. In addition, had it not been for the torches that the men held in tow, I would have not been able to see so much as my hand in front of my face. It was the definition of absolute darkness.

Reaching the base of the stairwell, we began to walk the long hall in search of what was to be my resting place for the night. I had ventured down this hall more times than I cared to count, but the eerie feeling that was now washing over me told me I could not remain here. Within the vault King Edric held his most esteemed possessions and his most disreputable enemies. For his enemies this would at least be temporary as King Edric rarely lets his enemies live for more than a matter of hours once within Castle Trocair. I do not believe that I fall within either category, but this may have been his way to rattle my cage. We both knew of the madness that could be found down within the hidden chamber. While in the custody of the guard, I had nothing to fear of the darkness or those that may have loomed within the chamber. Although, with each passing step we drew closer to our destination where his disreputable enemies would soon become very aware of our presence should any of them still live or have their sanity.

One of the cell gates was opened for me and I entered it without question. As the door closed behind me, I turned to face them, witnessing a look of shock that had returned upon their faces.

"Commander Elgar," one of the men spoke, "had I not been here to witness it myself I would not have believed King Edric would have turned on his favored."

His innocence and the slight concern that was heard in his voice pleased me for some reason. I felt a faint smile appear upon my face, just before leaving nearly as suddenly as it appeared.

"We all fall out of favor at some point." I placed my hands upon the bars that now separated us. "I hope you shall remain in his favor longer than I."

He nodded before turning towards the others in our company when I spoke once more.

"Would you remain here with me for just another moment? There is something I wish to ask of you."

He turned back towards me, eyes still wide with surprise. He must have been new.

"Of course, Commander," he bowed his head slightly. "What is it you wish to ask of me?"

I waited for the remaining guards to vanish from our sight before responding.

"There is a message that I need you to deliver," I

muttered.

"To whom is the receiver of this message?" he whispered.

"Kraciun," I muttered once more.

"Surely he has returned to the Ice Tower," he paused, "I dare not leave the castle."

I leaned in towards the bars and whispered, "Then perhaps I might be permitted a visitor during my stay."

"You know King Edric will have me beheaded if caught."

"Then best to not get caught," I winked.

"For whose company do you seek?" he uttered frankly just above a whisper.

"There is a young lad, often overlooked by most, but if Lavin is found in the garden, that is where he will be."

"And what do you want with this boy?"

I thought carefully for a moment, knowing all too well that even though this man and I were comrades in arms, he could never side with me over King Edric.

"My reasons are my own," I paused, "and I do not wish to trouble you further."

It was not my wish to place my men in the middle of the squabble I had started with King Edric, but something tugged at me once more, insisting I keep searching what he was trying so desperately to hide. The young lad was key. During my absence he was tasked with being my ears and I was anxious to hear what he was able to overhear.

"Very well, I will locate the boy and provide him with what he needs to find you."

He turned briefly towards the stairwell we entered the chamber from and then back towards me.

"But I will not bring him to you, and should King Edric discover him here, we never had this conversation…Understood?"

I nodded in understanding, not wishing to utter anything further for I have already kept him a suspiciously long time. He reciprocated the gesture before handing me his torch. Which is something I did not expect, but that may have been part of his cover to explain his delay. Bringing the torch into the cell, I watched as he stepped away to return to his duties. The cell was as I remembered it, grim and frigid, more so than what we encounter on the surface. As I continued to scan the cell for anything of use, I found that the previous occupant had failed to remain here long enough to use the gracious heap of timber that was to provide warmth for what should have been a long night. I crouched to pull a portion of it towards one of the corners in the cell. The hope being that once ignited the fire would not only warm my flesh, but the stone as well.

Continuing in my pursuit of warmth and repose, I ignited the timber with the torch before jamming the base of it within a crevice in the stone, holding it in place. The timber crackled as the fire took hold of its surface, crawling across each fragment of bark that remained. Initially the fire sent a cloud of smoke hovering above me, but it soon flooded out into the other cells that were found within the vault. Thankfully, new ventilation holes must have just been added or I would have surely been suffocated by the smoke as there was nowhere for it to go. Aside from the crackling of the fire, there was not a sound to be heard from anyone else that could have been left in my company. Could he have possibly executed them all in my absence or were they opting for silence as they now understood whose company they kept? The answer may not have mattered, but as the minutes would soon draw into hours, idle time was all I had. Forcing my mind to return to all that had been known to me, I dwelled on King Edric's reaction. He grew angry at just mentioning the vessel. What was it he did not wish Kraciun to find?

The thought troubled me greatly and I began to fear we had all been deceived. Though deception has never been his way, there may be something else at work here that I have not thought of. As I was scrolling through memories in my mind, trying to put it all together, there was a faint sound of movement towards the far wall. At first it sounded like something being drug across the stone's surface, but then the sound changed to a tapping of sorts in a rhythmic inflection. Tap, tap…tap, tap…tap, tap, tap, tap. I was unsure if this tapping sound was being given to me as a warning or was it possible that someone was trying to grab my attention? The tapping sound increased in frequently. Where it once sounded like one person could have been making the sound, now it could have only been controlled my multiple.

Returning towards the gate, I leaned in towards its spindles, casting my gaze in the sound's direction. The sound ceased the moment my face came into view, but with the light from my cell, I could not see the sound's source either. I pulled away slightly to note the sound resumed. I shifted my body, shielding the remainder of the vault from the fire's light, in hopes that would permit me to see further. As I returned to the gate, the light still pierced the darkened space, but not as it was before, permitting me to see the remaining cell gates. I leaned in once more, focusing my gaze on the direction the sound appeared to be radiating from. My eyes soon felt strained as I was not accustomed to searching the darkness. Just as I was about to give up the chase, I saw something faintly shining back at me. I squinted, straining my eyes even further, in an attempt to see what it was when all became clear. Although, I needed the light to see what remained in the vault with me, the light that pierced its way around me to connect with their gaze. I soon found a set of very bright eyes looking back at me.

Hovering there, patiently waiting for the man to speak, my legs soon grew tired. I returned to tend to the fire when I saw the torch once more. Taking it quickly within my grasp, I returned to the gate, forcing the torch back through one of the many openings. In one hopeful attempt, I tossed it towards him. It struck the surface just outside of the man's gate, where I was soon met with the realization, I was not in the company of man, but a beast. The eyes that once found me in the dark were connected to a very large, blackened wolf. Just as I was coming to grips with the fact King Edric had been hiding a beast within the vault, several more came into view. The feeling I once had of being comforted by the darkness turned to fear in their wake.

Drayk

It was without warning when King Ferand graced me with his presence. Upon entering the chamber to which I found myself, he remained just beyond the threshold. He appeared displeased.

"It is customary to rise just before bowing when your King enters the room," his tone gruff.

My hand remained locked on the stone I was holding to sharpen my blades, but its pace had been brought to an abrupt stop. I raised an eyebrow in disgust just before glaring at him through a narrowed gaze.

"While it may be your coin that I accept, do not presume you can order me about in private. The moment she was delivered to you our agreement ended as is *customary* for all our agreements."

He scoffed violently but did not utter a word for several moments. This man may have been the one in power, but without the guidance of others he simply did not know how to behave, nor was he quick to think on his feet making him an easy target should I wish to rid Tuiteam of his ignorance.

"What news do you have of the shapeshifter Bryn?"

I remained where I was and returned my attention to sharping one of my many blades.

"My sources tell me that there is one of such a name that resides in the Kingdom of Losgadh," I paused, "shockingly within arm's reach of your betrothed."

"What is his purpose there?" he uttered through clenched teeth.

It was clear he was aggravated at just the thought of another being near what he considers to be his. Oddly possessive over something he cared not for just days ago. Further proving I would never understand them.

"Of that I do not know, nor do I care," I said sharply, "for you asked me to locate him and I have."

I could see his cheeks flush, and his breathing deepen. My lack of concern was upsetting him further and I found I had taken delight in watching him squirm.

"Why would a shapeshifter be kept in the castle?" he persisted.

"Of that I cannot say. Perhaps they have a similar arrangement with them as you do." I paused giving him time to toil over the matter, "but then again perhaps not."

"Then I *desire* to employ you once more," he sputtered through clenched teeth.

I returned my blade to its resting place just before placing the stone upon the table next to me.

"Understood."

He turned to walk away when I spoke once more.

"However," my voice broke through the silence and stopped him where he stood. "There is the matter of my fee."

"Your fee?" he turned about suddenly. "Your fee to detain the shapeshifter has already been paid in full by my father," he growled.

I quickly slid the two blades that I keep carefully hidden within my gauntlets forward and advanced towards him. Before he was able to draw another breath, I slid them in against his flesh, one in front of his neck and one behind. His body stiffened at my sudden advancement. Even now as he began to sputter sounds towards me out of fear and anger, the blades only grew hungrier for him.

"I am not some mere cleric that remains loyal to the crown out of the goodness of their heart," I spat. "What you are seeking will cost more than just coin to retrieve. You will need my skill to lure him here and into the tomb."

It was then a sound caught my attention just before a smell forced my gaze to deviate from him. Upon following the sound downward, I found the obnoxious King Ferand to have violated his breeches. I disapproved greatly of his cowardice and as my gaze once more found his. I watched him carefully for several moments, he was clearly frightened. As he should be.

"Do we understand one another?"

When he did not utter a response for several moments, I focused my energy upon him and slid the blades inward a fraction forcing his cheeks to flush and his pulse to race.

Through choked breaths and a strained voice, he

muttered, "Whatever your fee," he paused, "you shall have it."

"Then we have a deal."

I grinned just before removing the blades from his throat and forcing him back towards the door.

"You may go now."

I gestured for him to see his way out. He stopped to say something, but no words were uttered. Was it fear that stopped those words or was he actually learning from his mistakes? Perhaps he wished to utter something of the misfortune that occurred within his breeches, but then again, he is not one to draw further attention towards such things. I watched him carefully for a few moments. The cogs of his mind were working overtime to pull together the words that would form the threat he was undoubtedly concocting.

"Dare I ask the fee you desire this time?" he mumbled, surprising even me.

I thought carefully for a moment, at what King Ferand's limit would be. How far would he be willing to go to secure these beings within his walls? Then it came to me.

"A favor is all that I require as payment." I spoke frankly.

"What sort of favor and when would you require it?" he asked sounding suddenly uneasy.

"Let us just say when a favor is needed, I will call upon you," I paused briefly. "It may be today or not for many years."

"And what if I refuse?"

"There will be no chance of that happening," I grinned. "As the blood oath I require cannot be refuted."

"And was my father required to take this oath?" his

voice dry and now reeking of fear.

"Aye, that he was."

"But was he willing?" he asked, though I am unsure why it mattered.

"Without question…however, his fee was very different than your own."

He advanced towards me slowly before muttering his question just under his breath, "What was it you asked of him?"

"An offering of blood," I paused, "to be named later of course."

"And did you receive your payment?"

"The Queen is dead is she not?" I spoke blatantly growing tired of his questions.

His back straightened and he charged towards me.

"You killed my mother!"

I held a handout before me as a warning to control himself or I would be forced to use less desirable means.

"I never said it was your mother that was taken."

He stood there for several moments, clearly unsure whether to be upset or angry over the assassin that been welcomed into his castle with open arms. Then there was a moment when light came to his eyes, and I knew he had figured it out.

"Prince Urie's mother was the one that was taken as payment," he uttered more as a statement than a question. "What did he ask of you for such a payment?"

"King Ferand, your father's desperation to secure your throne knew no bounds," I paused. "Just like the deeds you have asked of me for that same purpose know no bounds."

I raised an eyebrow, emphasizing and reminding him that I know of the secrets he keeps.

He cleared his throat before leaning into whisper, "No one else knows of what I have asked of you, correct?"

"Of course not," I grinned. "I would not be very good at my profession should I be babbling about my handy work."

He nodded repeatedly.

"Good, for the populace would not think so kindly of me should they find out I had anything to do with sending *their* Warrior Prince back into Boglach, weary and broken."

"Rest assured; your hands shall remain clean of that debacle."

"Has there been any word regarding him and his men? Do any of them yet live?"

"I have not heard such, but to remain disconnected from the matter, I refrain from inquiring to present my own anonymity." I smiled briefly, "As I am certain you can understand."

"Of course."

He turned once more to leave the chamber but stopped shy of the door.

"The man you sent to lure the vessels away from the port, does he know why you asked him to do so?"

"King Ferand, you toil too much over trivial information that will not change what has happened."

"If he does, then I will need you to be rid of him as a means of ensuring the purpose behind the action remains hidden."

"So quick to execute a man willing to heed to your call," I scoffed. "Bartholomew is not a lorvisad as I. He is merely a man out to secure a position within your court."

"And you offered this to him without consulting me?"

I glared at him once more.

"You tasked me with the challenge of purging any potential threat to your reign, that includes Tuiteam's Warrior Prince and the mischievous Prince Urie. Your permission is no longer required for anything I deem necessary to complete my task."

His face tightened significantly as if holding his breath or clenching his teeth would stop him from uttering something unwise.

"What of Prince Urie?" he blurted. "Did the Skogar truly take him or was this part of your doing?"

"Do not ask what you truly do not wish to know for the answers I can provide will not comfort you."

He nodded opting to not press the matter further.

"Then we have an understanding?" I pressed him.

"Aye," he mumbled now understanding the true cost of what he seeks.

"Then return to me now," I held out a piece of parchment for him to grasp, "for it is now that I require you to take the oath."

He turned towards me and held out his hand. I withdrew one of my blades once more and thrust it deep within his palm, forcing crimson to pool around the tip. He did not recoil from the blade, but the grimace upon his face showed his discomfort in the matter. Waiting only another moment, as to not let the blood congeal, before removing the blade and forcing the parchment into his hand. The parchment quickly absorbed the crimson liquid before forcing it to creep into the words that I had known to be found there. They flushed bright at first and then soon faded to the black as they were once found to be. I grasped the parchment within my hand before pulling it forcefully away.

"The oath has been set," I paused, gesturing towards the door, "you are free to go."

He did not appear to be pleased with me, but those in my company rarely are. After vacating the chamber, I gathered what was needed before opening the chamber door to flee through the back hall. During this time of day, there would be less congestion there and I could disappear amongst the shadows if I so desired. Although, most do not know of who I am even if seen, my elven ears and bright eyes make them frightened at the thought of remaining in my company for more than a moment. The treatment Conall received the night of his most recent return was what most elves would receive if they had mistakenly found their way into the city. They fear them here like nowhere else, but their reasoning is not validated. Of all those with magical abilities, I know few who would use it maliciously for them to fear and that being is human not elven after all. Elves of such magical skill would not flee from Lamprog or Tiene for that matter unless it was required of them. We need that tether between us for our magic to be at its most potent. The further we stray, the more strained the tether and feeble the magic. My tether along with my magic were broken the day I was reborn as a way of mutilating me for all to see. Being elven born, however, I would never fully be rid of it. I have since regained some of what I once lost and with each passing day in Haxa's presence, I feel it growing stronger still.

With no more than a few awkward glances I had broken free of the castle and was making my way towards the northern wall. On the northern side of the wall, there is a place where some may pass through without being seen for the guards rarely patrol there. The stone found sunken in the soil and clinging to the cliff's edge has broken away over many years of torment by the sea. Only those with considerable climbing skill could round it without heeding to the cliff's demands. Its presence and its weakness were known to King Baylon many years before his passing. Unfortunately, he opted to let the gap remain for any so bold as to attempt it would undoubtably be considered a sacrifice to the Gods that appeared constantly in a state of displeasure with our world.

It was nearly midday when I reached the wall. Upon taking its sun-kissed surface within my grasp, I swung myself across to grasp the other side. Hanging there for a moment, I watched the waves smoothly glide onto the shore as a faint breeze combed its way through my long locks that I had carelessly failed to draw back. For a moment, there was peace felt within, but that peace would be short lived for the pain in my chest that followed would soon grow. Enjoying the pleasantries of the afternoon light no longer pleased me and only brought pain. It was a reminder that I was without her and only the darkness could shield me from my suffering. It was a pain that I clung to and within its cruel grasp, I felt compelled to force those who caused it to experience it as I do. Out of fear, I cast peace aside and drew my attention back to the task at hand.

Stretching myself towards the other side, I leapt in one smooth motion permitting the soil to be met with my boots once more. The moments of peace that find me are few and far between and they are never welcome. The one I felt just now could permit weakness to brew within, that I could not allow. The agreements that are yet to be made or yet to be fulfilled would have no room for it. It was then I stepped off towards the port found near the sound. There is where I shall inquire as to the Warrior Prince's well-being. Though I do not presume he and his men would have made it out of the marsh alive, that man has surprised me on more than one occasion. I have learned not to underestimate him. Should he have survived, and I may no longer be given the luxury of letting Caladh determine his fate.

Reaching the port after nightfall was not without its challenges, but my stamina and lack of need for rest permits me to push the limits of the body I was given to the brink quite frequently. The port was quieter than usual, but that did not detour me in any way. I kept to the shadows as I observed all that were near for any prying eyes that should not have been there. All appeared as it should be. Though it would have been customary to call to the Port Master, I opted for that of covertness rather than what was customary. As I neared the building that housed the Port Master, I listened carefully to ensure that he was alone before entering. Only rustling parchment could be heard along with random muttering. He was alone. I pulled from my pack one of the Jagare's cloaks and drew it up onto my head, making sure to conceal my eyes from his sight once inside. I did not enter through the door, but a window nearby, only adding to the man's surprise as I now stood tall before him. He rose quickly from the chair he had been sitting at, sputtering something in confusion and fear.

"Calm yourself Port Master," I spoke softly but firm in my tone. "King Ferand sent us in search of Commander Berenger. We are not here for your head."

Speaking as they do and having their appearance would only further aid in my cover should the Port Master ever be questioned.

He grasped his tunic within his hands and pulled it downward in an effort to appear more presentable.

"My apologies, I was not expecting you at this hour."

"But you were expecting me?" I spoke plainly, though I was unsure what would have given him this impression.

"Of course, when I explained to Prince Berenger that the vessels were all sent away prior to his arrival," he paused. "I assumed a formal inquiry would follow."

I nodded as a gesture of understanding to aid in the ruse.

"And what of your findings?"

"The letter, while no longer in my possession, was not written by King Baylon's hand."

"Are you certain?" I asked already knowing that the handwriting was my own and untraceable to anyone other than one of elven descent.

"Aye, over the years the late King Baylon wrote many orders addressed to this port," he paused. "It was not until after

Prince Berenger left that I thought of this."

"Has there been word from Commander Berenger since he and his men departed?"

"Afraid not, they should have returned by now," he muttered as he began rubbing his hands together nervously. "But I fear they may belong to Boglach now."

"Thank you, Port Master. Should you receive word stating otherwise, please notify Tuiteam immediately."

I tipped my head downward slightly towards him.

"Aye, that I will."

He tipped his head downward in return. I returned to the window of which I gained entry and slipped through the opening without drawing in a second breath. As my feet returned to the wooden boards of the dock, I scanned my surroundings once more before setting off towards the edge of the marsh. While I had no intention of stepping inside at this hour, it was there that I would watch the port for any sign of Prince Berenger or his men. Should one of them have made it out alive and this is the first place they would go. If no word is received within a day, then I will venture along the edge of the sound towards the Kingdom of Losgadh where I will question their Port Master and the guard at the main gate if necessary. For now, I will rest here at the water's edge as I bask in the moonlight.

It was the smell of fire and ash that woke us where we lay, my ionuin still cradled within my arms. The ground beneath began to quake and as our gazes met, a feeling of panic washed over me. There was no time to enjoy the elation of a lover's embrace. We must rise and flee or perish in what was unquestionably coming for us. I rose first, only donning what I required before pulling her up from where she lay to do the same. No words were spoken between us, but I felt a growing concern pulling at us both, weighing us down. Upon taking her hand in mine, we both turned our gaze towards the north where the sky was now consumed by a dark cloud above a mountain of fire. It was like nothing we had ever seen before. The world we once knew was being consumed by fire and something undoubtably evil. Although, I longed to know the source of this evil, there was nothing we could do now but run.

Pulling her along with me, we fled towards the south with haste, but as our pace quickened, so did its. As we were struggling to outrun the fire's wrath, I felt her hand slip from mine, forcing me to stop as I were before returning to her. Crouching down towards her, I was attempting to help her up when the ground beneath me began to split. Before I could cope with what was truly happening, I felt her hands press against me in a violent shove. It took me by surprise and forced me off my feet and away from the crumbling soil. Scurrying to get my footing back, it was then that I saw her. She was clinging to what little soil and rock that remained as her body was slowly being pulled into the depths. I rushed towards her, reaching for her, promising to save her…but I was already too late. Beneath her flowed a river of fire that was consuming all within its path. I called to her, crying out her name, but she could no longer hear the words I spoke over the thunderous roar of our world collapsing around us.

Rather than let Caladh's wrath consume us both, she chose to cast me out of harm's way where I would hopefully be spared. It was in the fields where we first met and, in the fields, where we became lovers that her body would be no more. I felt fear consuming me as I watched her begin to fall into the fire. Though she did not appear afraid, I could feel her spirit abandoning her body in the hopes of returning one day. It was then I knew I could not rest until our spirits found each other once more.

The thought of her demise jolted me back to reality where I soon realized Eira was no longer by my side. My thoughts were beginning to spiral and in a moment of panic. I rose from where she once had lain to begin my search for her when I heard the water streaming inside the cavern a bit more forceful than usual. When I turned towards it, I saw her standing there, bathing in the water that was found streaming in. It was one of the most beautiful things I had ever seen. The way her vibrant locks flowed down onto her chest, cleverly covering parts of her body as she bent down to cleanse the sand and sweat from her legs. Just watching her made my heart race and my breathing deepen. I rushed towards her, desperate to feel her flesh next to mine once more, fearing a great deal that this was all an illusion. I stepped behind her placing my hands on her hips taking her by surprise. She turned about suddenly letting a soft giggle escape her before placing her hands upon my face, wiping away the tears that I had not realized had fallen.

"What troubles you?" she asked, her eyes widening with concern.

I shook my head before leaning in to kiss her. Just a nightmare I thought, but my body refused to relax just yet.

"Conall," she whispered, "there is something I have been meaning to ask you."

I felt my face tighten with uncertainty, unsure how to respond. I nodded as a suggestion for her to continue.

"Before when you said I had a memory," she paused, expression filled with apprehension. "That was a memory we shared, is it not?"

"Aye, that it is."

"How could that be? I had never seen your face before the morning by the stream."

"But you have," I paused, "just not with these eyes."

She shook her head slightly before muttering, "I do not

understand. How is that possible?"

"Do you recall ever being told what happens when our bodies are forced to pass on?"

"The body may pass on, but our spirit will live since that is what is immortal, not our bodies."

"Right…there is a reason you have had little desire to bond with another and you feel drawn to me despite believing you did not know me."

"We have met before," she uttered more out of disbelief than an actual question.

"Not just met," I kissed her once more, further tempting her to see what she desperately needed to see.

Her gaze now wandering across my flesh, she was starting to see it all come together.

"I pushed you away to save you…just before my body perished in a river of fire," her expression pained.

I wrapped my arms around her, pulling her towards me once more.

"My ionuin," I uttered breathlessly.

I could feel her expression change and her body relax.

"It was the memory that convinced you," she sounded surprised.

"Aye," I paused, "for you could have not known of that moment without being my ionuin."

"How is it I did not know sooner? How did you not know sooner?" her tone now quite sharp.

"Of that I cannot say," I whispered. "I have never met one of our kind that has found their way back. Perhaps they have been waiting for something…something I cannot understand as I have remained here alone nearly all this time." I leaned in and kissed her neck softly before continuing. "Though I could sense I was being pulled towards you…you did not appear as I once knew, and my own fear tried to keep me away. Telling me I had to have been mistaken. Once there was no denying who you were to me, I let all that fear and apprehension go."

She gazed upon my face for several moments before shifting her eyes towards my long locks and then her very own, twirling them amongst her fingers.

"I cannot recall much," she paused, "pieces of memories broken overtime and I am struggling to put them back together in my mind. Yet, the memory of laying in the field with you that night has remained unbroken. I just needed to find it again."

"That is the moment when we became bonded to one another and the memory of it cannot be broken so easily. That is, also, why we feel stronger together and why King Ferand must never know."

"But he already senses we feel something for one another?"

"Aye, that he does, and he is using it against us. The bond makes us more willing to cast ourselves into danger for the other, but, also, to bend to someone else's will if the other's life is being threatened. As a means of preservation, if you will. We can heal if maimed for the most part, but recalling a lost spirit has just not been done."

"But it is possible we could still find one another should we pass on, right?"

"Aye, of course or we would not be having this conversation, but who is to say when our spirit would return." I kissed her softly, before whispering, "I have waited centuries to hold you in my arms once more. I dare not tempt fate further for I do not believe my heart could take the pain of losing you for a second time."

She pulled herself onto her toes to place her cheek next to mine, where she nuzzled me instinctively. It was then I felt the nightmare I awoke to fading away. Had I but known she had the ability to make centuries of pain diminish in her presence and I would not have been so quick to push her away that morning in Coille or any moment since then. Thinking back on the moment now, I wondered if we both could have escaped or were we always fated to be imprisoned here. There was no way for us to know and I needed to remind myself that no matter the journey, she would always be worth the risk. Just the thought of her set my flesh ablaze and what started out as comforting nuzzles, turned into passionate kisses with a desire for one another that just would not cease. Wrapping my hands around her thighs, I lifted her up onto my waist before stepping towards the nearest wall where the cool stone clung to her scorching flesh. The sensation caused a gasp to escape her in between our kisses, which only excited us more.

The overwhelming feeling of ecstasy that we continually gave into felt inevitable, but just as we were about to, we heard a sound rushing towards us from within the chamber. It was faint, impossible for man to hear, but it broke through the air drawing our attention away from our burning loins. Though we were still very much in a lover's embrace, our attention fleeted very far from it. I lowered Eira's legs back onto the sandy floor, heavily focused on the sound we had heard. When we heard it once more. I turned to step towards it, pulling her behind me as I was unsure of what the noise could have been coming from. At first the sound popped like that of bubbles reaching the surface of a hot spring, but with each step the noise became clearer. In that moment, Eira and I both understood the sound. We rushed towards the coffin the young prince was placed within. We looked upon each other in utter disbelief before we knelt at the coffin's edge.

He still lives I thought, feeling disbelief wash over me. I was sure he would have passed on before now.

He is stronger than I would have guessed for such a young lad. Why was he brought here?

He is our leverage I suppose, should they still be searching for him.

How long has he been here?

It is difficult to tell, possibly several days now. I am surprised he wakes at all.

I have been caring for him when I could, but I worry that my care is hurting him.

I turned towards her feeling both concern and greater affection for her. She cared for this child of man despite who he was and the potential threat he may pose to our kind in the future. I watched her reach around me to brush her hand across his forehead, but he did not flinch from her touch as I would have expected. Clearly, he was becoming accustomed to receiving her comfort in the dark.

There was a time when I would have gladly traded his

life for ours, but as I look upon him now, I only feel fear for him.

You care for this boy.

She nodded, *That I do.*

I grabbed her arms and pulled her towards me, leaving nothing more than a thin margin of air between us as I hugged her gently.

Care for him if it be your wish, but I would not hold out on a hope. There is only one that I believe would come for him should he discover that he is here.

Who might that be?

Prince Berenger.

I know naught of who he is other than by name. What leads you to believe he would come for him?

We have found ourselves linked to one another since my capture. He is far from weak, but there is a pain that radiates from within him that for so long I emulated. While my beloved may have returned to me, his cannot, for she was laid to rest within this very cavern.

I turned to glance at the marker Prince Berenger was drawn to during what he believed was our first encounter. Her gaze followed mine briefly before returning to the young prince.

In my presence, he has challenged Ferand, and I believe he would do so again if given the chance. Nevertheless, Prince Berenger needs Ferand in a way I cannot understand, proclaiming nearly all his actions in the name of duty. The duty of men transcends the traditional barriers that we are accustomed to and perhaps that is the source of my confusion.

We do not bond with those not of our choosing nor would we give ourselves in service to another for mere coin or title. These are duties of man's creation that hold no value on a larger scale. Regardless of status or coin, their bodies will all become dust after they have met their end. Caladh was a place of peace and all who resided in its wake thrived, until man arrived. Birthed out of dark magic, yet they hold no innate gifts other than their own greed. They are the poison that feeds upon and seeks to devour the known world. Should it be the will of the Gods, I long to see a day when they are no more.

I felt her hand clasp the bottom of my chin turning my face towards hers where our gazes met. She slid her hand along my jaw cradling my face within her hand when I felt her other hand find mine. Clinging to it, she brought it onto her chest where I felt her heart beating in the familiar pattern, I had grown to take comfort in. With each beat, I felt some of the angst slipping away and though I would not wish to admit it aloud, I do not believe I would harm the boy unless there was not another option.

Very well, should it be your wish to care for him, then I will do what I can to aid you, but first you should probably don your leathers.

I winked at her just before scanning her very bare body with a wanting gaze. Her cheeks flushed with color before letting a soft giggle escape and I was overcome with a feeling that I had not felt in sometime. It was not relief...or worry...or fear...it was an overwhelming feeling of bliss and I clung to it desperately ever fearful it would be taken from me again. As she rose to her feet, the hand that was once placed on her chest, traced the curves of her body before falling back towards the sand that lay before me. She returned to the site where we tore the leathers from our bodies the day before and began donning what remained, piece by piece. I rose slowly before stepping towards her only to realize the breeches I once wore would need to be mended or they would be quite drafty if worn in their current state. As I searched for my remaining pair, I saw she had finished covering herself and was already returning to the young prince's side.

After a speedy search, I found my breeches and donned them quickly before stepping back towards them. Placing our hands upon the edge of the coffin's lid, we began applying pressure until it began to shift. Slow at first but soon it toppled off the other side and into the sand. There was a stench that wafted from within and out into the chamber in a cloud of unyielding decay. It clung to us, burning the lining of our nostrils and our eyes until we were forced to turn away. Another act of treachery by Haxa, had the young prince been sent into a dreamless state and his body would not have carried on as it were. What happened to him was far worse than I imagined. He had remained here, paralyzed, but otherwise very aware of where he was and all that had happened around him. Turning and gazing upon one another in dread as this revelation came to light. The moment of revelation left us feeling vulnerable and spiteful for what had occurred in this chamber over the past several days was not for a young prince's ears.

We must get him out of there or his body will soon fester from decay.

Alright, I will carry him.

Holding my breath I leaned over him, to witness his gaze now opening to mine. He did not appear to be focusing on mine, nor did he blink, just stared blankly in my direction. He was merely responding to the movement and my presence. I reached towards him and began unraveling the delicate braids that held his doublet together. As I worked to remove the doublet from his body, Eira removed his boots and woolen socks before casting them aside. It was then I noticed she was reaching for the strands that held his breeches upon his waist. Though, I knew her intentions to be pure, instinctively I took one of her wrists within my grasp, startling her. Her hand now quivering slightly at my sudden reaction. I shook my head, encouraging her to stop and step away.

He is a young man, probably never bedded a woman. So, for you to disrobe him, even if only to aid him, would not be welcomed I assure you.

Based upon the look that had consumed her face, this was not something she had considered. A moment later her gaze dropped to his while she thought the matter over just before nodding her understanding. I released her wrist from my grasp and watched her pull herself away from the coffin permitting me to continue disrobing the young prince until only his soiled tunic remained. I chose to let it remain since that would be all the privacy I would be able to offer him. Caring for him as it were reminded me greatly of when I was a young man and how I cared for my siblings. In our youth, shapeshifters keep to tight family groups due to our astonishing growth rate. From being birthed to sexual maturity it is little more than a year, perhaps two, which is why we rely heavily on seclusion during that time. Should we have chosen to live openly during such a time then everyone would know we were not as we appear. Even in times of peace, we have never been able to truly be ourselves while in the presence of others, a thought both comforting and frightening.

I returned my attention towards the young prince, and I believed he could remain there no longer. I inhaled deeply before leaning over him and sliding my arms into the filth that lay beneath his neck and thighs. The odor was potent and only grew stronger as I began to shift his body while trying to get a firm grip upon him. I tried my best not to draw in another breath or glance down towards him unless it was necessary. As I pulled him towards me, I was surprised how light he felt, even for a young man of his age. Upon reaching the dip in the sand where the water had been known to pool, I veered slightly to keep him just out of the water's reach. This being our only source of fresh water at this time, we could not afford to contaminate it. It was there that I placed him against stone and where I saw his eyes blink for the first time since they opened.

It was then when I noticed once more that there was more water trickling in than usual. Could the stone that supported this chamber begun to shift or was it possible that I was imagining the change in flow? Stepping towards it, I rubbed my hands along the various cracks that had grown since I could last recall, not finding any notable weaknesses. It would have been both a blessing and curse should a force so great have weakened the wall. While I would have loved to tinker with the reasoning behind it all, the young prince awaits.

Returning to his side, I found that his gaze had opened a touch more and his eyes were now fixed on Eira who was waiting patiently near one of the few angelic statues in our presence. I watched him, watching her for several moments, his gaze unwavering despite my presence. I reached for a bit of my torn breeches and dipped them within the water, it was brisk to the touch which may shock him, so I held it briefly within my hands trying to warm it slightly. Each passing moment felt like an eternity within the cavern and as I lingered there, quite uncomfortable with our current situation, I knew I could wait no longer.

Wiping his brow slowly, trying fervently to move past my resentment towards man to see this young prince for just what he was: a young man, quite ill and very near death. His body barely moved, even against my touch, and what once was the beating heart of a vibrant young man could now barely be heard. In between dabs and strokes to cleanse his body, I cupped small pools of water within my hand and brought it towards his mouth to drink. Most of the water ran in streams down his chin or unto the tunic below, but there was some that found its way inside. The drops that were able to take hold on his pale, cracked lips disappeared almost instantly portraying him as the human version of the ground Tiene is built upon. I watched him carefully during this time, unsure of what his future might be. Was this young prince destined to perish as a pawn in a game that had been being built since before his birth or would he survive to sit upon the throne many years from now? Neither answer pleased me.

Turning back towards the pool, I was reminded of when

I tended to Eira just days before. For a place built to house the dead, there was an alarming amount of healing and life that had occurred within. It was in thinking of her recovery that I turned towards her to find her watching me. Although she may not have recalled the moment for herself, she could now see it through my gaze. I watched as the corners of her mouth turned upward slightly and her gaze brightened. Just looking upon her as she were now, reminded me once more that there was nothing I would not do for her. This includes tending to the descendant of the bloodline who has imprisoned us.

Pulling the young prince towards me, the stench I once believed had dissipated, had preserved despite my efforts. I knew no amount of dabbing would relieve him of the filth that was the source of the foul odor.

"Eira, I need you," I whispered or so I thought.

As his body flinched, I knew I was not as soft spoken as I intended. I merely blinked when I felt the warmth of her slender fingers slide onto my shoulder and brush the side of my neck. The simple gesture comforted me greatly and without thinking I leaned towards her, brushing my cheek against her forearm. I gazed up at her, unsure what to say and possibly that was for the best. As I held him against my chest with his head lain upon my shoulder, she worked to pour water over his back, ridding him from the filth that had begun to eat away at his flesh. With each pass of water, we had less to drink, but the odor that once made it difficult to breathe had become tolerable. With little change to his breathing and heart rate, I worried all we were doing may not be enough. However, the longer I held his body against my own, the more his body relaxed. Almost like when someone exhales after a long-withheld breath. It was then that it occurred to me, it was my body temperature that comforted him, not being held. Being human and essentially trapped in a cave, there was no way to keep his body warm. If there was any hope of bringing him back from the brink, then we needed to warm his body and soon.

"That is the best we can do for now," she spoke softly. "There is not much water left and we will need every drop of what is there to sustain us until more is able to trickle inward."

I glanced towards the pool before nodding slightly, reluctant to move more than necessary for fear of startling him.

"We need to move him again," she whispered. "Being near the wall will not warm him and we need to bury the filth or let the chamber be consumed with its odor."

She made a very valid point and though I was reluctant to move him, we could not leave him where he was.

"Bring me what is left of my torn breeches," I uttered just barely above a whisper, "I will not leave him exposed."

She handed me what remained of them, and it was little more than what she wore upon her own body. I am certain the young prince would have wished for more, but this would have to suffice for now. We wrapped the remains around his torso, slightly looser, so when I stood with him, they could be lowered to cover his manhood. Eira remained knelt by the water's edge as I pulled him up with me, just before sliding everything in place and lifting back up into my arms. While he was still quite light for me to carry, he smelt much better, to which I am certain all of us appreciated. Unsure where to place him, I stepped towards one of the angelic statues, looking upon her face with curiosity before placing him at her feet. Her wings were curved inward, shielding most of her body from within them, but her hands I found the most interesting. They were held outward with her palms upward, almost like she was a sacrifice or waiting to receive one. There was something about it that gave me an eerie feeling, but I did not wish to remove him from her downward gaze.

After picking up the cloak that had become invaluable to us, I lowered myself towards him, sitting next to him in the cool sand just before tossing it over his body. He had curled himself inward slightly as a means of preserving what body heat he had left, but soon returned to as he was when the cloak fell in place. I placed a hand onto his back and massaged it gently, hoping my own body heat would transfer to him. It was not long before Eira joined us and placed herself just shy of the young prince's head. She reached for him, lifting his head slightly before sliding her legs underneath. The sensation of his icy flesh touching hers sent a shiver throughout her body and I watched her shake briefly before casting it off.

Thinking over our time together, the three of us each had a turn at being where he was. First, it was Eira who tended to me after I was badly beaten; then it was I who tended to Eira in her hour of need and now this young prince. The one not destined to be king, but like his brother, Prince Berenger, one of the strongest I have seen. Though they were clearly not birthed from the same womb, they were unlike the late King Baylon and nearly the opposite of their sibling, Ferand, who I refuse to accept as King. There was something there tethering them to this world, and I longed to know what that could have been.

Overtime, I was beginning to grow quite restless and with Prince Urie making little to no progress, it only further agitated me. I longed to be released from this prison. Should I have known the cost I might have been willing to pay it, if nothing more than to see the sun rise and fall in the sky. I miss the smell that flowers give off just after the morning rain or the smell of salt wafting across the fields of Feurach as the waves crash into the dunes below. While it was still all fresh within my mind, in here, time stands still, and we have no comprehension of the day or hour we find ourselves in. This made me restless even more so, and I could see and feel Conall's growing concern over the matter. Without hope of a different tomorrow, we remained as we were, locked in this state of uncertainty and peril.

It was not until quite some time later when Prince Urie stirred from his slumber, eyes soon peeled open wide with surprise just before they clasped shut again from the pain the light brought. Being that his head presently was laying upon my lap, I placed a hand just upon his temple, shielding his eyes from the light. They began to open once more. Slow at first, but once more they grew wide. He did not appear to fear me, but there was something in his gaze that felt peculiar. It felt personal, but not intimate such as the way Conall's gaze frequently falls upon me. Like this young prince knew something he should not. Reluctant to challenge him presently, I decided comforting him would be more appropriate in this moment.

"It is alright," I heard myself lie knowing all too well it was not. "You are safe now," I added in a soft tone trying not to frighten him.

I placed a hand upon his brow, gently brushing his unkempt, dark black locks back. His locks were smooth with no bends or twists to be found and it appeared to be kept long near the center of his head, while the sides remained cut very close to his flesh. Possibly as an act of rebellion, but that mattered little now. Watching him carefully, I noticed he was beginning to mouth something.

"Conall," I spoke quickly, but my gaze did not waver from Prince Urie's face. "Would you bring me some water? I think he is trying to say something to me."

Conall uttered nothing in reply, but as I felt his fingers slipping from their resting place on just above my knee, I knew he would bring me what I asked. I remained there with him, concentrating on the movement his lips were making, when I started to catch certain words. When taken out of context as it were, it was all quite difficult to understand. Conall returned to my side sooner than expected and I tilted Prince Urie's head upward slightly, encouraging him to drink. He took the water without question, gulping it rapidly just before gasping for air upon finishing. I was unsure whether he believed this may be the last of what he would receive in our company or if his will to live had returned to him. He began to mouth the words to me again, this time with Conall and I watching him intently. As he circled back to the same words multiple times, I knew there had to be something about them I was not understanding. I turned to Conall, desperate for his aid. Conall swallowed hard and his face tightened.

Though he has been taking comfort in our care, he is certainly fearful of us for we are elven and those of our kind are not welcome here.

I felt my expression grow cold, feeling a pain that I had not before. While I have lived a life in seclusion, when in the presence of others, I have never felt they have feared me for my elven ears. It felt cruel somehow and although, I knew I could not change what felt natural to this young prince, I desperately wanted to know why he felt this way. There had to be more to it than just an elf's innate magical gifts. Just as my thoughts were beginning to wander, I felt Conall's hand land upon my upper arm, startling me slightly, bringing my attention back to him.

He knows naught of what we truly are. Do not toil over the minds of men that we cannot change. For we may never fully understand their actions or their fears.

But they must understand that we are not monsters. I pleaded with him.

I feel they care naught of what we may or may not be. Years of deception poured into their ears has polluted them against anyone unlike themselves.

How lonely that must make them in the world.

He did not utter a sound in response, but as I watched his gaze return to Prince Urie, I could sense he felt as I. My attention returned as well when I noticed he was now mouthing something familiar, something I had seen another utter not all that long ago. *It is you.* It was uttered by the serf just before I helped death find him. Those three simple words should not trouble me but watching them be uttered by Prince Urie caused a knot to form within my belly. He knew something of me. Uncertain as to how, I felt a wave of fear sinking its claws into my mind, pulling me towards it, begging me to heed to its might. I held firm with my expression taunt, unwilling to give into the suggestion that there was something more to be found there. Unfortunately, Conall did not hold the same restraint and I soon heard his voice break through the silence. Prince Urie's gaze turned abruptly towards him.

"Have you seen her before?" his voice sounded unsure.

Prince Urie shook his head slightly.

"Did someone tell you about her?" he added sounding slightly hopeful.

He nodded slightly, never taking his gaze from Conall.

"Did someone tell you about me?"

He nodded again.

"Do you know why we were brought here?"

Prince Urie's gaze widened, and his focus began to falter, shifting slightly more than likely out of fear. When he did not respond right away, I gestured for Conall to step away for a moment with the hope that would coax him along.

"Prince Urie," I spoke softly, "we are trapped here just as you are. If you know anything at all, please tell us."

"I do not wish to die," Prince Urie uttered nervously and barely above a whisper.

I shook my head nervously; fearful it was us that he believed would be the bringers of his death when Conall returned to us. My gaze left Prince Urie to seek Conall's as a means of bringing my emotions in check and conveying my uncertainty. Conall's jaw tightened, and he once again knelt beside the young prince before tipping more water against his lower lip. Prince Urie drank until there was no more, and I felt compelled to press him about what was said.

"After all we have done for you, it is your belief that we would end your life?"

Conall's face turned towards me abruptly, eyes narrowed slightly in confusion. Prince Urie shook his head once more before raising one of his arms towards his brow and touching it briefly. The gesture felt like a riddle I desperately wanted to solve, but my mind was two steps back from where it should be.

"You fear he who wears the crown," Conall uttered sternly.

Clearly, his mind had not been compromised in any way and while I was curious to know how, that would be a conversation for another time. I glanced towards Conall, whose gaze was heavily focused on Prince Urie, when I, too, returned my attention towards him, anxiously awaiting his reply. Prince

Urie nodded once more.

"But he is your brother?" I felt the words tumble out across my lips in shock.

"He is no more my brother," Prince Urie's voice croaked, strained from dehydration, "than you are monsters."

"Do you know of what we are?" Conall asked.

Prince Urie nodded.

"You are not what any of us," he paused, taking a few shorts breaths, "were expecting."

"What were *you* expecting?" I added curious to hear the answer.

"Wolves," he paused again focusing his gaze on mine, "not elves."

A soft giggle escaped me unexpectedly and I quickly shielded my lips with one of my hands, but it was too late. Both Conall and Prince Urie heard the sound, but only Conall found Prince Urie's response as humorous as I did. I just could not fathom how man could have reached this conclusion even after all this time. It took only a moment to compose ourselves after receiving a look of disapproval from the young prince. I cleared my throat as a means of distracting myself as my thoughts returned to the discussion at hand.

"And you are kind," he whispered, "which is useless to Ferand."

"Useless?" we uttered in unison.

"Caladh cannot be taken by kindness," he whispered. "You cannot let him see this side of you."

His brow tightened as a means of having his point emphasized, I would presume. Having thoughts of us as nothing more than beasts would explain why they were inclined to treat us as they had. Their brutality could easily turn someone dark had that been their wish, but something about that did not set well with me. I understood that they would desire to use us as beasts of war, but why seek us out to begin with? Two shapeshifters would not be enough to bring down all the other kingdoms of men.

"After being in their company for some time, they could not explain why some would see me as a mysterious elf and others a large wolf. They believed me to be a warlock and vowed to execute me, but it was King Baylon who figured me out first. I do not believe he was seeking us out for he appeared genuinely astonished at his discovery."

"Then why risk so much to bring me here only to be imprisoned for a war that has yet to occur?" I posed the question to Conall, but it was Prince Urie who answered.

"The crown desires more," he spoke barely above a whisper.

"He must understand there are no more of us to be found," I insisted.

I heard myself lie once more as I was still unsure where the young prince's loyalty may be found.

"He has no further need to find others," Prince Urie cleared his throat once more.

Because he is hoping I will sire more for him.

Conall's thought was quite frank, not as the understanding of our situation as I would have anticipated. This thought either had occurred to him before now or he was beginning to understand the vile inner thoughts of the man who

now wears the crown. As his mind uttered those words, I felt
them push through me like a shockwave taking my breath away
and soon I could think of nothing else. Suddenly I felt as if the
walls were closing in on me and I could not catch my breath. I
glanced down towards Prince Urie and then back towards
Conall, who was now watching me with growing concern.

Calm yourself, my ionuin.

But I could not. My flesh was now crawling with rage,
and I felt any moment now I would collapse out of shear
frustration. I shifted myself out from under Prince Urie, taking
care not to drop his head too suddenly upon the sand below.
Once free of his weight, I scurried to my feet and rushed
towards the iron door, insistent on leaving. I reached the door
and began slamming my fists upon its surface violently.

"Ferand, come down here and face me you coward! I
am not a beast to be bred like cattle!" I screamed.

I was blinded by my rage and could see nothing of how
ridiculous I must appear to be nor what I was doing to my
hands. It was not until I felt Conall's hands clasped tightly
around my wrists before I stopped seeking my vengeance upon
the iron door. As he pulled my hands away from the door and
back towards my chest, I could now see all I had done. The
skin that once was smooth sun-kissed, now streaked with
crimson that lay over tattered and burning flesh. We both knew
the scrapes would heal soon, but I could not unhear those
words. He crossed my wrists in front of me, holding them
tightly to my chest, as he pulled me back towards his. I wanted
to scream, but as my rage soon faded, sadness overcame me
and all I wanted to do was weep. I felt my body soften against

his and although I was tempted to ask, I already knew he was just as disturbed by this revelation as I was. Closing my eyes tightly now, I felt the cool caress of tears racing their way towards my chin as the air from the chamber began to fill my lungs once more. I would soon be able to breathe again as normal, but each time my mind returned to those words I felt my breath catch.

How did you know that is what King Ferand now seeks? I stepped into his mind as I found myself unable to speak.

Too many of his actions are misplaced. As I watched him threaten to ravage you before me, there was something within him that I felt, and I still feel…he would have stopped at nothing to have you.

But he did stop.

Aye, but only after I told him that if he laid with you, he would be condemning our kind to death.

So, you knew then that this is what he desired of us?

No, not at all. It was not until just now that all the pieces came together. This must be why Drayk reaffirmed what I had said and kept Ferand from bedding you. He knew this is what Ferand wanted, and he refused to let those desires muck up the game he had worked so hard to stack in Tuiteam's favor. Why else would the young prince say there was no need for others? Because the crown already believes they have what they need to create others.

I opened my eyes once more to find myself staring blankly at the iron door, no longer feeling sorrowful, but clearly harboring a rage that was reluctant to be contained. Let it be the will of the Gods that this door shall open to us once more and in doing so, I will seek my vengeance upon he who wears the crown.

Do not linger upon this feeling as I fear it will turn your heart cold.

I felt his grasp relax just before his fingers stretched outward, clinging to the muscles in my chest by only his fingertips. His touch felt blistering, quite a few degrees above my very own. Though he uttered nothing of his displeasure with our new situation, every fiber of his being was screaming out in anguish. I could feel it radiating from him. This hurt him. Far more than any bones they could break, and as I thought over things carefully now, I had a feeling that this is what they would have wanted. They want us broken and desperate, for that is the only way they could control us. Turning myself somewhat, I brought Prince Urie into my peripheral vision. He remained as he were, clinging desperately to life, but his eyes were only focused on us.

For someone so young, he seems to know an awful lot more than he should. Would you not agree?

Perhaps there are other secrets his lips would wish to part with should he be encouraged.

My gaze found Conall's, and he appeared surprisingly optimistic considering everything that has happened. He released me from his grasp, and it only took a moment without it before I longed for it to find me once more. I flashed a glance towards him, slightly fluttering my eyelashes and in a moment, I could sense his hunger. It rushed through his body, heating his flesh to the brink of scalding. Had my own not increased as his and I would have surely been burnt. Together the putative tether between us was growing stronger, but what I had not predicted would be that my abilities would increase dramatically as our spirits were returned to one another. In just several hours' time, I could already feel things that I would not have otherwise, placing my senses dangerously above what I believed was their peak. It made me wonder if this is what we all should feel upon bonding with another of our kind or returning to the bond we once had. As Conall and I stepped back towards Prince Urie, he never veered far and with each glance I made towards him, it was always met with his.

Upon reaching Prince Urie's side, Conall reached for him, propping him up against the angel's legs, while remaining crouched before him. He appeared in discomfort at the sudden shift, but based on the sounds his lungs were making, he was breathing easier now.

"Aside from believing Conall could sire bairns within me, what else do you know?" my voice unyielding.

Even though, I was concerned for the young prince, I could not stop myself from pressing him for all he could possibly know. Prince Urie uttered nothing at first, but as Conall leaned in towards him, the young prince began to shift under the pressure.

"Nothing, I assure you," he mumbled.

"Forgive us, if we have trouble believing you," Conall growled.

"I have only heard whisperings," he muttered, "nothing that could be considered useful to you."

I lowered myself to meet Prince Urie's eye level before

insisting, "Perhaps we should be the judge of that."

"There were stirrings of a usurper and Ferand intended to silence the potential threat."

"Who was this usurper?" I insisted.

"It was believed to be my brother, Beri," Prince Urie paused and lowered his voice barely above a whisper, "but it is the warlock that concerns me."

He began licking his lips nervously and darting his gaze back and forth between us and the iron door.

"No one knows from which she came...but her body is beginning to rot."

I shook my head at him before insisting, "Rotting how?"

He glanced towards the door once more before returning his gaze to meet mine.

"Her once dark skin has begun to turn black."

"Blackened how?" I heard myself blurt out.

"As if she was dipped in oil," he added softly.

I turned towards Conall suddenly feeling very strange. He appeared to be focusing heavily on Prince Urie, but his thoughts were very far away. I felt his thoughts quicken, cycling through memories at a rapid rate, when I reached to clasp his chin just between my thumb and index finger.

Her hands were not as such when my first gaze fell upon her. Something has changed.

What could cause such a transformation?

Dabbling in dark magic for sure, but to obtain that level of decay this rapidly, she must be doing more than dabbling in it.

What do you mean?

Necromancy.

Have you ever seen such magic?

No, only heard of its existence. I have seen what dark magic can do to other beings, but I have never known a human to wield such power.

Then it could be feeding upon her.

Dark magic always has a price. Other than her own flesh, we need to be asking ourselves what is her offering to obtain such gifts.

What if we are to be her offering? I thought sending a winter's chill down my spine, forcing me to shutter.

"Do you know the land of which she came?" I pressed Prince Urie.

He shook his head before uttering, "It was before my birth. I was told she just appeared one day along the shore though I know naught if that were true."

"And they just welcomed her into the city?" Conall uttered sounding appalled.

"She is human," Prince Urie mumbled once more, "and my father was weak."

"Weak how?" Conall insisted.

Prince Urie's chin dropped towards his chest as he gazed at Conall through the top of his line of sight.

"I dare not wish to utter such things in front of a lady."

I admired his restraint and did not feel the need to press him further. His response told me everything I needed to know. There was little more he could tell us now and he needed his rest. Brushing his locks back from his brow once more, I felt the tension between us melting away. He lowered himself carelessly onto the sandy floor where he soon appeared to lose consciousness. No doubt out of sheer exhaustion and fright. I secured the cloak around him and left him to rest as I felt Conall beckoning me towards him. He had ventured towards the far side of the chamber where there was the least light, quite possibly the only portion of the chamber that was hidden from the mainline of sight. The space was a small alcove chiseled into the stone, probably from an expansion that had begun, but was never finished. It was there where we could be alone.

When I reached the alcove, I found him leaning against one of the walls, appearing intent upon all that he may have been listening to. As I stepped towards him, I began to hear it as well. The sound of water droplets crashing towards the surface, breaking against the rock, and colliding into one another. For a brief moment, I closed my eyes and believed I could smell the rain. Unfortunately, as my eyes opened again, I knew I had been mistaken. With a frown of disappointment growing on my face, it did not take Conall long to notice. Before another moment was lost to us, I felt him pulling me towards him. Our bodies clinging to one another like they did hours before. I looped my arms around his neck before sliding my fingers into his long locks and gently pulling his head back, exposing his neck to me. My lips greeted his flesh with soft kisses that soon turned to gentle tugs of his flesh between my teeth.

It was then that he shifted his back from the wall and turned to place me in between himself and it. Leaning his hips into mine, I felt pulled to him once more, drawn into the desires of not only our bodies but our spirits. Through breathless kisses and wandering hands, we found ourselves once more tugging at the leathers between us. It was then that something happened that we did not anticipate. The iron door to the chamber was opening. Our thoughts once so consumed by each other, could now only focus on that sound. It was a harsh sound. The squeaking and grinding of metal upon metal as the hinges fought to hold the large door as it swung open. Hidden within the confines of the alcove provided us with time to gather our thoughts and compose ourselves, but each time that door has opened, trouble was sure to follow. Just the thought of what may come, frightened me in a way I did not wish to admit.

Conall turned his head away from me, presumably to get a better view of the chamber, as my stomach began to turn. Living in seclusion as it were I believed was out of fear, but what I know now is that I knew nothing of fear until King Ferand found me. Though Conall's body never peeled itself away from mine, it did not stop the trembling that was beginning to run away with me. Through wide, tear-filled eyes, my gaze did not waver from where the light met the corner of the alcove. Should he who entered the chamber step across that point and there would be nowhere else for us to hide. The footsteps, though slow to advance, were growing louder now and it was difficult to hide the sound my heart was now making. Conall turned back towards me quickly, placing his lips upon my brow.

My ionuin, please stay here for I do not wish to bear

this world further without you.

Before a thought could formulate within my mind, he tore his body from mine and exited the alcove, undoubtably taking the intruder by surprise. I lowered myself against the wall taking care not to slide my body against it as it was Conall's wish that I remain unseen. I listened attentively.

"My apologies," the male voice spoke, "did I wake you?"

The voice rang familiar in my ears, but the words presented were far too polite for to come from King Ferand.

"Or perhaps did I interrupt something of a more *intimate* nature?" the man continued.

There was the tone I was growing accustomed to hearing. King Ferand had graced us with his presence once more. Conall uttered nothing in reply, which did not surprise me in the least. I never believed him to be the type to get rattled easily.

"Hmmm," King Ferand uttered, clearly displeased with Conall's lack of interest. "Bring me the she-wolf, for it is she who called to me."

"No," Conall's voice echoed throughout the chamber.

"I said bring her to me or I will have her drug towards me like the beast she is," King Ferand hissed.

"So, the mighty king of Tuiteam not only wishes to bed elves, but now beasts," Conall prodded. "How proud your people must be to have you as their *King*."

King Ferand's breathing had picked up in pace along with the beat of his heart. This upset him. I heard footsteps once more advancing in our direction and quickly, just before I heard the crack of flesh upon flesh followed by a scuffle. A few moments later, all was once again silent. I felt my breath catch within me, waiting anxiously for someone to make the next move or say something.

"Do not provoke me Conall or it will be her flesh that I shall lay my vengeance upon," King Ferand hissed once more.

"Perhaps you should not provide me with such an easy target then," Conall spoke frankly.

"Test me again and I shall summon the one of whom you both fear," King Ferand spat.

Haxa. We both thought and no sooner than her name graced our memory our thoughts turned to where she might be as King Ferand would have never left himself unprotected. I crept further towards the backwall, slinking amongst the shadows, until Conall came into view. The poor lighting in the chamber cast varying degrees of light and shadow upon him giving the illusion that the flesh of his back appeared to melt over the ample muscles that were found beneath. It presented him in a fashion that was both captivating and intimidating.

"That will not be necessary," Conall's voice cast towards King Ferand. "Before you wished me to beckon Eira on your behalf," he paused, "what is it you wish of her?"

"It appears I underestimated her intelligence, and I am here to answer her call," he sneered. "Eira, care to come out and voice your grievances against me directly or will you need an incentive?"

Conall spoke once more, breaking King Ferand's concentration, "There will be no incentive, but I have one for you."

"What is this you are carrying on about?" King Ferand uttered sounding confused as the sudden turn in conversation.

"It appears you are the sort to make deals and I shall offer you one now."

"You know nothing of the sort," King Ferand spat.

"The hand you thrust upon me moments ago is dressed to cover a wound that was inflicted upon your palm."

"What of it?"

"It reeks of dark magic," he paused, "perhaps a blood oath?"

King Ferand had begun to pace along with muttering incoherently under his breath. I needed to be mindful that if I could see him then there was a good chance, he could see me as well should his focus shift from Conall.

"There is nothing you can offer me that I desire."

King Ferand's voice sounded more confident this time, less taken back. Yet, he kept pacing. Whether out of distraction or nerves, I do not know.

"What about a life for a life?"

"Now, I am intrigued," King Ferand paused slightly in tone and step, "perhaps you wish to free yourselves."

"No," Conall's voice firm once more, "I offer the life of your brother to save the life of Eira's."

I felt my chest grow tight and my mind now pained as Conall threw pieces on the board that I did not believe we were ready to play. King Ferand exhaled heavily several times, clearly mulling over Conall's offer, but who was the brother he spoke of for I had none.

"I cannot," King Ferand responded, "Bryn will be

needed to sire bairns within her should you prove incapable of the task."

King Ferand's sharp tongue cut through me. What I believed was once so far away and safe, had been pulled towards me and placed within arm's reach.

How does King Ferand know of Bryn?

During your time with them, you mentioned him to stop the torment and Drayk is most certainly out there seeking him.

"Do so if you wish, but Bryn cannot sire bairns with Eira. Their blood would be as if oil was thrust into water and no use for the purpose you seek."

"How do I know the brother you speak of still lives?"

Conall stepped towards the angelic statue and pulled Prince Urie up and into the crook of his one arm. Prince Urie gasping and appearing disoriented from the sudden change.

"There is no downside for you in this arrangement," Conall spoke. "Your brother will be returned to you in exchange for your willingness to call off the hunt for Bryn."

King Ferand stopped pacing entirely and I found myself leaning further outward trying to observe his behavior. He had now stepped towards Prince Urie, but Conall's hand appeared to be thrust out before him, stopping him where he was. King Ferand's face was difficult to read. He did not appear overly pleased to see his brother, but he did not appear unconcerned either.

"And what makes you believe I would honor my word and halt my pursuit of Bryn?" King Ferand sounded skeptical.

"By sparing him from the treatment you have bestowed upon Eira and myself, I may be able to persuade her to give you what it is you desire."

I felt my stomach turnover and my body tightening from just the thought. King Ferand appeared to be mulling things over once more and returned to his pacing, never taking his gaze off Conall. He made several passes in front of the two of them, jaw taunt probably from him clenching his teeth and hands resting upon his waist, never far from his blade. When his pace suddenly stopped, and he once again advanced towards Conall. This time not in a threatening manner, more of a curious nature, as if he wished to get a closer glimpse of something.

"Urie," he shook his head, "always getting into mischief I see. What am I to do with you?"

He posed it as a question, but everyone present knew he was not requesting an answer. The room was silence for several moments when I thought I heard Prince Urie utter something. I had hoped he would repeat himself as he had before, but before I could blink, I heard a faint sound of metal grinding against metal. I knew the direction from which it came, but I could not see the source in time to stop it. Without a moment to react, I saw Conall's arms rise suddenly as Prince Urie fell towards the chamber floor, crimson pooling around his body. I closed my eyes tightly before covering my face with my hands and screaming within the confines of my mind. The chamber lay silent, and I felt myself begin to weep for the young prince. My heart broken once more and now questioning if this madness would ever cease.

The moon rose and fell in the night's sky, making way for the rising sun, but after finding my Rose in the arms of the Warrior Prince, I could not bring myself to go to her. Even though her kindness could have been nothing more than just that, my heart still felt betrayed. Upon finding them as they were, I opted to return to my bedchamber, unable to focus upon any other task and unable to rest. I remained as I were, frozen in time and space, as if I were a statue placed within the castle walls in error. It was not until the sun appeared fully within the morning sky that I was able to pull my focus back to the present in time to finish preparing for the journey ahead. Though I am not a pious man, I felt compelled to utter a prayer within the confines of my mind for a swift journey and the strength to withstand all that I should face upon our arrival in Tuiteam. They have never been fond of outsiders, and I felt confident that was a fact that would not have changed since I last found myself there.

There was a knock on the bedchamber door, "Lord Bryn," the page paused. "The carriages will depart for the port shortly. May we enter?"

"Aye, of course," I uttered while nodding knowing all too well they could not see the gesture.

The page along with three others entered my bedchamber, scurrying about as if their lives depending on whether or not my luggage was delivered to the carriages on time. Unsure if I should return to Losgadh, I reached for a tattered text that was frequently found near my bedside and clung to it with desperation, unwilling to let it be removed from my sight. Amongst the text were spells and incantations wound intricately throughout the picturesque renderings of fairy tales, leading most to believe this was a treasured keepsake of my childhood rather than what it really was. In addition to the text's magical contents, it now is where the parchments from King Itheal's secret chamber are held. Upon my life, those cannot be misplaced.

As the men tended to their duties, I fled the chamber with no more than the book in tow as I headed off in search of my Rose. I scoured the usual places to no avail, and it was not until I strode past the main hall when I spotted her. Although to me she appeared radiant in nearly any light, as she stood before King Itheal in a gown of golden lace, she was the light. I stood there nearly breathless, feeling my heart racing and my flesh smoldering at just the sight of her. As she turned towards me, the corners of her mouth upturned greatly, and I longed to take her in my arms before all who were present. She did not belong in a world of darkness as I feared that darkness would consume her light. Unfortunately, if she was to follow her duty and I follow mine, at least we would be in the darkness together.

She frolicked towards me with the joy of a youngling, stopping just shy of the threshold I stood beyond.

"Lord Bryn," she spoke, smile still plastered across her face. "I was worried you were unwell."

"Lady Roselyn, my apologies for worrying you. That was not my intention." I spoke softly and I held out my arm for her to grasp. "Would it be too forward of me to request your company one last time in the garden?"

"Lord Bryn," she paused, cheeks suddenly filled with color, "I would be delighted."

She placed her hand upon my forearm as we stepped across the threshold and into the garden she loved. Though I had not come to understand its meaning to her until recently, I wondered if leaving this place would sever what tether she held with Lamprog. Having never left the castle, the path she was choosing would test more than just her honor. In taking her lady's maid's advice, there was something I needed to ask her. I directed her towards a secluded portion of the garden, where not only our bodies, but our words would remain hidden. She followed me without question and upon our arrival, I pulled my arm before me, leading her to stop only steps away. I lowered my arm and watched her hand hover slightly, perhaps with anticipation for my hand to find hers, but it did not. I stepped towards her, closing the gap between us to little more than a slim margin of air. Her breathing deepened and I witnessed a slight quiver that had appeared to engulf her lower lip.

"Rose," I whispered, "there is something I wish to ask

you?"

I lifted my hand towards her cheek, grazing it delicately with my fingertips.

"Aye, what is it?" She spoke before turning to kiss my hand gently.

"Should there be another path for you, one that permits you to fulfill your duty while, in turn, providing you with your heart's desire, would you not take it?"

A soft giggle escaped her, "But of course I would, how could one not?"

Her response forced a soft giggle to escape me as well and soon a feeling of relief washed over me.

"It relieves me greatly to hear you say that."

She smiled before adding, "I half expected my father would disagree on this point, but it did not appear as such."

I felt my jaw drop, leaving my mouth agape and eyes wide like some blundering fopdoodle.

"You…spoke to your…I mean, King Itheal about such," the words fell out of my mouth awkwardly and I felt myself begin to sweat.

"Aye," she uttered through a smirk before leaning into kiss my cheek. "Are you feeling alright?"

I smiled faintly before reaching to pull at the neck of my doublet. Either the temperature rose dramatically in the last few moments, or it was beginning to cut off the blood flow to my head.

"Of course," I mumbled more than I intended.

I leaned into kiss her cheek, but she pulled away suddenly and began rushing back towards the main hall.

"Hurry now, Lord Bryn, for we shall not wish to be late," her voice raised considerably.

As I remained there, something about it all seemed quite off and what once felt like relief was rapidly turning to concern. What would possess her to tell her father or at least who she presumed her father to be, that she wished to be with me without at the very least mentioning it to me beforehand? And to second that thought, why would he be accepting of this? After learning that King Itheal and King Aldon came to an arrangement that Rose was to be raised as human, why risk exposing that by permitting her to marry an elf? He executed his own Queen over the very same offence. The questions were growing exponentially by the moment, and I was beginning to feel overwhelmed. While I wished to take a moment of rest, that would have to wait until we were all on board the vessel and cleared to make way across the sound.

Returning myself to my bedchamber once more, I found a familiar korp waiting there for me upon the window ledge. I had hoped he would be able to join me throughout this portion of the journey, but I feared for all of us should he be discovered. See, korpar are not just any sort of bird, they have the ability to alter their size and color if needed. They cannot entirely shift to another being or beast as I can, but those sorts of changes tend to be noticed as magical and not well received by those outside of Lamprog. Hence, why my primary communications to King Aldon were sent after nightfall. I stepped towards him and began stroking his head and his wings to which he bobbed about in delight. It was then I jotted a quick note on the remaining parchment that was found in the bedchamber and send him on his way.

"Until we meet again, dear friend," I uttered as I watched him fly off into the late morning sky.

Being that my presence was already overdue, King Itheal would surely be displeased over such an oversight, and I was not anxious to entice fate. So, I decided to forego my quest for additional time with the King in lieu of a certain lady that would be waiting for me. I fled the bedchamber one last time and sped towards the main gate. Having not left the castle much during my stay here, there was bound to be a certain amount of unwanted attention, but I felt able to handle it with grace. Bowing and nodding as I went, trying not to engage anyone directly appeared to be working and the carriage was now in sight. There I noticed Rose sitting upright and chatting up what appeared to be two soldiers. It was not until I ventured closer that I saw those soldiers to be Kenric and Prince Berenger, forcing my stomach to draw up in knots.

"Lord Bryn," Rose spoke, "so glad you could join us. I trust you remember Kenric and Prince Berenger."

I bowed and held the bow as customary, forgetting all too soon that the Warrior Prince was now sightless and unable to respond to the gesture. Though the bow was not without purpose, for out of my peripheral vision I saw Rose place her hand upon his.

"Rise Lord Bryn," he paused permitting me time to step into the carriage to be seated. "Please forgive my behavior at our last encounter. I was not myself and needed time to recover."

His hand turned to hers, stroking her fingers gently and

I felt the knots in my stomach rise uncomfortably within my throat.

"Princess Roselyn tells me you are quite the scholar and frequently challenge her in her studies."

Wait, what? How long had I remained in a trance before being drawn out of it this morning? Hours? Days? How was it possible for them to chat about my relationship with her when he has only just awoken?

"The Lady Rosalyn flatters me with her kindness I assure you Prince Berenger," I spoke modestly in an effort to hide my true frustration.

The carriage proceeded to break away from the castle grounds and onto the road that would lead us to the port. It would be a short trip and one that I was thankful for. The soldier, Kenric, appeared to be quite uneasy at being in such close proximity to me and I was unsure how to remedy his discomfort without drawing unnecessary attention to it.

"Honestly Lord Bryn, you are too modest," Rose continued. "You are both cunning in wit and strategy. It was gracious of King Aldon to let us make use of you for the time we have."

"Forgive me," Prince Berenger uttered, "did you say King Aldon?"

"Aye, that is correct," Rose responded with a touch of apprehension now in her voice. "Certainly, you are familiar with the elven king, are you not?"

"Forgive me once more Princess Roselyn," Prince Berenger smiled briefly, but soon cast it away. "I was not aware I was in the presence of an elven nobleman."

"My apologies, Prince Berenger," she spoke quickly before bowing her head slightly. "Lord Bryn was sent to us as an emissary of King Aldon and remains with us under my father's good graces and mine."

"Surely you must miss your homeland though?" Prince Berenger's tone changed, slightly hopeful and yet slightly insistent.

"Of course, Your Royal Highness, as I am certain you miss your own," I paused. "However, I am not unaccustomed to the ways of the mainland, nor do I feel compelled to flee from it until I am beckoned elsewhere."

Rose looked at me quizzically just before he bowed his head slightly, presenting his understanding. I felt the need to challenge him in some way, despite how petty-minded the reasoning behind it may have been. There was part of me that wanted to shout at him, demanding answers for the cruelty his people so wrongfully bestowed on the world. Should I choose to do so, and Rose might have rescinded her offer for me to accompany her. That I could not have.

"Have you ever ventured as far as Tuiteam in your travels," he paused, "during your studies or otherwise?"

"I have not been blessed with the pleasure entering the city, Your Royal Highness, but I have borne witness to the Falls of Saor. They are radiant when viewed in the morning's light."

"I know the location well," he grinned before leaning towards Rose and uttering, "of course, the beauty of the falls can only now be held within my memory. Should you wish it, and I would love for you to venture there if only to share your thoughts with me."

Due to his oversight and my keen hearing, none of his words were lost to me. Rose's cheeks flushed with color once more as he once again brushed his fingertips along hers. Their behavior was somewhat perplexing to me. Was he flirting with her or more importantly, was she flirting with him? I felt my heart betrayed once more by their interaction and I pleaded for this jaunt of the journey to end, so that I might speak with her privately. As they continued to schmooze amongst themselves, I found myself distracted by anything that was not in their direction. I could sense Rose was not pleased with me as her eyes were seen continually darting in my direction, but I could not bear to engage him further and Kenric seemed far from interested in just being next to me, let alone speaking to me.

With the port now in sight, I had hoped relief would find me, but knowing we were about to be locked aboard a vessel for what I would hope would be no more than a day or two, I felt restless. Just as the carriage came to a halt, I stood quickly and exited the carriage, waiting patiently for Rose to take my hand. When I was not immediately greeted with it, but Kenric's, my eyes grew wide with surprise.

"How kind of you Lord Bryn," he grinned, comment rich with mockery. "I had not anticipated you would be such a gentleman."

I faked a smile before returning my attention to Rose, who had now risen from where she sat. Unfortunately, Prince Berenger had, also, risen and stepped in behind her with a hand resting delicately upon her waist. The sight of it made my blood boil in a fury. I was desperate to separate the two of them.

"Prince Berenger, might you step forward, so that Kenric and I might assist you as you exit the carriage?"

Kenric shot a glance of disapproval towards me but returned towards the carriage step to stand just opposite me. Prince Berenger bent around Rose, using her as a guide for the boundaries of the carriage before reaching towards us and stepping downward.

"Very good," I uttered just before pausing to turn my attention back towards Rose, hand outstretched towards her. "Lady Rosalyn, will you give me the honor?"

She smiled and I felt my heart warm just at the sight of it.

"I would be delighted, Lord Bryn," her voice light.

She clasped her dress within one hand, raising it slightly, before placing the other upon mine just as she began stepping downward. In an act of fate, she stumbled slightly falling into my arms where I clung to her instinctively, fearful she would fall towards the ground and soil her exquisite gown. A gasp of surprise escaped her, but I soon found her gaze seeking mine as I held her body dangerously close to mine while her feet regained their stability. I felt her stand once more, but with her grip still firmly upon my arms, I was reluctant to release her until she insisted that was her wish. The entire ordeal may have only occurred over a matter of moments, but those moments felt like a lifetime to me. I cared not whose presence we were in, only that her gaze found mine and she was clinging to me, not another.

"Princess Rosalyn," Prince Berenger spoke before

stepping back towards us, arm outstretched, breaking the hold I had on the moment. "Are you alright?"

"Aye, of course," she spoke softly once more, clearly embarrassed by the mishap. "Thank you, Lord Bryn, for assisting me."

She released her grasp from my arms and reached to greet Prince Berenger's hand with hers. She bowed slightly as I returned the gesture, but it all felt quite distant from our usual manner. Almost as if just being in Prince Berenger's presence changed her somehow. Could this have been done out of fear or was there something else at work here? They walked towards the vessel, her hand upon his arm with Kenric following just a few steps behind. Nearly forgetting the text, I had clung to so desperately before. I gathered it just before the carriage was beginning its return journey towards the castle.

Turning back towards the port, I found the Port Master welcoming all aboard, although I was lost in the vessel's majesty. King Itheal's caravel was much smaller and lighter than most vessels that are found in the seas, making it ideal for short ventures primarily within the confines of the sound. Its sails were lateen and sharp edged permitting it to cut through even the most difficult of weather temperaments. We found ourselves filing one on after the other onto the main deck before several of King Itheal's guard proceeded to join us. Of them I paid no mind. I soon found myself drawn towards the caravel's forecastle where the sun was radiating from the sound into the inlet for all to see. It was not as if I had not witnessed the sound in all its splendor previously, but it appears quite different from the confines of the castle. The warm winds from

Tiene were flowing through, filling the caravel's sails, and forcing my long locks to billow in the breeze. I soon guided them back to be tied in order to keep this beautiful view from being obstructed.

It was not long before my presence was noted by nearly all on board as being elven and I soon felt quite self-conscious for the first time since my arrival in Losgadh. Most tended to whisper amongst themselves, but a few felt the need to utter such curiosities towards me directly. I sloughed most of them off with little more than a glare, but a few needed to be threatened with a King Aldon's wrath before they would see themselves away. Though, the populace of Losgadh is more accustomed to seeing elves than Tuiteam, they still do not appear entirely comfortable with my presence. It made me curious to see what their reaction would have been had I changed suddenly. Perhaps another day. I lingered amongst the soldiers as the nobles soon grew tired of the view and fled to their quarters while I longed to hold onto the moment for as long as time would permit me. Various creatures and beings arched out of the water's reach reacting to the caravel's presence, but it was their faces that pleased me the most. None appeared in distress or concerned in the least, merely just pleased to see someone new. The suggestion troubled me greatly as I worried, I would never feel as they do.

I remained there for hours, watching the caravel leave the inlet and into the openness of the sound. It was more beautiful than I remembered. It was there in the wonder of the sea and the ever-setting sun when Rose found me still lost in thought.

"It is beautiful," she spoke softly in my ear, "is it not?"

I flinched slightly with surprise as I had heard footsteps but would not let myself believe they were hers.

"Not as beautiful as you, Lady Rosalyn, if I am not too bold to say."

A soft giggle escaped her and once again I found her cheeks filled with color.

"You are too bold, Lord Bryn, but I dare not ever change you. For it is your kindness and your spirit that I hold most dear."

I glanced around to see if there were any prying ears or eyes nearby to which there were none outside of a few men, propped against the base of the mast towards the center of the main deck. I leaned towards her, brushing my shoulder with hers as we found ourselves leaning upon the banister overlooking the water.

"I know this may not be the time or the place, but I desperately need to speak with you," I whispered trying to appear as inconspicuous as possible.

Her smile softened slightly, and she whispered, "Aye, of course Bryn. What is it?"

I looked away from her, pointing at something in the water below as a means of drawing attention away from our whispers. She followed my lead.

"When you spoke of choosing another path, you mentioned you discussed this with King Itheal…what path were you referring to?"

She nodded just before sighing slightly, appearing ill at ease regarding the matter.

"I mentioned to him that I was having trouble controlling the battle between my mind and my heart and I wished to seek his counsel on the matter."

"And what was his reply?"

"The answer was as I expected, very tactful, but not inconsiderate of all that I was feeling. He believed my mind is overwhelmed and the desires of the heart are easier to fall prey to at my age but may ultimately end in a problematic situation."

"Hmmm," I mumbled unsure how to respond for I, too, have equally fallen prey to this conundrum. "Then unburden yourself to me. I have always provided you with reliable counsel, have I not?"

I smiled faintly, hoping that I was the one that tore at her heart when I returned my attention towards the sunset.

"Aye, that you have," she smiled, but it soon faded. "I am afraid that your counsel will not be impartial since…" her voice faded off as she turned to scan the main deck.

"Since I am in love with you," I uttered breathlessly, more as a thought spoken aloud than a statement or question seeking her reply.

She turned towards me, gaze wide and unwavering. She did not respond, just held the thought before returning her attention towards the water below.

"Forgive me," she muttered as she began to spin the golden hoops found within her right earlobe. "I never expected you to utter it so plainly towards me."

"Would it be to bold for you to know that you are in nearly my every thought? That when I wake my thoughts are only of you?" I paused, taking a moment to gather my thoughts and emotions before they ran away with me. "That the thought of you being with another, fractures my heart beyond repair?"

She looked upon me with genuine shock and awe. On some level she must have known that was how I felt, but in hearing it now, she could not utter a reply. I felt my jaw tighten now realizing how that must have all sounded. Although, I do not regret uttering it as such. I may not have been from her world, but in mine, life while infinite, can still be brief. There was not time for years to be spent in a drawn-out betrothal or courtship for we could never hope to live openly for that sort of an extended period. For shapeshifters, it was about the connection, solidifying a bond that was felt in an instant then spending the remainder of our existence nurturing that bond. Even though I felt confident she did not love another, I was unsure what was drawing her mind elsewhere.

"There is one more thing I must ask you," I whispered, "but I shall not utter it here." I turned towards her to bow slightly just before bringing my voice back into a normal register, "Lady Rosalyn, I thank you for joining me, but I must retire to my quarters."

"Rest well, Lord Bryn," her voice now elevated as well, taking the hint I had provided.

She bowed her head slightly and returned her gaze towards the nearly set sun. It was there that I left her, locks shifting faintly in the breeze as a touch of the night air was beginning to rush in ahead of schedule. I exchanged minor pleasantries to those who acknowledged me, but my focus was on finding my way into her quarters. A vessel this large would surely not keep her and Prince Berenger far from one another, but would it be far enough to be unheard by one another? I would soon find out. Once clear of the main deck, I began my search. There were a few sleeping quarters that were easily accessible from the main deck that I checked first to no avail. Thankfully, due to the hour, most were still upon the main deck or on the lower deck where there was undoubtably gambling and victuals to pass the time. I took no interest in either and continued my search. It was not until I had nearly given up hope when I heard her voice within. In order to remain inconspicuous of my intentions, I left the main deck appearing to venture towards my own quarters when in fact that placed me further from her very own.

Relieved to see the halls unguarded, of course I cannot say why this would surprise me, all aboard the caravel where there to insure her safe passage to Tuiteam's port. Well, besides me. I was there solely as her security blanket from what I could tell as no other purpose had been revealed to me as of late. I stepped towards her door, opting not to knock in case anyone happened to be nearby, before pulling it open just enough to slide my body inside before closing it once more. I found her there, gazing out onto the water as the sky grew dark.

"My darling Rose," I spoke softly but she did not turn towards me which made my heart grow cold.

I stepped towards her taking her hand in mine and placing it over my heart, covering it with my own. She turned her head towards me, but she did not look at me, only at where her hand now lay. I felt my heart thundering against the bones within my chest, growing impatient as I stood there on what felt like borrowed time. After several moments and when I felt my heart could take the silence no longer, I broke free of my worry and asked her what I came to ask.

"Do you still feel for me as you once did?"

I watched her body shutter as she exhaled from a long-withheld breath, but still, she did not gaze upon my face. I found myself growing worried of the answer she may bestow on me. As my heart began to beat in a terrible rhythm, I now felt my lungs following suit forcing me to cling to her hand for fear of losing it forever. Then I heard her voice break the silence and fill my ears with the sweet melody that was her voice.

"My mind wishes for me to give up on such childish folly as love, but my heart refuses to let me live without you even though I know it is improper of me to do so."

She spoke softly before taking a moment to look upon my face with tear-stained cheeks and watery eyes. I reached for her, trying to pull her in my arms, but she would not budge, keeping me at arm's length.

"Please let me utter my peace or the chance may forever be lost to me."

I nodded, unsure of how I was to feel in this moment.

"How can one choose to break their heart? This is what I asked my father and though he appeared understanding, his counsel was diplomatic. Ultimately, his answer was in time my heart would learn to love another, but I am not certain my heart is capable of such."

Kraciun

It was nearly midday when the cog departed into the Mar Deigh on a path unknown to us. The hull encumbered greatly by the vast number of crates, dropping the cog's keel deep within the icy water's grasp. It was the contents of those crates that now drew my attention. What could have King Edric been exporting with such magnitude that it would take several vessels to transport it all? The question was nagging at me. The purpose behind boarding the cog was to uncover the mystery of the missing wolf, but it was now my intention to discover the contents of these crates and the purpose behind them as well before the chance slips away.

While I felt confident the soldiers aboard haled from Tuiteam, I had yet to find anything concrete to confirm that. The serfs aboard were another story. They were surprisingly wordless even when the soldiers were not present. This set my teeth on edge and gave me concern for their comradery should they be tested by a common foe. They mainly stayed to themselves, muttering incoherently, or resting as I am sure the work that we now shared with them would be endless. Bart and I were quite exhausted ourselves, but we would need the cover of darkness and a resting crew to provide us with the time needed to search the hull. There would be no rest for us just yet. Taking turns being present while the other searched took some trickery and swindling, but we managed.

As the sky became blanketed by a cloth of endless night and the Mar Deigh was shrinking into the distance, our time had come. We broke free of our hammocks and began slinking our way across the wooden beams until we reached the hatch that led to the hull below. While I would have preferred a less obvious method of entering the space, there was none that were within reach and this one did not appear to be watched. Presumably for one of two reasons: either what could be found within the crates held little to no value or uncovering the contents would cost one their life. Both options would keep the serfs focused on their duties, as these men are rarely interested in anything other than coin. However, Bart and I were not what we appeared to be.

Upon closing the hatch behind us, we descended into the darkness below, where all was as expected. There were no windows and no light to be found, only the sound of waves crashing against the wooden hull. I had hoped for calmers seas as we ventured further away from all we had known, but so far, I feared the remainder of the world was not unlike our very own. Earlier in the day I was able to commandeer a candle from the soldiers' quarters I had searched and thankfully, the wick was still intact for us to light. Using a small blade, I kept secured upon the base of my leg, I struck its edge on a nearby nail, sending sparks flying. With each flick of the blade more sparks were cast into the room until finally one took, permitting the flame to grow tall forcing the darkness to keep at bay. The room was filled with rows and rows of crates as far as our widened gazes could capture. We began scanning them, searching for any variation or perhaps one that might have been damaged enough for us to gaze upon its contents.

Much time had come to pass, and we still had not uncovered what we were seeking. We had little choice but to either call off the hunt or break open one of the crates. The choice was simple as neither of us were the type to back down from a challenge. I gestured for Bart to come near where we began plotting our next move.

"There is a crate towards the back that was not nailed down properly," I whispered, "if we remove the crate from on top of it, we should be able to pry it open."

Bart nodded, "And if it refuses to heed to our demands?"

I grinned, "We use the crashing waves as our cover and split it open. Making it appear like a mishap if you will."

I winked giving Bart a clear understanding of my intentions and he nodded with his. We stayed low and moved back towards the crate, placing ourselves towards the one side, ever hopeful we could simply shift the crate over rather than bear the brunt of its weight by lifting it. Each crate took four grown men on average just to maneuver them about on the ice and into the hull, so should we have to lift it and it would be no small feat. Placing our shoulders against it, we began to shove.

Nothing happened. We tried again and still nothing. I was beginning to doubt my strength, when we would soon learn it was our wit that was lacking, not our strength. The crates appeared to be held in place with large ropes and iron slats, to prevent them shifting as the seas of our world are not often peaceful. Taking a moment to remove the restraints, we gathered our strength and gave it another try. The crate began to shift and soon there was enough room to as least lift the lid somewhat to give us a peek inside.

Inserting the tips of our blades we began to apply pressure to the lid, and it was beginning to open. I held the candle up towards the opening revealing the contents to be extremely dark and gleaming, very much like the stone Castle Trocair was built from. We needed to get a better look, but unfortunately our blades could not provide enough leverage for one of our arms to drop down inside to remove a bit of the contents. We withdrew the axes we had concealed against the small of our backs and waiting patiently for the waves to strike once more. With each crash of the waves, another strike was lain into the crate's lid and soon there was a space large enough for the contents to shine brightly with the aid of the candle's light. The crates were in fact carrying the very same stone the castle was built from, black obsidian. Since it is believed that Reothadh was largely volcanic at one time and what the mountains of Geamhradh were formed from, there is an abundance of this beautifully dark stone. Over the years this stone has been mined for several purposes, but Commander Elgar and I were just there, and we found nothing to suggest an operation such as this one was taking place.

Bart and I turned towards one another pondering the stone's purpose. There appeared to be a faint sign of recognition upon his face, but upon blinking it was gone. Perhaps I had been mistaken and it was the candlelight that was playing tricks upon me.

"Any ideas?" Bart whispered.

"Given the number of crates on board and with each crate carrying no less than several hundred pounds of stone, I cannot imagine one's purpose for it."

"King Edric would not be offering this stone to just anyone," he added.

"Aye and with the recent increase in cogs at our port, whoever these crates are being delivered to is planning something much larger than anything I would have guessed."

"Do you think King Edric knows of the stone's purpose or has he been blinded by his own greed?" Bart added.

"Of that I cannot say," I paused, "King Edric has not been himself for several years now and it is my understanding that even our beloved Commander is losing faith in his leadership."

His gaze narrowed slightly in suspicion pondering the undertone of what I had just uttered.

"You do not think the Commander would…" Bart's voice trailed off, suggesting the one thing we both were already thinking, just not of the man we were both thinking of.

I raised an eyebrow of suspicion, attempting to play along with his suggestion as only Commander Elgar and I knew of our conversation in the mountains of Reothadh.

"Though the Commander is not the man he once was, I

would not put it past him," I paused, "but I do not believe he knows of this operation."

"What bodes your confidence that he does not?"

"Commander Elgar appeared suspicious when I told him of the increase in cogs recently."

"But this did not concern you?"

I shook my head.

"We need supplies, and it is not my position to question what is returned to the sea, only what we receive."

"Understood," Bart nodded.

We returned what we took from the crate, but not before breaking off a shard that I quickly hid within my doublet. Its purpose yet unknown to me, but rather than risk returning to the hull I thought it best to take it with me now. As we began shifting the crates and their restraints back in place an eerie feeling began to wash over me. The once crashing waves had given way to soft ripples and there was an echo that could now be heard rebounding off the cog's hull.

"What was that?" Bart muttered.

I shook my head as my brow tightened.

"I cannot say for the sound is not entirely unpleasant, but something about it makes my stomach draw up in knots."

I crouched low towards the keel and followed it until I reached the rudder. The ripples were quieter here, permitting the sound to become clearer. It was an echo, but not the sort I would have thought. After handing Bart the candle, I placed my cheek against the side of the hull, I listened again. The sound I heard were voices. Not those from the serfs or soldiers above, but something below. In a language I did not know or understand, yet I could hear them clearly now singing a lullaby for all nearby to hear. I felt myself drifting towards the sweet sound of their voices and I longed to be near them, captivated by their sweet music. As my body relaxed, so did my mind and I felt myself drifting off. A moment later my attention was returned to me as I felt the cold, hard slap of Bart's hand connecting with my cheek and jaw. I rose to my feet with fist at the ready when I saw him raise his hands before me in surrender.

"Kray, it is me, Bart," he paused giving me a moment to adjust. "You were being taken in by their spell."

"What are you talking about? I am not under anyone's spell," I insisted.

"Then how did you reach the hatch?" he spoke frankly.

My gaze darting about us now, taking in our surroundings only to find Bart was speaking the truth. I had ventured nearly the entire length of the cog with no recollection of how I came to be there. At first, I was confused, but I felt anger growing within me as I do not take kindly to being deceived.

"How did this happen?" I muttered.

No sooner did the words exit my mouth and we heard footsteps shuffling above. The serfs were on the move, but not hastily by any means. They were waking from their slumber slowly before heading towards the main deck. I felt we should follow. Once the tapping of footsteps ceased, I lifted the hatch ever so slightly to scan our surroundings. All clear. We vacated the hull quickly before clearing the stairs and meeting the others topside. Nearly all were scattered about the railings feasting their eyes upon what lie below. The sound that was once barely audible below, now radiated through the air, captivating nearly all aboard. I, too, was once more draw towards the sound and found myself flocking towards the source. As Bart and I reached the railing and peeked overboard, there were women found splashing about in the dark blue water below. They were not distraught, nor did they appear to seek anything more than our company for with each face that appeared to greet them, the more they giggled with delight.

While their giggles and song may have found our ears, it was their bare bodies that now held our attention. Lush, supple skin that led to the scale covered tails that were found below the water's surface. The beauty of a maiden is one thing, but to behold the gaze of mermaids, was something entirely different. Found before us in all different variations of color and light, they were captivating in their youth and song. As I thought of it now, I was not entirely sure I have ever heard of mermaids being found west of Reothadh. The thought tore at me, but I soon abandoned that curiosity to gaze upon just as the others were.

It was not until the soldiers brought forth a handful of serfs when my attention was drawn away from the mermaids in the water. The serfs were brought forth willingly, but were bound, nonetheless. These men were meant for something more and I feared we would all soon find out what their purpose was. As the serfs made a path, the soldiers advanced towards the railing stopping just shy to remove several slats that were temporarily sealing off an opening. The bound serfs stepped forward and the maidens squealed with delight and their grins grew wide. For serfs and soldiers alike, there are seldom chances to see the bare body of a maiden, let alone be welcomed by that of a mermaid. This made us weak. A weakness they were now exploiting. It was then when I realized these were not mermaids, they were sirens. Vixens of our oceans with malicious intentions and hungry for the flesh of man. The bound serfs were to be given as sacrifices in hopes of appeasing that hunger.

I felt compelled to save those men, if nothing more than out of the sheer respect for life. As I stepped towards them, I soon felt Bart's hand grasping my upper arm, holding me back.

"It is not your place to save them," he muttered softly, "for a handful of serfs, the remainder will be spared. This is just how it is done."

I stood there for a moment, watching in horror as the serfs each stepped towards the opening before dropping themselves over the side. All of them blissfully unaware of the danger they were placing themselves in. What could have caused them to become so complacent?

I glanced back at Bart just before whispering, "This is not right."

"Let it go," he muttered, "or it will be you that shall become the one they offer next."

My attention returned to the opening where the serfs took their final steps and just listened, afraid to watch it all unfold. Upon impact the siren's trance was broken and the serfs began to cry out for aid. The sound pulled at my insides and made my mind ache. As the serfs flailed, the sirens grew more aggressive. They began strangling their victims just enough to calm their flailing before dragging their prey towards the watery grave that was anxious to greet them. It lasted no more than a few minutes. As the splashing died down, so did the interest and the main deck grew lifeless once more. The sirens had taken their fill and with that their song could no longer be heard. I could not move from that spot. While I have known men to be cruel, I have never seen sacrifices to a beast for nothing more than to gain safe passage. A clear difference between the world I was born in and the one that lingered just beyond the Mar Deigh.

To my astonishment, it was not long before one of the soldiers was drawn towards my vacant expression and statuesque stance.

"You there," he shouted, "return below deck at once."

I wanted to take him and toss him into the water below, but just as I was about to challenge him, I heard Bart speak up.

"We were just waiting for all to vacate before replacing the barrier and then returning to rest."

He lowered his head and I felt one of my eyebrows lift in disapproval. An expression that did not go unnoticed by the soldiers.

"Care to share what amuses you so?" he stepped towards us, and I felt Bart punch my torso as a means of encouraging me to take a hint.

I winced slightly now realizing I would need to learn to control the part of me that was Trocairian and start behaving as if I was one of their own. What would they have found amusing about all this that we would not?

I lowered my head slightly before muttering, "Just

wished I would have had a better view." I let out a faint chuckle, "I mean, how often does one get to see such luscious, bare breasts as those. Am I right?"

I was getting the sense I oversold it slightly when Bart's gaze was drawn towards mine, eyebrows raised. Although, I would have never uttered something of such a vulgar nature, I felt perhaps the serfs might of. I could only respond with a shrug.

The soldier laughed, "Clearly you have been aboard this vessel for too long!"

I let out a sigh of relief, not wishing to utter more for fear of being discovered and luckily the soldier opted to step away. Rumor has it that those outside of Reothadh believe Trocairians are nothing more than barbarians, perish the thought. Even with only being aboard the cog for a matter of hours, I could give quite a few examples of those exhibiting barbaric tendencies, and of those examples, none of them were from a Trocairian. Bart and I stepped towards the opening to begin closing it off.

"By the Gods, you are a clever bastard. Remind me never to cross you," he grinned.

I mirrored his grin with one of my own, "Probably for the best that you do not."

When the last slat was slid into place, we returned to the deck below in search of a much-needed hammock to be our resting place. The search was brief, and we soon found ourselves lost in dreamland.

We awoke with the others just after sun's morning light broke through what was left of the night's sky. Being that we were serfs now, the food was minimal and eaten quickly as we were soon beckoned topside where the soldiers required all to fall in line. As we reached the main deck, it was the warm air that I noticed first. The chill that seemed to never dissipate from my bones in Reothadh had merely vanished overnight and I found myself curious at the world I now found myself in. Though the soldiers had lined us up as if we were headed to the gallows, my thoughts were only of the land that could now be found in the distance. It was the first time I had seen land that was not snow covered since I was a varlet. Myself and some others were stowaways aboard a vessel that was scouting just off the coast of Lamprog. We were not able to see much from where we were hiding, but the lush forests and sandy coastline has always held a fascination for me. As I gazed upon the coastline with my eyesight keen, I could tell this coastline did not match the one that was found in my memory, but I was equally fascinated, nonetheless.

With my attention drawn elsewhere, I missed what the soldiers intended for us to hear, but I cared not. From the tales of others, I have come to know that soldiers aboard vessels such as these very rarely contribute to the operation of the vessel they find themselves on. Rather they are aboard to merely enforce justice and prevent the vessel from going rogue. I was confident these soldiers and this vessel would be no different. As they released us back to our duties, I found myself still wondering about all that lay before me and how fearful tales of the deep waters has kept the populace of Trocair frozen in an icy wasteland. I found myself pulled towards Bart in search of answers. I was able to get within earshot of him as he was now found fixing or rather feigning to repair something near the soldiers' quarters.

"Might I assist you?" I said, placing my bucket and rag aside.

"Of course," he paused, "here, hold these." He spoke as he handed me several pins needed to return an intricate carving to its original resting place.

"Where are we?" I whispered.

"Closing in on Tornen," he muttered.

"The Fallen City?" I heard myself utter, clearly questioning his response.

"Aye, but what once was only inhabited by the dead," he turned towards me before whispering, "has gained life once more or we would not be venturing there."

He returned his focus towards the task at hand and began hammering the pins in place as I handed them to him one by one. How could this have come to pass? I learned of the Fallen City when I was a boy, but I have heard no uttering of it in the remainder of my life. Though the renderings of such a city were undoubtably skewed by the storyteller, the mystery behind it still fascinated many. It is not often a city of man merely up and vanishes nearly overnight. There surely was more to the tale than all that I had heard.

"Have you ever seen the city?" my question rushed, but with a tinge of excitement.

He shook his head.

"But you are certain that is where we are headed?" I pressed him.

"Aye," he nodded as he finished hammering the last pin

in place. "So, did you have wax in your ears earlier or do you need me to recap the whole conversation for you?"

I shot him a look of disapproval to which he countered with a chuckle. Fortunately, my hand connecting with the back of his head shut that down. Now it was his turn to shoot me a look of disapproval, which he did promptly. It was one of the things I found most memorable about him. He never took the world too seriously. I dropped down to pick up my bucket and rag when a thought came to mind. Bart had completed several stints upon the seas during the time I had come to know him, but he never mentioned Tornen in all that time. Should there have been rumbling of a nameless face surfacing on the mainland and I would have thought that information would have been shared with me. It was in that thought that I began to question the company I now keep.

"Bart, before now, did you know about the Fallen City?" I whispered softly, trying not to draw attention towards us.

I heard the hammer drop towards the deck, connecting with the wood causing vibrations to be felt beneath my feet as he rose to his.

"Aye," he paused and the doubt that I previously felt lurking nearby was now gaining a foothold. "But Tornen lay dormant."

"I do not understand," I uttered quietly.

He shook his head and whispered, "There is life there, one can feel it, but nothing to be seen."

I felt terribly confused. How was it possible for a city to be dormant, yet new life found within? I did not turn towards him, only stepped a few paces away and pretended to polish some spindles nearby. Unable to pull it together in my mind, I opted to shift the focus rather than persist knowing our time was limited.

"Then why drop anchor there?" I pressed him.

I heard and felt him step towards me, "I know naught, but I do know it would not be without reason."

"Then I will head below deck to seek answers. Someone aboard this vessel knows something and I am going to find out who."

"Kray, I would not do such—" Bart began to utter, but I soon faded from his sight.

I dropped the rag into the bucket and headed below deck where some of the serfs had returned to their slumber while others had snuck off to a dark corner to engage in what the soldiers would deem as unsolicited behavior. It is that corner where I needed to be, and I had no intention of waiting for an invitation. Navigating my way around sleeping serfs and piles of unknown sacks of belongings, I found myself nearly face to face with the men I came to question. They were brutish-looking men, bodies heavily scarred and weathered by years of strenuous labor upon the seas.

As I drew closer, I could hear their laughter as they discussed the event from the night before. Jabbing the fallen at their cries for help, knowing all too well that it could have been anyone of them whom the soldiers selected. They just got lucky this round. My pace slowed and I lingered within the shadows hoping one of them may slip, exposing the information we needed. Watching and listening to them carefully, they appeared as any group of men would, carrying on and jeering one another. Nothing suspicious or unsolicited in their behavior in the least, how unfortunate. These serfs may not have the answers I need. I turned to explore other possibilities when I heard one of them call to me.

"You there," a gruff voice spoke, "care to join us?"

The man's hand extended before him. Though his words did not appear unkind in any manner, we are often deceived when approaching a lion in winter. Without another word from them, I accepted his offer. Stepping beyond the shadows into the bright amber light that was radiating from a nearby lantern where nearly all of their eyes were upon me. I scanned them all carefully, some older and some younger than I expected, but all appeared equally as battered as the man who spoke. Even though I may have been observing them all and my surroundings, I never felt his gaze shift from me. Very predatory in nature, but what they failed to understand was that I was unlike nearly all others on board. Sure, I was a man just as they were, but where they found themselves tasked with shifting cargo between ports, I was a soldier trained to slay beasts and climb mountains with my bare hands. I had the edge here and that gave me a confidence they did not expect.

"You are new here, are you not?" the man spoke again.

"Aye," I spoke sternly, not wanting to give them more information than they needed, but not wanting to appear unwilling to have a chat with them either.

"You are not a man from Tuiteam," he said frankly. "Where is it you hale from?"

"Does it matter?" I punted back to him.

"I suppose not, but we here," he gestured to the other men now surrounding me, "like to know whose company we keep. Understand?"

I thought carefully over what my response should be as I needed to remain here at least until another opportunity presented itself.

"Losgadh," I heard myself lie knowing all too well that had I uttered Trocair, and they may have executed me for treason.

"Ah, that explains it," the men began to chuckle.

I suddenly felt like the brunt of a joke, and I desired to know more of why that pleased them so.

"Is there something about Losgadh that you find amusing?"

"You are still pretty," one of the younger men spoke and I could tell I must have appeared taken back at his comment for the room erupted with laughter.

I was not sure whether to be flattered or insulted as no one has ever referred to me as being pretty before now.

"Do not look so insulted my friend," the older man insisted as he continued to snicker. "We should all be so fortunate."

I smiled, but that smile did not remain. I was ready to turn and walkaway when the man spoke once more.

"For someone so pretty, I would be wary of the company you keep."

I tilted my head slightly, pondering the meaning behind his words for the only company I now keep is Bart's. He must have sensed an impending inquisition as he did not wait for my reply before continuing.

"How do you know this man?"

I thought carefully before responding, "I do not particularly. Afterall, how well do we really know of the ones who we keep in our company?"

"Yet, you trust him?" he pressed.

"I trust no one," I insisted.

"Then you are as witted as you are pretty," he once again glanced at the others to find them snickering.

I was starting to believe I had fallen into a ring of mindless banter and though boldness is often found unfavorable when in the presence of unfamiliar circles, I was starting to believe they were not going to give me another choice.

"What do you know of the Fallen City?" I insisted. "Why drop anchor only to be welcomed by the dead?"

The room grew quiet and the humor that once was found plentiful had now ceased to exist. The man's gaze hardened.

"Your boldness is commendable, but it places you in a dangerous position for you know not the company you find yourself in," he uttered with a menacing undertone.

"I could say the same for you," I glared.

He shifted in his seat before crossing his arms, resting them against his chest in disapproval. Being that he appeared to be the leader of this particular band of vagabonds, he was not accustomed to being challenged and certainly not by someone unlike themselves.

"You are not aboard this vessel by chance I take it?" he

pressed me.

"No," I countered, "now tell me of the Fallen City."

He glared at me for several moments before shifting attention to the men that still surrounded me. Their attention had shifted and were now only staring at him, waiting for him to counter. I felt myself playing with fire and should this not go my way, I may have no other choice, but to flee into the Fallen City.

"Perhaps a trade is in order," he propositioned.

"Very well," I responded, "what is it you desire?"

"Blood," the man said sternly just before he snapped his fingers sending two of the others from the light in search of something in the darkness.

I felt myself swallow harder than usual as the knots from my stomach had begun rising within my throat. His response echoed in my mind, *blood*, and I felt my thoughts scrambled to grasp their meaning before the opportunity to counter would be lost to me. Much to my displeasure, the men that had previously fled were now returning to us, accompanied by Bart and mischievous grins. Had I misread the situation? I did not have long to contemplate what was happening before several men began grappling Bart until he conceded and was restrained upon the wooden table where we had just eaten our porridge earlier this day.

"For every word of truth you sputter, I will answer a question of yours," he paused pushing against Bart's cheek for emphasis. "However, for every lie the two of you spin, we will open the traitor up. Understood?"

The man's game held high stakes and I now knew the

doubt that had been seeping in previously was not without merit. These men knew something of Bart that I did not which irritated me greatly. Although, I was here to seek answers regarding the Fallen City and the crates below, my questions now only surrounded one word, traitor.

"Aye," I uttered, not wishing to provoke them by delaying a response.

"Being that you are the challenger, I will permit you the privilege of going first."

He gestured for me to present my question. I thought carefully over what I could ask and then narrowed that down even further by what I should. I desired greatly to know what was meant by calling Bart a traitor, but I decided not to inquire into the matter as I felt confident in due time the secret would be revealed to me.

"Why deliver crates of stone to the Fallen City?" I asked.

"Ah, someone has been busy," he responded. "To follow orders of course," he uttered frankly, and I suddenly felt foolish for asking such an obvious question.

"What is your purpose aboard the cog?" he asked.

"I seek information," I responded, adding fuel to the already lit fire.

Now knowing how these men intended to play, I had no intention of revealing my hand unless there was not another option.

"This one learns quickly," the group erupted in laughter once more. "We may have use for him after all."

I was not amused and immediately cast my next

question upon them, silencing their laughter.

"What purpose does Tornen have with crates of stone?"

The men's gazes shifted amongst one another, but their leader could not take his gaze from me. I knew more than I should. This caused something within him to tighten with apprehension and increasing curiosity.

"For the city is being rebuilt," he spoke firmly.

I felt my gaze narrow as my attention was now drawn to Bart. If the city lay dormant as Bart insisted, then why rebuild it and why out of stone from Reothadh?

"This man, who is he?" he leaned into Bart's back with his elbow causing Bart to grimace.

I was about to answer, when I noticed the man's attention was no longer on me, but on Bart. It was Bart of whom the question was directed, and it would be in his response of which I would know who's side he was truly on.

"He is a soldier," Bart muttered.

"A soldier—" the man started to demand when I cut him off.

"You forget yourself, for it is not your turn to ask a question," I spat to the man's displeasure, challenging him once more.

His eyes wide at first, but since narrowed to match his scrunched brow.

"On who's authority is the city being rebuilt?" I growled, growing tired of the game.

"We know naught," he spoke firmly before returning his attention towards Bart. "You said this man is a soldier, but what business would a soldier from Losgadh have upon a vessel of Tuiteam?"

Bart uttered nothing for several moments, only gazed upon me as I watched impatiently. The man clearly growing tired of the delay, lifted Bart away from the table before slamming his face violently against it repeatedly until blood spirt from his mouth.

"He did not speak falsely!" I insisted as I rushed forward and slammed my hands against the table's surface.

"To delay is to deceive," he growled, "and just as you are not here by chance, neither is this man."

The man leaned in once more towards Bart, placing his blade dangerously close to Bart's eye, pressing the tip inward and forcing his eye to bulge outward slightly from the pressure. I was struggling to comprehend whether my attention was drawn towards Bart as a tactic of misdirection or if the man's accusations had merit. Regardless of the direction I chose to pursue, I would not have long to decide.

"The Fallen City," I uttered, opting for misdirection, "who can be found there?"

The man and Bart were equally taken back by my question as evident by the vacant expressions and raised eyebrows. The bait was not taken, and should Bart need to be questioned, I would do so later of my own accord. When no response was directly given, I reached for the man's throat, grasping it firmly between my fingers and began to squeeze, watching the vessels in his neck and face engorge. His eyes widened just before releasing Bart of his grasp. The other men stood at the ready, but no one moved without this man's say.

"To delay is to deceive," I spat casting his own malice

back towards him. "So, let me ask you again, who inhabits the Fallen City?" I growled.

"Man," he mouthed as he was unable to speak.

I released him from my grasp and watched as he dropped towards the floor, panting, and gasping for air. I turned my attention towards the other men present and stepped towards them. With each step they drew back against the wall they found themselves near, clearly afraid of me for the first time since I arrived on deck the previous morning.

"Tell me of these men who now inhabit the Fallen City," I demanded. "Who are they and where do they hale from?"

"Tell him nothing," the man gasped still struggling to gain control over his breathing, "this man is a traitor."

Stepping back towards the man in a fury with my blade now drawn, I placed it just beneath his chin and waited for his rebuttal. There was not one uttered. I grasped his locks before jerking his head back towards me, permitting the blade to slide into the grooves of his neck. Still, he uttered nothing nor did the men advance towards me.

"They owe their allegiance to no one for we do not believe they are amongst the living," the youngest mumbled.

I brought the blade inward further, forcing crimson to pool around it and stream down the man's neck.

"Had that been true and no man would venture there," I insisted.

"Not spirits," he clarified, "men brought back."

"That is not possible," I whispered under my breath.

I thought over the young man's words, believing only

the King Aldon to have such power, but it would never be used in such a way for dark magic is forbidden.

"There is no one alive that can control such magic," I challenged.

"Then make sure to tell him that when you meet him," the young man spoke frankly.

"Him?" I questioned.

He nodded along with the other men.

"There is one who calls to the dead," the young man spoke again, "and they answer."

The revelation washed over me like a cold bath, setting my teeth on edge and my heart racing. I glanced around the room, taking a moment to lock eyes with each of them. None of them appeared to be taken back at what the young man had stated, and I knew then that the misdealings of the mainland were far greater than anything I could have anticipated. I felt the need to challenge this.

"You knowingly have interaction with a warlock, and I am the traitor?" No matter their reply there was none that would appease the wrath I was feeling. "Tell me of this warlock and I will release this man," I insisted.

"There is nothing to tell," the young man spoke once more, "for we have never seen him."

"Then how do you know he exists?" I countered.

"Enter the Fallen City and you will know," several of the men spoke and I felt an ominous feeling set in.

I withdrew my blade before pushing the man towards the floor and stepping away. The man that once appeared so powerful, now watched me from a child's vantage point and he uttered nothing further in his defense or in terms of the game we had started.

"King Ferand's fear is misplaced," one of the men uttered under his breath, but I caught the comment, nevertheless.

I stopped where I was and turned towards him.

"What did you say?" I posed to the room as I was unsure which man may have been the source of the comment.

"King Ferand fears what would happen if the Trocairians braved the Mar Deigh to attack him, but I think he should be more concerned with the soldiers of Losgadh," he paused. "Should they be anything like yourself."

I had not realized Prince Ferand had been crowned as of yet or that his father would have permitted such a lapse in judgement by allowing the young prince to delay his betrothal knowing what this would mean to Tuiteam should he pass on.

"The betrothal protects him from Losgadh," I responded.

"The betrothal is worthless unless he weds the Princess," one of the others interjected before the remaining men nodded in agreement.

I believed there was nothing more to say or learn from these men, so I turned towards the darkness to leave when I heard the leader speak once more.

"We are not finished here," he growled.

"You cannot best me on your own and there is nothing further you can utter that would be worth my time."

"But I am not alone," he stood slowly and gestured towards all the men that were found around us.

"There is no honor in what you are suggesting," I responded forgetting all too soon that only Trocairians believed in fighting fairly.

While I had hoped this detail would have been unknown to them or that the comment gone unnoticed, but I was not so fortunate.

"Lads, I believe we have another traitor in our midst," he grinned. "Your looks are deceiving, but your mouth rings to your true homeland."

Before he could utter his last words, I clasped my ax and cast it towards him, lodging it within his chest where it found itself buried onto the cheek of it. He fell backwards suddenly, slamming against the wooden floor with a thud, followed quickly by his gasping. The ax broke through all that he wore and made its home deep within one of his lungs. He was now struggling to breathe. With each breath, we could hear the crimson liquid clashing violently against the air he so desperately needed and soon it would all be over. The men turned to me, clearly unsure how they were to move forward, but I knew they would speak to me no more. The younger one who had been so bold before stepped towards his leader to pull the ax from his chest. I half expected him to challenge me, but he did not. He wiped the blade upon his breeches before tossing it in my direction.

"Should King Ferand learn of Trocairians aboard his vessels, and we shall all suffer his wrath," his voice solemn. "We are not soldiers as you are, and there is nothing more we can tell you that you would find helpful. Flee from this vessel and may the Gods decide your fate."

 Commander Elgar

Throughout my life, I had come to understand that uncertainty and fear were to become frequent bedfellows of mine, but it was not until I found myself within the presence of a pack of wolves that I truly understood the fear one feels in their presence. It was within their gaze that I felt my heart race and my body quake. With each breath they watched me, devouring me with their unyielding gaze and further tying my stomach into knots. The sound of their mouths watering and teeth clenching down in anticipation of the kill was nearly unbearable. Undoubtedly King Edric withheld their usual diet to keep them controllable, but perhaps it partly was to instill the fear I was feeling now. Had they been well fed, and the gates that held them would be of no match for their brutality. This amongst many other thoughts swirled in my mind as the hours dwindled onward and the light from the torch was no more.

It was the sound of small footsteps that woke me

sometime later. As my eyes peeled open, I found myself still clinging to the gate from where I watched the wolves in the darkness hours beforehand. The fire I had started was nothing more than ash with a few embers now. Upon noticing this, I stood quickly to come to its aid. Placing some kindling on the embers that remained, I exhaled slowly watching them grow bright once more. The smoke soon followed and once more there was fire within the confines of the chilled vault. When I turned to fetch more wood scraps for the fire, I found the young lad clinging to the gate, little hands wrapped firmly around the spindles as he peered through one of the openings. I let a gasp escape me unexpectedly as I half predicted the guard would have not heeded to my request.

"My apologies Commander Elgar," the young lad winced, "I did not mean to startle you."

"It is quite alright," I held my hands up, waving away his concern.

"The guardsman sought me out and told me of your wish, but I had to wait until the wee hours of the morning to come here as the throne room has been terribly busy this day," the young lad rambled.

"What is it they call you?" I interjected as a means to stop the rambling.

"Boy mostly," he shrugged.

"Your mother never bestowed upon you a name? Something she called only you?"

He shook his head and I felt myself stop within my tracks, holding several pieces of wood within my grasp when I felt a sinking feeling within my gut. Just as most of the young boys birthed in the city of Trocair, they are abandoned by their mothers without ever knowing a touch of their love and for a moment, I felt pity for the young lad. Never having been given a name is the equivalent of never having existed.

"Very well," I paused, "Would you permit me to bestow one upon you now?"

"I suppose so sir," he ducked his head downward slightly.

"Wren is what I shall call you," I paused, "is that pleasing to you?"

He ducked his head once more as a means of nodding I believe.

"Thank you, Commander Elgar," he paused, "I will try to remember that."

We both nodded in understanding.

"During my time away, were you able to do as I asked?" I spoke softly not wishing to frighten him.

Wren nodded.

"And what were you able to uncover?" I continued.

He swallowed nervously before turning and glancing towards his left then his right.

"It is alright," I assured him, "what did you hear?"

He swallowed once more before leaning in, pressing his face tightly against the gate's spindles, "There are whispering about the Queen."

"Our Queen?" I muttered not wanting to assume.

"Aye," he responded just before continuing, "she did not disappear."

"But how could that be? There has been no sign of her

since she vanished nearly twenty years ago," I had not intended for my voice to sound in disbelief of the young lad's words, but that is how it came out.

He shook his head violently before insisting, "She is alive, and King Edric knows where she is. I have not heard exactly where for her communications to him are vague, but she is on the mainland."

"Has it been uttered how she has survived all this time or why she left?" I pressed him.

"That was the plan from the beginning. They plotted her *disappearance* and they have been patiently waiting for something."

"No one else knew of this?"

"I am not sure," he said, "but I have heard King Edric speak to others regarding it. Very few mind you and never for more than a few moments at a time."

"Who are these others?"

"I am not sure," he shrugged, "soldiers perhaps."

"Did you recognize these men?"

He shook his head.

"Did anyone announce them when they arrived or when they departed as they do when I arrive?"

"If they did, I did not hear of it."

"And this thing they are waiting for, do you know what it is?"

He shook his head again.

"Do you think you can find out?"

His expression apprehensive, "Perhaps, if I were able to slip into King Edric's chambers there might be something in there?"

"Hmmm, perhaps."

I found myself now pacing across the cell. While I do not believe the men who held this secret were of utter importance, knowing what they were waiting for and why would be. Placing Wren in such close proximity to King Edric could be problematic for us both and I worried for the Wren's safety. With no guarantee he would find what I was requesting of him, I was reluctant to have him pursue the matter. However, the question of where King Edric would hide such communications and why perplexed me. I have never known him to keep secrets, but in questioning Wren, I was starting to wonder if I ever knew Edric at all.

"Search his chambers if you must, but I would rather you did not unless you are certain within those chambers is what we need."

Wren pulled himself away from the spindles slowly as his attention appeared to be pulled elsewhere. It took me a moment to follow the change, but as he looked towards the end of the vault, it was obvious. The wolves were growing restless and I, too, could hear their incessant hunger crying out.

"What is that?" he asked sounding uneasy.

"Wolves, though I do not know how many?"

"Why are they here?" his voice raised slightly, accompanied by a quiver only noticeable at the end.

"The space in which you presently find yourself in houses all that King Edric holds dear, including his most renowned enemies and his most prized possessions."

"Which are you?"

I chuckled slightly, "I would hope one of his most prized possessions. However, he is rather this displeased with me at the moment as I am sure you were able to deduce as much."

"And what are they?" his focus remained on the cell where the wolves were housed.

"Prized, of course," I grinned. "It is them that King Edric believes will shift the war in our favor."

"Why can we just not remain as we are?" he uttered, reflecting his innocence.

"I wish I had a simple answer for you," my grin faded. "There is one more thing that I need you to do for me."

"Aye, Commander Elgar."

"There is a man that is frequently in my company. The same man who led the search at the Ice Tower. Do you recall this man?"

"Aye, Kraciun," he turned back towards me. "Is that the man you speak of?"

"Aye, aye," I smiled, "that's him."

"He is the one King Edric is seeking," he spoke frankly.

"What do you mean seeking?"

"After you were taken, the guard sought me out, but not before I overheard King Edric's orders to have him apprehended."

"How long ago did those men depart?"

"Nearly a day now."

"Then there is not much time. I need you to venture back into the castle garden and call Lavin. Do not show fear, for he will sense it and flee. If he remains, pull yourself upon his back, placing yourself behind his wings. He will then take flight but must be guided towards the Ice Tower. Rather than guide him by tone, I suggest you pull at his feathers slightly in the direction you wish to go. He is not fond of this but will respond to your demand. You need to reach the Ice Tower before those men and inform Kraciun of what has happened here. He must not return to Castle Trocair under any circumstances. This is very important, do you understand?"

"Aye, alright," he nodded vigorously. "What shall I do if he is not there?"

"Then let us pray he is far from here as there is no telling what King Edric plans to do with him."

Wren nodded quickly before rushing back towards the stairwell, stopping just shy to return to me hastily. From within his pocket, he pulled a wad of fabric and thrust it through the gate towards me. I took it from his hand without question, but before I could unwrap it, he had returned to the stairwell to begin his ascent. The cloth was ragged, but I did not pay it no mind, for its contents is what held my attention. Within the fabric were several small, sweet biscuits, undoubtably prepared by Nan. She was an old woman who had been looking after me since I was a young man, and her baking was unmatched in Trocair. Though it was not her duty by birth nor position, but in world where it is not uncommon for mothers to abandon their sons, she took pride in standing by them.

I clung to one of the cell walls where I found myself sliding towards the stone floor as I thought of her. Initially, she saw me as any other, constantly underfoot and always up to mischief. However, as I grew, so did my position and what was expected of me. When I became a man of Kraciun's age, she would find ways to place women within my path, insisting that it was not proper or what was intended of a man to keep the fairer sex at such a far reach. From time to time, I indulged in her ideals to please her, but I never did decide to wed. It never felt right nor was it befitting of my position. Perhaps just like the mothers who abandon their sons, I was not confident that I would behave any different and they both would deserve better. With each sweet biscuit I tasted, another memory of her shifted to the surface and in those moments, I indulged myself in reliving a world that no longer existed to me.

Upon swallowing the final biscuit my initial reaction was to toss the cloth that held those biscuits, but knowing Wren already had so little, I decided to keep it close in case he may need it again one day. With little more than a faint light from the fire and surrounded by endless darkness to keep me company, I began toiling over the details of everything once more in a never-ending quest for the truth. The path chosen by King Edric had taken so many unexpected twists and turns it would be difficult for anyone to follow, but even more so now. Discovering our King had plotted with his Queen to deceive us all, left my insides torn and my mind aching once more. Man has always found reasons to deceive, but one of the things most Trocairians pride themselves on is their bravado. Had he been acting in the best interest of his people, and I would have thought he would have been willing to share this information. The reason may never be known, but I refused to let the matter rest while there was still life left in me.

Prior to becoming King, Edric was always bold in his

manner, believing that subterfuge was beneath him. During the years before he became King, he took comfort in announcing his intentions to usurp the throne. Of course, at the time, no one took him seriously because those who are so bold are rarely the ones who take action. Edric would soon prove to them that they were mistaken in these thoughts. However, the late King was not so easily fooled. When Edric arrived to slay him, he was not surprised in the least since Edric made no attempts to hide his mistrust or discontent under his rule. On the day of its happening, it only took a few moments for Edric to cross the war room's floor and impale the King with the blades of his axes. The guards did not even attempt to intervene. Of course, many would only see the brutality of act, not the purpose behind it.

As I thought over this and so many other things, Kraciun once returned to the forefront of my mind. He was ambitious, but not so much that he believed others did not matter in his journey. He was kind-hearted, but not so much that it made him weak. He was strong, both in mental fortitude and physique, neither of which were obtained nor maintained without sacrifice. Though, the thought of him becoming King seemed to weigh heavily on his mind when I suggested it, I could once more think of no one better suited. Still, the question that now came to mind was could he do what was necessary to usurp the throne?

It was not until I heard the voice of another when I had realized I had fallen asleep toiling over Kraciun and our missing Queen. The voice was soft and feminine, humming a melody of some sort to someone or something within the darkness. Not wishing to break her focus, I remained as I were, leaning towards the sweet sound. It was too dark to bring her into focus, but the melody she was humming sounded all too familiar to me. I had heard this before; I was sure of it. Unfortunately, in my exhausted state I was being quite lax in my control, and I had not felt my body shift off center, causing me to connect with the gate suddenly. The clash caused a clang to reverberate throughout the vault, silencing the humming I once heard. I waited for it to return to me, but it did not. Could this have all been an illusion or could the wolves and I not have been alone down here after all?

After several moments of waiting, I returned to my original position giving up on the hunt for the woman in the darkness. Upon doing so, I felt a chill once more settling in my bones and I felt myself scrambling in the dark for the flint that no longer appeared to be in my pocket. I was able to locate it after a short search, but not before shifting the pile of lukewarm ashes across the floor and in between my fingers. The cloud that rose from them filled my nasal cavity and lungs, forcing me to cough violently in hopes of expelling them. Through no shortage of attempts, I was able to expel the majority, but it would take time for my body to absorb the remainder. Pulling together the wood that was to become the last of my warmth, I struck the flint near the base and watched the bark turn bright just before engulfing the space once more in an amber glow.

It is an unusual thing being locked away in a place that you call home. Suddenly the things that brought you comfort now disturb you and every fiber of your being fights against them. Scanning the cell once more, I felt a distressing feeling wash over me and questions I no longer wished to think of again began to flood my mind now at an alarming rate. Was it King Edric's intention to have me executed for challenging him or was it simply to watch how my mind worked, like a predator toying with its prey? What of Kraciun? He already knew more than he should and what if the conversation that Wren overheard was true? There was something King Edric desperately did not want anyone to find, but what was it?

That was the piece I needed to toss about in my mind as just mentioning it seems to enrage him. I needed to think carefully, but even as I did nothing knew came to mind. Other than an increase in the frequency of vessels arriving at our southern port, there were little to no differences between them that were made known. Had there been any Kraciun would have surely mentioned them to me. Regrettably, like my mind, my eyes too, had grown quite strained from the struggle of fighting the darkness and I felt myself slipping away once more, lost into the moments of an endless day. Without the light from the fire, there was no way to fully comprehend the day or hour I found myself in. I realized then that is what would drive me mad should I remain here. With any luck at all King Edric would send for me to be released at any moment…aye, any moment now.

As luck would have it, the entry point to the vault was being opened. Soon I would find myself in the presence of another once more, but to whom answered my call? The footsteps echoing down the stairwell towards me were heavy and landed with thud followed by a gap before the next and then the next. Clearly not someone smaller in stature or the steps would have been lighter and much closer together. I stood with a groan, my body tired and stiff from resting upon the stone. Stepping towards the gate, I now noticed there was more than one pair of boots connecting with the steps. Should my calculations be correct, it would be safe to assume at least three, possibly four people were venturing into the vault. The who and the why had yet to be revealed, however.

Though I was standing, I did not place myself near the gate, but rather slightly off to one side of the cell, back facing the stairwell. A dangerous position no doubt should the ones entering bear me any ill will. The light from their torches began filling the chamber starting with a large rectangular beam that broke through the darkness and grew wider with each passing step, illuminating the stone that surrounded us. Had it not been a prison of sorts and it might have been beautiful. I did not have to wait long for the footsteps to change in tone, suggesting that the lead man had reached the base of the stairwell and was now walking towards me. Each step held a similar thud as it did on the stairwell, but it was the man's breathing that caught my attention. It was heavy and labored with a faint wheeze heard upon each inhaled breath. If I was to venture a guess, I would assume this man was quite unwell or perhaps suffering from an injury, but that still would not provide the information I was seeking. Who were these men?

I felt a tinge of suspicion and with that I withdrew a small blade that I kept tucked away beneath the padding of my doublet, bracing myself for whoever was about to appear, when I heard him.

"Commander Elgar," King Edric's voice broke through the silence. "Have you come to your senses, or would you prefer a stent within the walls of the Ice Tower?"

I turned to face him, blade still at the ready.

"King Edric," I bowed slightly, "aye, I have."

"Very well," King Edric pointed towards the gate, "release him."

The gate was soon unlocked and propped open for me to vacate the cell. It did not feel like a trap, but my legs struggled to shift from their current position.

"Commander Elgar," he growled.

I nodded just before pulling my feet forward. I barely crossed the threshold before the gate was slammed closed behind me throwing a loud clang to ricochet off nearly every surface. I wanted to cover my ears, but for one reason or another I did not. Stepping towards him I waited for his lead as no one was permitted to walk before him unless they were tasked with clearing a path for him. He placed a hand upon my shoulder and gave it a slight squeeze, feigning naught had occurred between us. It felt bizarre to me, and I began to wonder how long I had truly been down here.

"King Edric, please forgive my previous behavior, I was not myself. I will fetch Kraciun from the Ice Tower should you still require it."

The words stung as they exited my lips as lies frequently do, but I knew all too well that Wren would ensure he was not there for anyone to find and the journey I would be tasked with would strictly be to provide a distraction for King Edric. We continued towards the stairwell for several steps when he spoke again.

"That will no longer be necessary Commander," he paused, "for during your stent here I took it upon myself to silence him in the only way he would understand," he uttered boldly.

"Forgive me," I paused feeling taken back by his words. "What has happened to Kraciun?"

"I had his head removed before he was tossed into the Mar Deigh," his grip on my shoulder tightening. "As a *gift* to the Gods if you will."

I felt my expression tighten just before my lungs became paralyzed with what I felt was the last of my breath now trapped inside. It could not be I told myself. King Edric would not dare use his own to punish another, it is not our way. Thoughts and questions began colliding within my mind in such a way that I felt I could no longer stand, but as I closed my eyes, that feeling soon turned to rage. My eyes opened to find his face plastered with a diabolical grin, this is what he wanted me to feel, and he was waiting for my reaction. Would I heed to his call or defy him before all present? I attempted to swallow, but I felt I could not in the wake of his unwavering gaze. It was the first time I could recall feeling weaker while standing before him, incapacitated by feelings I did not wish to truly acknowledge previously and now unable to acknowledge them at all.

"You chose to slay one of your best soldiers in the night to protect your pride. Who is to say that I will not be next over something just as menial?" my voice strong, but spiteful.

"Come now Elgar, surely you can understand that he

was expendable," he argued trying to justify his actions.

However, there was no argument that he could make that would ease the pain I felt inside. Never having felt such a mix of emotions before, I was struggling to sift through them fast enough to formulate a decent response, but all I wanted to do was weep for him. As the tears began to pool at the base of my eyes, I watched his gaze change slightly, but not as I would have hoped. It was not a moment later before he and his guards burst out in laughter, mocking my pain. Channeling that pain, I turned towards him, thrusting my fists upon his torso in a violent display of my wrath.

Though I did not initially acknowledge what had happened, it was soon evident by the crimson that now pour from King Edric's body and mouth revealing the blade I had forgotten I held to slay my King. The men present did not attempt to attack me, nor did they flee from my sight. They only remained as they were with mouths agape and eyes wide in disbelief. I felt myself mirror their expression and in my distraught state, my fingers soon relaxed, releasing the crimson painted blade from my grasp to be met with the stone below. The stone floor soon became marked with streaks of crimson that were scattered further as the hilt of the blade connected with the liquid. All remained silent for what felt like an eternity, when one of the men decided it was time to break the silence.

"May his passing be mourned as we welcome a new day," he knelt before me, sinking a knee deep within the pool. "You have my allegiance, King Elgar."

Drayk

Although it was my intention to remain at the water's edge, as dawn broke the next morning, I began my search for the missing soldiers while keeping a keen watch on the sound. Upon entering the marsh's northwestern border, I found that the climate was altered from its usual and it now bordered on being tropical. Although, I could not see it with my own eyes, the increase in humidity made one feel as if I was walking through a wall of water with each step. It was not my intention to remain amongst the poison of the marsh for long, but with evidence of Prince Berenger's men still being found here, I needed to search further. With numerous tracks going in all directions, I could tell there had been some attempting to make it out alive, but I was not able to find any traces beyond the marsh. Which leads me to wonder, if someone or something from within drew them back inside or if they had fled the marsh to wander elsewhere. Neither suggestion would have surprised me.

Though the marsh was formed from dark magic, with each passing that I make into the marsh I can feel that magic still and it was growing. It was the poison man was created from in a sick and twisted sort of mutation. From what I remember, man was not birthed from their mother's womb, but out of the dark magic's residual poison as a means to punish the known world. Their cruelty and malice are merely a reflection of that and something they will never truly understand despite the evidence that supports this. While some have turned away from the darkness or perhaps their bodies were not so accepting of it, others cling to it tighter than one's true love. It was only when my own love was taken from me in such a way that I could comprehend their malevolent ways. With her death and the death of the bairn I placed within her, I vowed to see the demise of man through the end.

With each step towards Losgadh I felt the anguish of losing them all over again and was grateful for the solace the marsh provided. No blade, poison or magic could have wounded me as deeply as watching King Itheal slay his Queen because she loved another. Loss such as that, changes you. It was man's cruelty that destroyed me and the man I once was. Most view me as callous and vindictive, and although they would be correct, I was not always as such. It is what I wanted to tell Eira as we stood in the darkness of the passageway that day. Persisting would change her in ways she could not begin to understand and what I felt for her...what I still feel for her is not real. It is the binding these markings hold over me and will continue to hold over me. I will never feel the warmth of a lover's embrace or desire another without being drawn back to my Drusilla and with that, intense pain. That pain is what I wished to spare her from but her relentless desire to rush precipitously into danger was unyielding.

Rather than slough through the sludge of the marsh, I took to the trees using their trunks as coverage while, also, providing me a bird's eye view. There were things here unlike anywhere else and just as Eira was uncontrollably drawn towards me, I felt the same curiosity for this place. There was a darkness within it that felt oddly welcoming and familiar, but I could not place it. Was I the predator in this scenario, being welcomed home, or could I have potentially been falling prey to something much larger and more dangerous than a nathair? Those that resided here were no doubt basking in the sudden rise in temperature. I knew it was time to leave. It was not until I turned to vacate the marsh that I saw something unexpected. There were remains of something dark to be found here and as I now saw the ground beset with black putrid smears. Rather than flee in the direction of which I came, I opted to plot a new course aiming directly for the sound. It was difficult to tell the hour as the sun no longer shone through the treetops or the fog of the marsh, but my sense of direction was impeccable.

Remaining high amongst the treetops, I was able to move easier than if I were on foot, but it left me far from hidden. Even though I was not fleeing in a fright, I still drew some unwanted attention, mostly from insignificant prey that would soon become a meal themselves than attempt to attack me but, nevertheless. With each leap and bound I felt closer to my destination, but the pull of the marsh would not be soon forgotten. That familiar feeling, I tried to place with no success, but I did not doubt that feeling would resurface once more.

My pace suddenly came to a halt when I noticed a shadow lurking nearly at eye-level just a few trees off. The shadow was long and thin, moving much like man would, but it is here that man cannot survive for they are what so many in the marsh crave. This was something else. Something I found myself not too familiar with but feeling drawn towards it, unknowingly inching my way in its direction. Upon reaching the tree it so carefully clung to, I could now see that it was a woman, not a creature that drew my interest. She peered around the trunk of the tree, revealing her dark eyes and reddened hair to match. As she veered around the tree stepping towards me where I was able to appreciate more of her in all her splendor. Though she was wearing a long green gown covered with an even darker green cloak, I could tell she strode upon long slender legs with a torso to match, very elven in appearance. As she drew closer the fog between us vanished and her features came fully into view. Eyes crimson in color, which shone even brighter now as her flawless lily-white skin was seen surrounding them.

She moved as I moved, but though elven in appearance I felt she was not as no elf to my knowledge appeared as she did. Toggling through information in my mind, I was struggling to place her. As she took her final step towards me, stopping just shy of arm's reach, I could smell her now, she smelt old and of the marsh. Either she was cloaking her scent, or this was an illusion, a powerful illusion. She brought herself in towards me once more, closing the gap between us, placing her dangerously within my reach. She was smiling playfully and biting her lower lip as a faint giggle escaped her. I soon felt her hands caressing the back of my neck before being brought forth, tracing my jawline with her fingertips. I was beginning to feel groggy as if one had drunk too much ale. It was soon followed by a twinge of something inside me beginning to stir forcing my eyes to close unexpectedly. It was then that I felt her lips upon mine, pulling me towards her as she bit my lower lip. Though I believed I did not desire her, my thoughts were changing, and I felt myself think of her in ways I should not. A pain within me was taking hold.

Then it happened again, that same twinge only stronger this time. I felt my mouth open slightly, trying to catch my breath, but I could not for her mouth was fixed on mine in a desperation I did not understand. I felt her hands pulling at the neckline of my armor, permitting her fingers to find their way inside, tugging at me in that same desperation. I wanted to forget myself and get lost in a sea of passionate kisses, but I feared there was more to this. With that thought, the twinge grew violent and the pain searing. It soon spread and I felt my body now searing beneath her touch as if I were on fire. I tore myself away from her, eyes now open once more. With mouth agape, I now saw the fangs she intended to sink within me had she persisted, but what she did not foresee was that I was cursed, and she was one of the damned. Two ill-fated souls never destined to encounter one another, but out of our own greed we had.

"You are a fuil fae," I paused, "are you not?"

"I am not familiar to that of which you called me," she

spoke just before licking blood from her fingertips.

Blood, where had it come from? I wiped my neck quickly to be met with the warm touch of my own blood pooling at the surface. As I looked upon her once more, I noticed her fingers were not just any ordinary fingers for upon their tips were razor sharp talons. She intended to bleed me. Had I not pulled away as I did, and she would have surely fed upon me. I no longer felt the twinge pulling at me from the inside, but my mind, even in my groggy state, was screaming for me to flee.

"Might I convince you to stay a bit longer," she licked her lips attempting to entice me. "Let me unburden that broken heart of yours."

Although, man might have been tempted by her offer, I felt she no longer held a hold over me, but that did not mean she would be willing to let me pass should I but ask. The fog that previously clouded my mind was lifting and I was beginning to feel more like myself with each passing moment. I attempted to sidestep her, but she soon followed suit and into a tangled dance we went. We mirrored one another, making it difficult to gain the upper hand and soon our unrelenting dance within the treetops would gain an even hungrier following from those that were undoubtably watching below. When dancing with one of the damned sometimes we are forced to make a deal and I knew of one she would not refuse.

"Perhaps we could come to some arrangement?" I proposed and she looked upon me quizzically. "You are one of the fuil fae…a blood fairy, are you not?"

"Who are you?" she responded.

"That is not your concern, but what you should be concerned with is what I can offer you," I deflected.

She looked intrigued. I advanced towards her, placing my hand upon her jawline, luring her in as I placed my lips upon hers. Her body stiffened at first in surprise, but soon melted within my grasp. I felt the twinge jerk within me, beginning to sear my insides once more, like a flame taking hold of a field in a high wind. I held onto her for as long as I could as this part was crucial. The fae are obsessed with the chase and relish being desired. I needed her to believe that I desired her. I broke off the kiss and watched as one of her eyebrows raised itself slightly in wonder.

"Very well," she paused drawing her gaze from my lips and into my bright eyes. "What is your offer?"

"Blood," I paused, giving it a moment to settle in her mind. "I will *willingly* let you have a taste."

I could tell her mouth was watering as she began swallowing more frequently. She was hungry and I intended to exploit that. Tilting my head slightly, I drew back the neckline of my armor, permitting her to not only see, but smell the fresh crimson dripping down onto my collarbone. She let out a faint gasp and swallowed deeply, just before beginning to pant. She never asked what I wished for in return because part of me knew that she had no intention of just having a taste. However, what she did not know would soon be her undoing for I was not the prey she was accustomed to slaying and I knew of what she truly was. She nodded vigorously, accepting my offer without any further questions or debate.

Drawing in one final breath, I felt her lips connect with

the flesh of my neck as her tongue began drinking the flowing crimson. She had taken the bait and I would soon be out of time. The game I had grown to relish in was not without danger and I knew that all too well. With each breath I took, I felt my heart race a little more as the blood she devoured and thrived upon is also what gave me life. She was beginning to relax, relishing in the nectar of my lifeforce. This left her vulnerable. If I should wait another moment, I may not have the strength to get away for she would not relinquish the hold she had upon me unless there was not another option. It was then that I withdrew a blade of iron from the small of my back and thrust it into her neck, burying it up to the hilt. She recoiled from me with a spiteful cry that echoed throughout the marsh as a warning to all within of what I had done.

She began to stumble, and I reached for her, not wanting the blade within her to be lost to the depths below. Unfortunately, as she passed on, her body soon turned to ash, sending the blade into a freefall. I lurched forward, attempting to retrieve it, but I was not quick enough. As I watched both her ashes and my blade cascade throughout the limbs below, a sneaking suspicion that I was not alone came over me. I found myself stepping back towards the tree's trunk where I dropped myself against it, giving myself a moment to regroup. The gamble paid off, but I felt drained from the confrontation. It could be hours before I felt as myself again, but my biggest concern was I needed to stop the bleeding and leave this location and soon. The smell of blood is thick in the air and will travel far should a breeze blow in. I could not risk it.

Placing a hand upon my neck, I began to focus my

energy on the source of the bleeding and waited for the magic to take hold. It has never been as effective as when I focus it upon others, but I am able to channel enough to stop the bleeding. The remainder of the healing process will come in time. Within minutes I felt some relief, but I reminded myself that I could not stay. I would soon need to venture into the foliage in search of the lost blade. Venturing this far into the marsh was not my intention, but now that I am here, I would need that blade should more of the fae find me for iron is their greatest weakness. As I began my descent, I thought over the fuil fae once more. In all my travels and research, I had never known them to travel alone and never this far north. It was in the forests of Tornen they had made their home, keeping hidden amongst the dark timbers, and overcast skies. No doubt after the fall of Tornen they were driven mad by famine forcing them to seek the marsh. There they could be permitted to hunt an endless parade of wanders and soldiers who dare to cross its borders.

Upon reaching the base of the tree, I crouched low, concealing me in nearly my entirety, but the crown of my head. This limited my visibility but may save me from being directly seen by any creature larger than myself. The air at this level smelled and tasted quite different than what was found above, much like what I found when I first entered the marsh. I soon preferred what was found amongst the treetops though neither were ever pleasant. I concentrated on slower, but steady movements as a tumble into the foliage would not be advisable. It was not long before I located the ash from the fuil fae, scattered about in a wide net. Without consciously deciding upon it, I let out an audible sigh of my disgust. Feeling fatigued and impatient, I had already felt drained from the search, and it has just begun. Luckily, after only knocking over a few small bushes and decaying conifers, I found the blade laying upon the moss as if on display.

Creeping towards the blade, I snatched it up before returning it to its rightful resting place at the small of my back. It was there that it would remain hidden until it was called upon once more. My weapons are viewed as just that by the majority, but most do not understand the weapons I carry. These were weapons of the finest craftsman and unlike anything man could ever hope to achieve. No two blades that are elven made are ever alike nor are they capable of being wielded by anyone other than the intended. While my ability to heal is not what it would have been had I not been exiled, but my forging ability was still solid. The trick is using multiple materials, magic, and blood of the receiver to infuse within the blade, forcing it to only respond to the one who wields them. It is what makes them both unique and lethal.

Having freed myself from the marsh floor and crept my way back into the treetops, I found that the marsh had remained quiet, eerily quiet. As if a soundless echo had been forced through all within the marsh and now, they were waiting for me to bend a blade of grass giving them permission to come for me. I refused to give them the satisfaction. Despite the overwhelming exhaustion I was now feeling, I needed to press onward for soon the real monsters would come out to play and the marsh is not somewhere anyone chooses to be after nightfall. Giving up my search for the missing soldiers, if but temporarily, I drug myself from limb to limb until the air did not seem so fetid. It was there that I would rest momentarily as I needed to give my body time to purge the venom that was undoubtedly searching my veins for a place to burrow in. There would never be such a place I told myself.

My thoughts returned to the silence that was still heard and felt throughout, causing an uneasy feeling within me to grow. This place has always found ways to trick those that are daring enough to enter, but this felt different. What I felt was not an illusion nor was it magic. I was being watched, perhaps hunted even. With each step and each breath, I was giving away my position, drawing the predator further towards me. Tightening my body against the tree's trunk, I slowed my breathing and used only my eyes to scan my surroundings. Nothing directly lured my attention, but this game is grueling and there can be only one victor. I needed to hold out until they either gave up the hunt or moved first. The minutes drew onward, and I felt the sun would soon set. My body though not in motion was beginning to tremble from the strain of holding this position for so long. Very soon, I would need to break away from the tree in order to seek a more suitable place of refuge, permitting my body the time it needs to recoup from the conflict of the day.

Not wanting to greet my enemy unprepared, I slid one of my hands behind my back, reaching for one of the blades that was kept there. As I withdrew it from its hideaway, I felt it catch against the leather they were bound in, releasing a faint rubbing sound into the marsh. I scanned the marsh once more, still nothing. I permitted my body to shift slightly and that is when I saw it. Near the edge of a small pool of water, behind several large ferns were two brightly glowing eyes suspended in a sea of dark flesh or fur. It remained low towards the ground, using the foliage as coverage, just as I did. Keeping my gaze focused upon it, I stood slowly, wanting it to watch me all the while not understanding that I would be watching it as well. Its gaze followed me attentively, curious as to my sudden willingness to break away from the tree I had clung to for so long. Due to my position, I was able to watch the beast as attentively as it to me, forcing me to monitor it only through my peripheral vision.

Continuing to advance towards the next limb, I decided to stage a slipup and draw it out of hiding. Adding a quiver as I walked just before deliberately sidestepping the limb, pitching my body forward into a freefall. The beast withdrew itself from the brush before leaping towards me in anticipation of the catch, fangs, and claws fully exposed. It appeared to be a lejon, a large feline-like beast with elongated pointy ears accompanied by multiple whip-like tails to match and stalks the marsh upon six equally large limbs. They were known to thrive in the most stifling weather due to its dark amphibian-like flesh, making both dangerous on land and in the amongst water. This creature was made of pure muscle and did not need wit to overpower someone, though it had plenty of it as well. Their name was left unchanged even after the mutation, but they still resemble the large cats they once were. They have a habit of dealing immense pain upon their prey, thriving on killing them slowly, which made me wonder if they could have been human at one time. In addition to their harrowing method of torture, they are highly aggressive especially when their territory has been breached, much to my oversight. I had found myself careless and clearly, this one was not willing to overlook the misunderstanding.

Just as I watched the tree limb pass into my peripheral vision, I reached for it and made the connection, jolting my body back towards it. I felt my muscles burn from the strain, but it crucial for me to endure the pain until I assessed the lejon below. It remained curious over the elf that now hang over it, but more patient than I anticipated. Should I have attempted to flee, and it would only follow me. I must take a stand and challenge the beast. I shifted my gaze towards it and then towards our surroundings and back again. As I watched the lejon, it did not shift from its position or appear anxious, as if time mattered little to it. It was time for fortune to favor the bold. I pulled my legs up towards my chest, placing the blade I held between them and pointed it towards the lejon. Before another moment could pass, I relaxed my fingers and began freefalling once more. The lejon crouched down in anticipation of the kill, muscles taunt and eyes wide. I reached for the companion of the blade I held and pulled it from its resting place. Had I plotted my actions correctly and they would soon be greeted by the lejon's flesh.

The lejon leapt towards me, attempting to draw first blood, but its intentions were misguided. As we found ourselves drawn to one another, I relaxed my muscles in expectation of the tumble that would surely follow. I held my gaze, unwilling to blink, when I felt the lejon's claws reach calves, dragging their way into my armor and across my flesh.

I held firm, not willing to break from my position. The lejon's fangs breeched my knees with the intent to disembowel me, but what it did not know was there a blade concealed within. As it advanced, so did the blade and it found its way into the mouth of the beast, imbedding itself between its fangs. The lejon attempted to recoil, but it was already too late. As its backside returned to the moss below, the weight of my body came crashing towards it, further imbedding the blade within its skull. It writhed beneath me while whimpering. I thrust my remaining blade into the top of its skull crossing the blades within as a courtesy I am sure it would have never given to another. Its eyes soon grew dark and body limp, this one was no longer a threat.

Unfortunately, I did not have long to rest for out of the foliage behind me, something was on the move and fast. I pulled my blades from the head of the lejon and turned sharply to greet another one now lunging towards me. I pulled myself towards the ground, holding my blades high for the beast to impale itself upon them. Though that is what initially happened, I was unable to remove my blades in time to roll out of its path, leaving me trapped beneath its bleeding and moaning body. It would no doubt take several minutes to pass on and I was being suffocated from the weight of its body upon mine. Beginning to twist and turn my body about, I soon freed one of my hands, but the blade was still fixed inside it. I would need to remove myself from beneath the beast before retrieving my blades, but that would prove difficult since there was now another pair of bright eyes watching me closely.

With our gazes locked upon one another, I listened

carefully. The foliage was beginning to shift from something moving through it, accompanied by a low rumble that could now be heard. I focused on both the sound and the movement, however, I found myself surprised at my findings Whether it was another lejon or something else, there was clearly more than one and the sounds were now coming from all around me. The speed of the movement increased with each passing moment, and I struggled to free myself from beneath the beast. The bright eyes were drawing closer and soon the body cloaked from the darkness and belonging to those eyes broke free of the foliage. I found myself now in the company of two much larger lejons and I now understood that the ones that had been slain were probably their young and they were here to seek their vengeance.

Focusing my strength on breaking free, I continued to wriggle my way free, but not before they stopped within arm's reach of my body. Their white fangs displayed aggressively as they continued to growl, expressing their displeasure with me. With each growl, their gazes remained intense as saliva seeped from their mouths. With one on each side of me, I would not be able to flee even if I had not been pinned as it were. I worked to appear unscathed by their presence, but in truth, I was just buying time to free one of the blades from either the body or reach the one that clung to my leg. My movement did not detour their actions in any manner and as the male opened its jaws wide, I knew he intended to come in for the kill. As his weight began to shift, I thrust my hand towards him focusing all my energy on its eyes. The lejon began to shift his head from side to side in a fury trying to shake it off what it was now feeling. The energy I projected soon ruptured his eyes sending him back into the foliage in a fury. Quickly turning my attention towards his mate, she was now leaping towards me with jaws wide, but this time I would not have time to channel the energy I needed to stop her.

Refusing to turn away, I watched as she came for me, but just as her jaws connected with my shoulder, she was impaled with two very large bolts of energy. They were round and dark before turning into a bright white light, very common for magic of an electrical nature. Nothing that the beasts of the marsh would have seen or able to detect and even though I could not see the one who wielded this energy, I knew they were elven. I remained as I were, feeling the crimson pour from my shoulder, watching as the lejon's remains lay scorched and smoking from the encounter. When I attempted to reach for my shoulder to heal it, two figures stepped into my field of vision. Their locks long and dark, but their eyes were bright beyond compare in a shade I no longer found in our kind. Of the two, it was the male that crouched down before me and when our gazes met, a feeling of loyalty and yet mistrust took hold of my body.

"My, my, look what we have here," the man uttered with a mischievous grin.

With that I already knew there would be no living with him after this.

Conall

As Prince Urie's body fell before me onto the sandy floor, I felt utter disbelief at what had just happened. The cruelty of man was far greater than anything I would have imagined, and I was beginning to understand that we may never be getting out of here. King Ferand stood before me now with a look of indifference upon his face, one that I had not really seen before. He has always either tried to appear confident or his rage would run away with him. I wanted to wait for a reaction, but I now believed one would never come. We stood there for some time, unwavering and unyielding, when I heard Eira call to me once more.

I cannot take this much more. Her voice wavering out of frustration. *And I cannot sense Haxa's presence, should we...* her voice trailed off.

I think that is what they want us to believe.

Then tell him I will give him what he desires.

I will utter no such thing. I replied, feeling my stomach

turn sour.

Please Conall, for this is the only way he will leave.

He desires you and I will not let him have you.

Please do not misunderstand, I mean for you to offer him a bairn. Our bairn.

You cannot ask that of me.

We do not know if it is even possible, we just need him to believe it is and that we are willing. Perhaps this is the only way to stop the torment.

"We will give you what it is you desire," my voice stern.

"I desire her," he spoke frankly. "Surely that has not slipped your mind."

"You will never have her," I spat, "or dreams of me siring her bairns will be off the table."

He snickered, "You underestimate me Conall—"

I stepped over Prince Urie's body and advanced towards him, cutting him off.

"No, it is you who have underestimated us. I would sooner slough off the mortal coil that you know to be Eira than let you have her, so drop it," I hissed.

We were now staring one another down and it was he who broke away first.

"Very well," his voice sounding dry. "What is it you ask of me in return for your willingness?"

I thought carefully over what we would need to give us the upper hand as this would be our last chance to get it right.

"You will need to provide us with nourishment," I spoke bluntly, "and plenty of it."

"And why should I do that?" he countered.

"For bairns cannot be sired or birthed without it," I responded. "In addition, we will require bedding, rags, fresh breeches and leathers to cloth ourselves."

"Are you daft?! You are my prisoners, not my guests!" he blurted out.

"Then perhaps you will have to seek out others to fulfill your kingdom's needs," I hissed. "For I was under the impression it was my allegiance you valued above all else," I paused. "Or has that changed and you no longer wish for me to defend the populace of Tuiteam?"

He looked at me disapprovingly, debating my worth or possibly working to manipulate the situation in some way. Of course, had he fully understood the why we were asking portion, and there was no question in my mind that he would torture me for my attempt to deceive him once more.

"We have an agreement," he uttered never letting go of his disapproving look and tone.

I nodded, confirming my understanding, and watched as he turned to leave the chamber, slamming the door behind him. Despite executing Prince Urie before me, this was the calmest I had ever seen him, which unnerved me greatly. His behavior was like the calm before a storm and at any moment, I worried that the castle would begin to crumble above us, crushing us in its wake. Alas, probably not today.

No sooner than when the locks turned back into place, I heard Eira weeping softly within the confines of the alcove. The sound forced me to abandon all thoughts of anything else and go to her. Upon reaching her side, I fell to my knees before pulling her away from the stone and into my arms. Though I was confident she did not see what I saw, she heard it all the same. Urie meant something to her and although, I may never fully understand it, I respected her for what she tried to do. Had she not been here, and it was something I surely would not have done. As I clung to her, I felt her body change, trembling at first, but now boiling. I released her from my grasp and backed away until my back was greeted by the opposite stone wall where I watched her carefully. There appeared to be a faint aura of steam that was beginning to radiate from her body and though her eyes remained hidden behind the hands that guarded her face, I knew they were blazing.

This time felt no more than a blink and she had transformed before me. Her frame was slightly larger than I could recall, and her fur was much darker this time, a deep red inward towards her body with tips of black. She was beautiful. I gazed upon her for only a moment, then she fled into the chamber, towards Prince Urie's body where she hovered over him, taking in his essence. What had remained of him would not linger long and though they were not of the same blood, she tended to him as if he were her bairn. I wondered if there would ever be one for her. As I remained there pondering this thought, Eira began to howl. Long winded cries of her sorrow that she otherwise could not express in words. I sought to join her, but stopped myself as sorrow, such as this, is not meant for all to take part in. Her cries soon softened and then altogether ceased.

Eira broke away from Prince Urie's body and rushed towards a nearby statue, severing the angel's torso from its legs. Eira was enraged and there would be nothing to soothe that part of her nor could I stop her. She thrashed about in the chamber, breaking open several coffins before tossing the bones about as if they were flower petals billowing in a breeze. Had they not been decaying remains and it would have been strangely poetic. I stood slowly, walking towards her, but I stopped just shy of the one that I found Prince Berenger was frequently drawn to. This one, I could not let her destroy, regardless of her dismay. She advanced towards it, but I intervened, waving her away which was countered by her snorting loudly. Thankfully, she did not persist and returned to wreak havoc on all that remained including the chamber door and what remained of the vault behind the angelic statue she struck down first. It took longer than expected, but she soon collapsed from exhaustion and fell towards the sandy floor, panting heavily and clutching her head within her hands.

As I now surveyed the damages, including a sizeable dent in the door, it was not any wonder why she would be suffering now. She left nearly nothing unscathed and the debris was nearly in every corner of the chamber and only two things were spared: the one that belonged to Prince Berenger and the coffin where Prince Urie was hidden. Thinking over both carefully, I knew they were spared out of respect for another's pain, something that could not be taught and something that could not be taken away by another. I wanted to stop her pain. I wanted to take her in my arms and force her to forget all of it, but I could not. So, I remained as I were, watching her crawl towards the young prince, weeping all the while. Though I do not believe she had grown attached to the young prince, it was all that he represented to her that she was mourning, and I felt her desperation and loss all the same. I left her to grieve briefly before taking the young prince from her and returning him to the filth from which he came.

I never should have released him from his prison.

Forgive yourself for you did not know it would have ended this way.

I fear our own ending is far too near.

Should that be our path, then we must walk it without fear for at least we will be reborn again.

I covered Prince Urie with the cloak we all had desperately clung to at one time or another, before reaching for the lid of the coffin. As I began to pull it over him, I found Eira had returned to his side and was now assisting me. With a tear-stained face, she looked upon him one last time before watching the lid close over him, sealing him within for all time. Once closed she fell back upon her heels just before glancing around the room, stopping where I once stood.

Who is that to you?

No one, but to Prince Berenger that plaque held a great importance.

A mother or sibling perhaps?

His pain radiates as something more, something all too familiar. I believe they may have been lovers or wed in secret beneath a starlit sky. Each time he has been within my presence, his focus gravitates towards it unconsciously.

Like I to you.

Precisely. Should Prince Berenger have accompanied Ferand, I feel the events of today would have ended entirely different.

Do you believe he is weak?

Compassionate would be more like it. This feeling within him causes a clear struggle for power between the two of them, but ultimately Prince Berenger folds in the name of duty. I think if it were all up to him, he would abandon the folly of his father and brother to forsake it all.

She did not remain to ponder the matter, but brushed back the tears before standing and venturing back towards what remained of the angelic statue where Prince Urie was slain. Standing there for several moments, I grew curious as to what drew her attention and soon found myself up on my feet, closing in on her. At first, I thought her grief had placed her in a trance of sorts, but as my gaze followed hers, I could now see what captivated her. Beneath where the body once had been lain within the vault, there was a seam that ran the length of it near the base. As I stood there mouth now agape, she turned sharply and began rushing between what remained of the other coffins in search of the same seam. She returned to me quickly and leapt inside, before crouching low to follow the seam with her fingertips.

What is it?

None of the others have this seam, there must be a reason for it.

I helped pull any remaining bone and debris from within the space out and began scanning the seam with her as well. The seam encircled the entire edge, and it was now clear that the center piece was added at a later time. I wrapped my arms around Eira's waist, pulling her towards me before lowering her just on the outside of the vault's edge. We needed to see if the center slab could be lifted or removed. Unfortunately, the seam was quite small, and my fingers could just not take hold of it. Then it hit me, Prince Urie's wardrobe had buckles and we may be able to use them to pry it open. I rushed back towards the far wall of the chamber where the majority of his wardrobe still remained. Sifting through it quickly, I found more than what was intended. There was a blade hidden inside the breast of his doublet, something I did not expect. While I do not believe it is unusual for a member of the royal family to be armed, for one so young to bear arms, drew my curiosity. Taking the blade and buckles with me, I returned to Eira's side.

Where did you get that? She pointed to the dagger I now held.

Prince Urie's doublet.

Why would... her voice trailed off, clearly pondering the same thing I had just asked myself.

I was just asking myself that same question.

She frowned just before breaking the buckle from the leather strap it was bound to and I mirrored her action. Placing one on each side of a corner, we pulled back on them and felt the slab shift slightly. Not enough to permit our fingers to slide inside, but enough to where we now understood it was not attached to anything. We leaned into the action once more, shifting it further from its resting place.

Eira, use the blade. We cannot leverage it without it.

Alright, can you hold it?

I will do what I can. Just be quick.

She reached for the blade and jammed it into the small opening, before placing her full body weight onto it. The slab opened enough for me to place my fingers inside. Dropping into a squatting position, I slid my fingers inside and lifted with everything I had. After an initial push, I was able to flip it back without straining myself only to be greeted by a chill I did not expect to feel. The slab was covering a large, damp passageway that appeared to have been dug recently. We glanced at one another and then back towards the opening.

You should go. I insisted only to be met with a concerned gaze.

I will not leave you.

Just see where the passageway leads and come back to me. Feasibly there is a way out or it would not be here.

And what if King Ferand returns before I do?

Do not fret. I can handle him.

I turned towards her, placing my hand on the back of her neck, pulling her towards me to place my lips upon hers. I could feel and hear her heart racing. It was a sound I had come to seek frequently, and it comforted me greatly. She was concerned and that concern was understandable. There was nothing more I could do to calm that besides showing her what we were fighting for and what we would always be fighting for…each other. I felt her pull away just before placing her hands upon my face.

I will come back for you.

I just smiled at her knowing that neither one of us would have thought anything different, but she uttered it, nevertheless. I took her in my arms once more and began lowering her into the unknown. She caught the sides of the passageway with her feet and soon had a firm hold, but the passageway was terribly dark, and we had no way of knowing what could have made its home within or who could have created it. As I released her hands from my grasp, I watched her slowly descend into the depths. A moment later, she dropped, and I was sure she had found the bottom even though it was difficult for me to see. Her bright eyes then found mine and our gazes locked for what I very well knew could have been our last.

"You will always be my ionuin and we will see each other again."

Her face brightened even in amongst the shadows and then she was gone. I knelt back onto the sandy floor, waiting patiently while thinking over it all. Why would a secret passage be hidden inside a vault and more specifically, why this vault? Did Tuiteam believe their dead would rise again and would seek safe passage out? It did not make sense to me. I began searching through the debris for anything that could explain what all of this meant, but just as when I arrived, there did not appear to be anything to find. The stone to this vault was nearly identical to all that were within the chamber, leaving me no better than where I started. A thought entered my mind about whether the statues were indicators of some kind, but I quickly dismissed the suggestion as cryptic messages and puzzles did not appear to be the way of those in Tuiteam.

Fiddling through the debris once more, I found that some of the pieces felt different than others. Their initial appearance gave me the illusion they were nearly identical, but as I palmed them now, they were far from it. Some of the pieces felt lighter than others and had a pull to them. The more I held within my grasp, the more they were drawn to one another, as if they were moths flocking towards an open flame. They snapped together almost the instant they touched and the edge that was once there disappeared, making it appears as if it had never been broken. I pulled at the edges of the stone to see if it could be broken again and the pieces dropped into my hands just as they were before, broken but not. This statue was an illusion, though I am not certain of whom had created it or why, but it did not feel dark.

Out of sheer curiosity, I began to place the broken pieces in a pile to see if they would have the same effect and they did. Out of a pile of debris, there the angel emerged once more. I dropped the remaining pieces I held and reached to pull the slab away from the opening as I did not wish to trap Eira inside. Placing together the once broken pieces and it was beginning to look as it once did. Unfortunately, due to the weight of the slab, I was unable to move it more than necessary, but as long as the statue remained whole, I would see no reason for anyone to seek what would be hidden on the backside of it. However, much to my contempt, the door to the chamber was being unlocked once more and there was little more that I could do to conceal the escape attempt Eira was making.

As the door swung wide, the hilt of Prince Urie's blade caught my eye and I flung myself towards it, catching a bit more of it with my flesh than I would like, but concealing it quickly near the small of my back. The men who entered where members of the royal guard and while their pace may have been steady at first, it soon slowed to that of a snail as the destruction of their sacred tomb came into view. Eyes wide and mouths agape, they began to mutter and send shifted gazes between themselves. They did not approve and from their whispers I deduced their King would not either. They soon began to back their way out of the chamber, whether out of fear or something else I could not say, but within their grasps they held large baskets and burlap sacks.

"What brings you to the chamber of rot and ruin, gentleman?" I spoke with a slight upturn in my voice, quickly pulling their attention towards me.

"King Ferand will not be pleased," one of the men spoke up.

"I care little of what pleases your King. If he wishes for us not to behave as beasts then perhaps, he should not treat us as such," I hissed.

The men dropped all they carry in a series of sequential thumps as they hit the sandy floor beneath them. Some louder than others. Several of the men began to back away, when a familiar voice was heard breaking through the air.

"My, my, Conall," Haxa grinned, "you have been a wicked beast. Best learn to behave yourself or I will be required to force you."

She advanced towards me, giving me a clear view of the blackened hands Prince Urie had referred to. I cannot recall noticing them as such before today, but there was no denying the evidence before me. Even the lower portion of her forearm was now showing signs of the abuse and the decay would not cease until she did, leaving her forever stained. It surprises me though that no one else that has encountered her understands what those markings indicate, or they would fear her above all others. I quickly tucked the blade into the sand before rising to meet her, not wanting her to see or feel more than was necessary.

"Oh Conall, there is no need to rise in my presence," she taunted, "for I am no lady of the court. Besides, it is your beloved of which I seek."

I only had a moment to respond before my apprehension would surely draw attention, but nothing I could muster would not provoke her curiosity. So, I chose to remain silent and folded my arms over my chest, defying her. She began twisting her staff in between the fingertips of her left hand, rolling it back and forth until it had sunk into a circular groove that had been formed beneath it. She preferred to be the one in control and rattling cages. However, as long as I held firm and did not engage her more than necessary, I believe she will fold.

"Your beloved, Conall," she hissed. "Call to her or you will leave me with no other choice than to use force," a diabolical grin rose onto her cheeks, and I knew of what she meant.

"Why do you keep insisting she is my beloved?" I probed.

"For I knew the moment, I saw the two of you by that stream that there was something more than you were saying."

She stepped further towards me, eliminating any space that was between us before leaning inward to where she drew several deep breaths, captivated by an odor I did not notice.

"Perhaps the blood oath that was requested is no longer required."

"Have you decided to betray your King by not giving in to his demands?"

"Oh, Conall, I would do no such thing," she paused, "especially since it is clear you are already holding up your end of the agreement."

She sensed something on me that was not intended, and I was scrambling to keep up while trying to distract her from searching the chamber.

"I believe your time here has ended," I insisted.

"Perhaps so, but an oath is an oath, now call to your beloved," she hissed once more.

"I cannot call what is not near," I countered.

"Surely you must understand that neither myself nor King Ferand are fools. This chamber is a fortress, no one can escape or enter this chamber without my knowledge or skill."

I was backed into a corner, and I needed to come out swinging. I turned away from her, stepping towards the pool of Prince Urie's blood that remained near the base of the angelic statue. Upon scooping up a portion of it, I turned back towards her, holding it out for all to see. The crimson pulling itself downward onto the back of my hand, seeking the floor from which it came.

"Then here she is to take your oath," I growled.

Upon entering the passageway, I had interspersed feelings of what it all meant and where it could possibly lead, none of which gave me much confidence. However, something about it all did not add up and it was that feeling that beckoned me to go. With no end in sight and only the musty scent of damp soil to accompany me, I became fearful of being trapped within. This feeling forced me to glance back frequently at the rapidly diminishing light from the opening until it was no more. Though my eyesight was quite keen even in elven form, it far from desirable in the blackness of the tunnel, forcing my pace to slow and use my hands for guidance. Either I had ventured further than I realized or Conall had closed off the opening as a means of protecting me, but I wondered in my time away who would protect him should the chamber be found without me.

Unfortunately, the further into the depths I traveled the more I was beginning to feel suffocated. The passageway that once appeared so large and open, felt like it was closing in on me. Although, the walls were damp to the touch, they felt quite stable, further drawing my curiosity towards when it may have been created and by whom. As the path continued to narrow, I could no longer walk fully erect causing my body to ache from being hunched over and my breathing labored. The air was stale and full of moisture which wet my lungs, further adding to my discomfort. I was half tempted to turnaround, but I felt fear propelling me forward. Fear of being tortured to death, fear of being imprisoned for eternity and fear of being without him. With each day a few more memories would surface within my mind from my previous life, but the feeling I got with those memories is what I hold onto. It is more powerful than I would have believed it could be and that power is growing. It used to take several moments for me to shift, but now the process is nearly seamless. Prompting further interest of what else may have evolved in the process.

It was with those thoughts that I decided to shift once more in hopes of clearing more ground and easing the burden that was being placed upon my body. No longer feeling the need to focus on the change as much as just pushing through the movement was of great importance. The transition still forced my temperature to rise greatly, but this time I barely blinked before feeling the transition was complete allowing me to advance through the passageway quickly. With my heightened vision, the damp soil and mud of the passageway began to blur in my peripheral vision and what once was consumed by darkness, now shone brightly within my sight. There were very few minor twists and turns that were needed to veer around large roots, which led me to believe I was heading back towards Coille rather than towards the marsh as I would have suspected. This aided in my belief that it was the Skogar to whom created this passageway and prompted the question, why would they have created it?

Pushing myself to the brink, I continued onward into the unknown, when I soon came upon an opening. The opening was minor, barely large enough for a man's arm to fit through, but it was enough to permit the light to filter in along with fresh air. My pace slowed and I stopped several feet shy of the opening, listening carefully for anything or anyone that may have been nearby. I could not hear anyone speaking, but the sounds of nature were all around, relaxing my mind and body for the moment. The opening did not appear manmade, but not entirely natural either. It was there I found myself feeling weak and drained from the journey. As I dropped onto the soil beneath me, I soon found myself drifting off and although I wished to remain, I knew we were both on borrowed time. Rising to shake off the exhaustion, I found myself creeping towards the opening, ever watchful for anything suggestive of something lurking nearby.

The light above was fading, appearing as if nightfall would soon set in, blanketing the world in darkness and starlight. Had the opening been larger and I would have found a way to push myself up and through it, if only for a better view. It is easy to forget the sensation of the sun's warmth upon your flesh as you sit upon the sandy coastline or the calmness that is provided by the moon's light as you drift to sleep in the fields of Feurach until they are both lost to you. It is in those moments, not possessions, that we find ourselves most rewarded and most comforted. Regardless of our longevity, I always believed those were two things that could never be taken from me. It took King Ferand to show me otherwise and it was with the fear he provided, I returned to my pursuit, advancing onward faster than before. With nothing but the path to focus on, the minutes dwindled on like hours and I found myself feeling drained once more.

Luckily, as fate would decide, the passageway began to widen significantly just before a wall of soil came into view. The passageway that once appeared never-ending, now ceased to exist and there was no light to be found. As the feeling of being trapped once more clawed its way inside, I found myself panicking, thrusting my paws against the walls, ever hopeful an opening would be revealed to me. When nothing happened directly, I dropped myself onto the soil, which was much drier here than it was previously. Perhaps Tuiteam recently received heavy rainfall that Conall and I failed to take notice of or perhaps I had lost my way and was not near Coille at all. Forcing myself to change back, I felt a chill wash over me, almost as if I had jumped into Mar Deigh for a dip just before my normal body temperature resumed. I never did care for that sensation, but it is difficult to operate at those higher temperatures for long periods of time as they are quite draining on the body especially when already malnourished.

As I clung to the soil beneath me, pondering my options, I decided to make one desperate final attempt before being forced to return in defeat. Rising once more, I stepped back several feet from the wall and began pressing on the walls and ceiling with my hands, searching for any potential give in the soil. Nothing revealed itself initially, but as I stepped back towards what appeared to be a dead end this changed. At the point where the wall connected with the ceiling, the soil was very soft, allowing my hands to press deep within with minimal effort. I continued applying pressure and soon felt one of my hands break through, forcing the seal to be broken and large amounts of soil began to fall upon my head and shoulders. I turned my face away and began sputtering, trying to free the soil that had found its way inside. It was not particularly helpful since the soil was continuing to fall all around me.

Rather than continuing to inhale soil or wait for the remainder to fall, I began pulling the soil down towards me in large bunches. When the soil stopped falling, I took a moment to shake off what I could from my locks and face before searching the opening that now lay before me. It was equally as dark, but there was an opening. Using my hands as guides, I ran them along the edge of the opening before reaching to find something that I could use to pull myself out. My hands fondled anything within reach, several large groupings of tree roots were soon found, and I took them within my grasp. Their rigidity and girth boded confidence within me and with that confidence I rose from the soil and back into the night. The opening was not as I expected, and I soon found myself within the trunk of an immense tree. Had I not cleared such a sizeable opening beneath it and a few humanoids could have easily set up camp within its embrace.

Aside from its sheer size, the next thing that captivated

my attention was the gateway that would lead me back to my freedom. It did not need to be sizeable or grand, it just needed to be there, and it was. I reached towards it, noticing a faint tremor had begun taking over my hands, fearing the opening would be an illusion, but it was not. I had leaned into the reach with such anticipation that I nearly fell forward through the opening and onto the soil before me. I caught myself upon the edge just in time. Finding myself once more in awe of the world before me, I dropped onto my knees and began to shake violently, dispersing as much of the soil from my body and locks as I was able. I found myself still faintly covered in grains and particles, but I presumably appeared less monstrous. I leaned back upon my heels, glancing at the new world that I had found myself in. There were trees of plenty, and the air smelt fresh, filling my lungs with its intoxicating freshness with each breath I took. It was not home, but I no longer cared. I was free.

Night had fallen upon the land and as I rose to my feet, it was evident nearly everywhere. The land cloaked in darkness and nearly all life had fallen into a dreamless sleep, waiting for the sun to wake them once more. Unsure whether I should venture for aid or return to him, I stood there hopelessly paralyzed by indecision. When Bryn returned to my thoughts once more. It saddened me to realize I no longer thought of him as I once did and though there was a time, I would have done anything to save him, I now found myself holding a greater concern over my own well-being. Perhaps that is selfish of me, but perhaps not. We all must choose our own paths and though I felt neither of us stopped seeking one another, in a way we had.

Unsure of how long I had been standing there, contemplating the cost of my choices or the sacrifices that have yet to be made, I felt something change in the wind and the path became clear. I needed to feed, or I would collapse on the return journey and may not wake for days. Unfortunately, there was little nearby, but I could hear the trickling of water faintly in the distance. I began walking towards it, not wishing to consume more energy than was necessary. With each step, the sound grew more apparent. It started soft at first, water trickling along the edge of a bubbling brook, but then the water was rushing, crashing into nearby rock and debris. It was a river, and I could smell the water. I did not even need to taste it to know that my body both desperately wanted and needed it. Almost uncontrollably, yet instinctually I broke into a sprint, rushing towards it and upon greeting the water's edge with my feet, I nearly plunged headlong into it. Apparently, grace nor balance were qualities I possessed today. Dropping onto my knees a moment later, I began lapping up all I could pull within my grasp. The water's kiss soothed my aching muscles and coated the lining of my empty belly. It gave me the little boost I would need to venture back into the tunnel in hopes Conall would still be waiting for me on the other side.

It was in thinking of him that I returned to my feet and began trekking back towards the tree I had emerged from moments earlier. Although, when I found the tree, there was no gateway to be found, just the belly of a large bulbous tree. I began to wonder if I had mistaken this tree for the one I emerged out of, but as I searched the base of the trunk, several large piles of dirt had found their way out even though the path could no longer be seen. More than likely from when I rose from the soil, but before casting it off. Feeling the mother of all regrets rushing towards me, I began searching the trunk once more for any path inside. Perchance I could dig into the soil here and fall into the passageway, but then again perchance not. If someone wished for the passageway to be found so easily, they would not have hidden it within a tomb or a tree's trunk. I felt my thoughts and emotions start to run together accompanied by an overwhelming sensation of panic. I began slamming my fists against the trunk of the tree.

"I cry for your mercy," I pleaded with it, "I cry for your mercy..." my voice trailed off.

I began to weep uncontrollably as if my frustration had nowhere to go but out my eyes. It was there I gave into the demands of my emotions and the fatigue of my body.

It was the sound of movement that awoke me in the wee hours of the morning. The sound of foliage shifting and leaves bending underfoot. I quickly brushed away the dried tears and smudged dirt from my cheeks as I glanced around me, once more searching. I saw nothing, but quickly reminded myself that should I be in the presence of the Skogar, they may not appear as I, making it harder for me to locate them. I rubbed my eyes, further clearing away the dirt that had long set up camp there. The movement stopped.

"I cry for your mercy," I spoke clearly and waited for a reply. There was nothing, but I felt the trees closing in on me. "Please, I cry for your mercy," I pleaded once more.

"And you shall have it," a male voice spoke firmly

startling me. "Where is Conall?" he continued.

I waited for the man to come into view and when he did, he was not one I recognized. He appeared quite similar to the other Skogar I had seen, but this one remarkably like Yew, but not. Eyes wide and black as night, with long locks carefully braided away from his face. There was a softness to his face, maybe even kindness there I had not felt or seen in Yew, but I still was not comfortable in their wake.

"He is still," I hesitated, "trapped inside."

"Very well," he nodded slightly, "we shall go and fetch him, you will stay here."

"I will do no such thing," I sputtered.

"Had you heeded my father's advice previously and you would have never found yourself trapped inside," he paused. "So, I suggest you learn from your previous error and listen to my instruction once more. You WILL stay here."

His voice was firm and insistent, causing a brief, but clear feeling of fright to rush through me. There was something about them I did not entirely trust. They were not fond of man, but they did not appear to be against them either, making it difficult to discern which side they were on. Of course, there were moments I was not entirely sure which side I was on as the battle over Caladh would soon wage and the sides were not simply divided into good versus evil. The life on Caladh could never be found in such simplistic terms. There were times even I was neither, but often I could be seen as both, depending on the beholder. As I looked upon him now, I felt the same feeling of unease as I did when my eyes found Drayk in the darkness of the Ice Tower, but just as it were then, I felt I had no choice but to trust him. I did not shift from my position, knowing all too well what he spoke was true, but I knew my gaze had hardened. With a twitch of his eyebrow now, there was no denying he noticed the change. Control was not something I wished to relinquish, but in this moment, I had no choice for he would not permit me to accompany him, and I had no means to access the passageway without him.

"If I am to remain here until you return," I paused, "might I be permitted to bathe?"

He tilted his head slightly as if this amused him in some way.

"You are not our prisoner, Eira, so you may do as you please."

"Aside from accompanying you?" I posed it as a question even though we both knew the answer all too well.

"Precisely," he paused, "it would be wise of you to bask in our company, for we do not offer it freely to many."

I nodded, unsure of what else I could or should have said, but my mind reeled with questions. Questions involving the usual who, what, where and why, but not limited to such simplicities either. He watched me for several moments, presumably waiting for me to make or utter the next move, but when I did not, he did not even bat an eye. He gestured to the others something I did not understand, and I soon felt myself lifted onto my feet once more. Unlike previously, they did not opt to carry me, but he still did not shift from his position. Whatever his intention, he did not wish for me to witness it. As we faded further into the darkness of Coille, I glanced back once more only to find him still ever watchful of me. While

Drayk watching me never felt predatory, this one's gaze was unnerving, and I longed to be free of it.

As we continued trudging through the darkness, the Skogar in my company never uttered a word, but were frequently found gesturing towards one another with their hands and making noises with their mouths. The sounds heard reminded me of those in nature. Similar to the popping sound uttered by peepers in the spring when the ponds are full, and the foliage has begun to grow again or the call of a fowl during mating season. However, I am not sure how frequently either would be heard or seen here due to the forest ever growing canopy. Even now, the moonlight struggled to creep into their inner sanctum, further adding to the Skogar's illusion and appeal. They, too, drew my attention in a way I had not intended. The ones in my company tended to the forest as those before them, casually shifting their fingers back and forth as they walked, dropping seedlings with each step. I greatly desired to know of the magic they possessed and how they were able to execute what I was seeing. I have seen nothing like it in all my days.

"How are you able to create such life?" I uttered more boldly than I intended. "I mean, is it magical?"

They turned to one another briefly, but their expressions did not change, simply remained indifferent.

"Can all of you do this?" I pressed them.

They both stopped in their tracks, leaving me to step ahead unknowingly before I caught the change.

"Do you always wish to know such things of others?" the one to my left spoke accusingly. "Does it comfort you when others wish to know of what comes natural to you?"

Though I did not move, I felt part of me shrink inside now understanding the error of my ways. His tone was firm and monotone, but his words felt angered with me.

"Forgive me," I spoke softly, "it was not my place to ask such."

He uttered nothing further, just stepped off as if nothing ever was said. I followed just behind them, trying not to upset either of them further. As we drew closer towards their inner sanctum, all was not as it was previously. Though the sun would surely be rising soon, all life was still. There were no birds chirping or bees a buzzing, only silence. The stillness felt oddly familiar, like when prey can sense a predator, but who was I, the prey, or the predator? Despite the stillness and my curiosity over it, we continued onward until we reached what appeared to be the center of it all. Surrounded by several dome shaped hovels, we stood like statues, waiting patiently for someone or something. After a few moments, the Skogar in my company began making those popping and now clicking sounds once more within their cheeks when someone began to emerge from one of the hovels. I half expected the individual to be Yew, but it was not.

As a woman pulled herself upright, I watched as her long locks, the color of black walnut cast upon an ebony palette, flowed beyond her slender hips, shifting back and forth gently with each sway of her hips. She stepped towards me, graceful as a gazelle, leaving no trace of her movement neither by sound nor footprints left in the soft soil. She, too, dropped seedlings as she walked, but hers did not appear as theirs.

These grew slower at first, but after several moments produced tendrils that quickly coiled their way throughout the surrounding soil before sprouting tiny chartreuse green buds that soon blossomed into beautiful flowers with purplish centers. The flowers though tiny, tore my attention from the woman and onto them, leaving her to close the gap between us.

"Beautiful, are they not?" she spoke, her tone matter of fact.

She may have posed it as a question, but her tone left little option for a reply. My attention was drawn back to her, and my gaze was met by her ever-widened gaze. Every movement she watched with increasing interest, and I was beginning to feel as if I was acquired for a study without my consent. I soon abandoned that theory in lieu of my own curiosity. I felt her hands slough off some of the dirt that had fallen there, but her expression remained remarkably indifferent. She was neither threatened nor pleased with my presence and I worked to mirror that indifference. Once more I heard the popping sound within my ears, and it drew my attention towards the why. Why would they choose to communicate in such a way unless they were uttering something they did not wish me to hear? Was it possible that not all the Skogar could speak and understand as I? It was possible, I am certain, but highly improbable for they do not appear to be the sort to remain idle or wasteful of their time.

The woman sidestepped and gestured towards an opening that would venture towards the light. I stepped towards it knowing all too well the cost of resisting their aid. She followed alongside me as the males soon faded from my sight.

I found myself still drawn towards the trail of flowers that grew in behind her as she walked, and I took every opportunity to bask in their wonder. This did not go unnoticed by the woman, but she made no effort to call me out on it. We continued for some time, leaving the hovels and remaining Skogar to rest without us. She made no effort to speak to me during our journey, wherever it may lead, only focused upon the placement of her seedlings. As I glanced around us, I noticed the sun was now rising casting bits of its warm rays to pierce the veil of treetops above us. Though the light never found us, I could feel its warmth and it drew my attention towards a steamy pool just beyond a rock wall of sorts. Now knowing the Skogar were not only people of the forest, but the forest itself, I was unsure what having a pool such as this would mean for them.

The woman slowed her pace, extending an arm out before me, forcing me to stop or collide with it. I did what was asked of me. She stepped around the pool and stood like a statue at the far side revealing her surprisingly dark flesh. Just a few shades brighter than her ebony locks and smoother than the stroke of an artist's brush. Sheer perfection. Upon her body were no jewels or trinkets to be found, only draping of leaves covering the bits of her that were not fit for anyone but her lover to see. Her seedlings followed her to where she stood, glowing even brighter from the sun's reflecting light. The buds and blooms responded to her presence, stretching themselves towards the light and opening wide to reveal the delicate filigree petals within that were multiple shades of yellow and cream now. As I looked upon them now, I felt I had seen them before, though I cannot recall finding myself within the borders of Coille before I had found myself washed ashore here days prior. It was then I remembered the grove. Bright and warm, but with the same attention to detail that I was witnessing now.

"It was you," I spoke softly. "The grove I stumbled upon days earlier, you did that," my tone came across as accusatory though that was not my intention.

There was a slight upturn at the corners of her mouth, but they did not remain.

"The grove appears to those in need and those deserving of its treasure," her voice much softer than before.

"What led you to believe I was deserving of such a gift?" I responded.

"For you are as we are, forever hunted and misunderstood," her tone matter of fact once more.

Her response surprised me as I had not foreseen the Skogar as one of the hunted despite their proximity to Tuiteam.

"Do you not desire to rid the world of their malice?"

"Do you?" she responded.

I found myself hesitating for reasons unknown to me.

"There was a time I believed we could have shared this land," I paused, "but that belief was misplaced."

"Each one of us has a purpose to be found, but without knowing it you will stumble blindly through the darkness."

"Is that what you believe man is doing? Stumbling blindly, I mean."

"No," she paused, "you are."

I felt my face tighten into a scowl, clearly displeased with her brutal honesty. I felt attacked and I was unsure as to her meaning or the purpose behind her statement.

"What must I do?"

"You ask, but you are not ready to listen."

"You speak in riddles yet will not provide answers."

"My purpose is not to give you the answers you seek," she paused, "only to assist you on your path." She paused for a great while and I felt my lungs begin to ache, not realizing I was holding my breath in as she spoke. "Now, please step into the water and you will soon feel better."

She proceeded to walk the remaining edge back towards me creating a ring of beautiful flowers surrounding the pool. I looked upon the water once more but did not step inside. As I leaned towards it, I could see it was bubbling and the air above it was filled with sulfur. The odor irritated my nostrils, and I crinkled my nose in response. My apprehension did not go unnoticed, and I soon felt her hand upon my arm, guiding me towards the water.

"Do not let the water's appearance detour you for it will not harm you," she paused, "nor will anyone here. You can rest easy now."

The woman's hand dropped from my arm, and she began making her way back towards of which we came, but before she was able to venture too far, I spoke to her once more.

"Might I be blessed to know of whose company I have kept?"

"I am known to the others as Ceylon," she bowed her head slightly. "Should you seek my company once more and you only have but to utter such."

"But how—"

"The forest will speak to me for it sees and hears all within."

She bowed once more, and I mirrored her gesture just before she faded into the darkness of the forest, leaving only the blossoms as evidence of her presence. Returning my attention towards the pool, all was as I expected. While the odor and temperature of the water were not entirely appealing, I still felt drawn towards it. Slipping out of the tattered leathers that have been in my company for as long as I can remember and tossing them aside, I stepped into the water and felt the kiss of its warm embrace climbing up my legs and onto my thighs. The temperature did not appear as elevated as I would have imagined from the steam wafting above, which relieved me greatly since I already felt warm. I found myself slipping lower and lower until the water greeted my jaw. While my mind was still in overdrive, my body had conceded to the water's gifts, turning my muscles into lard on a warm day. It was then that I gave into the water and found myself drifting below its surface, thinking of nothing more than how long I could hold my breath.

In the moments that followed Rose's confession, there was part of me that felt I would never want to be rid of this moment and another part of me, that could not wait to be. Both of us were torn between a life of duty and the freedom to choose our own. In this moment, our thoughts and feelings synced, and we were choosing to break free of the ties that bound us to that duty for so long. We were choosing each other and although the path ahead would soon be muddied, my heart no longer ached, and my stomach no longer flipped from the indecision we were faced with. With each passing moment the anticipation was growing for me to say something or do something, and I felt if I should wait another moment, I would lose her.

Pulling her into my arms, I placed my lips upon hers, taking her breath away. I felt her arms loop themselves around my neck, closing the gap between our bodies and where I could feel her warmth radiating through the bodice of her gown.

Almost instinctively, I placed my hands upon her hips before dipping myself down slightly to pick her up, wrapping her legs around my waist. As she tightened her grip, I felt as if someone stoked the fire to her quarters causing me to pant in between our kisses. Turning to place her body against the windowpane, I pressed one of my hands against it in a pitiful attempt to cool myself down. While I was trying not to rush the moment, I needed to cool down some or I felt I would burst into flames at any given moment. I had engaged in private moments such as this before with her, but this time already felt different. Like I knew what to do but not at the same time. I felt rushed, afraid she would change her mind at any given moment, but how could she after all she had just uttered. I needed to banish those thoughts and focus on her actions. She was choosing me.

Wrapping an arm around her waist and placing a hand just behind her head, I carried her over to the bed and laid her down upon the duvet. Her legs relaxed as I hovered over her, kissing her softly. In between our kisses, I pulled away, removing the doublet and tunic from my body before casting them aside to return to her. The coolness of her cabin soothed my flesh greatly and even calmed my nerves as her mouth found mine once more. Her hands clung to the flesh of my neck and back desperately to hide the tremor that had recently begun to take hold of her fingers. I felt the need to comfort her, slow down the rush that she too was feeling. Pulling myself upright and back onto my heels, her body followed the movement and I felt her hold a breath in. Brushing her long locks back from her shoulder, I kissed it gently, waiting for her to exhale, but she did not. When she did not after several moments, I stopped, waiting for her eyes to open to me once more and when they did, they grew wide with surprise.

"Rose, my darling, is this what you want?" I had not intended for that to be what I uttered, but once it was out, there was no taking it back.

The doe-eyed appearance of her eyes softened slightly, and I soon felt her warm breath dancing across the flesh of my neck and chest. She was relaxing somewhat, but I felt the need to wait for a response of some sort.

When she did not reply, I leaned in to kiss her lips once more, but stopped myself, hovering just shy of them before I whispered, "Do you wish for me to stop?"

Her eyes fluttered closed just before she shook her head slightly in anticipation of the kiss. I wanted to hear her say that she wanted me above all others, but perhaps this is the one area that she struggles to find her words and being within my arms was her body's way of expressing her desires. I felt like my heart understood what was happening, but my mind would not let the matter rest, tugging at me with each kiss towards what I now believed was inevitable. My breathing deepened as the war between my mind and heart waged on. Just when I felt I could take it no longer, I felt her pull away forcing my eyes to open just in time to watch the bodice of her dress drop onto the wooden floor. In my distracted state, I did not even realize that she had removed it. Slipping her legs aside of me, she turned to stand at the bedside, permitting her gown to slide down off her shoulders. I rose to kiss her bare shoulders that I rarely had the pleasure of seeing just before tugging at the ribbon that held the gown to her body.

It fell towards the wooden floor with barely a sound, but both of us felt and heard it louder than any sound we had heard before. There was little more than a thin layer of linen between us now and though it was enough to cover her, I still found myself turning away out of respect. Out of the corner of my eyes, I saw her turn towards me before letting out a soft giggle, her cheeks flushed with color. Pulling my attention towards her with her hand, I now found myself staring into her eyes, keen to capitalize on our desires, but not at the same time. The passion she had previously witnessed was still felt within me, but my lack of experience was like tossing water onto that fire. I think she could sense something was amiss and pulled me towards her, kissing my cheek and then my neck. I ran my fingers through her locks before tilting my face down towards her, opening my mouth to hers, deepening our kiss. Cradling her face within my hands I held her towards me, unwilling to let her go for even a moment.

While I was unwilling to let her go, the continual kisses kept me distracted until I soon felt her hands fumbling at the buttons that held my breeches upon my waist. Without removing my lips from hers, I took her hands within mine and placed them upon my chest, where the trembling fingers relaxed somewhat, but the vibration from the tremor could still be felt throughout. I broke off our kisses briefly to remove my boots and breeches, feeling very exposed and surprisingly chilled as I stood back upright, neither of which I had expected. Rose must have noticed my discomfort for she did not gaze upon my body, only stared deep within my eyes and I into hers. In almost the same childlike innocence, my trembling hands had found her shoulders. She leaned her face towards each of them kissing them softly just before I felt the softness of her hand slide beneath mine.

The linen chemise she once wore had fallen from her shoulders and was now piled at the base of her feet, only leaving her long locks to cover part of her body from my gaze, but my eyes did not leave hers. I felt myself lean back towards the bed, pulling the covers down somewhat as an invitation for her to climb inside, but she did not. She looked at me with growing curiosity and I longed to understand what drew her sudden fascination. In thinking the matter over, I knew it could be nothing other than the naked male that now stood before her. Odds are she may have never seen one before and her gaze was relishing in the moment. I felt my own cheeks now flushed with color. I wrapped my arms around her, drawing our bodies towards one another where there was nothing but heat and flesh to be felt between us.

Guiding her body back and onto the bed, we slowly found our way beneath the covers where the trembling I once shown could no longer be found. It was in the silence and the breaths that we shared between us that I felt her body clinging to mine, taut and trembling with what I hoped was anticipation. Resting upon one of my forearms, I brushed the wispy strands of her golden locks back from her eyes as I kissed her gently. With the tips of my fingers, I traced the features of her face in smooth gentle strokes while watching her eyes flutter from the sensation. I leaned towards her nuzzling her cheeks with my nose between kisses.

"Be kind to this heart that I give to you for I do not

have one to spare," she uttered while waiting on bated breath.

Though it was not what I was expecting, it pulled me towards her in such a way that I felt my own heart would shatter should I turn away from her now. Taking her in my arms now, I channeled my energy in a single kiss. With it was all that I felt for her and all I could give her. This would be the kiss that would lead us down a path we shall not return from and banish the desire for all others, thereby changing the fate of our world. This was not as I would have intended the moment to be, but as I lay here with her now, there is nothing I would change.

The bliss of being with her in a post-coital embrace would not last, I am afraid. With swollen lips and tousled locks, there was a knock at her door. Unsure as to the catalyst that drew someone to her quarters at such an hour, I felt panic begin to take hold. There was nowhere we might venture that would keep me safe from the King's wrath should I be found here. I felt her body tense up as another knock was placed upon the door. Unfortunately, we did not have time to respond as the door began creaking its way open. I could feel our hearts joined together in a terrible rhythm ever fearful of who may have been stepping inside.

"Princess Roselyn," the man's voice spoke, but we could not yet see the man behind the voice as shadow still consumed his face. "I feared you were having a terrible nightmare and wished to check on you. Are you alright?"

The man who began to enter was Prince Berenger and though I rarely appreciate another's misfortune, I was extremely grateful for his lack of sight in this moment. Rose, not so much. Still appearing frazzled by his sudden appearance, she was clinging onto my body as if she were trying to climb inside of it. Had I not feared he would hear us, I would have showered her with kisses to calm her nerves, but alas that would have to wait until we were alone once more.

"Princess Roselyn," he spoke once more before crossing the threshold and closing the door behind him. "Are you alright?"

I nudged her to respond before his interest became perked enough to venture over to her bedside.

"Prince Berenger," she paused trying to appear as if she had just woken, "my apologies for disturbing you. I am quite alright. Thank you for checking on me."

"I am relieved to hear that. Being aboard a vessel chock-full of men, I half thought one of them might be taking advantage of your good nature." He giggled slightly as he lowered his head, clearly blushing from embarrassment. "You must think that trivial of me."

I did not have the heart to ruin the moment as we were all now slightly blushing: him for thinking his future Queen would do such a thing and us for doing exactly what he was thinking. It took all my restraint not to snicker at the childish folly that was playing out before us and though I took it all in humor now, I feared all too soon the danger would become all too real.

"Would you mind if I remain here with you, at least for a little while? I feel quite restless, and your presence has calmed that part of me greatly in the past."

Rose turned back towards me, mouth agape, completely

befuddled and unsure what to say. I glanced downward and back up hoping she would take the hint and provide the excuse that would send him away.

"Well, normally I would be honored, but I am afraid I am not dressed for guests," her voice sounding stiff and uncomfortable.

"Oh…uh," he paused sounding nervous for the first time while in my presence. "My apologies, I had not realized the hour or your current state of dress due to my…condition if you will."

In all the tales I had heard of the Warrior Prince of Tuiteam, this is not the man I would have expected. He may have looked the part by his muscular physique and battered armor, but his behavior now was more…well, more like my own really. From bold and courageous to meek and apologetic, it did not suit him and only proved the extent of the marsh's reach and power. He may have survived, but it came at a terrible price. He stood slowly and before turning and stepping towards the door, but as his hand welcomed the latch within his grasp, Rose spoke up once more.

"Prince Berenger," she spoke, and I felt my breath catch within my throat. "If you should give me but a moment, I can make myself more presentable for your company."

I felt the need to sigh heavily but resisted the urge. In most cases I would find her manners were of the finest caliber and appreciate them greatly. This was not one of those moments. Almost instinctively and quite regrettably, I scowled at her and watched her nose scrunch up in displeasure. Thankfully, none of this was heard by Prince Berenger.

He turned his head in our direction and nodded briefly, "Very well, I shall wait just outside your chamber door until you beckon me to return in an effort not to wake any of the others."

Then he was gone. I think part of me was hoping she did this to send him away, so I would have time to get out, but while he took the bait, it was returned to us in misfortune. As the door closed softly behind him, I let out a long-held breath which was greeted by a soft squeaking sound coming from Rose's lips that I would swear only the beast in me could hear. I clasped her upper arms and held her for a moment, trying to pull her attention back towards me.

"Just breathe," I whispered, "grab your things and don your dress, but do so without your typical grace." I paused, "He cannot be permitted to hear me here and now I have no way out."

"What of the window?" she pointed, "Could you not venture out through there?"

I pursed my lips before uttering, "Perhaps, but it would appear highly suspicious should I pop-up on deck dressed as I were from the night before and just above your quarters."

She closed her eyes tightly and let out a painfully frustrated sigh, a frustration I echoed. I slid towards the end of the bed, nudging her to do the same, but she appeared paralyzed, clinging tightly to the duvet. My toes touched lightly on the floor's surface, aiding in my balance as I reached to grasp all the pieces of her wardrobe that had been dropped or flung there along with my own. The floor creaked from the pressure, but I worked quickly drawing in what I could reach without stepping further towards the door. As I handed her things to her, I quickly donned my breeches and tunic before scanning the room for any place large enough for me to hide. With limited options and time running out, I turned back towards her to find the answer being where we just were. Prince Berenger was without his sight and therefore, would not notice me should I be so bold as to sit in front of him, though I dare not.

I dropped towards the floor, scanning the underbelly of the bed to see if beneath it would be more probable. The fit would be extremely tight for someone of even Rose's size, let alone mine, so I ultimately abandoned it unless there was no other option. I found myself drawn back to Rose as she was now standing beside me, looking even more radiant than when we first met. The memory flashed before me and as I looked upon her now, I could see our time together had changed her. She was no longer the naive maiden who had come to call upon me in the early morning hours in hopes of hearing whimsical tales of a world afar. She was the woman who I had given my heart and with that she had given hers in return. Before I could reminisce any longer, I felt her hand upon my cheek, its cool touch was enough to bring my focus back. She placed a quick peck upon my other cheek before scurrying towards the door, giving herself one last glance over. All was nearly as it should have been for the late hour.

"Prince Berenger," she spoke softly.

He must have been waiting just outside the door as he said because she barely uttered his name before the latch to the door lifted permitting the door to come ajar. I felt myself flinch, afraid of being seen, but as he stepped inside once more, the band he now wore over his eyes reminded me of the sight he had lost, and it was not his sight I should fear. Soon it would be his other senses that would grow stronger, and no amount of hiding could conceal my scent upon her flesh. It was almost barbaric how remarkable our senses were even in elven form. Just being across the chamber from him I could smell the cleansing soap he must have been bathed in the morning before and the residual sweetness of the summer berries he had noshed upon in the late evening. It is not difficult to understand why we would have once been the prevailing predator and why man would seek to use us as a weapon even now.

Fearful the resting upon the bed now would draw his attention, I slid myself back into a small nook just between the bed's frame and a large armoire of sorts. It was wide enough to conceal me should anyone else enter the chamber, but not so large that I could not observe them once within. They exchanged the usual pleasantries before she guided him towards a table just near the largest window near the back of the quarters. She stood there describing the moonlight and stars to him as though he were a youngling and never witnessed them for himself. Though I was not a youngling and I had frequently witnessed the wonder of the night's sky, there was something in the way she talked about it that always held my fascination. Of course, now knowing she is of elven blood, her relationship with the moon is all I would have expected.

My concentration was broken when they shifted from where they stood and seated themselves at a nearby table. Where she served them both a golden liquid the populace of

Losgadh call sotma. It was a drink served hot or chilled, but warmed your palate with its touch and left a sweetness upon your breath that could be appreciated even hours later. Rose drank it almost exclusively and it was a taste and scent I had grown to not only appreciate but seek. Clearly unaccustomed to such a drink, Prince Berenger sipped it slowly while lightly drumming his fingertips upon the breeches that covered his thigh. This could have been a nervous habit or perhaps he was using it as a means of distracting himself for a reason unknown to me.

"Prince Berenger," she spoke softly, "might you tell me of King Ferand. I know little of him, and I desperately would like to know of the man who is to become…" her voice trailed off and I found her gaze falling towards the floor before seeking mine, appearing unwell.

"King Ferand," he paused, "I mean, my brother," he paused once more clearly reluctant and unaccustomed to speaking of him in such an informal setting. "Princess Roselyn, after all the kindness you have bestowed upon me, I wish not to deceive you."

Her attention promptly returned to him and I, too, followed in her response.

"I do not understand," she uttered.

Bringing himself forward in his chair, he reached for her with his hands, placing them gently upon hers. His action was almost instinctive and though I would have believed such an action would have posed him difficulty without his sight, he did not fumble the gesture. I watched as her eyes darted between his hands and my gaze, unsure what the appropriate response or action should be when he spoke once more.

"My brother can be a cruel man, not unlike our father, and with our father's sudden passing it has left him little time to grieve or grow accustomed to the position he now finds himself in."

"Why tell me this?" her voice now defensive.

"To beseech thee for your forgiveness," he uttered.

"Of that I cannot give for it is not you who needs to be requesting my forgiveness."

She smiled slightly, but it was a smile he would never see. Beneath it was hidden all her apprehension that like any good noble she has learned all too well how to hide it. As I looked upon her now, the sudden changes in her breathing and posture were all too easy to spot. I had thought the conversation would have prompted her to send Prince Berenger away, but it did not, nor did she utter anything for several moments, causing an insurmountable tension to build up in the space around us.

"Is it for my life that I should fear?" her soft voice broke the silence.

"Yes," he uttered boldly, "for my brother sees you as a pawn just as I am to him."

"Yet, you protect him," her tongue sharp.

Prince Berenger's hands lifted from hers just before sliding his bottom back towards the backing of his chair before folding his hands in his lap.

"Your betrothed is not just my brother, but my King," he uttered with a slight sharpness to his tone as well. He did not take kindly to her challenge. "I am sworn by duty and blood to protect him," he paused once more as he leaned in towards her. "As I am sworn to protect you, the one who is intended to become our Queen."

She watched him carefully for a moment before responding, almost unsure of his intentions, as noted by her shifting and narrowing gaze, "I have lived my life in seclusion with nothing other than this betrothal as my one purpose," her voice sounding on the verge of weeping. "What good can come of telling me to fear the man whom I am to call my husband?"

"If you know what he desires than he will be more forgiving towards you and you may be spared," Prince Berenger's voice softer once more.

"What is it he desires?"

"An heir," he said frankly. "Should you bless him with such, and he will be more compassionate towards you. However, should you deny him such—"

"And he will have no further use for me," she muttered more as a thought spoken aloud than something she intended to say.

Prince Berenger nodded briefly before adding, "Then you understand," he paused, reaching to place a hand upon her cheek to which he did so effortlessly. Had I not known otherwise, and I could have sworn he was birthed blind. She did not flinch as I half expected which led me to believe he had touched her in a similar fashion before. "I tell you this not to frighten you, but to prepare you. My brother was once a wonderful man, but power and greed has tainted what once was. Yet, I am hopeful that your beautiful spirit and kind heart will return that man to us."

She smiled at his weak attempt to soften the harshness of the conversation and his thumb traced the change in her expression causing a smile to appear upon his own. There was something about the way he looked at her and the way he touched her that made me uncomfortable just as it did the morning before. Almost too familiar. Part of it was undoubtedly the jealousy that now raged within me whenever there was a suggestion of another man having her or touching her, but another part was something entirely different. Something I had not noticed or felt before as I rarely found myself in the presence of nobles until recently. They did not touch one another as he was now touching her, and it prompted my curiosity further. Could this have only been the way of nobility in Losgadh or was this Prince having a favorable response to his brother's betrothed? Rose noted my growing curiosity out of the corner of her eyes and reached to pull his hand away suddenly.

"My apologies once more, Princess Roselyn," he paused as he squeezed his fingers around hers. "I did not mean to make you uncomfortable in the least."

She smiled briefly as she glanced upon his hand squeezing hers before responding in a rushed tone. "You did not," she paused, "make me uncomfortable that is," she uttered sounding much calmer.

He smiled at her once more, followed by a faint laugh, barely audible but clearly present. They were drawn to one another, but whether by interest in courtship or a blossoming friendship remains to be seen. Had I not feared for our own safety, and I probably would have chucked him overboard just

270

to rid me of the distraction. Unfortunately, that would not be wise of me, for it is he who would know of the entrance to the Hall of Everfall and could protect Rose should I need to leave her side. Extracting that information from him may pose an issue, but if there was a chance I could repay the kindness she once had shown me, I needed to try. Thinking of it all now made my stomach draw up in knots as I remembered my last encounter with men from Tuiteam. I clutched my side with my hand almost instinctively as if the wound had just been reopened, rubbing it only to realize the scar was all that remained.

Lost in thought for several moments, dwindling on old memories, the conversation had taken a strange turn and it was I that was now the topic of discussion.

"Lord Bryn is frequently in your company I am told, has it always been such?"

"No, not entirely," she glanced towards me smiling. "Lord Bryn and I have grown quite fond of one another during his stay as I mentioned before and has become like family to me."

"Is it your intention for him to remain with you in Tuiteam?"

"It is, but I am told it cannot be such. So, he is to act in my father's stead and return to Losgadh after…" her voice trailed off once more.

"It would be for the best."

"Why do you say it as such?"

"Elves are forbidden in Tuiteam," he uttered frankly, "and my brother will not take kindly to a man being in such close proximity to his betrothed nor his Queen."

"You mean a man other than his own brother?"

Her response stunned me as I have never known her to be such sharp tongued.

"Should he ever know of me being with you as I am now without the supervision of another and even I would not be safe from his wrath," he growled.

She folded her arms in front of her chest in displeasure, but the gesture was lost to all but my gaze.

"Why are elves forbidden in Tuiteam?" she prodded.

"For they wield the dark magic that fractured the world of course," he uttered boldly, surprising even me.

I felt taken back by his response. Could the populace of Tuiteam really believe that all elves were to blame for what happened centuries before? While there are elves capable of wielding such power, I know naught of any that would desire to.

"Are there not others capable of such devastation?" she responded quickly. "Warlocks for instance, though few if any in number are believed to wield power of an equivalent vigor, would you not agree?"

"Perhaps, but I have yet to witness a warlock yielding magic with malicious intentions."

"Have you been met with many warlocks in your travels?"

"Not in my travels precisely, but there is one that has resided within the walls of Tuiteam's castle since I was a youngling."

"And yet you do not fear him?"

"No, not particularly as she is there for our protection."

"But how did that come to pass?"

"Of that I do not know."

"But yet, you trust her and cast away all others unlike your own?"

"She is fulfilling her purpose and she is human as you and I are. I may not always agree with the rulings of the kings of our past, but they cannot be challenged even by someone of my status."

"So, this is the kingdom I have been fated to rule, a silent queen next to a wicked king," she paused returning her attention to the sea and the rising sun. "May the Gods be merciful upon my soul."

Prince Berenger

As the words exited the Princess Roselyn's lips, I could feel her frustration. Tuiteam may have been ideal for those who have grown up amongst its walls, but it was clear that it was far from desirable to her. I reached for her, catching her upper arm within my grasp, and squeezing it gently. She pulled away from me slightly in surprise, but I had her attention once more.

"Princess Roselyn," I paused, "I can and will protect you, but that protection ends with you. Should you truly care for Lord Bryn as you say you do, you must send him away."

"I cannot," she uttered abruptly.

Her response surprised me and though I knew the two of them had grown close, there was something else there driving her response.

"He has been sent to act in my father's stead as I have already uttered. I will not send him away."

"Had King Itheal understood the problematic situation that Lord Bryn will be met with once in Tuiteam, and I am certain he would feel differently."

"No, he would not. For Lord Bryn is accompanying me of my accord, not his."

"You requested he venture to Tuiteam with you?"

"Aye, that I did," she paused. "I trust him above all others, and I have seen the kindness your men were willing to bestow upon him."

I was unsure as to what she could have been referring to as our interactions with elves has been extremely limited over the years. Other than the presence of Conall and Drayk, there have been no elves that have been detained or remained in Tuiteam since I was a young boy and none of which were permitted to leave Tuiteam alive. Conall and Drayk are the only known exceptions. While there have been some that have crossed our paths, most were forced to flee or found themselves beheaded. Lord Bryn did not appear to be headless or surely that would have drawn the attention of others. After I sifted through my memories for several moments trying to locate the one known as Lord Bryn, my thoughts returned to her response. There was something about it that did not sit well with me and as I thought over it now, she never spoke ill of him and never wished to part from him. Why would that be?

"Yet, knowing all that you know, you still wished him to make this journey with you?"

"Aye, that I did," her voice softer now.

I listened to her words carefully and thought over her actions. Though I could not see for myself the way the two of them interacted, I was not without sight. Her voice would sing whenever she spoke of him or when he was near. Although I could not see the flush of her cheeks, I felt certain they would mirror the warmth her hands exhibited when he spoke to her.

"You care for Lord Bryn," my tone presented it as if it were a question, but I was not asking.

"Of course, I do. Do you not care for those in your company?"

The muscles in her arm tightened in defense and she was deflecting. There was something she was hiding.

"I do, but not as you care for him," I added, prodding her further.

"How can you presume to know what I feel for him?" her voice and words strained in the attempt to adamantly throw me off the scent. It was then when I knew what it was, she was hiding.

"You love him," I uttered softer than I expected, but loud enough that there would be no mistaking that she heard me.

She pulled away from my grasp, nearly toppling out of the chair she found herself in. I reached to assist her, but she pulled away once more.

"How could you suggest such a thing? That would be treason to not only the kingdom of which I hail, but yours as well," her voice panicked and shrill.

"Your heart has betrayed you Princess for I am not a foolish man."

"Be wary of your words Prince Berenger for I do not take kindly to your tone."

"Then do not attempt to deceive me again and I shall not have to utter what we both already know to be true."

I could hear her jaw tighten, clearly feeling threatened by me now and undoubtedly displeased with her secret being pulled out into the open. She sighed heavily.

"It is true," she uttered before returning her hands to the tabletop and sliding her glass towards her, twirling it upon the wooden surface. "I love him," her voice unsteady and on the verge of tears, "but he knows naught of it."

I leaned back in my chair, taking a sip of the sweet and warm nectar that had once filled the cup before me.

"Are you certain of this? I have been told he frequently provides you solace and has been found on numerous occasions to be unsupervised while in your presence."

"No, but he knows of my purpose and would never jeopardize my betrothal, nor would I."

"Please understand I do not question you for lack of understanding, but merely out of concern."

"How could you possibly understand?" her voice oddly harsh.

"For I, too, once cared for another that was not meant to be mine."

"What happened?" she uttered now sounding hopeful.

"Many years ago, I was betrothed to wed a maiden from a noble house, but fate had a way of intervening, presenting me with someone I had not intended. She was the daughter of a seamster and therefore considered unfit to be courted by a man of my status. This did not detour me in the least. Our eyes locked one afternoon as my brothers and I were being fitted for some new garments, I then found myself making excuses to place myself within her company. A torn doublet…missing ties to my breeches…anything I could think of that would not draw attention to me being within her presence. Soon weeks turned into months, and I had fallen so far in love with her, I could not bear to think of myself with another. It was near the falls of Saor that we were wed, and my father's heart forever shattered for my disobedience. Our relationship was never the same after that and he never truly acknowledged the union between myself and the Lady Beatrice." I paused briefly now realizing that I had not uttered a word to anyone outside of my bloodline of our union until now. The thought of it just slipping out to the Princess Roselyn so easily amused me.

"What amuses you so?" her voice slightly uplifted.

"For so long I have been sworn to secrecy over her, as if uttering her name would somehow shame our family. It comforts me greatly to speak of her again."

"But you were wed, how could they not acknowledge her as such?"

"We are bound by duty, you and I, and matters of the heart have no place upon the throne."

"What became of her?" she uttered softly as I felt her hand slide itself onto mine.

"My love was taken from me one afternoon by raiders from the south. Rogues only seeking riches and they knew naught of who we were. I fought them off as best as I could, but by the time the men mounted upon the castle's wall heard my call for aid, it was already too late, and her wounds severe. I watched the woman I cared so deeply for utter her last words through dying breaths and it was there that I felt my own soul abandon me to be with her." I felt her reach forward to brush her fingertips across my cheeks, removing any evidence of the tears that had fallen.

"She is the loss you were speaking of the day you woke?"

I nodded, "Loving her changed me and losing her was nearly more than I could bear. So, please recognize that my understanding presents with merit."

She remained quiet for several moments, but I could feel her nearer to me as if she had repositioned her chair next to mine without my knowledge.

"What will become of him?" her words soft, but closely followed by her choking back her tears.

I thought carefully over what would need to be done with Lord Bryn and ultimately as long as what she told me was true, it need not go any further than this room, but he could not remain in Tuiteam after the coronation. My brother may be foolish at times, but I feel this would not escape him and her true feelings would soon be found out, forcing the elf she so desperately loved to greet his death much too soon.

"If you truly love him, you will send him away," I paused. "For an ill fate shall find him if you act upon your love or if my brother bears witness to what I was only able to hear. He is a possessive man and will not be as understanding as I."

"Thank you, Prince Berenger," I felt her hand upon my cheek once more, gently rubbing the flesh found beneath my eye. "For your counsel and for telling me of the Lady Beatrice. Though, I believe you misspoke earlier," she paused. "While I sense there is darkness within you as it is with all, your soul never left you for you are too kind and caring to be without one. Perhaps only a part of you remains with her as part of her remains with you always. The pain of such a loss never truly leaves us, but the scar left to remain will always be tender. Forgive yourself for being human."

I turned towards her now feeling the warmth of her face dangerously close to my own.

"He does not deserve you," I paused feeling and smelling her sweet breath float across my cheeks. "Though he shall never be convinced of such."

As we hovered there, I felt strangely drawn to her as if something about her was pulling me in, willing me to linger another moment, but I could not. I turned away from her attempting to sever the connection I had begun to feel and telling myself my mind was playing tricks upon me. It was her kindness I was drawn to, not her. This was to be my brother's wife, not mine. I must banish any thoughts or suggestions of her being anything other than that to me.

"Forgive me, but I must be going," I uttered.

I drew the cup towards my lips to consume what was left of the sweet nectar before I stood suddenly forcing her hand to trickle down along my side unexpectantly. I took it within my grasp before leaning to kiss the top of it gently just before she, too, rose to her feet. I sidestepped her in hopes of ensuring that I should not bump into her accidently as I made my way back towards her door. The attempt was futile as no sooner did I release her hand from my grasp I was met with the other being placed just behind my shoulder. She was guiding me, even though it was not asked of her and although, it made me feel incapable, I allowed it because it kept her close to me. We said our farewells for the time being and I heard the door close quietly behind me just before I was met with Kenric's backside. The hall was remarkably bustling for what I assumed the hour to be making it difficult to follow the constant noise that ran through the caravel.

"I never realized how noisy our armor can be until several of us are packed together in such a confined space."

"Aye, it is quite loud, even for my taste," he responded.

I clasped my hand upon his shoulder before stepping in front of him and pivoting bringing us face to face.

"Are we alone now?" I whispered.

"Aye, Commander Berenger, that we are," Kenric whispered in return.

"Do you recall Lord Bryn?"

"Aye, that I do, with eyes like those he would be difficult to overlook."

"What about his eyes?" I ask curiously.

"They are strangely bright," he muttered.

"It is not uncommon for elves to have bright eyes since they are a reflection of their inner light."

I dismissed his curiosity as lack of knowledge and was about to continue when he spoke again.

"Only elves have bright eyes?" he inquired.

"Aye, that is correct."

"Then how could the Princess Roselyn have them if she is but only human?"

"Are you certain they are bright?" I felt a sense of urgency seep within.

"Aye, as pale blue as the midday sky," he paused, "there would be no mistaking them."

I felt taken back as I have never known a human to have such eyes. I was not even certain how that could be possible and though possibilities were coming to mind, none of which would have held any merit. I have met King Itheal on a few occasions when I was a boy and cannot recall him being anything other than human as was Queen Drusilla.

"Lord Bryn's eyes, are they of a similar shade?"

"No, not at all," he paused, "quite the opposite actually."

Lifting my one brow in confusion and slight disapproval, I prompted him to elaborate without uttering a word.

"They are bright and radiating like candlelight. Brighter towards the center nearly appearing as sunlight but darken the further from the center you view."

I thought over this detail carefully as I felt confident, I had seen eyes as those before. It was just a question of where. Tracing all the names and faces I could recall through my memory in rapid succession, it came to me. Conall's eyes appeared similar to me even in the dimness of the Hall of Everfall he now found himself in, but could they all be as such? Was it a trait of shapeshifters to appear with such eyes or were those just his? The suggestion of another gave me pause and I had to think carefully over my next move. I did not wish to alert him to my suspicion, but he would need to be watched carefully.

"Commander Berenger, are you unwell?"

Kenric's voice brought me out of my thoughts and back to the matter at hand.

"Of course not, just lost in thought."

"Did something happen while you were with the Princess Roselyn?"

"Nothing that I wish to discuss further while presently out for any prying ears to hear," I added. "I need you to watch her quarters without appearing as that is your purpose." I leaned in closer towards him, bringing my face within a narrow margin of his ear. "And take note of anyone that should enter or leave her quarters. Is that understood?"

I pulled myself back as he whispered in return, "Understood."

I nodded before turning to make my way towards the steps that would bring me topside. Using my hand as a guide, I walked along the long hall feeling quite tired, but I could smell the fresh air wafting into the hall from the nearby staircase. The scent propelled me forward and soon I found myself rising out of the belly of the caravel towards a new day. The air that greeted me was humid, but not so much so that I felt suffocated by it. The main deck was bustling for what I believed was early morning, but none of the men appeared in distress. As I approached the railing, my face was greeted by a faint breeze which tossed my curly locks back from my forehead. The sensation permitted me to relax if but briefly as I did little more than just breathe for several moments. Listening carefully to those around me, I was able to infer that we had crossed the midpoint in our journey during the night and should reach Tuiteam's port before nightfall. The thought of returning home both comforted and terrified me as I was still struggling to cope with all that had happened.

I felt my mind slipping back to that afternoon in the marsh. The air was suffocatingly damp, so much so that it felt as if we were breathing water rather than air. I cannot recall how far we ventured within, but as I tried to focus on it now, the memories started returning to me in short bursts. I could hear the men's blood-curdling screams repeatedly, clawing at my mind from within. I raised a hand towards my head, clutching it while trying to steady myself against the growing breeze. Then suddenly the screaming stopped, and I released my hand from my temple, thinking the memory had passed. As I began exhaling a long-withheld breath, it came rushing back to me. My eyes opened to see my arms thrashing before me as I gasped for air, but there was none to be found. My body had been pulled beneath the water's surface and I was flailing to no avail. The water that surrounded me was dark green with an ever-growing darkness that crept up from beneath me, cloaking me from all others and concealing the heart of its darkness. I watched as what remained of the air from within me worked its way out and floated to the surface in a chain of orbs seemingly unaffected by the violence in their company before all went dark. Had it not been for the brutal assault that I now felt upon my chest, and I would have assumed I was no longer amongst the living.

It was not until someone approached me that I realized it was all just a memory, but if it was just a memory then how could I taste the water?

"We are near Boglach, are we not?" I uttered ever

hopeful I was mistaken.

"Aye, Commander Berenger," the man paused, "but how could you know that?"

"I can feel it somehow," I paused turning away from him. "I cannot explain it."

And that was the truth. Ever since I awoke in Losgadh I could feel something pulling at me, a darkness perhaps…its darkness. Placing myself near its energy once more was as if a beacon had been ignited, alerting it to my presence. I felt it calling out to me, like the whistle of the wind before a storm sets in. With each passing moment, the sound grew louder and louder, until it was no longer a sound but a voice speaking my name repeatedly. I clasped my hands over my ears trying to drown the voice out, but it only provoked it. My heart began to thunder against the bones within my chest sending pain throughout as the increasing pressure pushed upon my already broken ribs. I could not acknowledge the voice; it was not real. The more I denied it, the louder it grew until words could no longer be heard, only a deafening shriek.

"I cannot take it anymore!" I screamed, "I cry for your mercy!" Feeling my body and mind were nearing the breaking point, I collapsed onto the wooden deck clutching my head within my hands. "Take me now, I beseech thee! Grant me mercy!" I shouted.

A moment later, I felt the cool rush of water upon my face, and I felt as if I was drowning once more. I began to flail as the water washed over me once more but was met with resistance. There was someone restraining me and with that thought the voice ceased to be heard.

"Commander Berenger! Commander Berenger!" a man shouted.

I felt a wave of energy surge through me, taking my breath away. The warmth of it radiated throughout my body causing me to break out in a fever and I would soon feel sweat beading up upon my brow. It was like nothing I had ever felt, but just as lightning striking a sandy beach, it was leaving its mark. I reached towards my chest, firmly grasping my doublet within it, and pulling incessantly, hopeful the pressure was from an external source. I was mistaken.

"He cannot breathe! Send for the Captain!" another man shouted.

Though I could not see them, I knew this one was not the one who spoke before. I listened carefully to those around me. There were several and most of them were shouting or whispering amongst themselves, which I did not approve. Just before I thought my lungs were to explode within my chest there was a crashing sound nearby and my breath returned to me just as quickly as it was taken. I inhaled several deep breaths, feeling the warmth that once nearly consumed me fleeting and with it the grip upon my doublet relaxed.

"Prince Berenger," the Princess Rosalyn spoke, "are you alright?"

I shook my head, "Of course," immediately contradicting myself.

"He's disoriented," her voice quieter now. "Please take him to his quarters where he can rest. I shall be down in but a moment."

I was brought to my feet a moment later and although I

was upright, I was quite unsteady. The men guided me back towards my quarters where I was greeted by Kenric near my bedside. While Kenric uttered little, it was manner that was unmistakable. He was gentle and soft spoken, two features rarely found within a soldier. As I lowered myself upon the duvet, I heard the men step away, but they did not vacate the space.

"Thank you for your assistance," I paused. "You are dismissed."

They said nothing, but I soon heard the door close behind them. Just as a wave of energy washed over me topside, I now felt a wave of emotions flooding my mind, causing me to be unsteady once more. I fell back onto the duvet and curled myself around its softness. I wanted to disappear within it should the Gods have given me the option, but that was not their way. I was to remain here, struggling and fighting for my purpose that had not been revealed to me as of late. Losing myself to a sea of misfortune while in the company of the only one I could trust, seemed like the only path that made sense at the moment, but it was not meant to be.

"Commander Berenger," Kenric whispered, "I was able to obtain what you asked."

It took me only a moment to shift my focus and though I was quite tired, I knew the answer he held was worth starving off my exhaustion.

"Very well," I muttered softly, "I shall have it now."

"I remained below deck after news of your illness reached my ears and waited to see if the Princess Roselyn would flee her quarters to come to your aid," he paused.

"Which of course she did. However, that was not the strange part."

"Go on," I mumbled.

"After fleeing her quarters, there was someone who left shortly thereafter," he paused leaning in towards me where I soon felt his breath upon my flesh. "Meaning you two were not alone in her quarters when you spoke earlier."

I sat up in anticipation, waiting for her secret to be revealed.

"It was Lord Bryn that fled her quarters," he muttered softly.

I felt my breath catch forcing my response to sound airy and strained, "Are you certain?"

"Aye," he paused, "for him to have found his way into her quarters prior to the hour you knocked upon her door, he would have undoubtably been there since he retired the evening before."

Pondering the conundrum that lay before me, there were only two paths that presented themselves: expose them for their treachery or use their bond to our advantage. There was clearly more to them both than meets the eye and now I had the advantage.

Kraciun

Not much time had come to pass, and the cog was beginning to drift into the port of the Fallen City. Though Bart and I were permitted to remain amongst the land of the living, it was made abundantly clear that we could not remain aboard which left me to contemplate the city we would soon find ourselves in. The pieces provided by the men aboard I am certain had their purpose, but they were presented as a riddle rather than the map I was hoping for. Should any of it be true and we should all be made fearful of what may be found within. I stood near a railing on the starboard side, watching as the once bright sky was choked out by the mist and fog that rose from the land. The water, a once vibrant shade of cerulean, now heavily polluted by something much darker and the current that once pushed the weighted cog along with such force, had vanished.

My attention returned to the crew as several of them were now flooding onto the main deck. They looked upon Bart and I with growing displeasure, but I cared little for their pleasure or approval as we would soon be out of their reach. We watched a rickety dock come into view and just beyond it lay several wooden crates, similar to the ones onboard. Rather than wait for an open invitation to flee the cog, I signaled for Bart to follow me as I made way towards the stern castle. There we could slip over the side and into the water's grasp without alerting the remainder of the crew. He appeared skeptical at first, but soon followed me with little more than an upward glance. Upon reaching the stern castle's rail, I glanced overboard, now realizing that with the height of the cog, one leap towards the water would end with a manhunt through the water and into the unknown. There must be another way.

As I was scanning the railing and all that could be found below, I felt Bart's elbow connect with my ribs forcing a sound out of me I had not intended. Just as I began rubbing my side, an unfamiliar and quite unwelcoming soldier came into view.

"To what do I owe the pleasure of serfs upon my stern castle?"

"And what makes you think this was going to be a pleasure?" I responded with a fair amount of sarcasm and almost instantly regretted it.

The man grinned with delight; a response I could not have foreseen. He stepped towards us, and I glanced towards Bart for guidance, but there was none to be found. Sidestepping the man, he reached the railing and glanced overboard.

"You are new aboard," he glanced towards me and then back towards the water, "are you not?"

"Aye sir, that I am," I spoke confidently.

"Be wary of the water's edge," he glanced towards me and then towards Bart, "and of the company you keep." His eyes narrowed briefly before he turned about to step away from the railing. "Now, fall in line or I shall have you flogged."

I nodded, unsure what was customary. No sooner than when he dropped out of my sight, I took the railing within my grasp and flung myself overboard, clinging tightly to it as my feet worked to find a foothold. Feeling the pressure mounting, I abandoned my search for a foothold and relied on my hands to shoulder the burden. Without winter's icy grasp needling me, it was easier to maintain a grip than I would have anticipated, and I soon was greeted by the water's touch. There was something different about it. Inviting, yet not so. I lowered myself into its grasp just before taking a deep breath and dropping below its surface to be greeted only by the water's stillness. Almost immediately throngs of seaweed began cluttering up my field of vision. I glanced upwards to find Bart had not followed and I should wait no longer if I intended to reach the shore without being detected.

The water was remarkably clear, but quite dark, appearing as it would just before nightfall. Although, the field of seaweed I now found myself in was all but unseen from above drawing my curiosity towards it. I pressed onward trying not to disturb life below the surface as I was yet to understand the soldier's warning. Using the seaweed as a guide, I veered around them, twisting and turning my body until I found the water had grown even darker forcing me to return to the surface for guidance. I floated upward slowly, tipping myself backward just as my brow broke through. It was difficult to hear much with my ears still below the waterline, but I parted my lips just enough to draw in a few breaths as I glanced towards where I believed the shore to be. It was indeed closer, but my exit had not gone unnoticed, and the men aboard were flocking onto the stern castle. The only advantage I had was the cog had not connected with the dock providing the time I needed to reach the shore.

I returned to the depths and quickly sped towards the shore. While it might have been wise to continue twisting myself about the seaweed, there was not time as the men would soon reach the shore as well. As my speed increased, I no longer felt alone in the water and as I glanced behind me, I noticed the once docile seaweed appeared to be coming to life. The leaves were stretching their way towards me, scrambling to take hold of my legs and boots, but I continued to pull away. With each flick of my boots outward and each pull of legs inward I felt their presence waning on me. Even though I could not see the shore I knew it was there. As my focus on it intensified, I felt a pain growing within my chest. It started out as an ache but was rapidly spreading throughout and clamping down on my throat. I would soon be out of breath. I needed to surface, but should I stop for breath and surely the depths would find a way to keep me.

Stretching myself further in the water, I soon felt sludge forcing itself into my nailbeds before surrounding my hands in its grimy hold. Jerking my legs away from the seaweed, placing them beneath me, I dug the toe of my boots in and began crawling towards the surface. It was in the struggle that my lungs began to burst, and I began gasping for air, only to be met with a flood of muddy water racing inward. I felt the surface of the water break over my back and even though I was choking upon the water, I only needed to hold out another moment. Pulling myself onto the shore, I began expelling the water from my lungs. Unfortunately, just as I had tackled one challenge, I was about to be met with another. The cog had reached the dock and I could hear the men rushing towards me.

Struggling to gain a foothold, I grappled the sludge and overgrowth as I coughed until my lungs were sore. I returned a disapproving glance towards the water and that is when I saw them, brightly lit orbs peering from just beyond the main body of the seaweed. I was unsure how I was even able to see them now when I could not before, but the longer I concentrated on them, the clearer they became. It was not the seaweed that attacked me while I was within, but something else. Something much darker and sinister. My pace slowed, feeling drawn back, not wishing to remove myself from the water's edge. It was there I knew it was only a mere matter of luck that I survived, and should we meet again I may not be as fortunate. The voices of the men grew louder, they were closing in, and I closed my eyes trying to break the hold the water had over me. I felt the draw lessen and as my eyes reopened, I found myself able to pull away from it all now.

With the men nearly upon me now, I found myself rushing and struggling to break through the overgrowth. There were dark wooded vines nearly everywhere now and though they appeared to be rotting, they were still quite tough to snap. Each step through felt exhausting and very little ground was gained. I found myself throwing my body weight towards them as a means of breaking more at once, but each leap was not without consequence, and I soon found myself nearly skewered by previously fallen timber. Turning myself over, I stood slowly as I scanned my surroundings, searching for an easier path. While nothing immediately jumped to my attention, I noticed the men's voices had nearly all dissipated and the suggestions that brought terrified me to my core. A feeling I had not felt in ages. The sensation caused my gut to draw up in knots and a tremor to appear in my hands. This was not the mountains of Reothadh of which I had grown quite familiar nor was I in good company. I should tread lightly if it is my wish to survive beyond day's end.

I found myself seeking the men with my eyes, searching for them through the overgrowth and fog that had consumed nearly all around me. Aboard the cog the fog was seen, but it did not appear as thick as it is now. While previously bits of it were transparent, now it had become so thick I was not even sure if sound could penetrate it. Almost like the land was shielding itself from the eyes of the world, but why? What was here that the world should not see? I felt those questions burrowing into my mind, further straining it. Unfortunately, I would need to abandon my quest for answers in lieu of seeking asylum or I would soon be taken captive. I turned away from the cog in pursuit of another path, but I found myself greeted by a remarkably stealthy Bart. I was half startled by his sudden appearance, but did not utter such, just watched him with growing curiosity. How could he have trudged through the muck without making a sound? I felt my eyebrow raise in slight amusement and disapproval when he gestured for me to follow him.

He turned abruptly and began mumbling barely above a whisper. "Perhaps you could have thought of a less obvious way to flee the cog," his voice thick with sarcasm of which I did not approve.

"Subtle has never been my style," I struggle to say, my throat still raw and tender. "How did you reach me so quickly?"

He glanced back before muttering, "I know this land better than I should."

I pulled my boots out of the mud and scurried towards him, clasping his doublet just below the nape of his neck. He had been here before.

"What is it you are not telling me?" I hissed.

He stopped but did not turn to face me.

"Seeking the wolf was all just a means to distract you. You were never meant to reach the mainland so soon."

"What?" I heard the word escape me, but more as a sound than an actual question. I tugged back on his doublet, nearly pulling him off his feet. "Tell me what you know," I growled.

"She wanted you safe," he whispered.

"Who?" I insisted.

"The Queen, of course," he spoke plainly.

"The Queen is dead," I spat in return.

He shook his head, "Not dead, merely hidden is all."

"Does King Edric know? Have you seen her?" I pressed him.

"Aye, he does, but I have not seen her as of late."

"Then why the charade?"

"It was necessary."

I released his doublet from my grasp and gestured for him to keep moving.

"Why me? What am I to her?"

"Of that I do not know," he muttered frankly, "she just says you are important."

"Important how?"

He shrugged.

"Where is she now?"

"Not far," he added.

"Take me to her."

He turned sharply, "I cannot, and we cannot remain here."

I thought carefully as my endless questions yielded little fruit.

"Why did the men warn me of the company I kept?"

"For in their eyes I have no loyalty," he paused, "and that makes me dangerous."

I felt my legs stop where they were, frozen in time like a statue. Though I have known Bart for many years, his vague responses were building a growing concern within me. He was telling me just what he needed to appease me, but he was holding something back. I could sense it.

"If they truly believed you were a traitor," I paused, "why permit you aboard?"

"For they fear the one who wakes the dead," his voice rang clear and with those words I felt a chill crawl up my spine.

"Necromancer," the word came out dry, but we both heard it the same.

Bart nodded slowly.

"Have you seen this necromancer?" I whispered almost fearful of the word.

"No, but his presence can be felt quite strongly here."

"He is the one raising the Fallen City and that is what the men were referring to…he's building an army."

Bart nodded again, "We must go now."

He turned to walk away and although I should have wished to follow him, there was something pulling at me, telling me not to go. It was only a few moments before he noticed I had not budged from my position.

"You said the men fear the necromancer and that is why they let you aboard," I spoke plainly feeling a great deal of it all was not adding up. "You have made a deal with this necromancer and that is why they call you a traitor."

I felt the wind get knocked out of me and I longed to be rid of his treachery.

"Kray," he muttered, "we must—"

I cut him off, "How can I trust anything you say?" I looked upon him with eyes wide and burning.

"Everything I have done has been for Trocair," he said frankly.

"You knew of a necromancer, and you sought to help him!" I spat louder than I intended.

"It was at the Queen's behest!" he yelled back.

"Dark magic is forbidden! It is what has polluted the mainland and yet you help the one who wields it!"

I tossed my hands into the air in disgust as he clearly would see no error in his ways. When did he abandon all reason to blindly follow orders?

"Who is the necromancer to the Queen?" I pressed him.

He sighed heavily but uttered nothing.

"Who is he to her?!" I pressed him again.

"Kray do not concern yourself with such" he paused. "You are the king in this game of chess and all the pieces upon the board either seek to conquer or protect you."

"What are you blabbering about? I am just a soldier in the King's army."

He pressed his lips together tightly just before muttering, "That's what you were always meant to think."

I drew my blade as I rushed towards him, clearing the muck beneath me as if it was never there, to place the blade at his throat.

"Who am I then?" I growled.

"That is not for me to utter. It is too soon. I just know that you are important and must reach Tuiteam alive," he muttered.

I stood there, muscles taut and gaze narrowed. The man before me was infuriating and I no longer recognized him as the man I once called my friend. While I cannot be certain that he knows naught of the answers I seek, I now know he has no intention of divulging that information to me. Whether it was his fierce loyalty to the Queen or a corrupted mind I knew naught, but he could not be trusted. Withdrawing the blade from his neck, I let my arm fall towards my side before sidestepping him to continue onward. I had nothing left to say to him. Several steps into the unknown and I heard his footsteps fall in line behind mine.

"You are no longer welcome in my company," I said frankly and kept walking.

"Welcome or not, my company you shall have. It is not safe for you here."

"I could say the same for you now."

The ground grew firmer the further from the water we ventured, but my mind remained disheveled. I had hoped Bart would have parted with the answers I sought, but it was not meant to be. I was now destined to face the wonders and dangers of the mainland with an enemy at my side rather than a friend. Several hundred paces from where I broke free of the water's touch, I heard voices muffled in the air. Dropping low towards the ground, we inched our way in their direction when the remains of a large stone castle came into view. The walls were large and pieced together with stones of grey, not black obsidian as I half suspected. The shell that remained was now covered in dark, overgrown vines that sent an eerie feeling throughout me.

Tornen was once a great city of man. During its peak it was filled with all the promise and wonder of a bustling metropolis. The land was plentiful in its gifts and its populace thriving, yet it all appeared to vanish overnight, leaving only traces of what once was behind. It was rumored that Tuiteam had grown bitter and sought to seize control over the city, but no remains were ever found. It was as if the populace just vanished into the breeze forcing it to become known as the Fallen City and the source of frightful tales told to the younglings of man as a warning to control our greed and curiosity. The city was not meant to be. Even now, I feel this land is cursed.

Peering around what I can only assume was once the castle walls, I could see people moving in the distance. Sluggish in their manner but carrying large quantities of stone all the same. The same black obsidian that we found being transported in the crates, but what were they doing with it? I squinted, trying to bring them into view, but it helped little. They appeared to be man but not like any I had seen. There was something about the way they moved and their appearance. I stretched myself towards them but was soon pulled backwards onto my heels.

"It is not wise to enter the city," he whispered.

"I thought you said the city was dormant?" I insisted in a whisper.

"From the shore it appears to be," he responded.

"What do you mean?"

"From there none of this is visible to our eyes, but if one ventures too far inward, the unseen becomes seen."

"Have you seen this before?"

He shook his head, "Never have I ventured past the dock. I may be in the Queen's good graces, but I know little of the necromancer."

I scowled, "Then it is time we caught ourselves a glimpse of this necromancer. Afterall, he is just but a man."

He glared at me before uttering, "Kray, the necromancer is no ordinary man and I think tempting fate further today would be unwise."

"Then you can stay here, but I cannot stand futilely by while such a man builds an army."

I did not wait for a reply before rising to my feet and trekking inward, using the large stone walls as cover. The populace I had witnessed earlier came into view, revealing what was previously confounding. Could these have been the ones that were brought back? They moved slower for their bodies appeared malnourished and taut, presumably from residing beneath the soil for countless years, but was such a feat even possible? While they uttered words, they were not clear as mine were now which prompted another look around. Within the masses were several soldiers, such as the ones aboard the cog. Armor freshly donned and breeches unsoiled by countless battles or long stents upon the sea, but how could this be? Was it possible they were under some sort of spell or had they, too, passed on and were brought back by the skill of the necromancer? My interest in him was growing stronger.

Upon scanning the vicinity, I found he was not nearby or at least not to my knowledge, so I began winding my way back from which I came in hopes the adjacent side of the shell would lead me to him. As I ventured back, I encountered a very frustrated and impatient Bart who was now insisting through countless gestures that I return to him where he remained hidden in the overgrowth. Refusing to heed to his demand, I continued in my pursuit, only stopping briefly to glance around the corner to ensure that there were no surprises waiting for me. A moment later I rounded the corner and disappeared from his sight once more. This wall was much longer than the others with only minimal vines and overgrowth to shield me if needed. I stopped frequently to keep my breathing calm and take in my surroundings. A lesson I learned quite young as panting like a beast revealed my location quite quickly on numerous occasions to men and beasts that were within earshot of me. A mistake I could not afford to make often and certainly not now.

I crept along the stone wall, trying to pace myself but, also, moving quite quick. After losing my ability to trust Bart, I could not be certain of anything he uttered, including what he knows to be here. The populace here appeared birthed out of the muck that formed the ground beneath me but did not appear as someone who had previously passed on. Not that I would particularly know what that would look like. Could it be that the fright of the necromancer was all a hoax, and these are all that remain of Tornen's original inhabitants? Or what really happened to the populace who now find themselves here? Just as the sounds of the once charging serfs vanished from my ears without a clear explanation, who is to say that what I see before me has an explanation? There is little to reference on such things and until now, I did not even believe necromancers were entirely real as I have never known anyone to have seen one. Perhaps that was part of what propelled me forward, an incessant need to prove him wrong, so I could rid myself of his deceit without the guilt I presently feel. I tend to pride myself on my persistence in the pursuit of the truth, but as I now find myself creeping through an overgrown land of mystery a thought was nagging at me in my mind. Could I have taken that pursuit too far?

Remarkably, I was able to reach the far side with

minimal effort and entirely unseen…or at least that was my impression. I shifted my gaze behind me and then around the next corner, when something caught my attention, forcing the hairs to stand up on the nape of my neck. Suddenly, the noise of the populace that once consumed my ears had vanished and the forest, I found myself within, was utterly silent. Like the calm before a storm, there was not so much as a rustle of a breeze through the nearby branches or the sound of water breaking against the shore nearby. It was as if the world stood still and suddenly the youngling within me began to tremble with fear. I was not alone. Every fiber of my being could sense it.

Although, my body now stood paralyzed in fear, I found my gaze was shifting rapidly between all the points within the limits of my vision. I captured nothing within my sight, but I could not shake this feeling. As my body began to tremble further, I soon realized I had been holding my breath in anticipation and my lungs were prepping to burst. I felt them give way just before a rush of air forced my lips to part suddenly. The action was much louder than I would have hoped, but when nothing came of the action, I forgave myself. My shoulders soon relaxed as my breathing return to normal, but still only silence could be heard. The silence set my teeth and senses on edge, much like a wee bairn the first time they greet darkness alone. It was nearly impossible to shake. In that moment, I opted to abandon my search for the necromancer and flee back towards Bart. I desperately wanted to be rid of this feeling.

I took another moment to peer around the corner, still

unsure what I may be searching for, but I performed the action instinctively rather than purposefully. There was still nothing and the silence remained. My gaze took towards the sky, ever fearful that death may come from above, but still nothing. I began to lower my gaze, but something felt off. There was a feeling of being watched and I could sense it now. I reached back and withdrew the blade that I kept near the small of my back before turning the pommel in my hand to allow the blade to lay flush with my wrist and lower forearm. Should there be a need and I shall be ready. Pivoting slowly upon the balls of my feet, I began to turnabout when I was greeted suddenly by a large, cloaked figure. I lowered myself, stretching one of my legs out, attempting to sweep it beneath the figure to knock it off balance, but I was outmatched. Before I could even execute the move, I was flattened out atop of the ground and out of breath once more.

The figure, which I could now see was male, only watched me with growing interest, yet said nothing. While he wore a cloak of dark fabric, his hair was quite light, almost white in appearance and nearly identical to the flesh it surrounded. Yet, it was his eyes that drew my attention more than the color of his flesh or the vacant expression his face now dawned. His eyes were surrounded by darkness, almost as if that portion of his face had been slathered in charcoal and permanently stained from the encounter. This along with the shadow the cloak had undoubtably cast upon them made them appear as a void rather than the window to one's internal light. Their color was all but unknown to me. However, that did not stop me from trembling under their menacing gaze.

"Rise," his deep voice demanded.

As he gestured for me to stand, I felt my breath return to me once more. Though I did not wish to hold his gaze any longer, looking away would make me appear weak and his tone left little room for negotiation. I brought myself upward, blade still clasped tightly within my hand, his gaze unyielding. His eyes, now able to be seen, were not as I expected. They nearly as dark as the charcoal stain that surrounded them, but with a redness that could be found huddling near the center. Never had I seen such eyes before, not in man nor beast. They were truly unique and though they perked my interest, gawking at them as I were, was surely not acceptable. I found my attention drawn towards the man's other features. We were nearly the same height, but his demeanor was far more imposing than mine. With his shoulders broad and gaze unwavering, I felt childlike in his presence.

"It would be unwise of you to think of using that blade," he spoke plainly.

I swallowed out of nervousness before uttering weaker than I intended, "I dare not." I paused before continuing, "For should I choose such a course and I would be struck down before the blade grazed your flesh."

"Then you understand who I am," he added, his voice low.

"You are the necromancer," my voice started off stronger this time but quickly faded making the last word nearly inaudible. I cleared my throat before trying again, "You are the necromancer."

He nodded before gesturing to lead on, but I still felt

paralyzed with apprehension. The questions that would have normally been flooding my mind nearly all vanished and now only one thought remained. What purpose do I serve to the necromancer?

"You need not concern yourself," he spoke plainly once more. "Had I wished you ill will, and you would have already received your answer." He gestured once more, "Now, if you will or shall I give you an incentive?"

His gaze narrowed, making the whites of his eyes barely more than slits and I did not wish for him to elaborate on to the means of his incentive. I nodded before turning to round the corner where a much calmer Bart stood motionless before me. My eyes grew wide, and I desired to warn him of the company I now kept, but there was not time. A moment later I watched as his eyes grew wide and I knew that the necromancer had made his appearance known.

"Bartholomew," the necromancer's voice boomed, "you have done quite well in your task. She will be pleased."

My intuition had been correct, Bart was working with him and all that I knew to be true had become a sea of deceit. I felt my mind beginning to ache from it all. Bart knew the vessels and the serfs; it was clear by their behavior when we were aboard. While the tale he had spun to me was filled with partial truths, they were correct in all they uttered of him. None of this was by chance and he was without loyalty. He conveniently appeared in the Ice Tower just after the wolf's disappearance and opted to flee upon one of the cogs with me to ensure I ended up here. He knew of the necromancer and of our missing Queen. Bart is the piece that ties them all together.

He has betrayed us all. I felt enraged at just the sheer sight of him, and I could find myself in his presence no longer. I rushed towards him, overcome with resentment and rage, where I flipped the blade within my hand before imbedding it into his belly.

"May Caladh now be free of your treachery," I spat.

Bart looked upon me with genuine shock before turning his attention towards the necromancer. Though I could not hear any words being spoken, his lips were moving, clearly giving him a message. I withdrew the blade and watched the crimson pour down his doublet and breeches in thick flowing waves. It was only but a moment more before he dropped towards the ground and his eyes blinked no more. He was now in the hereafter, where his deceit could no longer find me.

"Had he always displeased you," the necromancer paused, "or was this display purely on my account?"

I scoffed as if I would ever do anything for his benefit.

"Maybe not yet, but in time you will."

King Elgar

The men in my company soon rose from their feet and waited for my command.

"The late King Edric is to be prepped and set ablaze in the forge as it is our tradition," I paused. "In addition, I would like Kraciun's body found and returned to Castle Trocair to be treated with the same kindness as he was one of our finest."

"King Elgar," one of the men spoke. "The late King sought to mislead you in an effort to expose your feelings for Kraciun and search your response for any resemblance of betrayal as he heard stirrings after the search for the wolf."

I felt my brow furrow and eyes narrow.

"Are you saying the King I pledged to give my life for if asked deceived me for nothing more than to see if I cared for a soldier in his army?" The man shook his head and I felt infuriated further. "I care for all the men in his army!" I shouted.

"He was concerned of an uprising," the man replied

hastily, sounding defensive.

"Well, I hope his concern was worth his life," I paused, "because that seems like an awfully high price to pay when asking me would have done just as much."

I sighed heavily as I now looked upon the man I had followed for decades and a man I called my friend for even longer. Although, our relationship may have been met with challenges, I would have never imagined us parting in such a way. The feeling of being set free from his reign soon gave way to an unsettling and far more troublesome feeling that I would not be rid of so easily. The stirrings King Edric heard had merit and should Kraciun feel compelled to seek the crown, it would be my life now that would be sacrificed rather than the one we had intended.

"Give me a moment alone with him," I commanded of them, and they fled the vault without so much as an upward glance.

It was then that I sought the torch that I once had tossed upon the stone. I struck the flint upon the stone and watched as sparks cascaded down upon the stone in a slow shower of light. Just as I felt the need to strike twice, there was a growl that escaped the cell nearby. I crept towards the cell gate, stopping within arm's reach of the spindles, when I struck the stone once more. The sparks shot into the air once more, casting a faint light upon my face and the surface of the spindles where I could clearly see eyes watching me once more. It was in their menacing gaze that I opted to strike the stone again, igniting the torch I held and setting the vault a glow from its light. The once pair of eyes I saw turned to many and I soon found myself in the company of several large, blackened wolves. Against the blackness of their long dark fur, glowed their bright eyes that felt all consuming and I met each one of theirs with mine. Their eyes appeared just as marbled as a stormy sky with shades of grey, silver, and white swirled throughout. They were exquisite and each one a distinctive pattern all their own.

Just as I was beginning to lower the light from their eyes, the one furthest from me caught my attention. While the attention of the others was clearly fixed upon me, this one would only glance upon me in short bursts. Something a young maiden would do in an attempt to hide her flushed cheeks, but this was not a maiden. I found myself leaning towards the spindles as Wren did previously, lured towards them by my own curiosity. The wolf saw that I was now focusing on it and began to turn away from me. Only the beast failed to do so before I caught sight of its eyes. They glowed even brighter than the others against its dark fur and I felt a tug of recognition at just the sight of them. Its bright golden eyes were nearly identical to the wolf that was captured and placed within the Ice Tower. Its coat, however, was all wrong. The one we captured was rust in color, not black as night as this one. Could it have been possible that two were in existence and seeking one another?

"It was you whom I heard in the night," I paused, "humming a lullaby."

The wolf turned slightly back towards me and held my gaze. Not only had it heard me, but it also understood me. Could this being have been what I believe it to be? Though I knew naught whom the elf from the tower to be, the once farfetched thought of a shapeshifter suddenly felt very probable. Perhaps this was all just some elaborate ruse, and I was fooling myself into thinking I had stumbled upon something extraordinary. Should any of this ring true and the questions of their presence here and now would soon flood my mind. I wanted to those questions to find me. I needed them to. Though the purpose behind seeking these wolves at one time made sense, I now feel that it was all in vain. Perhaps the diluted misguiding of an aging king nearly the end of his reign and desperate to leave something noteworthy behind. Unfortunately, I now see that the wolves are not what will tip the scale in our favor since holding onto them has been met with such challenges. As I look upon these wolves now, I see the error of the one whom came before me. They must be set free.

"Guards!" I bellowed.

It was only but a moment or two before I heard the echo of footsteps rushing towards me through the narrow passageway.

"Aye, King Elgar," he paused sounding slightly out of breath, "what is it you desire?"

While I understand the change in title happened before even King Edric's body turned cold, it would take me some time to adjust to it.

"Your name, good sir, what shall I call you?" I asked politely.

"I am called Pendar, Your Majesty," he spoke plainly. I nodded.

"Very well Pendar. Do you see these beasts?" I spoke

clearly as I did not wish there to be any confusion and pointed towards the wolves.

He nodded.

"They are to be fed…well fed and then I will assist you with releasing them back into the wilds."

"Aye, it will be done," his words reflected his understanding of the request, but his expression shown that of confusion.

"Is there a problem with my request?" I uttered.

"Not at all," he paused peering around me slightly, "I just never imagined we would release them."

"I feel they do not belong to us any longer and I now understand what it is like to be caged. It messes with you in ways I cannot describe." I turned back towards them, "Who am I to impose such a fate upon them?"

"Their King," he replied innocently enough.

"They belong only to the mountains of Reothadh, not I," I added not taking my gaze off them. "Now, fetch a freshly taken boar for them. In addition, the young lad that has been frequently found in my company. He has taken Lavin to the Ice Tower on my bidding. Upon his return, bring him to me. Do so with haste."

He bowed slightly as was customary and fled the vault along with several others. Only to be replaced moments later by a different grouping of soldiers. Other than my ears taking in the presence of their footsteps I acknowledged them little for my eyes remained on the wolves. They had begun to pace as they watched me and the others with growing concern. These wolves were not the ones my team and I detained at our king's behest, but that matters little until now. These particular wolves were foreign to me, but how they came into the King's possession was a detail I could afford to avoid no longer.

"These wolves," I turned back towards the men who were now cleaning up the late King's remains. "Where did they come from?"

"I know naught," he paused, "I was told once by another guard that within them was a gift, but before the guard could elaborate further, he was silenced."

"Silenced, by whom?" I inquired.

He glanced over his shoulders several times towards the others before leaning towards me and whispering, "King Edric."

"Why would he silence his own guard?"

The man shook his head, "Not guard, but guards. There were several that went missing, so we stopped asking questions."

"Do you know why these ones were kept here as opposed to in the cages near the west gate with the others?"

He shook his head again and I nodded with my understanding. I gestured for the man to return to his duties as I found myself in need of a few moments to ponder the actions of the king before me. Within them was a gift, I repeated to myself. Within them? Had the wolves themselves been the gift, why would one conceal them beneath the castle rather than display them proudly for the realm? Could he have perhaps known there was a shapeshifter amongst them and that's what was meant by within? If so, keeping it hidden would have been as much for its protection as ours. Though it was the gift part that still struck me as peculiar. Did the source know of what he or she had in their possession and sent the shapeshifter to King Edric in error or was this intentional? Had it been intentional, it would have to have been a Trocairian or he would have refused such an offer immediately dismissing it as a trap. But who? Who would have not only had the access, but the means to detain such a creature? My mind was feeling drained from all the questions and just as I felt myself wanting to abandon the search, the answer came to me. The Queen.

Without a word, I pivoted and bolted towards the stairwell, drawing the attention of all present and they were now scrambling to pursue me. I felt my tired muscles screaming for me to stop, but with King Edric no longer with us, now was the time to search his things for word from his Queen. Though I do not know how she would have found a shapeshifter, she would have been someone to send him such a gift and he would have kept it hidden for nearly all in Trocair believed her to be dead. The light from the throne room found me and I burst onto the main floor, not stopping for breath or to chat. What started off only a few in tow, turned to several and soon more joined in the rush, frantic over what drew their King's attention. In a streak of color, I sped through the halls, stopping just shy of King Edric's chamber…well my chamber. I found myself now hunched over, gasping for air.

"King Elgar!" the men shouted, "Are you alright?!"

I held up my one arm, waving them off, "Stop making such a fuss," I spat.

"But King Elgar, what brought you here with all haste?"

314

"Step aside men," I took a deep breath, "for this matter does not concern you."

"But you are—"

"Out of breath, aye, I am," I uttered still panting. "It happens when you spend too much time eating Nan's cakes instead of in the training yard." I paused, "Now, off with you."

I thrust my hands upon the door with a thud, forcing it to burst open and into the stone pillar that was nearby. I stood there panting and taking in the space. It felt different than the last time I found myself within its walls. It was dark, like much of the castle, but the bedding and drapery were stained in shades of burgundy, Queen Nimue's favored color. The room was just as she left it and that was the last time I can recall be invited into the chamber. He very rarely spoke of her after she left. Part of me wondered if it was because the thought of her hurt him so, but now I understand that he was protecting himself. I reached for the door and forced it closed again, despite the growing desires of my audience to understand my purpose here.

Wedging the door back in place, the latch dropped into its slot with a clang, but I suddenly felt calmer and quite tired. Not because it was to now be my space, but it was the first moment I had to take in all that had occurred in such a short period of time. Walking over towards his bedside, I felt the weight of it all crashing down upon my shoulders and the weight was nearly more than my body could bear. I sat upon the duvet, allowing the softness of it to brush along my legs and hands as they now rested at my sides. If only I could rest but for a moment, that would be all I need to see things clearly once more. I leaned back slightly, trying to pull my legs unto the duvet, but I was so stiff from sleeping upon the stone in the night they just would not bend in the direction I wished of them. Instead, I fell back upon the duvet and felt my back crack as the bones must have fallen back into alignment. Years and years of weathering the storm has taken its toll and I was beginning to understand why King Edric appeared as he did. He was a curmudgeonly old man, but he was not always so. Thinking of him in his youth made me smile and that is what I wanted to hold onto.

The moment of peace would not last and though my body was temporarily at ease, my eyes and mind would not rest. I found myself scanning the room as I lay upon the duvet, surrounded by its soft embrace. The chamber was remarkably tidy, even by my standards, which prompted a new interest within me. I returned myself upright and began searching for anything out of place. When nothing directly jumped out as being off, I began to search for unlikely things out of place. Perhaps a loose stone or…a piece of furniture that just does not quite belong. I saw the chair just in front of the only large picture window that was found in Castle Trocair. Most were tall and thin, very easy to peer out of but not in. They were carefully designed to prevent one from getting in or out as well, adding remarkable security to the castle, but it was the chair that now had my full attention.

I stood slowly and began walking towards it. While most things in the room were showing appropriate signs of wear, this piece was nearly perfect, almost too perfect. As I stepped towards it, a significant wear mark was found in the

316

fabric. It was near the base of the seat, but on the side where the fabric meets the wood. The rivets that once held it in place had been pulled away so many times that they no longer could hold themselves in place and were found jutted out rather than flush as they should be. I reached towards the arms of the chair and lifted it slightly, tipping it side to side slowly to check its balance. Its balance may not have been off, but I could hear something shift within. I tipped it again, only faster this time. I heard the noise again followed by another noise. There was something inside. I quickly flipped the chair onto its side and grasped the edge of the fabric within my fingertips. In one quick jerk, the fabric ripped exposing the contents for all to see. There were numerous pieces of parchment held within.

I felt myself draw in a deep breath and hold it in anticipation of what may be found within. Upon reaching in, I grasped several pieces of parchment to withdraw them. Judging by their exterior, most had either been through something quite awful to get here, or King Edric handled them frequently. I could be certain of neither at this point. I dropped them onto the floor before reaching back inside to withdraw the remainder. There were so many. Of course, thinking over the number of years since the Queen's disappearance, this was minimal for what could have been found here. I returned the chair to its original position before scooping up the parchment and tucking it into the crook of my arm before whisking them off to the bedside. I placed them upon the duvet before I, too, returned to sit upon it. With no particular notion of which to read first, I just grabbed the one that lain atop of the others and waited for the answers I sought to find me.

The contents were not as I expected, and I half debated to abandon the matter in lieu of something more productive. Something pulled me back though. While most were letters from a love lost, others had not made their purpose known. The letters became significantly shorter and the hand they were written in had changed dramatically. At this point, I could not even be certain that they were written by the same person. I scattered the pieces across the duvet, trying to place them in an unforeseen order, when the order became known.

My dearest Edric, the journey here has been daunting,
but I believe I may have found a way inside.
Please forgive me for what I must do.
All my love, Nimue

My dear Edric, the most wonderful thing has happened.
I have found myself with child. Though you are not
with us, he will know your name.
With love, Nimue

My Edric, the Gods have accepted my offer
and I birthed a healthy bairn.

With love, Nimue

Edric, the bairn will be raised in secret
for as much his protection as ours.
Do not attempt to seek him out.
In time, all will be revealed. Trust in me.
Nim

My King, rumor of an illegitimate child
has surfaced here. This bairn may be the key to
the King's undoing. Be patient.
Nim

I have found a gift for you. It is within its bright eyes
you will find it. Keep it secret at all costs.

Rumor of another has been found though I know naught how.
The secrets these men kept are far greater than anything

I would have anticipated. It will be their undoing.

The tides are turning in our favor.
The King's heir is within our grasp.
Let him not slip away.

Keep him close and let him not venture far.
He will be needed before the end.

When darkness consumes all,
send him without question or delay.
It is he that will unite all under one banner.
Their end is near.

      I fumbled through the remaining parchments, curious to the identity of the heir that was spoken of and even more so as to which kingdom he may have been a part of. While some questions were answered, even more now found their way inside and once more my head was throbbing from the assault they were casting upon and already tired mind. I desperately wanted to search further, but I was just overwhelmed. Without intention, I found myself falling back onto the duvet where my eyes closed tighter than a trapdoor. The trauma and strain of the day would have to wait. I was exhausted.

Drayk

"Either have your vengeance or get this beast off of me," I spat through gritted teeth.

The two elves looked towards one another, grinning with delight at their find, just before I felt the tip of Caid's blade slide into the grooves of my neck. While these elves were technically kin, they came from a bloodline that only those who find themselves frequently within the wilds tend to stumble upon. They once inhabited Angof, an island just off the coasts of Lamprog and Reothadh but fled due to rising threats and frequent raids by the men of Trocair. The few who remain are frequently found alone or in small groupings and often mistaken for lorvisad by man. These particular two have found themselves in my company previously on a few occasions, but never for any noticeable period of time.

Their names were Ailios and Caid. They were identical twins which was a rarity amongst our kind and with-it remarkable gifts were given. They had the ability to feel each other's pain and it had been known to manifest itself physically at times, creating an issue on more than one occasion. Though they never spoke of it, I felt confident that they felt more than just the other's pain. They both were beautiful in physical appearance as most elves are, but due to their region of origin, they did not appear as those I was most familiar with. Their locks, while straight, were long and dark. The color of fertile soil just after it has rained and with eyes as bright as my own. Although, the coloring of their eyes was all wrong. Just like the shapeshifter, elven eye colors can give away just as much. That is how Eira knew I was an elf of Lamprog before I was able to utter as much. Elves of Lamprog are found to have eyes that are a shade of green or blue; elves of Tiene are usually red or orange; and elves of Angof produced those with shades of purple and pink. As if our magical abilities were not enough to set us apart from the rest.

While similar in appearance their difference in gender made things simpler for those outside of our race. Ailios was female and Caid was her male counterpart but was the younger of the two by only moments. Quite different in their studies and fighting styles, but in combat they are lethal when isolated. Ailios is a master at harnessing her body's physical and spiritual power to perfection while using her magical abilities to strengthen those attacks or take down foes from a distance. Caid, is a lot like me and perhaps out of the two we have grown to appreciate one another for our similarities. I have known him to use magic little, but do not be fooled, he is well versed in his abilities. We just rely on more physical qualities to complete our tasks rather than magical ones. Not to mention we are both scoundrels in our own right, he is just bolder in his manner than I. This could be due to the company I keep, but that matters little now.

"You were the last person we would have expected to find here. What is your purpose?" Caid inquired as the two of them began shifting the lejon to one side.

"I could ask you as much," I responded, just before pulling myself out from under the beast with a groan.

"Coin," Ailios spoke frankly.

"Aye, of course," I muttered as I pulled myself upright only to feel my arm grow dampened at the rush of crimson that was continuing to flow.

"Best tend to that before you bleed out or my sister's magic would have been all for naught," Caid pointed to my shoulder and smirked.

He was a cheeky bastard. I placed my hand upon the wound and focused my energy upon it. It burned briefly. A moment later, I drew my damp hand away and wiped what was left of the blood onto the leathers I wore. It would fully heal over soon enough.

"I would be careful doing such while in Boglach," Ailios spoke once more, "the beasts here will flock to you as long as you wear what they desire."

I shot a look of disapproval in her direction, "Perhaps you and I should get better acquainted then as that would make your job so much easier. Would it not?" I winked at her to emphasize my meaning, but she understood me well enough without it.

Ailios frequently wears a drape across her cheeks and

nose that falls onto her collarbone, as a means of protection and shields her expressions from others. Due to this draping, all I could see now was the rise of her one eyebrow. The gesture made me snicker if but for a moment.

"So, is that a yes?" I pressed her.

"Drayk you are incorrigible," she scoffed and rolled her eyes.

I snickered again just before turning back towards Caid.

"Who is it that paid the highest price this time?"

"King Aldon," he said frankly before turning to walk from the way I just came.

"King Aldon has no desire to study beasts of Boglach," I spoke confidently, "why are you really here?"

"We are seeking someone, just as you, but must take more secluded paths in pursuit of them rather than pursuing them openly," Caid responded.

"They are one of man then," I spoke plainly for had King Aldon been seeking an elf and nothing of their behavior would have been questionable.

Caid continued walking, Ailios and I soon followed suit while I waited for his reply. Both were dressed in full leather with plates of metal shielding their shoulders and knees. Ailios's hair was drawn back as was mine, but Caid left his free flowing with only a large red band across his brow to stop it from falling into his line of sight. They glanced to one another as they walked, clearly trying to work out what may have already been known and what was not. By their lack of response, I already knew the one they sought was one of man and either from Tuiteam or within the city's wall or they would not be venturing through the marsh as they were. What I needed to know is why King Aldon was concerned with the fate of man.

"The one I seek is in a position of power and clearly elven in man's world," I opted for boldness rather than remain cagey as this is often met with resistance when speaking to kin.

"We know of whom you seek," Caid interjected.

"And does he remain in Losgadh?" I pried.

"No," they uttered in unison.

He must have boarded the vessel with the Lady Roselyn significantly easing the burden of my search. In doing so, would lead him straight into the mouth of the beast.

"This pleases you?" Ailios probed.

"Having one's target unintentionally seek its attacker is always pleasing," I grinned.

We continued back towards where the fuil fae once found me and though an eerie feeling had found me once more, I had no intention of letting the two of them see it. I was about to break the silence when Caid spoke once more.

"The new King seeks them, why?"

"You know man in their foolish ways. Always seeking that which they believe will make them appear stronger than the others."

"You and I both know those beings cannot be contained by mere stone or metal restraints."

His pace slowed slightly, and I sensed his mind was beginning to wander. He was remembering something, and I could feel his emotion change within a blink. Confident to questioning and concerned.

"This King…is he worth destroying the world for?" he spoke plainly and his voice unwavering. The memory that made him soften was gone.

"It will not come to that," I responded.

"You speak it as if you already know such to be written in the fates of all," he returned with haste.

"The King is but a pawn—"

"And the shapeshifters?" he interrupted.

"One in the same," I returned. "They are a means of distraction to focus upon until the veil can be lifted."

They both stopped and turned towards me. Expressions reflecting that of perplexing thoughts.

"Of what wickedness do you speak?" Caid uttered much softer than I am sure was intended.

Unfortunately, elves can cleverly evade a question or response, but when attempting to be outrightly deceptive towards our own kind we are often found out. In speaking with these two, they would undoubtedly sense it should I speak falsely.

"Caladh will fracture once more, and the world of man will fall," I spoke plainly without revealing our hand.

"But without dark magic it cannot," Ailios spoke up.

I sent a dangerous glance her way, knowing all too well that we both knew dark magic exists and she was naïve in thinking otherwise.

"You know of the one who means to use it," Ailios uttered barely above a whisper, but all present heard her speak plainly.

I nodded.

"Why help this person? You could not possibly be indebted to them," she insisted sounding agitated.

"You and I both know that man cannot control their greed and lust for power," I paused. "This is just the means we must use to force their ending upon them."

"And what of the world they leave behind?" she added.

"Caladh as we know it will return to what it once was for *we* have powerful allies that have grown tired of man's tyranny as well."

"These allies, who are they? King Aldon would be interested to know," Caid sounded insistent.

"I care not for King Aldon's interests or concerns," I spat.

Out of my peripheral vision, I watched as Ailios cringed, pained by my own disregard for the one who demands all elven loyalty. A moment later she turned away from us and placing a hand upon her head. Clearly feeling the strain of taking it all in at once. I watched Caid step towards me, bringing his face dangerously close to mine.

"Spoken like a true lorvisad," his voice aggressive and spiteful. "You betrayed your kin to lay with one of them and now you call yourself one of us?"

"I was weak!" I shouted defensively, "Betrayed by my own heart!"

"Is your broken heart worth the known world?" he fired back in return.

"Aye," I hissed, "it is." I paused trying to calm my enflamed nerves, "I was tortured relentlessly by King Itheal and then again beneath the crushing weight of King Aldon's magic as he stripped me of all that I was. Then in a twist of fate, I watched as King Itheal executed his Queen along with the bairn I placed within her belly. A broken heart cannot begin to explain my pain."

"Queen Drusilla was with child?" Caid muttered sounding inquisitive and I saw Ailios turn back towards us, her eyes wide.

"Aye," I added quite confused at his response.

"Are you certain the bairn was slain along with Queen Drusilla?" he insisted.

"I was there that day!" I bellowed, frustrated with his prodding when it struck me, I turned away from them when her eyes went dark. The bairn was taken before her passing and tossed aside. I never heard its cry, and I cannot recall if they returned to it. "No," I mumbled feeling a weakness in me struggling to overtake me. "I did not witness its death, but I never heard its cry."

I felt that weakness turn to crushing pain at the realization that our bairn may have lived and I knew naught of it. The two of them shot glances between one another and though my own emotions were fighting for control, I could sense something was off with theirs. They knew something they were not stating, and it was setting my teeth on edge.

"What is it you know?" I pressed them.

"Since King Itheal never remarried there have been rumors that the Princess Roselyn is illegitimate," Ailios spoke softly. "In addition to the sibling we know her to have. Although even fewer are aware of the sibling's existence."

"What are you saying?" I pressed her.

"The Princess Roselyn is the bairn you believe you lost," she added.

"That is not possible," I added, quickly dismissing the possibility. "King Aldon and King Itheal would have never permitted a half-elven bairn to survive." I stepped away from them shaking my head violently before clasping it with my hands. "King Aldon showed me what would become of them and that is why I ventured to Castle Losgadh on the day of their passing. I knew she was to be executed and even though my heart could weep for her no more nor could she be saved I could not stop myself from venturing there."

I felt Caid's hand land upon my shoulder, squeezing it gently before uttering, "He showed you what he needed you to see to reinforce the bond of the marking. Without its painful grasp forever within you it would not be effective. He needed you to believe there was no other way." He leaned in and whispered, "You know he has the ability to make you see what is intended as punishment for your crimes."

I threw my hands up, sloughing off his touch, "Then how in all my years would I not feel the pull of my own blood calling out to me?! Or how would I have not heard the bairn's cry after being torn from its mother's womb should it have lived?! Tell me how!" I shouted at him.

"Perhaps what was intended was not what had occurred!" Ailios shouted.

I felt a fury within me growing and though I had little magic left from all King Aldon took, there was enough left to make me dangerous should I be provoked. Though I was not focusing my energy, I still felt that energy surging, ripping through my veins like a fire in a high wind. I needed to refocus my thoughts to calm my nerves.

"The sibling you spoke of," I paused, "where is it now?"

"We know naught," Caid paused, "for it could be anywhere if hidden by the right person."

"Both would be of a similar age, but in hearing your tale it is clear that King Itheal's daughter—"

"Yet she does not appear as I," I cut Ailios off.

"Well, we are not exactly certain of that," Ailios sounded apprehensive.

I turned about and glared at her, "You dare bring this to me and you are not certain?"

She glanced towards her brother and then back at me before clarifying, "King Itheal forced her to live a life of seclusion for her protection we have been told, but we cannot be certain how she has survived in plain sight being half-elven as very few have laid eyes upon her other than those within the castle's walls. We are confident she is your daughter. King Aldon would have little interest in her otherwise."

"Why are you venturing to Tuiteam?" I blurted out desperately trying to stop the bleeding.

Ailios muttered, "King Aldon could condemn us to your same fate should we utter anything further."

"Then you were foolish to save me from the lejon," I spat. "Why not rid this world of my ill will and continue on with what you feel is your purpose?"

"Not all elves feel as King Aldon does," Ailios paused, "and though we may not agree with your choice, to endure such pain for eternity is already a high enough price to pay without being forsaken by your own as well."

"Our task is to ensure the Princess Roselyn weds King Ferand and consummates the betrothal," Caid blurted out, drawing the attention of both Ailios and myself.

I found his brutal honesty both commendable and cruel. To force a half-elven woman to bond with man would condemn her to an eternity of suffering for he is mortal and their years together quite few. What would possibly be worth such a sacrifice?

"King Aldon seeks to control Tuiteam," I felt the words slip from my mouth as the thought struck me.

"But Tuiteam cannot be ruled by a queen," Caid uttered.

"Only if the bloodline has ended," I found myself muttering louder than I anticipated.

Of course, I knew all too well that Prince Berenger presumably perished in the marsh and Prince Urie in the tomb beneath Tuiteam's castle leaving only King Ferand. It was he that I could not figure out how King Aldon intended to unseat from the throne. They were observing me now, studying my emotions and I was reminded they were not privy to this information, but could have easily been within the marsh at the time of Prince Berenger's passing. However, there was something about the way they were watching me that caused me unease. They did not appear genuinely shocked by what I had to say, only curious. It was then that my mind relaxed and I understood their purpose. King Aldon would not have chosen two elves such as these to merely ensure a forsaken half-elven princess bedded her betrothed, their task was of a greater importance. They were there to execute King Ferand once she was with child and all others that stood in the line of succession. King Aldon who appeared to be abstaining from the affairs of man had been dabbling in them all along.

"You have been tasked with ensuring the gateway remains intact," I said boldly, "and what do you intend to do with me now that I know his secret?"

"Drayk, you care nothing for the world of man. So, as far as we are concerned this encounter never happened," Caid responded.

"And what of the Lady Roselyn? Who else knows of her true identity?" I pressed them.

Ailios shrugged, "If someone else does know of it, they are not acting upon it."

"Is there a chance that she may know?" I added feeling concern wash over me.

"We know naught," Caid paused, "but let us hope she does not, and it remains that way. It would be troublesome for her should she become aware and opt to flee the betrothal."

I closed my eyes and exhaled slowly. The web of truth and lies tore at my insides and made me despise King Aldon even more than when I was cast out from Lamprog. The encounter, though insightful, has placed me at odds with my kin once more. I would never be rid of the pain and even if what Haxa promised me could be given, it would not be as it once was. Perhaps we were just as damned as man and there was no good left to be found in this world or maybe I was just too damaged to see it.

"I admire King Aldon's patience and the two of you for your honesty, but should I be given the choice again, I would do just as I have done. The two of you have reminded me that though we may be superior beings to man, we can be just as flawed and vengeful." I glanced towards them both before stepping off in the direction of the port, "May the Gods have mercy upon us all."

While it was understood we were all venturing into the west, I found myself drawn towards the north, where I knew the falls to be. The danger the marsh presented at this hour forced me to rush towards it with an urgency I had not intended. Though I had countered and abandoned the intended path, Ailios and Caid followed me in relative silence. It was in the wee hours of the morning that the monsters of the marsh continued to flock towards our footsteps and between the three of us, those monsters plummeted towards our feet in defeat. It reminded me of when I was first reborn. Not being accustomed to much of the mainland since man came to power, I used to flock to where I knew there to be little as a means of strengthening my muscles and reflexes. At the time, the monsters here were few and much smaller, but the feeling I got was the same.

By the time the canopy of the marsh had begun to thin overhead, the sun had already risen in the sky and all we could see was light. It burst through any opening it could muster and poured a wealth of warmth into the already blistering air. It felt stifling at first, but as we continued onward it was the smell of the salty sea air accompanied by a freshness that was carried upon the breeze that we all clung to. In the few deep breaths, we all drew in, you could watch our bodies begin to relax. Though the battle for the marsh would never be over, the events of the previous night were already fleeing our minds.

As we stepped towards the water's edge, we watched the water transition from a beautiful and vibrant shade of blue into a blackness that could be found in nearly all the pools within the marsh. Just the sight of it sent the warmth that clung to us for so long far away and allowed a chill to set in our bones. It was in darkness that I always found comfort. It had the ability to make the seen unseen and it was then I could see all that I had lost without anyone the wiser. However, the darkness of the marsh has only the power to hurt, and it never sleeps. As I glanced over my shoulder towards its ever-watchful gaze, I felt the darkness call to me, but it was not a call I had the strength to answer. I turned back towards the falls and began my ascent towards the mouth of the falls, where the sound would come into full view. Provided my calculations are correct, the vessel carrying the Lady Roselyn should be nearing the port just as the sun would be beginning to set.

As we hiked our way towards the summit, the crashing sound of the falls drowned out my thoughts and the voices of my companions. Though it may have all just been mind numbing chatter by this point, I longed to be free of it. Just as I valued the darkness, seclusion provided comforts not all have the ability to understand. Upon reaching the mouth of the falls, the sound came into view and a strong wind fought to topple me back down on the rock below, providing another victim for the marsh to consume. Today it would not be so lucky for it would take more than a gust from the Gods for me to enter the marsh again so soon.

"Incredible is it not?" Caid uttered.

I turned sharply not realizing how close he had gotten in the few moments I found myself staring off into the sound.

"Perhaps," I replied.

"Yet here you stand," he added.

I did not reply. We stood there like two pins set against a backdrop of water and light waiting for the darkness of the marsh to be filtered out of our minds and bodies.

"Quit gawking like two pigeons on a perch," Ailios called out, "we have work to do if we plan to reach the port before they do."

I had not realized how long we had been standing there just taking in the breeze until her words broke through the air and shattered the hold the sound had over me. It was not often I found myself feeling drained, but the power found within the marsh could never fully be understood nor could it be contained.

Haxa was greatly displeased by my response and took little time before voicing that displeasure.

"You lie," she spat, "you could never do what you are suggesting."

"Could I not?" I growled, "After all, what do you truly know of our kind?"

I cast the now congealing blood back onto the sandy floor before returning my gaze towards her. Her eyes while generally dark in appearance often appeared lighter to me while being embraced by wandering silver strands of her long locks. Only now, even the light her locks brought upon the flesh of her face could not shield me from seeing the darkness that was gaining a foothold around them. Should she opt to continue as she were and soon the dark magic would consume her for its own. A fact either that has escaped her or was knowingly part of the arrangement.

"I had not taken you for someone who could be

silenced so easily. Consider myself flattered if you will."

"You may leave us," she paused clearly addressing the royal guard, "for now."

"What should we tell King Ferand?" One of the men shouted, "He will be greatly displeased should the Hall of Everfall be left in such a state."

"Leave King Ferand to me. Tell him nothing of what you saw," she glanced back towards them, "or heard here today. Is that understood?"

The men nodded vigorously clearly threatened by her, but I would not be so easily rattled. As the men began to flee the chamber her gaze returned to mine, and I felt her picking apart all that she could with her eyes. Not willing to admit she may have overplayed her hand or presumed knowledge she had not earned. With so few of us in the known world, it would not have been possible for her to truly have any understanding of what to expect from us and I intended to keep her on edge for as long as I could hold out.

"It is upsetting to me really that you opted to devour your beloved without so much as offering me the courtesy of watching. I thought we had a better relationship than that."

I raised one of my eyebrows in disapproval.

"The dark magic you wield, has it polluted your mind?"

"Come now, Conall," she grinned, "I have never been better."

"The relationship you believe exists is solely a figment of your imagination as my mind cannot be so easily fooled as that of man."

"But it can bend to my will," her grin widened.

"Attempt to bend it if you will or perhaps even shatter it if you must, it matters not for you cannot alter what I have already done."

A smug smile found its way upon my cheeks as I folded my arms upon my chest.

"There is one thing that has been nagging me for days though," I uttered, "care to humor me if but briefly?"

"When King Ferand learns of what you have done here today, he will conclusively request that I free your soul from your body...so I suppose I could entertain your curiosity if but for a few moments."

She sounded surprisingly interested and had there been doubts before of who was behind seeking us, it was clear it was not Haxa. Genuinely displeased with the suggestion of Eira being devoured, but not irate as I half expected. There was something about it all that did not settle well within me. Nothing she did was impulsive. It was whom that she was acting on behalf of that I needed to seek.

"Is it not painful?" I gestured towards her hands.

Her brow tightened as her hand became fixed upon the staff she had been twirling previously.

"You pose this as a question, yet of anyone I would believe you would recognize the cost of one's own sacrifice," she responded. "Is this the question that has been taunting you?"

"Not in the least, merely curious about it is all," I responded casually. "What I cannot place is who you are trying to protect or save if you will," I added honestly.

"What if it was only myself? Would that surprise you?"

She stepped towards me.

"No," I spoke, "but it would not be the truth." I leaned in towards her, forcing her to stop advancing. "You are mortal, so the price you are paying for *this* illusion," I extended my hand towards her face, bringing my fingertips just shy of touching the flesh that covered it before curling them back towards me. "I hope the person you are protecting or buying time for understands you are paying for it with your life," I added.

"Conall," she smiled, "do not let yourself forget that I am no ordinary mortal and the web of lies you are spinning to me now is only to buy yourself time. I can sense your beloved upon your flesh and though you may be a powerful being, just as she." She stepped towards me before placing a hand upon my chest. "You do not have the fortitude of mind to destroy her…even if it would set you free."

I stood there uncomfortably trying to maintain my composure as she gazed into my eyes. She was reaching for something within me, perhaps trying to break me, but I shall not let her. It was in her gaze that I felt a dire need to flee, and I knew then that she was casting a spell. In her own way, she had distracted me enough that I permitted her to place a hand upon me and that cracked the door for her to step inside. It was then I remembered the way she indulged in my flesh days before and I knew what I needed to do. Leaning in towards her, I brought my lips dangerously close to hers and waited for the flutter of her eyes to beckon my kiss to find her. Her gaze widened at first, but then softened as she waited patiently for me to continue in my pursuit or withdraw from her. She had not taken the bait as I had hoped and the thought of being this close to her turned my stomach. I feared she would not waiver without me continuing in the pursuit of her. She needed to feel that want, that desire, even though she had to have known it was not sincere. I lowered my arms before closing the margin of air between us, bringing my body next to hers. Her breathing deepened and I knew that I had her.

With my face nearly upon hers, her gaze had nowhere to venture but into mine. I inhaled slightly and her body mirrored the action. In the brief inhale, I withdrew the blade from the small of my back and lodged it just below her ribs. Her eyes widened just before trying to pull away. I placed my other arm behind her back, forcing her to remain with the blade inside.

"You know nothing of real pain," I whispered before twisting the blade inside her. I began to watch the blood seep from the corners of her mouth when I spoke to her again, "So, consider her oath fulfilled."

I desired to lob off the head of the snake, but this all seemed too easy. As I held her within my grasp, I felt weaker by the moment. When it struck me, as she stepped towards me, she tethered us together if but temporarily as a means of insuring there would be no foul play afoot. She knew I would attempt to harm her. Should I attempt to execute her now and I, too, would be taken. I released the hold I had on her and watched her body fall backwards struggling to stay afoot. She faltered briefly but regained her balance as her eyes fell towards the blade that remained lodged within her ribs. A diabolical laugh escaped her.

"You should understand by now that nothing is as it seems," she paused to wipe the blood from the corners of her mouth, "and I cannot be overcome so easily."

I smiled knowing all too well of the secret the statue held. Had she been as keen in her observations and less distracted by her own ego, she might had sensed it. Regardless, I could only hope Eira was faring well in her journey, for I may soon find myself hurdling into the tunnel behind her to escape Haxa's grasp. It was not long before my smile soon faded as I watched her hand clasp the hilt of the blade just before beginning to turn it. A grimace appeared upon her face only to be followed by a menacing grin as I felt my lifeforce being siphoned. It was in a swift motion she pulled the blade from her side and crimson began to rush outward in a wave of color that soon saturated a large portion of what she wore. To my surprise though, the drops of crimson soon ceased to fall, and I felt overcome by weakness. Within moments, I no longer felt I could stand, and I fell onto my knees, watching her through half-lidded eyes. She slowly walked towards me appearing quite displeased.

"Should you long for death, I would like nothing more than to give it to you, but that gift is not mine to give." She crouched down before me and placed her hand upon my cheek as she gazed into my eyes. "Such a shame that you could not see all that I could have given you for so little of your time." I felt her hand fall onto my shoulder just before digging the tips of her dark fingers into my flesh. She leaned in towards me, bringing her face next to my ear before she whispered, "This might just hurt a little."

My eyes widened briefly, but I did not have to wait long to understand her meaning. The blade she had removed from herself had been thrust into my stomach and she was dragging it downward, splitting me open. The pain was excruciating.

"I suggest your beloved return to you with haste," she hissed, "or I will not be so kind next time."

Thankfully, I did not remain conscious for long, and darkness soon welcomed me.

As I lay within the pool's grasp, my ailments melted away and I soon felt new life within me. Unfortunately, the peace I had found there was broken when a pain arose within the walls of my chest. I pulled myself towards the pool's edge, clinging to it as the pain worsened and began climbing towards my throat. With each moment that passed the tightness grew and I soon found myself desperate for breath. In what I believe would be my final breath, I uttered her name, Ceylon.

"Calm yourself Eira," she whispered, "this will soon pass."

I heard her plainly, but she was nowhere to be found. The pain now crippling.

"Eira," she whispered once more, "you must breathe my child for it is not your life that is in peril."

I heard her words, but I had yet to understand their meaning. I closed my eyes to hear them once more. *It is not your life that is in peril.* Conall. Something is happening to

344

him, and I can feel it. With what strength I could muster, I pulled myself from the pool and collapsed upon the soil, pleading for mercy to an unseen foe. When I thought of him once more. I must return to him. You will get up I told myself. You must get up now. Turning myself over, I felt my lungs give way and the air that previously felt it had been taken from me found me once more. I lay there gasping for a moment or two before my hand found the leathers I had removed earlier. Scrambling to don them quickly, I pulled my legs beneath me and rose to my feet.

It was as I began rushing back towards the tunnels, I realized my muscles no longer ached and my body that was once terribly broken had been reawakened from the pool. My pace slowed and I turned back towards it. In the moments since I pulled myself from its grasp, it was already working to mend itself from my presence. Nothing in this forest appeared as it were and though it piqued my curiosity once more, I did not have a moment to spare. Turning back towards the north, I found myself greeted by an all too familiar face. The lady, Ceylon, had returned to me.

"You must go no further," she held a hand up before me.

"I cannot stay," I muttered still feeling slightly out of breath. "Something is wrong, I can feel it."

"Aye, you are bound to your lover, and you will feel what he feels," she spoke frankly.

"Is he going to die?" I uttered fearful of the answer.

She watched me carefully for several moments. Her head tilting slightly as an animal would while watching something that amused them so.

"You are permitting fear to guide you." She lowered her hand, "You must first listen and feel for him. Should you find naught, then you will need to learn to see through his eyes."

"How is it possible that you know such things?"

She smiled and a soft laugh escaped her.

"Just as you, my body may be new, but my spirit is...well...much older one would say."

"But you are unlike me?" I spoke posing it more as a question than was intended.

"Precisely," she spoke firmly. "I am merely here to give fate a fighting chance and should you wish it, I will grant you a boon of your choosing. Should you favor that path, I suggest you choose wisely."

"How is this your gift to give?"

"The means are not important, what will be of your choosing is."

"Are there limitations?"

"But of course," she smiled once more. "After all no one has limitless power. I cannot turn back the hands of time and give you a world that has since been lost to us, but I can do many other things."

"Could you destroy the world of man should I choose it?"

A soft laugh escaped her once more, "I offer you nearly anything your heart desires and your first inkling is to rid the world of man." She smiled, "How surprising of you."

"Should I waste such a gift on my heart's desire, and I

would feel selfish in doing so when Caladh will soon be on the brink of war," I uttered softly.

"This boon is for you and you alone. Choose wisely for I already know what it is you seek."

I felt betrayed in that moment by my own thoughts and though I was curious as to her means of learning my heart's desire, I was terrified of losing such a rare gift.

"I know I cannot ask how you have come to know my heart's desire, but should I ask it of you, would you grant it?"

She smiled just as she folded her hands before her. "Of course, though I believe in time Conall will prove more than adequate in the task."

I found myself smiling uncontrollably at the thought.

"Can I call upon you at any moment to grant me this boon or must it be granted now?"

"There is still time, but you must know my offer will not transcend time."

"I understand," I nodded, "and though I know it is not wise, I need to return to Conall."

Just as I was about to step off towards him once more, I felt something within me shift and the pain returning to me. My gaze found her, and I felt my eyes pleading with her for aid when I began to wonder if this was her doing. Perhaps this all was another distraction and the Skogar really did side with Tuiteam. I must perish the thought for not all whom offer aid have ulterior motives. I felt the pressure growing and my chest tightening.

"Stop fighting the bond and start using it to help him."

Her response angered me, and I felt the pain growing

stronger with that. I did not understand how to do what she was instructing me to do. I needed her help. I needed to find him.

"Take that pain and turn it into power," she insisted, drawing herself in towards me. "Eira, use it," she insisted once more.

"I cannot," I uttered through strained breaths.

"Then you are not worthy of his sacrifice," she spat. "You will do it, or he will perish."

Her words cut through me like blades, that only enraged me further. I wanted to strike her, but rather I dropped onto my knees and slammed my fists into the ground. Though they were not strong enough to make the ground quake, upon connecting with the soil, the pain burst through my hands and soon ceased. As the pain stopped, something else was felt and I closed my eyes trying to focus upon it. It was dark, wherever he was, but I could hear him breathing. Strained, wet breaths as if he were drowning and in one final breath, I felt his call.

"Something is wrong," I paused, "I must go to him."

She crouched down beside me before insisting, "I implore you to reconsider."

I thought carefully over her words knowing I had failed to heed the advice of others previously leading to our recent imprisonment, but I was deeply concerned over the feeling I now felt. Closing my eyes once more, I pushed myself to reach for him, struggling to tear down the barrier that was found between us. As the pressure within my mind began to grow and it was then I heard a death rattle escape him. The sound forced me to power through the struggle. He needed to be found. I felt her hands come forward and place themselves upon my shoulders. When they did, I felt a surge of energy push through me, taking my breath away just before I was taken. Surrounded in darkness, I now found myself seeing through his eyes. He was being drug away by something or someone unseen. I tried to shift my gaze, but only darkness could be seen. I felt her fingers tighten upon my shoulders and my vision grow stronger. I used his eyes to scan his surroundings. He was within the confines of the tunnel and appearing quite unwell. What happened to him? I felt her release her hands from my shoulders and the surge I once felt vanished with them.

"What was that?" I mumbled while reaching to comfort my throbbing head.

"One of the many gifts you shall discover once you cease giving in to your impulses."

Upon reopening my eyes, I attempted to stand, but tumbled back onto the soil.

"The first attempt is always the most difficult," she paused to lean forward and wipe the blood from my nose that I had not realized had fallen. "In time you will learn to channel it with more finesse than you are able to presently."

"If my spirit is not new, why do I appear to not understand what should come naturally for me?" I spoke inquisitively, feeling consumed by confusion.

"For your bond with him is," she smiled once more.

"But we became bonded centuries ago," I paused, "did we not?"

"Aye, but the bond is at its strongest when you both are physically present upon Caladh, as you are now. You will understand it all in time."

"Does he know of this power?"

"Of that I am certain," she paused, "but he has just had more time to get acquainted with the skills his body possesses than you."

"But how do we learn if not from another?"

"In time, all will come naturally to you, provided you heed to their call," she took my arm within her grasp and helped me stand. "Patience, however, is not a virtue you possess," her gaze narrowed, "it would be wise of you to learn it."

I felt like a bairn being scolded. Though I did not yet know of whom she truly was, I did not wish to displease her by not heeding her advice at the expense of the boon she so generously offered. I swallowed deeply thinking of what I may request when my thoughts once more returned to him. I felt desperate to be near him, but powerless against her counsel. There was something about her that I just could not place. She remains unphased by nearly everything with a knowledge pool that appears endless, who is this being? No sooner did I think of who she might be when suddenly I knew.

"You are one of the ancients," I uttered breathlessly, "one of the Gods." Her focus pulled towards me, looking amused. "How have you come to be here?"

"I can be anywhere of my choosing as you must know," she smiled. "I *choose* to be here, for this is where I am needed, and all of this was birthed from my grasp."

She turned her attention towards the treetops and then towards the blossoms that were now huddled all around where we stood. Once more blossoms of vibrant chartreuse that added light to the darkened forest. Extending an open hand towards me, I watched intently as from her empty hand sprouted a sapling, that soon grew tall and fled from her hand. She looked upon it with nearly as much wonder as I and upon reaching the ground, it scurried away just after its first branches began to extend from its trunk. It was miraculous.

"When the forest calls to me, as it did before I found the grove, it is you that I hear calling me," I spoke softly.

She nodded.

"Though I cannot take all the credit," she smiled playfully.

"Does it not hurt you when your forests are poisoned?"

"But of course, as it would pain any mother to watch her bairns grow ill."

"Can you do nothing to stop it?" I pressed her.

"The answer is not so simple, and I am not the only one with vested interest in the rise or fall of life on Caladh."

I was taken aback.

"You mean there are ancients who would rather see our world collapse?"

"For some, they wish to begin again, and others believe there is still time to mend what has been broken." Her focus shifted and her body turned towards the north, waiting for something I had yet to see. "It is not us who will decide the fate of your world, only those upon Caladh have that ability." She glanced back towards me briefly before outstretching a hand towards the north, "Choose wisely in your course, for the fate of all may rest within. Now, go forth and comfort your beloved. He will need your strength to survive."

I followed her hand and watched as several Skogar broke through the darkness of the forest carrying a very bloody Conall. Though I wished to thank her for her counsel as I turned to do so, she had vanished. My mind started to wonder if perhaps she was an illusion or an ill-fated omen, but the mystery of Ceylon would have to wait until another day. It was Conall that now needed my full attention. I rushed towards them, dropping onto my knees before them and stopping them where they stood. I clasped his face within my hands, franticly searching his face for any sign of recognition, but there was nothing. Conall's eyes no longer opened to mine, nor did he respond to my touch. Searching his body for the source of the bleed, I found a large opening in his torso, clearly cut by a blade. Could it have been possible for King Ferand to have hastily gutted him over my disappearance or was there something else at work here? I looked towards the Skogar for guidance, but they only appeared displeased by the interruption in their task.

"Eira," Yew's voice cut through the darkness, "leave them to their task as there may still be time to save him."

I released my hands from his face and watched as his head fell forward towards his chest. I closed my eyes before reaching towards him in my mind, calling out to him, begging him to remain on Caladh with me. All was silent and only my cries could be heard now. He did not appear conscious nor was he in any pain, but it was the beat of his heart that I found I missed the most. When I opened my eyes again, they were gone. I searched the ground for any sign of them, but there was not so much as even a blood trail of what once was.

"Yew," I called out, "what has become of my beloved?"

"Presently he is battling the Gruamach, the bringer of mortal death, to remain amongst us." He stepped towards me, stopping just shy of arm's reach where his dark eyes seemed to pierce through me. "For now, he has become a wraith," he added.

"A wraith, but why? If he has passed on, should he not have already shed his mortal coil and his spirit become free?"

"Is that what you wish of him?"

"Not in the least," I said hastily.

He watched me carefully for several moments as he mirrored the same head tilt, I witnessed by Ceylon earlier.

"In a cruel twist of fate, he has become tethered to the warlock, Haxa." He paused, "Thereby forcing his spirit to cling desperately onto his mortal coil."

"And I felt this because I am tethered to him…" I mumbled barely above a whisper and more as a thought than an actual question or statement, but Yew responded regardless.

"Precisely," he spoke confidently as he folded his hands before him. "However, unlike the tether shared between a bonded pair, the tether they now share is quite different, and I know naught of its purpose just yet."

"Is it possible to fracture the tether?" I asked.

"Possibly, but it will take time."

He began walking and I soon fell in step with his own, unsure as to where he might be going. Though my mind was still riddled with questions, I remained quiet. Following the path back towards the pool I took comfort in, it was there we found him. His body lay just beyond the water's edge where several Skogar were tending to it, cleansing him of any blood and filth that may have found its way inside.

"How much time do you need?" I whispered, never taking my gaze from Conall.

"More than he may possibly have," he spoke softly.

I stood there deep in thought for several moments before a thought came to mind and my curiosity would not let the matter rest.

"While I am bonded to Conall, is it possible to tether my lifeforce to his?"

"You wish to give your life for his?"

"Will it come to that?"

"Should you tether yourself to him in his current state and your life may be forfeit in order to pull his back from the brink," he spoke forthrightly. "Do not choose forfeit his boon needlessly."

"His boon?" I uttered, "Then he knew of what could be found here and that is why he seeks the comfort of your realm."

I felt myself taken aback once more. Conall knew of the ancients present here, but why not disclose this to me?

"For he could not, it is forbidden. I shall advise against the questioning of your beloved's motives for they have been nothing, but for your wellbeing."

"The boon you spoke of," I paused, "are you able to tell me of what he requested?"

"Should I utter it and it will not be possible to unhear it. Do you still wish to know of it?"

I nodded just before swallowing deeply.

"Very well," he nodded.

He placed his hands upon my shoulders as Ceylon once did and I felt a similar energy rush through me. In a blink, I saw Conall being greeted by the Skogar at spear point, almost as I did. As I blinked again, he was playing with the saplings as they tussled his locks before taking comfort in his company. With another blink, I found him with Yew, pleading for something unseen. When finally, I saw him mouthing a word that had become all too familiar to me, *ionuin*. I gasped and felt him release the hold he had on me.

"It was I he wished for," I spoke knowing all too well this was already known to him.

"I implore you to reconsider your course as in doing so could possibly forfeit his own."

"Can he be brought back by other means?" I was feeling desperate.

"If necromancy is what you seek, then you would be choosing the one who has placed him within the Gruamach's grasp in the first place."

That would explain the decay she was experiencing, but who or what was she bringing back? It was then that I knew the answer would not change my course.

"Bind us," I uttered, "and should the Gruamach seek me for his own, may he take us both."

It was in the remaining hours aboard the caravel that I found the most discomfort. Though I had been given the virtue of the Lady Roselyn, all was far from bliss. There was an air about the vessel that was difficult to shake and the rumblings regarding Prince Berenger's ill-fated behavior were beginning to quake. It was a source of mystery for all aboard and just as he was being watched, I now felt I was too. It was in everything that was seen and felt. I was probably just being paranoid and although, it was not my place, I found myself eavesdropping upon all those aboard whenever an opportunity presented itself. I needed to know more about Prince Berenger's behavior.

When Rose had not resurfaced after the incident and the sun now high in the afternoon sky, I returned to her chamber. Upon knocking on her door, I found only silence greeted me. I knocked again and still nothing. I slowly began to open the door, unsure of what or whom I may find inside.

"Lady Roselyn," I paused waiting for a reply, "please forgive the intrusion."

As I opened the door, she came into view, radiating from the sunlight that now shone through the windowpane. Upon stepping fully inside, I now noticed there was something different about her…something I had not quite seen before.

"Good day to you Lord Bryn," she paused. "Might you close the door behind you."

Her voice sounded odd to me as it was in a tone I had not heard from her previously. Stepping towards her now, I could see something sprawled out before her upon the table where her and Prince Berenger once exchanged words. It was the text I once carried and the parchments from within had been removed. It was clear now the tone that I had heard. She was distressed at what she had found.

"How long have you known?" she spoke nearly breathless and now on the verge of tears.

"Since just after I sought the chamber found in your father's…I mean, King Itheal's study."

I stepped towards her, reaching to take her within my arms, but she would not budge from the table at which she found herself.

"How could you keep this from me?" she spat just as she turned to glare at me.

"I did not wish this to sway your decision."

"Did you ever plan to tell me?" she sounded more hurt now than before.

"Aye, of course," I insisted. "I kept this from you to save you."

"Save me from what?" she sounded angry now.

"The wrath you shall face if anyone learns of what you are."

"You make it sound as if I am a monster," she spat.

"To them you would be should they ever discover the truth," I muttered.

I reached for her once more, only this time, she held her hands up in defense. As if my touch pained her in some way.

"You must be mistaken," her tone softened slightly, but was now quite defensive. "I have but no magical abilities and no *pointed* ears."

She brushed her long wavy locks back from her ears to reveal what we both knew would not be found there. I felt compelled to tell her the tale of how she came to be, but even the thought of it hurt me. I reached for her once more, clasping her hands within mine.

"It is you who has been misled my darling and though I could not see it initially, maybe perhaps because I did not wish to, but as I look upon you now, there is no mistaking it."

Now appearing quite doe-eyed and lost, I longed to ease her burden, but I feared nothing I could utter would do such. I leaned forward and kissed her cheek softly.

"I know of no others that are as you are and though I cannot begin to understand the sense of betrayal you are feeling, we are not so different."

"I do not understand what you mean," she whispered softly.

"I, too, am not what I seem. Only nature has taken care of hiding what needed to be hidden from others, not man."

I looked into her eyes, and I felt a coldness I had not seen before. I began to regret keeping the letters and bringing the text aboard and for uttering such foolishness while aboard a vessel we cannot escape.

"What are you?" she spoke barely above a whisper.

I watched her carefully for several moments, not wishing to upset her, but also fearful of her reaction should I be so bold as to tell her...I had to tell her. Sometimes love just is not enough and I felt worried more so in this moment than I had in nearly all others. Should she reject me, and I could be exposed, forced into the limelight, forced to find myself on the run once more. Should she accept that I am what I am and my love for her is genuine, we would be forced to flee out of fear, but we would be together. The life I had become accustomed to in recent years would vanish along with all she had ever known. I could only hope that fate would present me as the victor today.

"You undoubtedly heard of my kind through fairy tales that were read to you when you were young. There were once many of us, but now there are few. I appear as I do for my protection, but as you can attest there is something about me that often entices you and feels primal. Though few know it, the answer can be found in my gaze and within the warmth of my flesh for there are no others that appear entirely as we do."

"Shapeshifter," she uttered faster than I expected, "you are a shapeshifter." She shook her head, "How can that be possible?"

"We are immortal spirits my darling," I paused, "despite the efforts of man, Caladh will never fully be rid of us.

Most are merely dormant or in hiding as I was before I was taken in Losgadh."

"Taken? By whom?" she insisted.

"That is not important. What is…is how you plan to use the information I have just given you."

I watched her carefully once more. Though her voice appears defensive and even slightly accusatory at first, her actions exhibited nothing of the sort. Her hands remained in mine and her gaze fixed upon mine.

"This is why you speak as if you are from another time…a time that has since been lost and why you speak of loss like no other. I often wondered what you could have endured to speak as you do and now," she tore one of her hands from mine and slid it beneath my doublet, grazing the scar the Jagare blessed me with. "I am beginning to understand."

I stood with her, ever mindful not to make any sudden movements as I did not wish to provoke her. Though I believed her heart remained loyal to mine, what she has just heard tends to change people and not always for the better.

"The first night after you took me into your arms, you uttered something to me that I did not fully understand," she spoke softly.

I nodded, quickly trying to replay the memory within my mind when I realized what she may have been referring to.

"I said I would bind myself to you," I uttered.

She wrapped her arms around me and whispered, "I have never heard it uttered as such. What does it mean?"

I looked at her for several moments, allowing myself to get lost in the depths of her crystal blue eyes as I took myself back to the night she spoke of. Embraced by the moon's light, it was there I decided to forsake the life I was born to have in pursuit of my heart's desire. Had she decided against giving herself on that night or any other and I still do not believe my love for her would ever cease.

"Bryn," she spoke softly, "where did you go just now?"

I shook my head slightly and smiled, "Forgive me my darling, I am here." I exhaled heavily before adding, "Being what we are, our kind is bound by laws unlike those of man or elf. Though we may love whom we choose, the consequences of acting upon that love are absolute and irreparable." She still appeared unsure and rather than leave it up to interpretation, I decided to continue further down the rabbit hole. "Should you pass on or choose to abandon that love, however unintentional, and I will forever be yearning for you, incapable of loving another."

"That would be heartbreaking," she muttered before glancing towards the far side of her quarters.

"It would be should I have to endure it," I leaned towards her, kissing her softly, "but I am hopeful that I will never have to."

"Bryn," she whispered just as I felt her heartbeat increase.

"What is it my darling?" I whispered as I pulled her towards me before showering her neck in playful kisses.

"I am afraid," she whispered.

Her words stopped me as I were just before whispering in reply, "Of what?"

Though I believed I already knew the answer I felt

361

compelled to hear her reply.

"Should Prince Berenger find out I spoke falsely, and King Ferand find out I am what you say I am…they will kill us, will they not?"

I felt my breath catch, surprised by what it is that she truly feared. Although, part of me wished to correct her as should we be discovered and we would face a fate far worse than death, but a larger part of me opted for restraint as that would not have been kind.

"Perhaps it is best that we not think of such things," I replied.

We stood there for several moments, both lost in thought and suddenly very aware of what we had done. I found myself lost in the thought of being tortured to death and possibly enslaved to man and her banished from both the worlds of man and elf. Yearning to exude the confidence she needed, I felt myself struggling to maintain my composure in light of these terrifying thoughts. It was then that I thought once more of the union she was still bound by duty to uphold, and my concern soon pivoted. Though I cared for Eira greatly, she was no longer within my reach, and it was my Rose that everyone would soon be coming for. If she were to leave with me, we would need to do so and soon or within their painful grasp we would find ourselves.

"Rose," I uttered softly just as I pulled myself back slightly bringing her eyes into view. In moments like these when tears of fright begin to consume her eyes, how could I not offer to stop her pain. "Run away with me," I uttered desperately, but she did not reply. Only gazed upon me with tear-stained eyes and I felt my heartache just being in their presence. "Rose, please say you will take my hand and run away with me for that is the only way we can be together. Please make time stop and be my eternity," I pleaded with her.

Just as I felt panic beginning to set in at the deafening sound of her silence, I felt her lips pressed tightly against mine, kissing me repeatedly. Lost in a sea of her sweet kisses, I felt my flesh ignite and I was hungry for her once more. I pulled at her gown, drawing it upward in an effort to feel the softness of her bare legs within my grasp. It was in the moments between her tearing the ties to my doublet and my lips finding the flesh upon her chest that the door to her quarters swung wide. I turned sharply, before pulling her behind me, shielding her with my body. She drew in a quick breath, attempting to slow the pants her body was displaying for all to hear. The gesture failed to do so and was now in unison with my own, appearing louder than either of us would have intended.

Into her quarters stepped two men, one I knew to be Kenric and the other unknown to me, followed closely by Prince Berenger. Of all who may have discovered us, these were the ones we were to fear.

"Princess Roselyn," he uttered with a surprising calmness within his voice as he closed the door behind himself. "When we spoke earlier, I thought we had an understanding. Did we not?"

She said nothing and although I knew what he was referring to, I dare not speak of it to him for fear of angering him further. I felt her hands upon my arm and one upon my waist, clinging to me as they began to tremble. She knew naught of the encounter that exposed her mother nor of the cruelty that followed, but it was all I could think of in this moment. Our love exposed now just as theirs and soon there would be no escaping. I watched the men interact with one another, shifting slightly as they were to whisper things into Prince Berenger's ears. Nothing particularly noteworthy, mostly just observations that he could no longer witness. They appeared terribly concerned about me, almost fearful and this time it felt different than it had previously. There was something they now knew that they did not before, and I wondered what it was that shifted their focus upon me.

"Princess Roselyn—" Prince Berenger began to utter, voice demanding.

"She heard you," I cut him off, "I can assure you."

The men looked at me surprisingly, a look that falls upon me frequently as I must not appear the type to be so bold. Rose did not shift from where she stood and while I knew I could not protect her forever, I would until there was no other option.

"Then why does she not speak for herself?"

"Would you if you were in her situation?" I fired back.

"What is before me is treason, punishable by death in Tuiteam's high court—"

"Even more incentive for her not to speak to you in this moment," I cut him off once more. "You will hear nothing of what she says only the web that the men in your company will choose to spin for you."

"You speak as if you will not endure the same fate," he uttered much calmer than before and almost quizzically.

"You, Prince Berenger, will not decide my fate," I spoke bluntly. "The only fate you possess control over is your own and the men in your company. Perhaps you should consider their lives before attempting to exert your power here for nothing here is what it seems."

I watched him carefully, shifting slightly where he stood just like the men in his company. I do not believe it was fear stirring him, but something else behind the scenes that moved him about like a marionette for its master.

"Though you and I are foreign to one another, your kind is not. Perhaps you should rethink your course should you wish to be reunited with one of your own."

His tone while direct, was soft, attempting to invite me in. I did not wish to take the bait and I felt my flesh heating up.

"Unless you intend to take the lives of all aboard, I *suggest* you recant your claim to King Ferand's betrothed or in irons you will find yourself," he persisted.

On some level he knew something about me was different, but I knew naught how and the words he spoke rang true. We could not escape the vessel without being known and without rivers of blood following us. Though I would have wanted to, I did not wish for her to see the beast that is kept within me. Our options were rapidly diminishing, and I felt we would soon be with our backs in a corner.

"Do you believe you are a man of honor, Prince Berenger?"

A smirk appeared upon his face; I am unsure as to the reasoning behind it.

"But of course," he uttered.

"Then I will go with you freely," I felt Rose tugging at my doublet, "but should the Lady Roselyn come to any harm, and it shall be you that I come for."

"You believe me so barbaric that I would harm the maiden that is to be Tuiteam's Queen?"

"No, but should King Ferand learn of what you believe you have found here, and it would be the harm he would inflict that concerns me."

Prince Berenger pushed past his men and stepped towards us. He whispered, "As far as I am concerned, your love for one another will die here or you shall," his voice sharp with intent. "I will not sacrifice the success of my brother's reign so easily. Do not presume that because we share blood that my brother and I are anything alike."

Something within him shifted and I could feel it now. His behavior swinging wildly like a pendulum. At first, threatening us with accusations of treason and now, willing to let the matter drop. Something did not add up in my mind, but though I would have wished to break apart this puzzle, now was not the time.

"This is for neither of you to decide as my body is my own." I heard Rose speak loudly as she stepped around me, clutching her gown within her hands, covering the chest I so playfully exposed before their entry. "This betrothal is now null and void. We will drop you at your port, but the vessel along with Lord Bryn and I will return to Losgadh," her voice insistent.

Her response may have forced a scowl to appear on Prince Berenger's face, but I could not have been prouder.

"Princess Roselyn," he paused, "that is where you are mistaken. Just as I am a pawn under my king's command, so are you." Her eyes widened. "King Itheal commands this betrothal go through and your union with King Ferand be consummated. This is not up for negotiation and your body now property of the crown, not your own."

"What if I deny King Ferand what it is he desires?" she uttered boldly.

"That would be unwise of you Princess Roselyn," he responded, "and I could not protect you should you choose such a course."

I was unsure what she was attempting to do, but I felt that she was playing with fire. Yes, we were in isolated quarters upon the caravel, but we were not alone. These men were both of Tuiteam and Losgadh with vested interest in this betrothal. Treason should not be our only concern. I must do something to put out the fire before we cannot turn back.

"Prince Berenger," I interposed, "she will do what is asked of her." I felt her gaze now upon me appearing deeply concerned. "However, upon *your* honor I humbly ask that she remains unharmed and what you and your men have witnessed simply become forgotten." I turned towards her slightly trying to comfort her, but there was little I could do in the moments we had. I reached for her hand with my own, squeezing it gently. "Do we have an understanding, Prince Berenger?" I added.

He stepped further towards us, imposing on what little space that remained before quickly pulling Rose towards him forcing a gasp to escape her as my hand was pulled from hers.

It was in the shock of his sudden movement that I failed to see the blade that he was drawing and placing against her. He moved with a precision I had not expected due to his condition and though he appeared feeble only yesterday, today he was already much stronger. What was it within him that gave him such strength?

"Though I do not wish to harm the one who will bear the bairns of Tuiteam," he paused, "I will not make a deal with a shapeshifter. For I know the strength and power you wield."

Prince Berenger

Although to my knowledge his position did not shift, there was something within him that did, revealing to me that so much of his life force was now tied to her. I could not understand it. Not being a stranger to the extremes a passionate embrace will force you to go, I have never known them to push someone this far. Princess Roselyn was willing to sacrifice all she knew and all that was expected of her…for him and he willing to do the same for her. I half expected there to be surprise heard in her voice when I mentioned what I now felt confident he was to be, but there was nothing. Could it be that she was already aware of what he was or was she remarkably gifted at disguising her feelings when needed.

When Lord Bryn did not respond to me in the timeframe I would have liked, I pressed the blade inward slightly, feeling her body jerk ever so slightly.

"Please," his voice insistent, "do not hurt her. I will do as you ask and so will she."

She did not appear pleased with his response, and I felt her body tighten significantly. Even though the purpose was to provoke a response in him, the longer I held her the more something within me began to change. The darkened cries of the marsh that flooded my mind while topside, were nowhere to be found and the aches that were nearly all consuming had nearly vanished. I soon found myself scrambling to remember what it was that brought me to them and what it was about her that my body so desperately clung to. Then the thought returned to me, forcing the blade I held to fall upon the wooden planks beneath us. This man that stood before them, threatening them was not me. I cared little for threats as they rarely serve a purpose other than revealing the hand you have yet to play and, in this case, the threat was a decoy as I would never hurt her.

"Commander Berenger," Kenric rushed towards me, picking my blade up from the floor. "Are you alright?"

"No, I do not believe that I am," I mumbled which was unlike me.

I found myself struggling to understand what I intended to say or why I was holding her as I was. I released the hold I had on her, feeling the softness of her flesh graze my heavily callused hands. Suddenly, I felt as if I had violated her in some way and the thought sickened me. I reached to pull the cloak from my back before holding it out for her to grasp.

"Princess Roselyn," I spoke softly, "please use this to cover yourself and forgive my touch."

I felt the fabric jerked from my grasp before her light footsteps were heard moving away from me.

"I do not understand," she uttered ever so softly.

And neither did I, I just did not have the heart to utter such. Upon waking in Castle Losgadh, I felt so much that no longer made sense to me. My body, which clearly felt as my body, was no longer my own and though the bits of my actions I can recall, there are a great deal of them that do not appear as my own. Even now, I was angry with her for attempting to deceive me, but I would never have approached them in this manner. I needed more time, and should the cause not be revealed to me, then I will seek the aid of the only one that might know, Haxa.

"Forgive me," I paused, "for I am not myself," I uttered honestly as I knew little more to say.

"Commander," Kenric paused, "what shall we do with them?"

I thought carefully for a moment. I was not a heartless man, nor did I wish to appear as such, but what they shared must end now or it would only get worse before the end.

"The two of you will accompany Lord Bryn to his quarters where the three of you will remain until needed elsewhere or upon our arrival at the port. Should he change or attempt to flee, and you are to execute him. Is that understood?"

"It will be done," they replied.

"I will remain here in Princess Roselyn's company for the remainder of our journey to prevent her from doing anything rash."

"What will become of us upon our arrival in Tuiteam?" she spoke softly sounding very concerned.

"Princess Roselyn, it is there you will greet and wed your betrothed as you are bound by duty to do so."

I heard her exhale violently, almost like a shutter ran throughout her, just before she spoke once more, "What of Lord Bryn?"

"He will be chained and taken to join his kin within the castle. There he will never be far from you, but never yours again." I paused, thinking carefully over what I was about to utter and all that had been uttered before. "As I said before, your love shall die here or you shall," I paused, "and I meant that. It may not be in this moment, but it cannot continue, or both of your lives will meet their undoing."

"How will you explain to King Itheal of why his emissary has not returned to him?" she pressed me.

"You need not worry about such things now. All will be taken care of in a manner of which I see fit. Now Lord Bryn, I suggest you take advantage of my generosity and make your parting moment with Princess Roselyn memorable as you may not be given another chance to do so."

I heard the two of them shift slightly before beginning to whisper. There were vows uttered to find one another and the yearnings for more time. She was concerned for him and the pain he shall suffer should she be forced to abandon their love. I assumed she was referring to the heart that would soon break as that was something I was all too familiar with. Their words soon ended, and I knew he had taken her within his arms, kissing her repeatedly. The soft keening, she exhibited left little to the imagination, and I was starting to regret my generosity. I gestured for Kenric and the remaining guard to take him now. As they stepped towards them, Princess Roselyn began pleading with me, though I knew naught why. Could it have been possible that she truly believes I would have let them go if she only but asked? Perish the thought.

Upon their departure and the door shut behind them, Princess Roselyn collapsed onto the floor, weeping uncontrollably. There was little I could do to comfort her as I was the source of her pain but hearing her now as she was felt crueler than I could have imagined. It was not often during my upbringing nor once I became a man that I was forced to listen to such an act, but it always set my teeth on edge. Should it have gone on longer than a few moments and I would undoubtedly cave just to make it stop. Something of which I cannot do in this case, so I was forced to endure it while it lasted. I lowered myself towards her, resting my weight upon my knees and I reached for her. Initially, she slapped my hand away, but upon the second or third try, she caved. I placed one of my hands delicately upon her shoulder and massaged it gently.

"Forgive me for what I must do," I whispered to her, unsure what else to say.

In truth I was deeply remorseful for being forced to sever the ties that bind as I did, but I saw no other choice. While thinking over this one choice, a decision partially of duty and partially of my own heart, there were many more that came to mind that I now regretted. Within me was a lifetime of regret and I now believed I chose wrong. I should have provoked Lord Bryn further in hopes he would have bestowed upon me the courtesy of ending a life filled with regrets.

Although, I rarely made a misstep during all my years, within this moment and listening to the two of them…I saw myself and all I could have had if I was just willing to look the other way. I sacrificed so much in the name of Tuiteam and my *duty* that it became all that I had left. It made my heart ache thinking of it all. I decided to cast it away for her moment of suffering was not my own and none of this was about me in the least.

"Princess Roselyn," I whispered.

"Do not speak to me," she spat. "You say you are nothing like your brother, but within you I see a darkness taking hold."

"What is this you speak of?" I uttered feeling lost.

I felt her turn towards me, sliding my hand from her shoulder and down onto my lap. Though I could not see her, I felt her gaze upon me and the tears that were once so uncontrollable, now barely seeping.

"When you awoke in Losgadh and all the moments that led up until you found yourself within my quarters in the wee hours of the morning, you had presented yourself with honor and grace. More than I could have ever expected from someone in your position." She paused, taking my hand in hers, "But the moments that have followed, you have been someone else. Someone that I fear as you are becoming unpredictable."

"Princess Roselyn," I paused, "I would never hurt you unless there was not another option."

"But you have," her voice insistent.

"Because you gave me no choice!" I shouted suddenly feeling her grip tighten. "What you feel for him may be real, but is it worth the fate of our world?"

374

She sat there for only a moment before uttering, "I believe it is. Would you not have done the same for her?"

I felt my expression tighten as I thought of Beatrice and though I would have moved mountains for her, the fate of our world did not rest on my shoulders.

"Of that I cannot say, for what your betrothal means to our kingdoms cannot be compared to the love I shared with her." I covered her hand with my own as they both now lay upon my lap. "The choices the two of you are making are not just against our laws and there will be consequences. I just hope you have thought them through before..." While my thought was still strong, I could not bare to think of her laying with a shapeshifter, let alone utter such.

"Before what?" she asked.

"Perhaps it better that I not utter such things," I felt my cheeks flush which made me feel quite childish.

A soft giggle escaped her, and I felt my heart flutter at the sound. What was it about her that made me feel so different? As I thought over what she said moments ago, while it did not make sense, I was starting to see what she was seeing. The further from her I found myself, the darker my behavior. There was something about her that pulled my spirit back from the brink and kept it towards the light. This prompted my curiosity greatly, but I knew naught how to test this theory.

"Princess Roselyn, were you trained by a skilled cleric by chance?"

"No, I have not been," her voice now skeptical. "Why is it you ask?"

"The darkness you saw or felt within me, do you feel it now?"

"Aye, but it is much quieter. When you and Kenric were brought to us from Boglach, it pained me physically to be near you, but I remained."

"Why?" I asked curiously.

"Partially out of duty I suppose but," she hesitated, "another part because I was drawn to you. Captivated by a man so different from any I had seen in Losgadh with a physical and mental fortitude unmatched by any other…and you were kind. During the worst of it and even before you knew who I was, you were kind to me and concerned for me. I did not expect that."

I reached to place a hand upon her cheek, trying to feel if they were flushed in any way as I could no longer see them for myself. She turned away slightly, but my hand remained.

"As I think back upon it now, I believe I was hoping Kenric misspoke and you were my betrothed," she paused. "Of course, it was probably just foolish wanderings of an idle mind now that I think of it."

She was smiling slightly as I could now feel the subtle upturn from the corner of her mouth followed by a warmth felt within her cheek. For a moment, I felt as if she may have been flirting with me, but I cannot imagine that would be true. I felt the need to redirect, if only to take our minds off that moment.

"Forgive me for asking, but your mother, Queen Drusilla, was she a gifted healer as well?

"No, not at all actually," she was smiling once more. "King Itheal tells me she was once a radiant songbird, captivating all with her voice, although, I was never able to hear it for myself as she died when I was quite young."

"Were her eyes blue, like your own?" I questioned trying to piece together what I now believed to be true.

"How do you know the color of my eyes?" her expression changed just before she turned back towards me sharply.

"Were they blue?" I pressed her.

"No," she paused, "they were not," she paused again. "How did you know my eyes were blue?"

"I was told of their remarkable beauty and wished I could have seen them for myself."

I felt the need to press her further, but while that may be appropriate, it may not yield the results of which I desire. There were things at play here that were once surprisingly rare and difficult to comprehend, but now appeared to be becoming the norm. When did the tides shift to reveal a world so different from the one I grew up in? The once elusive and mysterious were coming out to frolic amongst us. Something none of us could have been entirely prepared for and I found myself in the company of someone that appeared to be like myself, but not. Though those with elven blood are known to have bright eyes, I was beginning to wonder if perhaps she might have been something else entirely. Maybe a member of the fae? I could not be certain and as such, I was reluctant to act blindly.

"Prince Berenger," her voice soft, "are you alright?"

I nodded, "Quite," I paused, "just found myself lost in thought for a moment there. Nothing to trouble yourself over."

"Perhaps you should lie down regardless," she sounded

insistent. "Had it been my decision and we would have remained in Losgadh until you were well again."

"I may never be well again," I uttered, "but we both already know that."

She sighed, "I think you should rest now."

She began to stand just before taking my hand in hers, guiding me upwards where I found myself remarkably close to her once more. Though I could not see her, I could feel her breath upon the exposed flesh of my neck in warm swirls of sweet honey. It was intoxicating. Her gaze upon my face, I longed to see what she saw. A man that both enticed her and made her wary. I found she now also held the same fascination for me and that caused concern to brew within me. With that concern, my thoughts began to wander, to places I had not wished them to go. I thought of my brothers, all desperately seeking something within our own right, but it was the wickedness that ran throughout our veins that gave us strength and made us weak to those whom were stronger. Was it that wickedness that she kept at bay or was she feeding it what it required before something much darker revealed itself?

Kraciun

Upon locating me just outside his city, the necromancer guided me towards an undisclosed end and where the fear I felt never ceased. It was unlike anything I had ever experienced and though I longed to be released from the hold he had over me, my mind would let me think of nothing else other than my own negligence. How could I have been so foolish to get caught up in all of this?

"Why do you not ask me what it is you really wish to know?" his voice boomed once more from behind me, startling me.

"If I but had the courage to ask, would you tell me of what I wish to know?" my voice shaky.

"There is no purpose in deceit. However, it is not courage you lack," he spoke plainly, "you fear the truth as you always have. It eats away at your mind and even now distracts you."

I felt myself stop where I was, frozen in place and

entirely of my own accord. As I watched him step before me, I felt the bairn within me crying out, knowing all to well that he already understood me better than most.

"You fear the web of lies that has been spun around you breaking down. You fear your identity becoming a lie." He raised an arm towards the sky before adding, "And though you seek the unknown, you fear it more than your own death."

As he lowered his arm, just beyond it appeared a castle formed of black obsidian. While there were two large towers accompanied by numerous buttresses, flying buttresses, pointed arches, and gables of plenty, it had more of a whimsical feel than one of defense. My gaze was drawn towards its center where there rose a central tower, possibly a spire, that stretched towards the sky attempting to pierce the veil. I scanned the castle in wonder. Within the darkened overgrowth of the Fallen City, a new evil had awakened, and it was beckoning me to stay. I found myself being pulled towards it by an invisible tether, unwilling to turn away, but incapable of such at the same time. Glancing back towards him now, I saw he had not shifted from his position and the gaze upon his face had remained unchanged. Neither pleased nor disgruntled with my reaction, his indifference was remarkable.

"Should you choose to venture within my keep, and I advise you to be wary for all within is not what it seems," he uttered, voice commanding to all who were near.

"You state this as if I have a choice," I replied. "Am I not your prisoner?"

"No, you are not," he uttered quite bluntly.

"Then release me from your grasp, so that I may be on

my way," I spoke quickly.

"Your comrade warned you of drawing near the Fallen City and yet you persisted," he added sharply as he stepped towards me, eyes burning brighter now. "My grasp is not the only one you should be concerning yourself with."

I felt my throat tighten just before I swallowed deeply, and I once more found myself wondering why I ever was curious about the mainland. The horrors found within the mountains of Reothadh paled in comparison to this one city…and this one man. As I thought of who he could have been referring to he began walking once more. We reached the base of a large stone staircase, wider than it was tall and where the steps tapered inward until the summit was reached. While they appeared as nothing more than stone steps initially, as he began his ascent, the steps began to exude minute smoke clouds from them. I stepped back, unsure of the wickedness I now found myself in the company of.

"Should you desire to be rid of that fear and you have only but to ask," his voice menacing.

How was it possible that he understood my every emotion without even being near to me or seeing my reaction with his own gaze? Could this man have been more than just a man or perhaps not a man at all?

"Perhaps you should worry more about what I can offer you than what I may or may not be?" he responded as if I uttered such aloud.

Casting caution to the wind, I rushed up the staircase towards him in search of answers. Upon reaching the summit, he turned towards me quickly, nearly knocking me off balance.

I recovered quickly and glanced back to find that the steps I had taken left imprints upon the stone as if the stone were molding itself to me. I squinted trying to bring the steps into focus, curious as to life that had found its way into the stone when I felt his hand upon my shoulder. It startled me slightly and brought my focus back towards him, where our gazes met with only a small margin of air between us. I did my best to control my breathing as I did not wish to appear rattled more so than I already was. Yet, I was beginning to believe nothing I did would be unknown to him as my thoughts and emotions no longer appeared to be my own. Had this been true and he would have undoubtably been elven at least in part. He raised an eyebrow, and I knew he had heard me.

"Are you always this inquisitive?"

The whites of his eyes struggling to win a battle over the blood and darkness they found themselves in.

"No," I paused, "but…" my voice trailed off.

"You have never encountered someone like myself," he spoke bluntly before removing his hand from my shoulder.

I swallowed.

"Hmm," he mumbled, gaze unchanged. "I did not think so."

He did not appear amused as he stepped towards two large metal doors that opened just by his presence and nothing more. As they opened, they revealed a dark corridor with little more than a faint light near the end to guide us. As we stepped towards the light, the doors behind us closed and with each step nearby candles found themselves igniting spontaneously without flint or fire. I had never seen anything as such. Nearly everything here responded to him with just a glance or shift of his body and I was reminded of the words he spoke earlier. All within is not what it seems. Could this have all been an illusion? Part of me desired to ask him what he meant, but the instant the thought entered my mind the more childish I felt. Only younglings ask questions on every thought that enters their mind and a youngling I was not. If I was to remain here, willingly, or otherwise, then I should at the very least work to extract any and all information I am able to.

"The information you desire is yours for the taking, provided you understand that there are limits," his voice echoed throughout the long corridor.

"While you will tell me what I wish to know," I paused, "you will only do so if it does not compromise your intentions."

"Precisely."

In my distracted state, we had reached the end of the corridor to find ourselves in a large, ribbed vault lined with elaborate tracery and stained-glass windows. While there was little light to be filtered inward, what did come through was nearly as dark as the stone it was formed from. There were faint streaks of color that found their way upon the stone we walked upon, but little more. The beauty of the castle's architecture was overshadowed by an ominous feeling. Perhaps that was what was intended as it was being created or perhaps it was a favorable accident. I half expected to find tables ridden of carcasses and talismans, but I was pleased to find there were none in sight.

"Do not be daft," he spoke, "those items are beneath us

and just past the middens where their odor can be masked."

I was unsure if he was attempting to be humorous or if he was being legitimate. I was tempted to ask, but ultimately decided against it knowing all too well that he had already heard my thoughts regardless.

"I do not understand this humor you speak of," he replied, and I was growing frustrated.

"Would it be not easier for you to simply converse with me as any other?" I spoke sharply.

"No, it would not," he paused, "for your incessant thoughts are daunting when heard once, let alone twice."

I half believed I heard a tinge of sarcasm in his response, but just like humor, he probably did not understand it or use it. Regardless, I felt a scowl appear upon my face to accompany a firm feeling of disapproval I now felt. I decided not to utter anything else until we reached out destination, provided there was one. Unfortunately, while I intended not to utter anything, that did not stop my mind from running wild. The necromancer uttered nothing as we continued onward but being that he was walking in front of me I had no doubt he was probably rolling his eyes in disapproval.

As we continued throughout the castle, the remainder appeared very much as the outside. This was built more like a basilica than a castle as the defenses appeared limited on the exterior and interior. However, knowing its inhabitant was a necromancer I am certain there would be little need as few would risk challenging someone like himself. Upon entering a large dark chamber, we were soon welcomed with light, only candlelight was not the light we found. There were several large metal basins of which equally large purplish flames that hovered above them. At first, I figured it had to be some sort of illusion or trickery to fool lesser beings as myself, but as I stepped towards one of them, they appeared quite different. Reaching a hand towards one of them, I found that they were not flames of any sort as they radiated no heat, just appeared as such. I felt the need to touch it as I have never seen anything like it, but I reminded myself that it would not be wise.

"Wise decision," his voice broke through the space. "They do not take kindly to those unlike themselves."

They? I was unsure as to what he could have meant by that, but I opted not to pursue it presently. Shifting my focus, I turned my attention back towards him, he now sat upon a throne of sorts. It differed greatly from its surroundings but was not entirely out of place either. It appeared to be crafted from pewter with a filigree pattern carved throughout giving it a delicate appearance. He sat upon it looking just as I half expected, remarkably indifferent, but there was an aura about him that I could not place. Was it magical or just his general appearance in the light that radiated from the basins? The hood of his cloak had fallen revealing very human features, but nothing else about him appeared human. His long locks were as white as they appeared before and the shadowing upon his face no less dark. He wore darkened fabrics, black mostly, to match the leathers that his tall boots and gloves were crafted from. Sitting upon his throne, his legs were crossed, almost feminine like, but the way he watched me was anything but.

I turned my attention towards the remainder of the room, scanning it as I found a need to step away from the basin

I had grown to near to. The walls were no different than any other we passed on the journey here, but the ribbing was isolated to the perimeter of the room, drawing my attention upwards. As my attention followed their lead, to reveal a beautiful stained-glass ceiling above us. The light from above shone down through the glass casting an aura upon all within and I now understood that was the aura that surrounded him. My attention soon returned to him, ever curious of what was to come next. I scanned him more carefully now, trying to place if he could have been known to me, but I did not believe so.

"No, you would not," he stated boldly permitting his voice to echo through the chamber. "I have never set foot upon Reothadh, though I have heard it is *pleasant*," his voice sounding smug.

"Necromancer, is that your given name or do you prefer titles as opposed to identifiers of a more personal nature?"

Though I was not smug, the sarcasm found within my voice was quite thick. As expected, this affected him little.

"You seek things of little value to mask the fear that still quakes within you," his words cut like blades, exposing me once more.

"You deflect," I spat out of anger knowing just being in his presence struck a nerve. "Why?" I soon added.

"Then do not think or ask me questions of little value as I am not here to please or amuse you," his voice unwavering.

The basins within the room blossomed greatly and startled me with the sudden change. Was it possible that those basins were connected to his power or emotions and that is why they reacted as they did? Could it have been that I angered him or was there something more that I could not comprehend just yet.

"You were encouraged to inquire as to what you seek previously and yet you have not. Am I to assume that was mind numbing banter within your mind or are you being demure?"

"There is little that escapes you," I uttered feeling defeated.

I watched him place his chin against his hand, with an index finger propped against his one cheek and remaining fingers coiled near his mouth. I found myself stepping further towards him. It is difficult to understand one's enemy from afar.

"I am not your enemy," he spoke frankly, "it will serve you well to remind yourself of the company you keep."

"Though you are not my ally," I responded.

"In time you will see otherwise."

"Bartholomew stated I was the king the game was built around. Why would he say such?"

He lifted his head upright and he appeared amused. So, there is life within that dark shell.

"You are the true heir to the Kingdom of Losgadh."

"You lie," I spat out of shock more than actual belief that he was attempting to deceive me. "How is that possible?" No sooner than the words exited my lips I already regretted them as they would undoubtedly be met with a brutally honest response. "Strike that," I added. "If that were true, how did I end up in Trocair?"

"Does that really matter?"

"No, perhaps not, but I cannot help wanting to know."

"King Itheal bedded a lady's maid of Queen Drusilla's. Upon learning of you, she was sent away. Little else is known."

"What of the Princess Rosalyn, would she not be the legitimate heir?"

A faint and brief laugh escaped him to which I was not prepared.

"The Princess is not of the King's loins nor what she appears to be leaving Losgadh vulnerable and the betrothal they cling to worthless."

"That is why Queen Nimue believes I am important. She intends to use me to take control of Losgadh."

"Precisely," he paused, "you catch on quickly."

"What of the Princess?"

"She is not your concern."

"But she is of my blood," I uttered sounding more concerned than I probably should have been for someone I felt no allegiance to just moments ago.

"You feel too much," he spoke, "let me pluck out the pain and fear and give you a new life."

I stopped thinking of what he was offering and knew that should I accept; I would never be the same. It was then that my thoughts returned to Queen Nimue. I now understood who I was to her and in time the pieces would begin to fall into place. Nevertheless, the thought nagged me, and I needed to know who this necromancer was to her even though I found myself fearful of the answer. Just as I was about to inquire as to their relationship, I felt the fear melt away and with that an intrepid spirit uncovered I had not felt since I plotted our course to flee the Ice Tower. Then it came to me, this change was his doing.

He wanted me to hear the answers I sought, but knew the fear was holding me back.

"While this feeling is temporary," he paused, "should you be willing to make an offering and it can be yours always."

His voice was confident and persuasive, but it was the offering that held me back. An offering of what and to whom? I thought carefully over this when my thoughts returned to Queen Nimue and the man before me. Before my intrepid spirit returned to its hiding place, I found myself finally willing to ask what had been on my mind.

"While I now understand a bit more of who I am and what has been happening I feel I must ask, who is Queen Nimue to you?"

He leaned forward upon his throne, uncrossing his legs and resting his elbows upon his knees, hands folded before him. Eyes now growing brightly and fixated upon mine. Yet, I felt no fear even now. It was invigorating.

"For she is my mother and with her sacrifices all of Caladh will be ours."

www.ingramcontent.com/pod-product-compliance
Lightning Source LLC
Chambersburg PA
CBHW021755190726
48290CB00005B/1286